Kim Lawrence lives  her university lecture arrived as strays and one or both of her boomerang sons. When she's not writing she loves to be outdoors gardening, or walking on one of the beaches for which the island is famous—along with being the place where Prince William and Catherine made their first home!

Lorraine Hall is a part-time hermit and full-time writer. She was born with an old soul and her head in the clouds—which, it turns out, is the perfect combination for spending her days creating thunderous alpha heroes and the fierce, determined heroines who win their hearts. She lives in a potentially haunted house with her soulmate and a rumbustious band of hermits in training. When she's not writing romance, she's reading it.

Also by Kim Lawrence

Awakened in Her Enemy's Palazzo
His Wedding Day Revenge
Engaged in Deception

The Secret Twin Sisters miniseries

The Prince's Forbidden Cinderella
Her Forbidden Awakening in Greece

Also by Lorraine Hall

A Wedding Between Enemies

Rebel Princesses miniseries

His Hidden Royal Heirs
Princess Bride Swap

Work Wives to Billionaires' Wives collection

The Bride Wore Revenge

Discover more at millsandboon.co.uk.

WED IN A HURRY

KIM LAWRENCE

LORRAINE HALL

MILLS & BOON

All rights reserved including the right of reproduction in whole or in part in any form. This edition is published by arrangement with Harlequin Enterprises ULC.

This is a work of fiction. Names, characters, places, locations and incidents are purely fictional and bear no relationship to any real life individuals, living or dead, or to any actual places, business establishments, locations, events or incidents. Any resemblance is entirely coincidental.

Without limiting the author's and publisher's exclusive rights, any unauthorized use of this publication to train generative artificial intelligence (AI) technologies is expressly prohibited. HarperCollins also exercise their rights under Article 4(3) of the Digital Single Market Directive 2019/790 and expressly reserve this publication from the text and data mining exception.

® and TM are trademarks owned and used by the trademark owner and/or its licensee. Trademarks marked with ® are registered with the United Kingdom Patent Office and/or the Office for Harmonisation in the Internal Market and in other countries.

First published in Great Britain 2025
by Mills & Boon, an imprint of HarperCollins*Publishers* Ltd,
1 London Bridge Street, London, SE1 9GF

www.harpercollins.co.uk

HarperCollins*Publishers*, Macken House, 39/40 Mayor Street Upper, Dublin 1, D01 C9W8, Ireland

Wed in a Hurry © 2025 Harlequin Enterprises ULC

Last-Minute Vows © 2025 Kim Jones

Pregnant, Stolen, Wed © 2025 Lorraine Hall

ISBN: 978-0-263-34472-1

07/25

This book contains FSC™ certified paper
and other controlled sources to ensure responsible forest management.

For more information visit www.harpercollins.co.uk/green.

Printed and Bound in the UK using 100% Renewable Electricity
at CPI Group (UK) Ltd, Croydon, CR0 4YY

LAST-MINUTE VOWS

KIM LAWRENCE

MILLS & BOON

For people who welcome rescue animals into their homes and hearts, and the real Mouse cat and his furry friend Arthur, the very sweetest dog. Sadly, both were no longer with me by the time I finished this book, but they were an inspiration.

PROLOGUE

Two years ago

HEAD DOWN, thinking wistfully of the jacket that in her haste she had left slung over a chair, Lizzie walked straight into a puddle. She was approaching the flight of shallow stone steps that led to the impressive porticoed entrance of the exclusive hotel hosting the meet-and-greet dinner for the two families about to be joined by matrimony. Hosted and paid for by Lizzie's own father.

It was a generous gesture considering the bride was not his daughter but his niece. Although her dad, the head of a successful firm specialising in maritime law, could afford the gesture, and, as he often said, he couldn't have been any more proud of Deb if she had been his own daughter.

Lizzie, who was his own daughter, rarely—actually, never—elicited the same sort of rave reviews from her parent. This had been the case even before her cousin had burnished her already glowing golden child crown by marrying into the Aetos shipping family, who happened to be her dad's most important client.

While her dad had never come right out and said so—he was not an unkind man—Lizzie knew she was a bit of a disappointment. Their relationship had actually improved since she'd stopped trying to win his approval, and she could see his point of view. Unlike her cousin, she was not a professional asset and no one had ever called her dynamic.

As for working the room, her dad frequently forgot she was in the room, a situation that suited Lizzie fine—she didn't like to be the centre of attention.

Swearing softly under her breath, she decided not to look at the puddle damage to her pale-coloured suede heels—the only bit of her outfit that worked—and her spirits lifted a little as she saw a uniformed doorman holding an umbrella rushing forward. Her half-smile withered as he hurried past her to someone he presumably considered more deserving.

Someone who wasn't going to arrive looking like a drowned rat, she thought, adopting a tight-lipped stoic stance as she sidestepped to avoid a couple running down the steps wielding a large brolly like a battering ram.

A snatch of their conversation reached her as they passed by. 'I don't know what you're worrying about…'

The words, though not the supportive intonation, threw her mind back to her last conversation with the bride-to-be. There had been nothing that could be construed as supportive in Deb's voice, just bored irritation as Lizzie had admitted she was really nervous about being her cousin's bridesmaid.

'I don't know what you're worried about. Nobody will be looking at you.' Deb had dismissed Lizzie's comment as she'd tossed her river-sleek silver-blonde hair in a practised flicking action, a complacent smile curving her lips as she'd caught the rippling effect in the wall of mirrors. They had also revealed Lizzie in her mushroom-coloured gown with puff sleeves—she'd looked awful but then she defied anyone to look good in that shade.

'They will if I fall over this walking down the aisle,' Lizzie had pointed out, holding up the acres of drab fabric that had pooled on the carpet.

'Don't be ridiculous. There will be a hem and you won't be wearing heels.'

'I won't?' Lizzie, who stood five two in her bare feet, had responded to this information with a depressed grimace before reminding herself that in this dress no one would see her legs, which, while not supermodel length like her cousin's, were pretty good.

'And I want you as my bridesmaid. You're like my sister.' Deb had pouted, air-kissing either side of Lizzie's face. 'Everyone knows that.'

Actually, not everyone. Just Lizzie's dad.

Lizzie sometimes wondered if her dad really believed they were like sisters or if it was wishful thinking because Deb was the sort of daughter he not so secretly longed for.

It had been her dad who had offered a perfect solution to a single parent's dilemma, when, soon after Lizzie's own mum's premature death, Deb's mum's modelling career had experienced a revival. She had become the face of a global cosmetics brand, upping her profile and offering opportunities that entailed whisking her off to exotic locations around the world.

'Deb can stay with us...she'll be company for Lizzie.'

This arrangement had resulted in the two girls, who were of similar age, being virtually brought up together, and when Deb's glamorous mother had been home Lizzie had often been shunted to their apartment.

They said that opposites attracted but, in the case of

Lizzie and her cousin, they really didn't, which was partly why Lizzie had been surprised to be asked to be bridesmaid, but not flattered, after her cousin had explained she didn't want a gaggle of attention-seeking bridesmaids all trying to upstage her.

Lizzie had responded with a thanks, but no, thanks and explained that she didn't feel she was the right fit for the role.

Deb had gone straight to her uncle in tears, heartbroken that Lizzie wouldn't be her bridesmaid.

Her dad had been disappointed.

Deb had continued to be dramatically heartbroken, weeping without ruining her make-up.

What chance did Lizzie have? She could have held out against the pressure but what would have been the point? Better to gracefully concede defeat because she knew that what Deb wanted, she got, especially, historically, if it was something that Lizzie wanted.

Her cousin was very competitive.

The things that Deb had wanted down the years had included the special boyfriend that Lizzie had imagined herself in love with—so much in love and convinced that he was the one, she had brought him home to meet her dad.

Big mistake.

It had taken Deb just a few pouts and head tosses to make him forget that Lizzie existed. Lizzie had pretended that the flirting over dinner between her cousin and boyfriend was just light-hearted. But when she'd set out to see if he had got lost finding his way back from the bathroom, it had been impossible to put a positive spin on discovering her boyfriend enjoying a very close encounter with her cousin on the bathroom floor.

She could nearly laugh about it now.

Well, at least the early and very important lesson had taught her that loving someone gave them the power to hurt you. Lizzie was not keen on being hurt, so during the head-on collision with something that resembled a stone wall she definitely did not enjoy the sensation of having the breath knocked out of her lungs in a soft, shocked whoosh.

The impact caused her to step backwards, and she tensed in anticipation of the inevitable jolting impact of hitting the step below, her arms windmilling wildly cartoon-character style as she sought to regain her balance. But a large hand clamped itself around her forearm, attempting to drag her back onto the step while simultaneously Lizzie reached out, her hand closing around fabric that slipped through her fingers.

A split second later her centre of balance was restored and her hand was cushioned between a much larger hand and a hard, warm, male chest. She could feel the stranger's heart beat and in that odd moment of intimacy felt her own heart rate react, seeming to slow and quicken at the same time, which was, she knew, an impossibility.

'Watch where you're going!'

The voice, velvet, deep, dark, with a gravelly edge that emphasised the terse impatience, shook her free of the weird light-headed moment.

Lizzie shook her head, the impatience in his voice pressing pause on her instinctive apology. The tendency to apologise for everything from the weather to someone standing on her toes was a habit she was trying hard to break.

She tilted her chin and looked up, a long way, as it turned out.

On one hand she was familiar with this face—you'd have to have spent the last years on a desert island not to be—but not familiar in the 'up close and personal' way she now was, near enough to see the faint darker shadow on his close-shaven jaw delineating where stubble would emerge.

Close enough to be uncomfortably aware of his personal forcefield of raw masculinity and conscious all the way down to her curling toes of the overpoweringly earthy, sensual quality he exuded from every perfect pore.

Everything about him in real life was more, from the dramatic symmetry of his carved features, the square jaw, hawkish nose and sharp sybaritic cheekbones, to the heavy-lidded eyes fringed by preposterously long lashes beneath thick, slightly slanted ebony brows and the chiselled sexuality of his mouth, which it was claimed had fuelled a thousand fantasies.

As she took in the healthy glow of his olive-toned skin Lizzie was no longer sceptical of this extravagant claim.

Adonis didn't pause to analyse the strange reluctance he felt to release the small hand pressed to his chest or the fact it took a conscious effort to uncurl his individual fingers as he studied the face turned up to him.

Not a beautiful face, but heart-shaped, and her skin had a startling clarity, a clarity highlighted by the freckles sprinkled over her rounded, smooth cheeks and the bridge of her small nose. Her kitten eyes, a startling sky blue, were too big, as was her mouth, which was wide, the cushiony full lips almost indecently sensual.

He felt as if he had walked into a wall of mind-numbing lust, something basic and raw—something about that face shook loose a hunger in him. As his eyes sank lower his glance landed on the billowing fabric across her middle and he experienced a flash of sense-cooling reality—the woman was pregnant.

'Are you all right? You really should be more careful in your condition.'

She discovered that the man who had been called the sexiest male on the planet was not looking at her face.

'In my condition?' she began, her voice vague as she struggled free of the weird inertia that chained her to the spot.

She was silently awarding him a brownie point when she realised that he wasn't staring at her boobs—so many men equated the size of a woman's breasts to their sexuality and availability, and hers were not small—his gaze was riveted lower on her middle, where her dress was ballooning in the wind.

His frowning regard returned to her face as he proceeded to lecture. 'In your condition you should take more care.'

Her confusion gave way to dawning horrified comprehension. Did he…? Was it possible he thought she was pregnant? Humiliation pumped through her in a red-hot stream.

Her colour fluctuation alarmed him. He really didn't fancy the idea of having a pregnant woman faint at his feet. 'Are you all right? Do you need to sit down?'

She made a batting gesture, even though he was not making any attempt to touch her. 'Me take care!' she snapped, nostrils flaring. 'I like that! You barged into me. One thing I really hate is people…men…who act like everyone has to get out of their way and are happy to trample on anyone who doesn't! And don't say, "Don't you know who I am?" Because I do and I don't care.'

Taken by surprise, he didn't immediately react to the attack, coming as it did from a totally unexpected diminutive source. During the short static silence that followed her fiery outburst he read the anger and, yes, contempt blazing in her azure eyes.

'I wasn't going to. But good to know.'

The sarcasm and insincerity of his soft response made her teeth ache.

'But actually you bumped into me.' He had no idea if her outburst was the result of an unhinged personality or pregnancy hormones, but his willingness to cut her some slack was limited. He would never normally tolerate being spoken to that way.

'We could debate this,' she tossed back with a haughty sniff, 'but I have better things to do.'

He watched her stalk off, sections of her rich chestnut-brown hair confined in a knot at her nape coming loose and falling down the back of the nightmare of a dress. The aggressive little vixen clearly did not follow the current trend for showing off a baby bump in clothes that clung and celebrated a burgeoning bump.

Pregnant... I do not believe it, she thought, fuming as she stepped inside the gilded entrance hallway.

'And I actually felt sorry for him. Almost,' she mumbled under her breath.

The conversation that had elicited this sympathy replayed in her head as she took a couple of deep steadying breaths and told herself to calm down.

Deb had been force-feeding her the contents of a glossy magazine, reading out all the captions below the photo spread of her and her future husband, along with a detailed description of what she was wearing, name-dropping designers who were falling over themselves to give her freebies because of the Aetos name.

Lizzie had let the words flow over her.

'I was worried about the new colourist...he came highly recommended though.'

'Oh, your hair looks lovely,' Lizzie had said.

'Adonis thought it was a joke when I asked him if he'd ever thought of going a bit lighter.'

'He is very handsome,' Lizzie had conceded, glancing at the man who had stared out from the pages looking moody and broody and quite impossibly gorgeous.

At the time she had told herself that no one was that good-looking and it was the lighting and a few clever filters. Now she knew it wasn't.

She felt a lot less inclined to feel sorry for him now as Deb's response replayed in her head.

'Handsome? Well, obviously I wouldn't marry an ugly man no matter how rich he was. He's not as gorgeous as Luke or Stephan, beautiful boys for fun, but not really keepers.'

It had taken Lizzie several seconds to realise that it wasn't a joke. Her cousin really had been comparing the man she was to marry unfavourably to the pair of clones with blond-streaked highlights and tans that stayed just the right side of orange that her cousin had dated.

Actually, she might not have been putting the right faces to the names—there had been a few others whose names Lizzie couldn't recall. She just remembered that her dad and aunt had been pleased that Deb was getting out there. Their approval was connected, Lizzie suspected, with the nameless married man that her cousin had got involved with in her early twenties.

'I know he's rich, but you don't need his money. You don't have to marry him if you're not in love.'

'You are such a child sometimes, Lizzie. Of course I want to marry him—he is Adonis Aetos. He thinks I'm perfect, which is what counts. Everyone else wanted him and I got him.'

Which, from her beautiful shallow cousin's point of view, was the main thing, hence the fleeting sympathy Lizzie had felt for the groom-to-be. Now, having met him, she felt that they deserved one another.

As Lizzie stalked past a massive gilded mirror, her heart still thudding after her encounter with the tall, rude Greek, she caught sight of herself.

Her anger melted into horror. She looked, she decided, like an inflated balloon about to take off in the mustard-yellow silk—the colour of the season, she had been reliably informed. The cut fell from an elaborately smocked bodice that flattened her boobs and at the same time made them seem even bigger, if such a thing were possible!

She had only herself to blame. She had chosen to believe the perfectly groomed, stick-thin sales assistant who had spoken about unflattering lighting.

She shrugged, her sense of humour coming to her rescue. It was just a dress. If she avoided every reflective surface she might get through tonight, so long as she wasn't arrested by the fashion police.

When it came to things she cared about, Lizzie could and did fight her corner, but when it came to clothes, she didn't care that much, and by the time she had fought her way into this dress she had been standing waist deep in a pile of rejected but safe black and brown—coincidentally cheaper—dresses.

Actually there had been two, but it had felt like a lot, and though Lizzie could have argued the saleswoman's claim that darker colours were really not slimming to larger ladies, by that point she had lost the will to live. Added to which she had already been late for her meeting with the new illustrator so she had taken the line of least resistance, working on the theory nobody was going to be looking at her. This was Deb's evening.

But of course they would be looking and for all the wrong reasons. She lifted her chin, pasted on a smile and thought, *Man up, tomorrow the full frilly horror of it will be donated to a charity shop.* And it wasn't as if it would be her worst fashion mistake. She had form—that had been falling out of her halter-neck bikini playing volleyball on the beach.

She had spent the rest of her holiday in a kaftan while her 'friends'—she'd discovered on their flight that she had only been invited to make up the villa numbers and cut down the cost—had flaunted their flat abs and perky boobs in nearly there bra tops.

This did rate as her most expensive mistake, but then her exasperated rather than generous father was paying, because, as he had said, he didn't want the Aetos family to think she was the hired help.

Actually, Lizzie could have afforded her own expensive clothes had she wanted them. It had yet to dawn on her dad that her 'little hobby' paid.

When her first self-published book—*The Feline Feminist*, a story about the comic romantic disasters of a twenty-something woman written from the point of view of the heroine's cat—had become an overnight success, Lizzie had been as surprised as anyone.

Now there were four books in the series, she had a publisher, an agent, the whole deal and while her dad had pronounced himself happy she had a suitable hobby he had advised her not to do anything foolish like pack in her day job.

Catching sight of a row of tasteful vanity units and mirrors as a door swung open, she detoured. A few minutes spent repairing the damage from the rain to her face and hair would be well spent. Standing in front of the mirror, she patted the frills that made her square shoulders look enormous and took a deep breath, reminding herself that, to quote Deb, no one would be looking at her.

The reality was she could have been a six-foot supermodel, not five feet two, and they still wouldn't be looking at her, not with Deb in the room. Her cousin had the indefinable something that made every other woman invisible.

Deb sparkled.

She was sparkling when Lizzie slipped as unobtrusively as possible into the room where the two families, champagne in hand, were mingling before the formal get-to-know-one-another meal.

Lizzie stuck to sparkling water and the wall, where she blended in with the flocked wallpaper, and stayed there long enough to assess the level of awfulness to expect from the evening. One or two women had gone for floaty, one was even wearing the same colour as Lizzie, but there the similarity ended.

It was in the red zone of her awful monitor.

Across the room Deb was wearing a necklace, presumably the one she had triumphantly told Lizzie was worth a cool million, that glittered around her swan-like neck and was matched by an equally hefty diamond ring on her finger.

She really was living the dream, or at least her dream. All the diamonds in the world would not make Lizzie embrace a life spent as tabloid fodder dodging paparazzi.

Surely no man alive, certainly not the one striding across the room and carrying all eyes with him, would be worth that? She watched the tall figure weaving his way with sinuous grace towards Deb, making Lizzie think of a very well-groomed and outrageously handsome moth flying towards a flame.

The way he moved was riveting, in a 'jungle cat stalking its prey way' riveting. You didn't want to watch, but you couldn't not!

The people who weren't staring at Deb were, like Lizzie, watching her future husband, Adonis Aetos, the heir to a Greek shipping fortune, his dark hair with the distinctive widow's peak pushed back from his broad bronzed forehead.

His carved features had been called perfect, the high sharp cheekbones, the planes and hollows so symmetrical they could have made him look effeminate, especially when you considered—as many did—the lush sensuality of his full upper lip, but he wasn't. He was undiluted raw masculinity.

Her stomach flipped as she remembered the charge she had felt when she had been staring into those eyes, before he had assumed she was pregnant.

She watched a possessive arm claim Deb's waist as her cousin tilted her beautiful head to receive the kiss on her cheek. He murmured something that made Deb's silvery laughter ring out.

'Lizzie, I need to go powder my nose.'

Lizzie gave a start and plastered on a smile to greet her godmother, who was examining her dress.

'Your dear mother had such excellent dress sense,' she bemoaned.

Lizzie, who expected nothing less than brutal honesty from her elderly relative, kept smiling.

'I need the ladies' room. Come with me,' her godmother said imperiously. 'You could do with doing... something to your hair.'

It was ten minutes before Lizzie slipped back into the champagne reception through one of the arches that led into the chandelier-lit space, her hair looking pretty much as it had done when she'd left.

She stopped dead. A few feet ahead of her stood her cousin and Adonis Aetos. They remained oblivious to her presence.

An image formed in her head of her stepping forward and revealing herself, cool, composed, hand outstretched.

The image stayed where it was. A better option, she decided, was backing quietly out, less a cowardly retreat and more conserving her energy. Tonight would be an endurance event.

She had not put her slip-away strategy into action before Adonis's deep distinctive voice reached her.

'Your cousin, the one you invited to be your bridesmaid?'

'Poor darling Lizzie. We are more like sisters.'

'She works with you in the family firm?' Lizzie heard him ask in the same casual offhand voice.

'God, no, darling Uncle tried, bless. He gave her all the opportunities.' She gave a theatrical sigh that made

Lizzie's fists clench, her nails digging into her palm. 'But you know how it is with some people—they have no staying power. She only lasted a week.' Another sigh. 'But it's sometimes that way with these little mousey people—they have no drive. Seriously, she is scared of her own shadow. I hate to say it—'

But you're going to say it anyway, Lizzie thought.

'I'm afraid she is just your typical little rich girl. Her daddy pays all her bills, her rent, the lot. I think she does some voluntary sort of stuff. Oh, she's very mousey, and apparently she dreams of being a writer. Don't we all, darling?'

'Mousey?'

From where she stood Lizzie could see his dark brows draw into a straight line above his masterful nose.

'Have I got the right woman, the tiny one in the yellowy tent?'

Deb laughed at the description. 'Oh, God, yes, the dress. Lizzie and fashion are not really friends. She favours the tent. They are usually black though, or, if she is being very frivolous, navy or brown. I've tried to encourage her to make the best of herself.'

'I realise you are fond of her, but, honestly, do you think it's a great idea to have a pregnant woman as your bridesmaid? She might give birth in the church.'

Deb's mirthless cruel cackle made Lizzie wince. Her mustard-encased boobs swelled against the tight fabric as she took a wrathful breath. 'She isn't pregnant, darling. She's just…how can I say it tactfully…?' she purred as she reached up and stroked his lean cheek. 'Stout?'

As Adonis emerged from Deb's long lingering kiss, he looked across her shoulder and found himself staring directly into the bright burning blue gaze of the mousey cousin.

If looks could kill, he'd be lying stone cold and very dead on the floor, a mouse's claws in his vital organs.

If it had been a scene in a drama, she would have undergone a Cinderella transformation, losing twenty pounds and returning midway through the film to have her revenge on the man who had humiliated her by making him fall desperately in love with her. Obviously, she would have rejected him and he would have crawled away a broken man.

The triumph she built in her imagination crumbled as reality kicked in. This wasn't a drama. It was real life and she was not a teenager who believed in fairy tales.

She had believed in fairy tales longer than most—she had still believed in them the day she went to buy her first bra, a long-awaited event as she'd been a late developer.

She remembered the fluttery feeling of excitement when she had spotted the rows of pretty lacy bras that her cousin had headed for. But her aunt had ushered her past the colourful racks to another row without any colour or lace, to what she had explained were minimiser bras, which she had reassured Lizzie would reduce her by a full cup size.

In the real world she wouldn't be losing any weight, partly because according to the charts she inexplicably wasn't overweight, and partly because she enjoyed food. She turned her back on the happy couple and accepted a canapé.

CHAPTER ONE

ADONIS STEPPED OUT of the shower and shook his head, pushing his fingers through the drenched strands of his dripping ebony hair. A quick glance in the steamed-up mirror told him it was time for a trim—the waves were damply curling on his neck in a way he found irritating.

Quickly drying off, he had pulled on a pair of boxers and was reaching for his razor when his phone rang. He saw the caller ID and picked it up, a half-smile curving his mobile, sensually sculpted lips.

'Thought you didn't get up before noon on vacation, Jack.'

'It's hard work to maintain the illusion I'm an entitled hedonist.' His friend's languid response, accompanied by an exaggerated yawn from the workaholic lawyer, drew an ironic grin from Adonis. 'I thought as your best friend, possibly only friend—'

'Thanks for that,' came the dry interruption.

'It takes a very determined person to get past your iron ring of security, and of course your trust issues. Not everyone has an angle, you know.'

Adonis grunted, thinking, No, but most people do.

'But back to the reason I called—it was of course to congratulate you? I'm kind of hurt that I am the last to know.' There was an audible question mark in the light teasing response.

Adonis looped a towel around his neck and walked over to the glass wall of his penthouse apartment, rubbing a hand across the dark stubble on his jaw as he glanced from the numbers on the screen of the laptop set up on his desk to the iconic view of the city far below.

'Last to know what?' His dark brows twitched into a frown. Had someone leaked information on the deal he had spent the last month putting together?

'About your marriage plans. Have you set a date yet?'

Adonis's eyes narrowed. He was not very amused by the joke, particularly given the significance of the date.

Two years ago today he had been meant to be exchanging vows with his beautiful bride.

And Deb had been beautiful, he thought, an image of her face floating into his head along with a wave of genuine sadness. She'd had her whole life ahead of her. She'd had everything, including him.

An ironic, self-mocking smile tugged at the corners of his mobile lips. Beautiful Deb had taken him for a fool, a fact that he had not discovered until after her death when, along with the helicopter pilot, a third body had been found in the wreckage.

Identified as an older man, neither wealthy nor influential, a married man, and, it turned out, her long-standing lover. This fact was not general knowledge, though how his grandfather had buried that little pearl he didn't know. He must have pulled in one hell of a lot of favours, which meant that the world didn't know that Adonis was a fool. But he did.

His pride had taken a massive hit when he'd discovered he'd been played.

The rumours of his infallibility, he conceded with a cynical grimace, had been grossly exaggerated.

The fact he had been confident that she would have been faithful seemed beyond laughable. It was even more disturbing that in his arrogance he had so readily accepted her word when they had struck their very civilised bargain. Which seemed, in hindsight, irredeemably stupid.

If Deb had actually produced the one child they had agreed on when they had hammered out the details of their practical, mutually beneficial arrangement, which was obviously no means a given, there was a big doubt that any child would have been his.

But that was academic. There was no wife, no child, not even an ignominious divorce. He'd been blinded less by her beauty than by the fact he had been utterly convinced he had found his version of the perfect bride: beautiful, ambitious, driven, and not clingy or, most importantly, in love with him. A fact she had quite happily admitted when he had initially thrown the idea of marriage out there.

He'd been upfront, said he wasn't in love with her, and had had his instincts rewarded when she'd told him that that was not an issue.

She had not recoiled in horror at the possibility of divorce if things were not working, and he'd congratulated himself on finding his perfect bride. For many people, marriage was about staying together and raising kids. For Adonis the staying together aspect was deeply unrealistic, but kids?

He would have happily stayed single but his grandfather's influence on his younger self meant he was fully aware that it was his duty to provide an heir to continue the Aetos legacy and family name. Of course, it was possible to father a child outside marriage, but it remained a fact of life that legally a marriage contract made a father's rights a lot more secure.

He had never been looking for a woman who thought she was his soul mate—the last thing Adonis wanted in his life was the sort of love that his devoted parents shared.

The sort of romantic love that to his mind had more in common with an obsession than a partnership, mutual obsession that led to emotional stormy fights, and equally emotional making up. As a child he had learnt never to relax. The most peaceful moment could without warning become full-scale no-holds-barred vicious war.

And he had been in the middle. Some of his earliest memories were of being asked to side with one or the other in their current row. He much preferred the times when they had forgotten his existence, sometimes literally.

He had been glad when they'd packed him off to boarding school at seven, arriving with what he'd considered an advantage: he hadn't spent the first weeks crying because he'd missed his parents. There had been weeks before school when Adonis had seen more of hotel staff than his parents, though he had found the food at school not up to the standard of the room service offered by the five-star hotels his parents favoured and he'd spent a great deal of his young life living in.

After he had exchanged hotels for school, he had been

offloaded on his grandfather and extended family, spending his holidays on the family's private island, which had suited all involved. While his parents had drifted from one fashionable watering hole to another being beautiful in love people, he'd run wild on the island while being taught the responsibilities that came with being an Aetos, along with privileges that he should never take for granted.

He had nothing against beautiful things or people. He could see the attraction of beautiful... Deb's exquisite face floated into his head. He fully appreciated the irony now that he had been impressed when she'd countered his honesty with some of her own, admitting quite openly that, being married to him, she would enjoy the status and, she was sure, the sex too.

'And on that note... I'm sure the sex will be great, but considering this is a contract situation I'd prefer to wait until the ink is dried?'

He hadn't liked the idea, even for him her attitude was clinical, but he could see the logic. It wasn't as if he'd wanted to stake his claim, own her the way his father wanted to own his mother and vice versa.

At least he hadn't loved her. How could a man who didn't believe in the existence of love find himself a victim of it? He wasn't congratulating himself—being a victim of his own arrogance and lack of judgment was not something to celebrate.

He had messed up big time, but he wouldn't be repeating his error, and he wasn't going to be pressured into marriage, despite his grandfather's growing frustration.

His friend interrupted his chain of thought, pulling him back into the moment. 'So was it a secret? It isn't any more.'

'Enough with the cryptic clues, Jack...get to the punch-line. I have a meeting in an hour. I'm not on holiday.' He closed the laptop lid with a decisive click.

'No punchline, no joke. I have the proof in my hand.' The rustle of paper echoed down the line, along with laughter. 'Imagine my surprise when I stumbled across this. And I suspect it won't just be me that stumbled. The notice of the engagement that the families are happy to announce between Mr Adonis Athan—you kept that quiet—Aetos to Miss Elizabeth Rose Sinclair.'

His phone was wedged to his ear as he entered the walk-in wardrobe and selected one of the suits that hung there. 'I don't even know any Elizabeth Rose Sinclair.'

'The daughter of Rafe Sinclair?'

In the act of selecting a tie, he paused. 'Rafe Sinclair? He has a daughter?' Which made her Deb's cousin. A face floated into his head, big kitten eyes, rounded cheeks, a pointy little chin, that mouth... The so-called mouse with a spark of molten anger in her eyes, the die-a-pain-ful-death glare.

Not his idea of a mouse. Was she feeling the pinch now her father's finances were in a death spiral? Was that what this was about? Was she looking for another source of income to replace Daddy? he speculated grimly.

His thoughts continued to fly as he grabbed a fresh shirt and stalked back into his bedroom.

'She is...was Deb's bridesmaid, or she would have been.'

Instead the next time, the last time, he had seen her, had been at the funeral. Wearing a black tent, she had walked right up to him, her eyes huge in her pale face. Like her cousin, she did sincerity very well. Her lips had quivered as she had delivered the formal platitude.

'Sorry for your loss.'

The rest of the time she had been supporting her father. Someone had had to be—Rafe Sinclair had seemed on the point of collapse—and now it seemed the supportive daughter was part of some sort of plot to trap Adonis into marriage. Obviously she hadn't been working alone. He could see his grandfather's fingerprints all over this and, considering his financial woes, her father's also. How complicit was his new bride? he speculated, his lips twisting into a cynical smile.

He was angry.

He was curious.

Had his new bride been aware when they'd met that her cousin had had a married lover tucked away? Was that what had given her the audacity to think he would fall for this sort of obvious trick?

'So I am engaged. Interesting… Thanks for the heads up. Speak later.' He hung up.

His next call went direct to his PA, who was in charge of his carefully choreographed life. She didn't let him get a word in before she launched into a litany of exclamations.

'Engaged! Why didn't you tell me? I've been inundated and I don't even have a quote!'

He cut her off. 'Cancel the meeting.'

'Cancelled.'

'Maybe cancel my day, Jenna.'

'Is it true?'

Adonis, sifting the possibilities in his head, continued to keep his options open. 'That remains to be seen.'

Lizzie was running late. She twisted her thick hair into a loose knot and pinned it on her head, ignoring the thick waving strands that escaped to cluster around her face, without even glancing in the mirror.

She snatched the slice of buttered toast she hadn't got around to eating and glanced automatically at her phone before she slid it into her bag.

The sight of the number of missed calls and messages made her dark feathery brows twitch.

'No time now,' she muttered, narrowly avoiding tripping as her annoyed cat wound herself around Lizzie's legs demanding attention. Not proof against the animal's pathetic miaow and reproachful stare, she paused to pour some dried food into the half-full bowl.

'You're getting fat.'

The cat gave her an eloquent 'look who's talking' superior feline glare, and walked away from the bowl, tail twitching.

Her phone rang. She saw her dad's number and ignored it. She'd ring back later. Actually she'd been a bit concerned he'd cancelled their last Sunday lunch, which since she'd left home had become an established tradition, and the last time she'd seen him he'd not interrogated her on her love life or lack of it. He'd also told her she looked nice, which was as unusual as it was untrue.

Glancing at the time on her phone before she slid it back into her bag, she debated whether to ring and warn the stables she'd be a few minutes late before deciding it would be quicker just to get a move on.

Her dad approved her work ethic and also approved that she had kept her day job. Approval was relatively rare from her parent so she had not bothered telling him that she now helped at the disabled riding stables where she had worked since leaving school on a voluntary basis.

She might not be getting paid but that was no excuse in her mind for bad timekeeping.

Her cottage had an upside-down arrangement, the open-plan living area upstairs and the two bedrooms and bathroom downstairs. She flew down those stairs, hitching her bag over her shoulder as she flung open the front door of her red-brick Victorian terraced cottage.

Normally she would step out onto the path between the tiny square of lawn and the fragrant lavender-lined border, except there was no lawn and her lavender was crushed. There was just a sea of bodies and faces. The sea stretched beyond her garden and onto the street, where more faces were creating a wall of noise.

Disorientated and confused, she stood there blinking as questions came at her from all sides. Like a trapped animal, she half turned and glanced back at her front door, which was now hidden by a jostle of bodies who had moved in all around her, essentially cutting her off from any avenue of escape.

Lizzie hated crowds. Panic flared in her belly as she fought her visceral response, the horrid impression that she was suffocating under the press of bodies, the same way the coats had been pressing in on her when Deb had 'accidentally' locked her in that wardrobe.

'Excuse me, please, I think you've got the wrong person. Excuse me…' Polite having failed, head down, she tried to elbow her way forward taking small shuffling steps. It was like fighting a living tide.

Nothing she said made any impact, nothing paused, nothing stopped—if anything the bodies pressed in closer, not respecting anything resembling personal space. Lizzie, who had massive issues with claustrophobia, focused on her breathing and struggled to slow her hyperventilation as a rash of red dots danced and whirled dizzily in front of her eyes.

She had never fainted in her life... This would be a very bad time to start.

'I'm from the...'

'Exclusive story...'

'Where's the ring, Lizzie Rose?'

Her eyes darted from left to right, stilling as they located a figure who was head and shoulders above the crowd. He moved with a negligent broad ease through the packed bodies, his face hidden by the tinted visor of a helmet.

She had been watching his progress but it was a tummy-flip moment of shock when he appeared at her side. She didn't react when his hand closed around her arm, her eyes just slid from the point of contact upwards. It seemed like a long way upwards. He was very tall, broad-shouldered and athletically lean.

She found herself looking at her own reflection in the visor of the helmet he was wearing. All that was visible of his features was a strong jaw and a sensually sculpted wide mouth.

As she stared up at him for the space of several frantic heartbeats the clamour and the frenzied mob seemed to retreat, unable to compete with the stranger's overwhelming presence.

She had no idea how many seconds ticked by before she shook herself free of the weird thrall.

'I didn't order anything,' she said apologetically as her temporary respite from the babble ended.

Adonis, who had never been mistaken for pizza delivery before, swallowed the unexpected rumble of laughter he felt in his throat.

'If you want to get out of this, come with me.'

Maybe it was his unrealistic confidence that she reacted to, but he was offering her an escape, whereas previously she hadn't been able to move. The crowds seemed to part as, with his hand in the small of her back, they moved through the small garden and onto the street.

They were still surrounded and now she was not the only focus of the stream of questions, though Lizzie didn't take in anything other than the name.

'Adonis... Adonis... Adonis!'

'Did love grow from your mutual grief?'

'When did comfort turn to passion?'

Clamped to his side, not because of any pressure on his part but because of the shelter it offered, Lizzie turned her head. Yes, the jawline was unmistakable and the mouth that had fuelled a million fantasies... Adonis Aetos. Of course it was!

To retain her composure and not be fatally distracted by the hard male muscle or the warm male scent that was making her stomach quiver, she trained her eyes on her toes until they reached the edge of the pavement.

Where now?

Her question was soon answered.

'Oh, God!'

Instinct, not always practical, made her close her eyes as he stepped without hesitation off the pavement, taking her with him. If the lorry didn't get her, the double-decker bus behind it definitely would.

She reached the other side of the road while the bus was just rumbling past.

'Move, woman!' A helmet was shoved unceremoniously in her hand.

She bit back a retort, her eyes narrowing to angry blue slits as she resisted the temptation to tell him where he could shove the damned thing.

People got her wrong sometimes just because she took the road of least resistance when nothing was at stake that she cared about. That did not mean she was in any way pliable. She might look like a brown mouse—no one had called her that since she left school—but she wasn't one.

It could on occasion work to her advantage when people underestimated her. She didn't think this was one of those occasions.

'Get on!'

As the bus trundled along, the mob waiting to cross was revealed. Lizzie decided it was not the moment to argue so she hastily pulled the helmet on and climbed onto the gleaming monster of a motorbike.

'Hold on.'

He didn't even bother with polite pretence. It was an order.

She looked at the leather-clad back of the man in front of her and, holding her breath, she tensed the same way she would have if she was about to duck her head under cold water.

A small yelp was wrenched from her throat as, with a roar, they pulled away from the kerb.

Underneath the leather he was hard and lean.

She was riding pillion with Adonis Aetos.

Could be she was still asleep?

If so, it was a very realistic dream or rather a continuing nightmare.

The cliff-edge emotions she struggled to keep in check surged, sending her thoughts into a flashback moment of childhood terror, when the hide and seek game had left her locked in a wardrobe with no Narnia behind the coats when Deb had forgotten they were playing.

Escape from the memory was not much better. She was bombarded with sensations, her palms damp, her heart pounding, fingers laced tightly into the strap of her bag, digging into her damp palms. She pressed her cheek against his leather-clad back and screamed as he rounded a corner at what felt to her a ridiculous, actually reckless, speed.

She heard, or rather felt, his laugh and bit her lip, determined not to offer him any more opportunities to mock her, when he took a sharp right down a narrow cobbled alley, navigating a number of obstacles at a pace that made her teeth rattle.

It would have been an exaggeration to say that she relaxed as the journey progressed, but she moved beyond the conviction she was going to fall off or die. She refused to acknowledge the zing of exhilaration the combination of speed and hard male body shook loose inside her, and as her thoughts moved beyond survival, other thoughts rushed in to fill the vacuum.

She was clinging not because she was afraid of falling but because she liked the male scent of him, the heat of his lean muscled body filling her senses, blocking out everything else.

Doubtless she was living a lot of women's fantasies. She took a sense-cooling moment to remind herself that this was not her fantasy.

He was rude and arrogant, but annoyingly her dislike

was complicated by the fact she felt sorry for him. He had lost the love of his life!

At least he'd had a love.

She didn't envy him. It was an awful thing to lose the person you loved. She'd been twelve when her mum had died, not suddenly but slowly, losing a little part of herself every day.

Early onset Alzheimer's was rare and very cruel. At the time Lizzie hadn't known that. She had just known that her mum, her best friend, the person she loved with a childish ferocity, was dying.

She hadn't known it was her mum who had made her feel safe, secure in the knowledge that she was her Lizzie Rose. The most important person in the world to her. The one person she knew would always be in her corner no matter what.

She hadn't known that until her mum was gone. Not on the day they buried her, that person was gone long before, but Lizzie had still loved her.

She had discovered young that loving came at a price and it was one Lizzie wasn't sure she wanted to pay. The popular theory was you didn't have a choice about falling in love, but Lizzie didn't buy into the what the heart wants mantra.

She had vowed to disprove this theory, and so far she had.

She had never been in love.

Obviously she'd felt sexual attraction, but she'd not allowed it to go farther... Why risk it?

When people said it was 'better to have loved and lost' she thought of her mum, felt everything her twelve-year-old self had felt, and murmured, 'I really don't think so.'

* * *

Adonis waited until he was sure he had lost the couple of journalists who had stayed with them following in cars. Even then he did not head directly, instead he took a circuitous route, to the building that housed his penthouse apartment. It was possible there might have been a reception committee and that some enterprising journalist would have beaten him there but this proved not to be the case.

He drove directly into the gated underground parking area, where he pulled his bike into its allocated space between his cars before he dismounted.

With far less elegance, hardly surprising considering the disparity in their leg length, and the fact her knees were shaking, Lizzie followed suit.

She staggered slightly, righted herself and looked around before unfurling her fingers from around the strap of the bag she still clutched in one hand. She flexed her numb white fingers to encourage the blood flow before she dropped the bag and pulled the helmet off. After a tussle she managed it, though the last of the pins her hair had been confined by came with it, leaving her hair to spill untidily down her back.

Adonis's eyes followed the spectacular progress of the rich chestnut-brown waves that bounced softly as they uncoiled, framing the creamy pallor of her pixie-chinned heart-shaped face.

'Where are we?'

Her voice, quiet, soft and surprisingly low, had a breathy catch. At least she wasn't having hysterics, which was a plus, but then her shock horror might have been an act…even though he would have sworn it was real, so real it had kicked him into protective instincts he hadn't known he possessed.

Luckily he no longer went solely on his instincts.

'I live here. Don't worry, there is security, the building is gated, and, besides, I lost them.'

'And I nearly lost my breakfast,' she told him, thinking it would have been almost worth it to see how he coped with that situation.

He winced at the rather literal admission.

'Lost who?'

'The press pack who followed us.'

'Why?'

His shrug, the unconvincing dumb act, fed Lizzie's growing exasperation.

'Why were they there? Why were they following me? Why did they think—?' She couldn't go on. It seemed too crazy a question to voice but there was no escaping the things she had heard.

Below the visor his lips curled. 'You don't know?' he said, loosening the strap on his helmet.

She looked at him, really resenting his tone, his attitude. Him! 'How would I know? But you appeared. You knew what was happening,' she accused.

He laughed. 'So you don't have a clue… You are just an innocent bystander?' he suggested, not bothering to hide his scepticism.

'Sure, I invited that mob to breakfast. What can I say?' Sarcasm thinly disguised her growing antagonism.

'So you had no idea at all?' he pressed.

'Oh, for God's sake. You can be as sarcastic as you like, you can sneer as much as you like, but it doesn't alter the fact that I don't have the faintest idea what you are talking about,' she finished on a breathless quiver of sheer frustration.

'If there is a conspiracy, no one has filled me in on it!' she yelled, not much caring by this point if her response thickened the tension in the air or his sneery hostility. 'And I am not going anywhere until you tell me what the hell just happened!'

He studied her face for a moment before giving an almost imperceptible nod.

'Not here,' he said tersely. 'Let's carry this discussion upstairs… My apartment,' he added as she looked back at him with eyes that were brilliantly blue and even more unrealistically so than Deb's. Did she wear the same lenses that Deb had and exchange them for green to match her outfits?

'Not possible, just explain what just happened, and why it happened. I need to get to work.'

His dark brows lifted at her peremptory tone. 'You work?' He didn't bother to disguise his scepticism.

'I volunteer at a stables,' she said, explaining the basics.

Pretty much confirmed what Deb had suggested. She lived in a house that Daddy paid for—the property prices in that exclusive little enclave did not come cheap—and she brushed horses. Also, her mouth was not made for pursing.

It was made for kissing. He pushed away the unhelpful observation while noting the fact the lush, pouting curve appeared to be an untouched natural rosy pink.

Did any female not wear any make-up at all? Not any he knew, but he had to admit Elizabeth Rose Sinclair could get away with it and then some. Her skin had a

Celtic creamy pallor marked only by a designer sprinkling of freckles across the bridge of her small straight nose and softly rounded cheeks.

Lizzie could feel the prickles of antagonism under her skin as she replayed the disdainful note in his voice, but she could not prioritise her desire to tell him to stuff it because she needed him to unravel the mystery.

What had made the media mob assume that…? God, it was too crazy. She couldn't even think it, let alone say it! She felt as if she had just fallen down the proverbial surreal rabbit hole, and she hadn't reached the bottom.

She really needed some help here. It wasn't just the gaps she needed filling in, it was the entire thing. There were too many hows and whys in her head to count!

'So what's going on?' she asked, telling herself that the answer would make her laugh and not really believing it. 'You didn't roll up in leather like a modern-day knight by accident?'

As she paused for breath she realised that the surreal events were catching up on her in a physical way… Suddenly she could feel the crushing pressure of the baying mob, her dry mouth meant she had to moisten her lips every few seconds and the little internal tremors as she watched Adonis Aetos bend to remove his helmet were a big obstruction to calm, logical reasoning.

This logic bypass was probably the reason she couldn't stop cataloguing his perfect features. It was an embarrassing compulsion but at least she wasn't being too obvious—he was standing in profile and couldn't see her ogling.

Was it his good side?

She seriously doubted he had a bad side, with the broad

forehead, the chiselled cheekbones, strong jaw and the mouth that had launched a million fantasies.

His glossily abundant raven-dark hair was ruffled sexily, standing up in spikes on his perfectly shaped skull. The carved angles and strong planes, the dark stubble on his chin and jaw, added to the air of danger he exuded.

She blinked away the fanciful thought. Danger, she reminded herself—some things couldn't be said too often—could not be attractive. This fact established, she was shaking her head, not ogling like a sad pathetic creature, when he turned his head sharply, possibly sensing her scrutiny.

His night-sky eyes really did have silver flecks... Where had she read that?

One brow lifted. 'After you...' With an elegant flicking motion of his long brown fingers he gestured to the doors of a lift she had previously not noticed.

It was as if he had not heard her at all.

Lizzie could take being tuned out by her family but enough was enough. There had to be a cut-off point. Tension added extra rigidity to her spine as impatience mingled with trepidation and she pulled herself up to her full and deeply unimpressive five two.

'Just tell me,' she said, refusing to be ushered anywhere. His expression suggested that he had never had any woman refuse the invite to his apartment before, though the invitation on those occasions would have been issued in very different circumstances.

His frown reflected his momentary confusion, the confusion of man who was accustomed to people falling in with his wishes.

'You are being—'

In a voice that was deliberately slow and calm she cut across him. 'I have never seen how sitting down and having a cup of tea makes bad news better, and it doesn't take a genius to see nothing you are about to say is going to make me break out into spontaneous joyous song.' By the time she paused to catch her breath, calm and deliberate had become shrill and emotional.

As the breath she tried to catch remained out of reach she pressed a hand to her chest. The tightness felt like an iron fist as she struggled, fighting for oxygen, but not panicking.

She recognised the symptoms, unlike the very first time she had experienced the claustrophobic chest tightness.

Hand shaking, she dipped into her bag and pulled out an inhaler. Fitting it to her lips, she breathed as deep as she could, once, then again, and felt the tightness lessen almost immediately.

Panic over, she waited, arms folded, for him to respond.

'Are you OK?'

'OK?' she echoed, not appreciative of the concern in his voice. 'Who the hell would be OK after this morning? But if you mean...?' She waved her inhaler at him before realising what he was referring to and slipping it back into her bag. 'Oh, I have asthma—mild asthma.'

Adonis didn't buy into the mild, neither did he underestimate how serious asthma could be. He still remembered the kid in his dormitory who had been blue-lighted to intensive care in the middle of the night. He'd never come back and for the rest of the term Adonis had thought he'd died. It wasn't until the next term that he'd discovered the boy's parents had decided to take him home.

'What triggers it?'

Lizzie stared at him, thinking, *Are you serious?* 'Actually a few things, but now I can add a white-knuckle ride on a motorbike driven by a raving lunatic.' She omitted the being pressed up close and personal to a virile male body.

Startled by the less than flattering description, he laughed, his austere expression melting into a grin in the blink of an eye.

He had a sense of humour and an incredibly attractive grin that made him look years younger. Lizzie's own sarcastic smirk faded as she fought the urge to join in his laughter. She was almost relieved when he stopped looking human and frowned accusingly.

'You should have said,' he reproached.

'Oh, yes, I start every conversation with, "And by the way I have asthma." Don't be ridiculous. So, no, I am not OK. I am very not OK.'

'So I take it you did not find the ride exhilarating?'

'Exhilarating?' She snorted, choosing to forget the illicit thrill and instead directing a withering look at him. 'I am not some sort of weird adrenaline junkie. I was terrified!' she retorted. 'You know—in-fear-of-my-life terrified?'

In reality the ride had been nothing compared to the cumulative effect of the media frenzy followed by the close intimate contact with a man who had received a double dose of pheromones.

He looked mildly amused. 'You were never in any danger. Obviously if I had known you had health issues I would have made allowances.'

'I don't have "health issues",' she said, framing the words in angry inverted commas. 'And I don't want or need any allowances from you.'

'Yes, I am getting that.'

It wasn't the only thing he was getting. Adonis was getting the militant sparkle in her narrowed, rather spectacularly blue eyes and the stubborn set of her jaw.

He'd expected her to be either another, slightly more subtle and therefore more dangerous version of her cousin, capable of conniving in this scam. Or innocent, shy, and overwhelmed, perhaps unable to believe her luck to have her name linked with his. Over the years there were enough women who had tried many and varied means of achieving this, some quite inventive.

The pursuit could have left a man believing that he was irresistible had that man believed that his attraction lay in his smile or his charming personality, but Adonis had not fallen into the trap of believing his own PR machine. He was well aware that it was his image, his lifestyle and his money that made him irresistible. Yet had not fate and a design error that had grounded the entire fleet of helicopters intervened, he would have married Deb, who had wanted nothing from him but his money and lifestyle while she carried on an affair with her lover.

'But I would like an explanation and please don't make a big song and dance about that. I simply don't like motorbikes.'

It was impossible to miss the silent addition of 'Or you' that her blue eyes were messaging.

'As modes of transport in the City go, it is a good way—'

'The only place for high-speed chases, in my opinion, is on a cinema screen.'

He laughed and, to her irritation, managed to look even more gorgeous. 'That was not a high-speed chase. I didn't break any speed limits.'

She'd never had much sympathy for women who were attracted to men with a bad-boy persona, but for the first time she felt some sympathy as she watched, exasperated by her inability not to, as he unzipped his leather jacket to reveal a white tee shirt that was fitted enough to hint at the corrugated flatness of his belly.

She felt the heat curl low in her belly and countered the shame by rushing into accusing speech.

'You were there, you knew this was going to happen...' Her lashes swept downwards before fluttering up again as she fixed him with a suspicious blue accusing stare. 'How could that be, if you didn't plan it?' She shook her head. That sounded even more crazy than it had in her head.

'We should discuss this situation calmly and in private in my apartment.'

Her social mask refused to stay in place. 'Don't patronise me. You know what happened. You knew it was going to happen. You weren't just passing, so tell me.' She stopped short of stamping her foot but only just. It had been a long and very confusing morning.

'Calm down... You'll give yourself another attack,' he said, concealing his genuine concern behind irritation that was genuine too.

'I happen to be perfectly calm.' His laugh made her push the helmet she was still holding towards him hard. 'And this is yours.'

He pulled it into his stomach, his fingers grazing hers. Lizzie froze, her eyes automatically going to his as the electric current of sensation sizzled along her nerve endings.

'Keep it, if you like, for our next road trip.'

Even a mocking suggestion of a repeat trip with her

breasts crushed against his hard back, the male scent of him in her nostrils, sent a shameless rush of liquid heat through her body that pooled between her thighs.

Her little rabbit-jump step back caused her backside to hit the gleaming monster of a sleek designer car behind her and set off the alarm. Wincing at the high-pitched shriek, she pressed her hands to her ears and backed away from the car.

'Do something…' she shouted above the din that bounced and echoed around the cavernous space.

Presumably he did because the noise stopped abruptly and Lizzie's shoulders sagged in relief as she let her hands fall away from her ears.

'Thank God!'

CHAPTER TWO

ADONIS RAISED A hand to acknowledge the two uniformed figures who had appeared from a concealed side door. 'Will you excuse me a moment?' He tossed the words over his shoulder as he strolled decisively towards them.

Lizzie expelled a long sighing breath as her eyes followed his distinctive stride, and she focused with fierce determination on not thinking too much about the finger-in-the-socket electric contact.

Obviously the prohibition had the opposite effect and she relived the moment all over again and again...and what about the disturbing pull she experienced when she came within his orbit?

She needed to be objective and not overthink it, and, in her defence, he possessed an overwhelmingly powerful physical presence, mind-numbing in its strength.

The obvious way to cope with someone like him was to listen and ignore, so why did she feel compelled to challenge him? It wasn't as if she didn't have experience of alpha men. Her dad was a classic case, and she had learned that keeping quiet and going her own way was the simplest, most pain-free route for both of them to deal with what she privately thought of as his man-child tantrums.

Why wasn't she utilising this tried and tested tactic

now? Whenever he delivered one of his pronouncements that always came with the subtext that he was right and not agreeing was not an option, she felt like a cat having its fur brushed the wrong way.

Having ascertained that he now appeared to be deep in conversation with the security guards, she took the opportunity to ring the stables, not just to distract herself, but because they were short-staffed this week due to some sort of bug going around and she felt guilty leaving them in the lurch this way.

The security guards were chatty. It was several moments before Adonis could extract himself from a motor-racing-related conversation—one guard was a fan and had seen him in the VIP area of a race meeting the previous month.

When he did escape he saw the diminutive figure was looking at her phone, her frown suggesting she had discovered there was no signal down here.

This was confirmed when her crude curse echoed around the space.

Adonis's lips twitched. He was beginning to realise that he had made the mistake of forming a character assessment on one meeting, an awful dress and information sourced from Deb, who had turned out to be not the most scrupulously honest source.

Lizzie was not the mousey, not too bright nepo baby too fragile for life outside her overprivileged little bubble. The alternative was a slightly more subtle version of her cousin.

She fell into neither category. She resembled a mule more than a mouse. She was no Deb lite, she was another species.

Though physically, he conceded as his eyes lingered

on her soft profile, the little pointy chin, softly rounded smooth cheeks, she resembled neither a mule nor a mouse.

Obviously she was no great beauty, her features did not have the required regularity, but the combination of the big dramatic blue eyes, fake or not, and the sexy mouth was striking, and her freckle-sprinkled skin had an almost translucent quality.

What she was wearing today was not terrible, but the thigh-length tunic topped by an oversized chunky sweater over badly cut jeans did not shriek style, or a woman who wanted to showcase her femininity.

Strip off a few layers and she might even have a figure, he acknowledged as he walked back to her side, gesturing towards the lift and suggesting once more, 'Shall we take this up to my apartment?'

'No.'

His high-voltage smile faded. He was not accustomed to people who did not fall in with his plans, especially women, and he had put real effort into the smile.

'I'm late,' Lizzie said to soften her abrupt response. 'So if you could just explain the situation and I will be...' She made a fluttering gesture, the action making the loose sleeve of her sweater fall back, revealing a very slim wrist and a scar.

She saw him looking and pulled her sleeve down.

'I'd be grateful if you could, erm...set the record straight, as soon as possible,' she said, aiming for scrupulously polite if a bit distant.

A waste of time. He acted as though she hadn't said anything at all.

'Late for what?' he said, looking her up and down in a way that made her want to wrap her arms around herself or at least add another layer even though the scrutiny was, if anything, impersonal.

Since puberty hit she had suffered a thousand moments of wanting to do that when she had been on the receiving end of crude remarks about her breasts, before she had discovered that layering and baggy and shapeless achieved the desired concealing effect.

'I have told you. Work.'

His dark brows rose towards his darkly defined hairline. 'Wow, you really would be a nightmare interview. Have you signed the Official Secrets Act or what?'

His sarcasm brought colour to her cheeks and ignited wrathful blue fire in her eyes. 'What is it with you? You want to know how the other half lives?'

'Rafe Sinclair's daughter thinks she knows how the other half lives? Give me a break.' Though she might learn sooner than she imagined if she was genuinely ignorant of Sinclair's precarious financial situation.

His dismissive drawl made her fists clench. He really was, she decided, a deeply unpleasant man!

'Actually I volunteer in a stables,' she snapped out, not bothering to describe the non-profit establishment that, alongside an animal rescue, ran classes for disabled children and adults.

'Great stuff, admirable, though I suppose some people might suggest when Daddy is paying your rent you can afford to volunteer.'

'Some people? If you're going to be judgemental and sneery you might as well have the balls to own it!' she snapped back with a sweet, achingly insincere smile that transitioned in the blink of an eye to contempt as she read his expression. He was outraged. How very predictable, she thought, feeling a little glow of superior pleasure. 'And before you start getting all "how very dare you", can't you just tell me what happened back there? Those people? Who fed them that false information?'

How very dare? Adonis was starting to think that this woman would dare pretty much anything! His curiosity was piqued, he had to admit it, that stubborn chin, those glorious lips... Out of nowhere he found himself wondering how hard it would be to hear hoarse gasps of pleasure on them, not contemptuous insults.

'And why,' she continued, wishing she could control her antagonism, actually wishing he were not such an aggravating man, 'did they think that we were a...?' She stopped, unable to finish the sentence. It was just too embarrassing.

He looked more curious than alarmed as he queried, 'Did you say anything to them?'

'About what?'

'Our engagement,' he drawled sarcastically.

Her eyes widened to their fullest extent before squeezing tight closed as she grabbed her head between her hands, her fingers sinking into the rich silky strands of her hair.

Nostrils flared, she sent him a drop-dead glare as she snapped out a resentful reproof. 'I'm glad you can laugh about it.'

'If this came out of the blue for you, I can see it is a difficult situation!'

The concession drew a hoot of laughter from her. 'Of course it came out of the blue,' she snarled, thinking, But not to you.

'But don't pull your hair out.' It was very pretty hair, rich, like glassy silk, with the sort of gloss you rarely saw outside a shampoo advert. Did it feel as silky as it looked?

Her hands fell self-consciously away from her head. 'I'm not. This may seem amusing to you, but it's not to me. None of this has anything to do with me, and I want my life back without people camping on my doorstep. So fix it!' she bellowed.

'Calm down!' he said warily. The last thing he needed was for her to work herself into another asthma attack, but he was also fascinated by the heaving of her breasts against the thick wall of her heavy sweater. 'Apparently an announcement was put in several newspapers today.'

She went pale digesting this information, finding the slow drip-feed of information torturous.

'Saying what?' she snapped back, feeling as if he was playing with her and not much liking it. 'I know you think I'm dim but nice. Actually I am neither.'

He gave a sardonic smile. 'I am not finding you particularly nice.' He was finding her a lot of other things, which he suspected were shading his decision-making to some degree.

For the first time he was taking on board that this woman with an abrasive quotient way out of proportion to her size might not be a person who wanted sympathy, actually hated it, probably hated it almost as much as he did.

'It was an announcement of our engagement placed by our respective families.'

Lizzie had been focused on a point over his left shoulder. She gave a wild little laugh, her thoughts twirling dizzily, and her horror-filled eyes met his.

'How?' she said, clinging to her denial like someone drowning… This could not be happening, but actually it was the first time any of this made sense. This was a case of mistaken identity. He was engaged and somehow her name had appeared instead of his new fiancée's.

'Oh, I'm so sorry,' she breathed. 'Your fiancée!' She gasped, thinking, If I feel ill at the thought imagine how she must be feeling! The woman he was actually engaged to. 'Well it can be fixed with a retraction and I'm glad you're...' Like he cares about that, Lizzie. 'It's been two years. I'm sure Deb would have wanted you to find someone,' she murmured, falling back on the conventionally polite lie.

In reality Deb had always been very possessive, and if she couldn't have something she had made sure nobody else could have it.

Lizzie was immediately ashamed of the uncharitable thought. Poor Deb was tragically not here to defend herself, and Lizzie was no longer twelve. Though even after all this time, she could still see Deb's look of triumph when she had handed back the princess doll that had been in Lizzie's Christmas stocking, not her own... with its golden tresses hacked off.

A fiancée?

Find someone?

His brow furrowed in bemusement as he struggled to make sense of her sudden change in attitude. She seemed relieved.

'I'm sure she, your fiancée, must be very upset, but it's easy to put right.'

And until then her own life was where exactly?

It would be a story, wouldn't it?

And she would be at the centre of that story?

Her nightmare was being at the centre of anything. Her publishers had been incredibly frustrated when she had refused to do any publicity, but of course in the end the mystery—Who is this woman?—and the ensuing speculation had sold it, which, as her agent had told her, was all that mattered.

Fascinated, he watched the play of emotion across her expressive face. 'I'm not too happy discussing my marriage plans in the open,' he proceeded cautiously.

If he immediately corrected her mistaken belief that this situation was about a misprint, which appeared to be the conclusion she had jumped to, he could see them spending the night in this damned garage with her arguing the odds. 'How about we take this upstairs?'

Take this upstairs...

She brought her lashes down in a protective screen as her wilful imagination lent those words a very different meaning.

She shook her head, willing the guilty fire in her cheeks to cool. 'Is that really necessary?'

'I think so, yes.'

'Oh, all right, then.' She huffed out an eloquent sigh. 'I wish I could start this day all over again.' If she had she would not have got out of bed. While she liked to think she didn't run away from tough situations, burying her head in a duvet held a lot of appeal at that moment.

She flinched at the light touch of his hand on the small of her back and tilted her head upwards. The hand was no longer in contact with her skin but she could feel the warmth, which the logical part of her knew was an illusion. Even so she allowed that warmth to guide her into the lift.

She didn't say a word as the lift swished silently upwards to his apartment, but he decided he preferred her sly digs and outright antagonism to this silence.

He was convinced now that she had not been party to any of this, unless she was an award-winning actress.

It might not have been his doing, and he was as much a victim of his grandfather's machinations as she was, but he felt a stab of inconvenient guilt anyway. His grandfather wouldn't give a damn about collateral damage so long as he got what he wanted, but her father must have been complicit. He had to be.

The private lift opened directly into the sort of apartment she had imagined someone like Adonis Aetos would call home.

Dizzying high ceilings, pale wooden floors, acres of glass with a view she wasn't interested in, blonde, bland and expensive, she silently decided, her knees folding as she was pushed into a chair.

A glass with something amber in it appeared, and, not looking at the person delivering it, she swallowed it all in one gulp, ignored the burning sensation, and held out her hand mutely for a refill.

After a pause the refill, or at least a small one, arrived, and she disposed of that.

'I don't actually drink spirits,' she mentioned after the fact.

His mobile lips twitched. Strangely she was the sort of woman who made you want to laugh and hug her at the same time. He'd never been a hugger and he couldn't see any man hugging her without being able to resist the invitation of that lush mouth.

'No, I can see that.'

'I'm quite hot.' She struggled to pull off her outer layer, a heavy Guernsey sweater, before dropping it and subsiding in her seat.

Adonis watched as she folded herself into the chair,

the action revealing a gap of bare flesh between the floral tunic that had ridden up dramatically and her jeans, which had slipped down to hip level, the belt appeared to be the only thing holding them up and it was cinched in as tight as it would go. Either she had lost a lot of weight or she habitually wore clothes two sizes too large.

He suspected the latter.

The busily patterned fabric of the tunic pulled tight across centrefold breasts—not that he had personally ever seen a centrefold. Did they even exist any more? The bare area extended from the edge of her ribcage to just below her waist and the section of smooth skin had a pearlescent quality. Her waist was so narrow that he found himself speculating that he could span it with his hands.

Her body, the bits he'd seen, were a total revelation.

The woman hid this body, very successfully, in a world where… He expelled a deep sigh and tore his gaze free. Who knew? barely covered his shock or his… He filtered the thoughts in his head and chose confusion—it was easier to admit to than arousal.

How was this even possible?

The phrase kept playing in his head like the needle on an old-fashioned vinyl record stuck in a groove.

'Sorry, I lost it there for a moment there. Things caught up with me, but I'm totally fine now,' she promised, fixing him with a solemn, slightly glazed, sincere stare. 'Your fiancée, she must be a bit…cross? Tell her I'm sorry, though actually I really haven't done anything, have I? I'm a victim…' The discovery came with a grimace of distaste. 'God, don't you hate being thought of as a victim? I do. I think I might have drunk that…?'

'Brandy.'

She nodded sagely. 'I thought so. Nice. It stings but so does whisky, I think, and I might have swallowed it a bit too quickly. Let's be honest, it was wasted on me. I'm more of a prosecco and soda girl or maybe a white wine spritzer. Don't touch a cocktail—they are lethal, don't you think? There's a lot of snobbery about alcohol, I think. You do know...' she added, noticing the clinging leather she was sitting in but not his fascinated expression and thinking, I have to stop talking '...this is a really awful chair, and I bet it cost you a fortune, but they saw you coming. All style over substance. I'm really going to stop talking now... Can I have a coffee? Maybe several.'

'That might be a good idea. I'll organise it.'

He returned a few moments later minus his leather jacket and carrying a tray with a coffee pot and cups.

'Oh, my...!' she said, staring at his white tee shirt.

'Is there a problem?'

'Oh, no, you just have... You must work out,' she said, her eyes fixed on his biceps.

'Upon occasion.'

After several coffees interspersed by a few intervals when she fought off the impulse to close her eyes, Lizzie tuned back in.

'Do you have anything to eat—a sandwich maybe? I'm starving.'

Adonis watched as his visitor—or should he call her his future wife?—tucked into a cheese sandwich, the production of which had exhausted his culinary skills and would have won the scorn of Dmitri, who was due to come back today after a week's downtime.

Dmitri filled his freezer with edible and healthy things. He did a lot of other things that Adonis missed when the older man was absent. After Dmitri had quit his job as Head of Security to help his wife care for their autistic son, Adonis had persuaded him to return and take on a more wide-ranging, flexible remit. There were few people that Adonis trusted implicitly and Dmitri was one of them. Considering the fact that he and Adonis's PA were married, Dmitri already had access to Adonis's diary—the role was almost a job share and the couple had complementary skills.

Initially the older man had been reluctant to accept what he had suspected was a charitable non-role, but he had soon realised after a short trial period that Adonis really did need him.

The line between employer and friend had become invisible. Next week Dmitri was sifting through the candidates for a new member of Adonis's security team, today he was meant to be coming here, officially to discuss the forthcoming trip to California but Adonis knew he would be trying to persuade him to attend his parents' anniversary bash.

He'd fail.

'Sorry, I can't drink,' Lizzie admitted, self-consciously brushing the crumbs off her upper lip. 'But you have to admit... Your poor fiancée. You have to sort this out.'

'I don't have a fiancée.'

She blinked. Her voice, which he had noticed was warm and throaty when she wasn't screeching at him, sounded hoarse as she stammered, 'I—I don't understand. Why...? H-how?'

'The why is fairly simple: my grandfather thinks I need a wife. He decided to...intervene.'

Simple, he said. It didn't sound simple to Lizzie. Aware that she was in danger of hyperventilating, she tried to slow her breathing but it was outside her control. Her sense of confused outrage was escalating, not receding.

'How? Your grandfather did this!'

The heaving bosom, the narrowed, outraged blue stare that fixed on him like a laser—literally nothing could have been farther removed from the angry gaze he remembered at that dismal dinner party. It was focused on hating him in a much more personal way.

'Well, I don't have a signed confession, but his fingerprints are all over it. Do you need your inhaler?'

Her response to his concern was devoid of any gratitude; instead, there was plenty of exasperation. 'Oh, for heaven's sake, relax. I have been managing my asthma since I was ten years old. I'm fine. Your grandfather, really…that is just a…a wicked thing to do.'

'Possibly…' There was a fractional hesitation before he added, 'But he is dying and I am actually quite fond of the old bastard.'

He gave a bleak smile as his magnificent shoulders lifted in an accepting shrug.

She was totally disarmed, not just by this bombshell, but by this chink in his almost inhuman control. Her glance drifted to the vein beating in his temple as the small crack in her outrage widened before, like ice cream in a microwave, it melted into gloop.

'I'm sorry,' she said awkwardly. 'I didn't know about your grandfather.'

'It is not widely known outside the family and,' he added, his hard stare so obsidian dark it was difficult to believe the glimpse of vulnerability moments earlier had not been an hallucination, 'I would prefer it stayed that way.'

Did he think she was about to blab to the world?

Swallowing her indignation at the implication there was a danger she would not respect his family's privacy, she nodded then hesitated, emotion swelling in her throat as she reminded herself that just because he was far too good-looking and had thought she was pregnant, that didn't make him an evil person. She almost hoped he'd do something awful so she could put him back in that convenient box labelled 'toxic and no redeeming features' in her head.

'I'm sorry, it's hard, I know, when someone you love… I hope…'

Adonis watched her blue eyes fill with tears, the muscles of her throat working as she swallowed before she pinned on a smile and, after a small hesitation, said brightly, 'Do you possibly have a glass of water?'

He arched a brow. 'Brandy?'

Tears still sparkling in her eyes, her husky laugh rang out. The throaty sound made his dark eyes widen. That was a sexy bedroom laugh from somewhere in his subconscious. An image of her shedding another layer and standing, or preferably lying there in her… Realism intervened and he realised there would not be silk and things involved. Never in his imagination or outside it had utilitarian white cotton aroused him more.

Her loud sniff brought him into the moment and out of the rapidly escalating strip-poker fantasy playing out in his head.

'I think I'll pass. Just water, that would be lovely.'

'Water it is. Give me a moment.'

Before he had risen to his feet, a figure appeared wearing an overcoat that his vast shoulders stretched. He stood there, an expectant expression on his craggy features.

'Hi, boss. Water, was it?'

'Impeccable timing as always.' Dark eyes flickered to Lizzie. 'Biscuits?'

She shook her head.

'Sure thing.'

She felt the hooded gaze move over her before he vanished. Obviously it wasn't her place to ask who he was but even when, unexpectedly, Adonis reacted to her unspoken question she was not much the wiser.

'Dmitri is my… He is… Actually he doesn't have a title, but you can trust him.'

'I don't trust you.'

He leaned back in his seat, extending his long legs, and crossed one ankle across the other, the action pulling the faded black denim close across his thighs as he studied her for a long uncomfortable moment before asking, 'Do you always say what you think?'

'Hardly ever.' It must, she decided, be the brandy.

'Then,' he said, executing an elegant mock bow from a sitting position, 'I am honoured.'

Lizzie was alarmed because she felt pleased, as if they were on the same page, which they clearly were not, so she said nothing.

The water arrived, ice clinking on glass delivered on a tray. The character without a title was now in sleeves rolled up to reveal tattooed forearms. 'No biscuits, but there is a cookie mix in the freezer I could…'

'No, I'm fine, thank you.'

She waited until he had gone. 'He cooks.'

'No, but he has a sweet tooth and my housekeeper adores him.'

'Is she here too?' She looked around as though she expected people to materialise from the walls.

'No, here at least I can be alone. Susan does the housekeeping and makes sure I have no sour milk in my fridge. She and Dmitri fill my freezer with meals, unnecessary, because I rarely eat in and delivery from...' he mentioned a Michelin-starred establishment that made her eyes widen '...is simple.'

She wondered whether he actually believed the three-Michelin-starred establishment did takeout, or whether his bubble was so secure that reality never impinged on it.

'Thanks...' She lifted the glass and took a sip, eying him over the rim as she admitted, 'Alcohol at this time of day.' Actually, alcohol at any time of day was an issue for her. 'I might have overreacted. I'm sure you'll sort it and things will go back to normal. Is your grandfather... confused?' she wondered tactfully.

Lizzie knew that people did not always like to discuss dementia and she of all people respected that privacy, the need to protect loved ones from speculation.

'Confused?'

'Your grandfather?' she repeated. An image of a craggy-faced man at the awful dinner, with his blade of a nose and a mop of silver-shot black hair, flashed into her head. She had been introduced and been slightly repelled by his black heavy-lidded stare, not that she had held his attention for more than a moment.

'What makes you say that?'

'Dementia, it can be hard for the family.' And it would totally explain the announcement. 'My mum once left me in a department-store restaurant and went home.'

'How old were you?'

She shrugged. 'Around ten.'

'She must have been very young?'

Lizzie nodded.

'No, my grandfather does not have dementia. Spyros is as sharp as a tack.' And as ruthless as a wolf. 'However, he is dying...cancer.'

The curt delivery was calm, almost cold, but the telltale quiver around his taut jaw suggested that he cared a lot more than he wanted to let on.

'I am sorry...'

People said it, the words were an automatic reflex, but the difference was she meant it. The growing suspicion that it was not an act with her, that it was never an act with her, disturbed him.

He found deceit much easier to manage.

'He's already lived six months longer than they gave him. It is not common knowledge.'

She ignored the second implication that she would blab his personal business to the world.

'He wants me to marry and provide an heir, hence the engagement announcement as a way of forcing my hand.'

This time she allowed the implication that she had no say in the matter to pass because surely it wasn't the only hole in this crazy theory. 'Surely not.'

'Two years ago to the day I was meant to be marrying Deb.' Her stricken look made him grin in what she might once have considered an utterly heartless way, but now she suspected it was all part of hiding his true feelings.

Then again, maybe he didn't have any true feelings to hide.

'I didn't realise.'

'Why would you? Before your earlier shock-horror gasp, I was about to explain that my grandfather let it be known to me at Deb's funeral that six months is an acceptable period of grieving and then you get on with it.'

'He said that?' She studied his face. 'No, not seriously.'

'No one has ever accused my grandfather of possessing a sense of humour.'

'People in pain say things they don't really mean.'

He looked at her, curiosity shining in his hooded eyes. 'Have you always believed everyone has good in them?'

Her chin lifted in response to the mockery in his voice. 'I am not naive or gullible, if that is what you are suggesting. Whatever your grandfather's motivation, he can't think that just because of an announcement in a newspaper you'll marry, even if I would agree, which obviously I don't,' she began a little incoherently, then paused, her blue eyes narrowing. 'Why me?'

'I think it is possible this was a collaborative approach.'

She shook her head. 'What are you talking about?'

'Your father.'

'You are not suggesting…?' She fixed him with a grim glare and slammed her glass down on the table, sending splashes across its surface.

'Your father. Is it Lizzie or Elizabeth or Lizzie Rose?'

She just glared back at him.

'Your father is in a financially compromised situation.'

Choosing to be offended by the suggestion, she shook her head, not wasting words on her response. 'Rubbish!'

'He is within a hair's breadth of going bust, being declared bankrupt.'

She opened her mouth and closed it. He watched her face, a study in stillness, her eyelashes flickering against her smooth cheeks.

CHAPTER THREE

'IS THIS YOUR version of inarticulate rage?'

Lizzie expelled the breath she'd been holding and slung him a killer look. 'That is me thinking,' she snapped, pointing at her face.

He arched a brow. 'I hardly dare ask.' She looked at him blankly. 'What you were thinking,' he elaborated.

'You really don't want to know,' she snapped.

He threw back his head and laughed.

'Even if what you said about Dad is true, and I don't believe you...he would never trade me.'

Studying her set expression, he let it pass, feeling a pang of sympathy for how she was going to feel when she realised the truth. Her parent was willing to use her—a lesson he had learnt early in life.

'I'm willing to hear any alternative theories.'

'I can see your situation is difficult but if you speak to your grandfather I'm sure he will understand everyone grieves in a different way. Grieving is... There can't be a timetable for such things, and Deb was so very beautiful.'

'Do you still believe in Santa Claus and the Easter Bunny too?' he drawled. 'There is no well of human understanding. My grandfather has always lived by his own rules, and now he has been robbed of that by a disease that doesn't care he is Spyros Aetos. He has no control over the disease, but there are things he still does have control over.'

'You, you mean. Then I feel sorry for you, but my dad would have no part in something so mad, so crazy.'

'Being in financial difficulties makes the crazy seem perfectly legitimate. I do understand his position…the fait accompli is all my grandfather though.'

'My dad doesn't have financial difficulties.'

'Your father has had money problems for some time. He overextended himself after Deb died. He made some reckless moves. Some very ill-judged decisions that could have paid off, but they didn't. He was greedy.' He acknowledged her angry little squeak of protest with a sardonic lift of one dark brow.

'I would know.'

'The banks have refused to give him another extension.'

'What are you saying?' She shook her head, not leaving him space to answer. She knew exactly what he was saying. 'I can't believe that he would not have told me.'

'You can believe it, though, can't you?' he said, studying her face. He had rarely seen anyone who was less able to hide their feelings. 'Of course, you know him better than me.'

'My dad is very proud of what he has achieved.'

'And how do you think he'd react to losing it?'

Her chin lifted at the sly insertion. 'He'd never, never sell me…'

'Well, let's be honest, that is exactly what he is doing. I have some knowledge of your father and he has never struck me as a man who would admit his own failings, especially to a woman, and a woman who is his daughter.

'But he is... A lot of people work for him. What will happen to them?'

'I'm impressed you are thinking about others,' he said, not sounding at all impressed. 'But you've never been poor.'

She flashed him an impatient look. 'I can look after myself.'

'You planning on getting a paid job at the stables? That might involve getting your pretty hands dirty mucking out. Wouldn't you miss your pretty cottage, your allowance?'

Her laugh cut off his taunts and she had the satisfaction of seeing a puzzled expression flicker across his lean face. She had surprised Adonis Aetos, and she was willing to bet that not many people managed that.

'You think you know me, but actually you know nothing about me.'

'Then educate me.'

She hesitated and then shrugged. 'Fine. I don't have an allowance. The cottage is mine.'

He shrugged, assuming that she had received an inheritance from her mother's estate. It didn't really change the essentials. She didn't possess the skill or the will to earn her own living.

'As for getting my hands dirty?' She extended her hands palm upwards and turned them over, displaying her neatly trimmed, short, unpolished nails. 'I have no problem with that, no problem at all.'

She paused, her eyes widening. 'How much money does Dad need, do you think?' she wondered out loud.

Her brief flare of hope faded. The investment that she'd only last week signed off on meant that she had no access to her money for four years. Money she had thought she could not possibly need.

'How much do you suppose my cottage is worth?'

Her first instincts appeared to be shockingly selfless. A day-old chick probably had more self-protective instincts than this woman.

'It would not make a dent in what your father owes the bank.'

'There must be some way,' she murmured under her breath.

'There is…' He paused, clicking his tongue as he leaned forwards and removed her white-knuckled hands from the arms of the chair and laid them on her lap.

Her blue eyes flew to his face.

'You'll cut off the circulation,' he said, unable to take his eyes off the specks of blood on her full lower lip where she had worriedly gnawed at the soft flesh. She had a mouth that fantasies were made of.

'Don't worry. I think your father has found his own way—'

'You can't say that,' she tossed back angrily. 'This is guesswork. You're just—'

'Not exactly,' he interrupted. 'I have an inside source in my grandfather's office who—'

She launched to her feet. 'Spies for you! That's disgusting. You spy on your own family!'

'I do not spy on my family,' he contradicted, looking irritated by her emotional response. 'I have someone close to my grandfather who has his best interests at heart. He did not reveal any secrets, but when I suggested a hypothetical scenario that involved your father pocketing cash and us walking dutifully up the aisle he did not deny it.'

'That sounds like spying to me,' she countered, clinging to her denial as she started restlessly pacing the room, pausing to finger a lamp or stroke a cold marble surface tinged to a warm glow by the sun shining through the tinted plate-glass wall.

He watched her, able to feel the tension emanating from her as he got to his feet in one lithe motion. 'So you accept we have been set up.'

She paused and turned. Her height advantage had only ever been an illusion and as he uncoiled to his full height with lazy elegance she recognised it as such.

She nodded, pressing a hand to her forehead as the words filled with pent-up emotion burst from her. 'I know I'm not the son, or even the daughter, especially the daughter, he wanted, but how...how could Dad have put me in this position?'

'Desperation makes men do reckless things.'

'Crazy things!' she contradicted.

'Semantics and your moral outrage aside, you say this is a crazy action?' He shrugged. 'And yes, but it is fuelled by desperation. Will you listen for a moment?' he snapped, cutting off her imminent protest and grabbing both her wrists before she could continue her agitated pacing.

He loomed over her, capturing her eyes with his.

'Will you listen?'

After a moment she nodded, mainly because she couldn't escape his dark stare.

'My grandfather knew about the seriousness of his condition for six months before he informed anyone in the family, which was when I approached someone who is loyal to him.'

'Your spy?'

'He agreed to inform me if there were things pertaining to his health that I…we as a family needed to know. Last month he was given the news that he only had weeks to live.'

The muscles quivering along his taut jaw gave a lie to his emotionless delivery. Despite the situation, Lizzie's tender heart ached for him, though she was aware he was not interested in her heart, tender or otherwise.

He cleared his throat. 'The latest scans show there are more secondary tumours, this time in his brain.'

'Your family—'

'This is not news I have shared except with you. My father would have him declared unfit if he got wind of it. They have never…got on.'

'You think this explains…' she spread her hands wide and shook her head '…this…today.'

'Who knows?' He held her eyes in a stranglehold grip, the message in his dark-lashed compelling stare grave and sombre. 'I'd like my grandfather to die a happy man.'

She didn't pretend not to understand what he was saying.

'Would you being engaged…? Would it really make that much of a difference to him?'

'Me being married, the idea that I would produce the heir he longs for, but I think it wise to keep a closer eye on things, which is why I was making arrangements to go home, but events have moved on. Now I think the best way to deal with this is… Well, cut out the middleman.'

'How do you mean?'

'I'm sure that the matchmakers have their next move planned. Your father will appeal to your better nature. You clearly have one,' he observed, making it sound like a flaw. 'My grandfather will... Well, let's face it, he has the winning hand. He is dying.'

'Not really a winning hand... Sorry, I didn't mean to be flippant.'

'You're just being factual, but I'm assuming you get my drift?' he said, as though it was obvious.

'Not really.'

'I think we should get married!'

CHAPTER FOUR

'You are certifiable!' Lizzie said with deep conviction.

'The fact is your father does have a financial black hole that my grandfather is willing to plug if he persuades you of the advantages of marrying me. The engagement was apparently the first act, meant, I assume, to set the ball rolling.' He dropped languidly into a seat. 'It would be easy for us to call their bluff, but, as I say, I'm fond of my grandfather. Where's the harm?'

His casual offhand question made her leap out of her seat. The sight of him sprawling there looking so relaxed sent her temper soaring.

'Are you off your head? Harm. Harm!' she spat out, stabbing the air with a finger before pointing it at him. 'You know what I think? I think you are deranged! I think this is all some fantasy you have created. Well, I'm not buying into it.'

'A fantasy where I need to blackmail you into marriage?'

His sarcasm brought an angry flush to her cheeks.

'There is an easy way to settle this one way or the other. Call your father. Ask him.'

She blinked, taken off balance by his suggestion. 'Call him?'

He nodded. 'Why not? Unless you are scared of the answer you get.'

Her chin went up. 'I'm not scared,' she lied.

'Fine. I'll give you the room.'

He returned twenty minutes later to find Lizzie still pacing the room. She paused when she saw him. He studied her face for a moment and experienced a rare stab of compassion—her expression told him everything he needed to know.

'I've spoken to Dad.'

He watched her gather herself and didn't push. It was not a leap to assume she hadn't liked what she had heard.

'I always thought that he was confident but really... he's—' She couldn't bring herself to say weak. She loved her dad and she always would.

'The man is in financial trouble. He's desperate and he's proud,' Adonis said.

The defence coming from the most unlikely source made her shake her head. Amazingly, Adonis Aetos was showing more compassion than she felt able to at that moment.

'Proud, yes, he is, and he's self-entitled.' Shocked by the audible bitterness in her voice, she put her hand to her mouth. Snippets of their recent conversation flying piecemeal into her head. Her dad had gone from denial to anger, to pleading.

'He didn't say sorry. Nothing was his fault.'

Had it ever been?

An image of him sitting on the sofa, his head in his hands, when the doctor had explained that Lizzie would always have a scar after the scalding incident.

'You should have stopped her,' her dad had yelled. 'You should have come and got me. This wouldn't have happened if you had watched her.'

Lizzie, shamed, had said, 'Yes, Dad.' Even though he hadn't been there to get—he rarely had been during the latter stages of her mum's disease—and Lizzie had been watching her. She had only gone outside for a few minutes to play with the new kitten. Mum's carer—by that point she had needed full-time care—had been upstairs turning off the bath tap before it overflowed again.

When Lizzie had come back in, her mum, wearing a glittery and saturated evening dress, had been in the kitchen and there had been a full pan of boiling water bubbling furiously on the stove.

Lizzie had got between her mum and the pan but when Lizzie had stretched up to switch the gas ring off, her mum had made a grab for the pan.

Most of the boiling water had spilled harmlessly on the floor, except for the amount that had hit Lizzie's wrist before she'd jumped back. The scarring would have been worse if the carer hadn't returned and immediately plunged Lizzie's arm under cold running water.

'Your father needs validation and approval. He can't admit a weakness or own a mistake.'

She blinked, her lashes fluttering against her cheek at this objective and painfully accurate assessment.

'Do you think people change?' she wondered.

'No.'

She nodded, then said defensively, 'I love him,' before adding, 'You love your grandfather and he's not perfect!'

'Unlike you, this comes as no great shock to me and I have always found perfection a dead bore. Did you tell your father you would save him?'

'No.'

'Only human to want him to stew for a while.'

She gasped. There were just so many things wrong with that statement. 'I do not want revenge on my dad and you are speaking as though I have already agreed.'

'Your father thinks you will. He is relying on it.'

She gave a bitter little laugh and addressed his claim with weary resignation. 'He thinks I'm a pushover and so do you!'

'Maybe you're just too lazy to push back?'

'Do I come across as someone who cares what you think about me?' she flared.

'I think you sell yourself short, which is entirely up to you,' he drawled. 'No judgement. Your father, on the other hand, needs the world's approval. He sees himself through the eyes of others and yes, actually, plenty of judgement there.'

Not you, she thought, staring up at the tall alpha male figure. On many levels he remained an enigma to her. Superficially he and her dad were two generations of the stereotypical alpha male. But her dad was playing a part. His confidence was a thin veneer hiding his inadequacies. Adonis's was not an act, was not a veneer of confidence. It was at a cellular level. She was betting he had never needed anyone's approval in his life. His confidence was not based on how he was perceived by the world. It came from an inner certainty.

He waited, watching the emotions she wore so close to the surface running across her expressive little face.

'You were right... I was wrong about Dad. I am sure he's ashamed deep down. He...he... I think he was crying.' She took a deep breath, the emotional exhaustion she was determined to hide creeping into the tremor in her voice.

Her hunched shoulders, the bruised hurt in her blue

eyes, dragged a surge of something he chose not to recognise as protectiveness.

She straightened her shoulders. 'So how would this work?'

'My family, including my grandfather, are at present at the island. It belongs to our family, totally private. There would be no press intrusion for you to deal with for the weeks or months.'

'So the plan would be?'

'We marry, go there and play the newly-weds until the charade is no longer necessary.'

'You make it sound simple. You can't just get married. There is paperwork?' she persisted, hopeful of a flaw in his reasonable-sounding plan.

Reasonable? At what point did insane become reasonable?

She supposed it depended on how it was sold, and Adonis was a very good salesman.

'It is not simple,' he agreed. 'But you don't need to worry about it. I will sort the details.'

'You're relentless, aren't you?'

'I prefer focused.'

'I don't like being organised.'

His lips quirked. 'Yes, I am getting that.'

'So if I agree, in three months' time I'll be married and separated.'

'I thought you already had agreed.'

'That's because you only hear what you want to.'

He laughed then, adopting a more serious note, added, 'Divorce is not a stigma any longer.'

'It's not divorce. It's marriage. It's something I always vowed… I never intended to get married ever.'

His brows lifted at her vehemence, then he watched as the frown lines in her forehead smoothed.

'But this wouldn't count, would it?'

'Legally it will, but, well, obviously it is a transactional arrangement.' Head tilted to one side, he considered her face. He was still adjusting to the fact that he was attracted to her. The more he looked at her face, the more he enjoyed looking. The glimpse of the suggestion of the body underneath the awful clothes had tweaked his interest. Perhaps this was a perversity in the male of the species, the hidden more erotic than flaunting acres of flesh.

Next he'd be getting turned on by a nicely turned ankle.

'Or are you talking about sex?' he said, thinking about it as his eyes sank to the curves she tried hard to conceal.

Her little gasp sounded very loud in the silence that followed.

'No, I am not!' she cried, making a red-cheeked recovery. Angry as much with herself for reacting to his taunting when she was sure he had barely noticed she was a female. 'It had not even occurred to me!' she said with lofty disdain.

'Well, it had occurred to me.'

Lofty disdain vanished as her jaw dropped literally.

He had said it so casually, she would have assumed that he was winding her up if it hadn't been for the gleam she glimpsed in his dark eyes before his heavy lids half lowered.

Imaginary gleam or for-real gleam, the fact that the man frequently billed as the sexiest man on the planet had just said that he had thought about sex with her... Lizzie worked very hard at keeping her face blank, but her defence mechanism failed her, probably due to the fact her hormones were going crazy.

Get a grip, Lizzie, she told herself. *This is a wind-up.*

His dark eyes crinkled at the corners as his head tilted to one side in what she was recognising as a characteristic gesture. He slanted her a curious stare. 'You look shocked.'

The mild surprise in his voice made her want to hit him.

'Just stop! We both know that you already have me, so you can save yourself the bother of resorting to the tired old seduction routine.'

'Tired? I'm offended,' he mocked, his eyes shining with amusement and something else she tried hard not to see.

'If I agree to this, there won't be any sex. I assumed that was a given,' she said, recalling the occasion when Deb had offered Lizzie her leftover lovers until Lizzie had realised that showing her visceral distaste only encouraged her cousin, who had taken great delight in mocking what she'd seen as Lizzie's prudery.

'A given?' He allowed himself the painful indulgence of wondering about her glowing skin. Was it that smooth and pale all over? Did the freckles extend beyond her pretty nose? 'I think you have not thought this through. We could be together for weeks.'

'I thought that was the idea, me not thinking it through,' she countered, her spiky interruption drawing an unwilling grin from him. 'You rush me into saying yes before I can think about it. And I think I'll be able to last a few weeks without sex.'

He threw back his head and laughed, a warm and uninhibited sound that delivered an extra tingle to her already thrumming body. 'What if I can't?'

Impelled by desperation rather than inspiration, she heard herself blurt out defensively, 'Have you even looked at another woman since Deb?'

Any hint of humour faded from his face—effectively it became an austere, beautiful blank.

A blank that hid a world of pain, she realised, her tender heart aching for him as guilt bit deep.

'Sorry, I didn't mean to… That was a callous thing to say,' she admitted in a small guilt-laden voice.

'I do not want to discuss Deb.'

'No…no, obviously, of course not and neither do I. I knew you were not being serious, I just…' She paused, relieved when he cut across her.

'Histrionics aside, my grandfather is ill, not stupid. To convince him, we are going to have to display some… affection, if we are to sell this to him.'

'He won't expect us to be overcome with lust and have sex on the dining table, will he? Or is that a quaint Greek custom like smashing plates?' The smart words came back to bite her before she had stopped talking.

It was ultra hard to maintain an expression of amused indifference when her wilful imagination supplied the visualisation of the torrid scene she had just described. A gleam in his eye and a few provocative words and she had become a bundle of raging hormones.

God, what was happening to her?

That, she told herself, was a question for later. Right now her priority had to be concealing the fact. She needed to focus and take control of her rioting hormones.

'My family has its moments but on the whole they are

conservative...mostly. Tabletop sex is optional and conducted in private.'

'Have you...?' she began, able to still her tongue by biting it hard, but not the images playing in her head.

The raw lust that was sliding through his body made it hard for Adonis not to react to the open goal she had gifted him. He focused instead on managing the lust, which he assumed had something to do with the drought of late in his sex life.

It wasn't grief or guilt that got in the way of him moving on, it was distrust in his own judgment and boredom. Strange that it took a woman who made no attempt to please him, made no attempt to seduce him, to jolt his libido into full sinful life.

Maybe he needed a challenge, he needed surprises?

She definitely surprised him, though for such a self-possessed female she also had a vulnerability that made him step back when every instinct made him want to move in.

'The point is we are going to be living for a short period in close proximity.' He paused to allow this fact to register and, from her worried expression, it did. 'For some weeks, possibly months. We will have to act as though we are intimate even if we are not.'

'Months!' The moment the exclamation left her lips she was regretting it. 'Not that I'm wishing your grandfather—'

'I know exactly what you mean.'

'Look, bottom line,' she began awkwardly. Given the circumstances it felt right to explain. 'I am not a very sexual person.' Despite her best intentions, she couldn't hold his gaze when she made this big reveal.

She really believed what she was saying. What or who the hell was responsible for that? he asked himself, feeling contemptuous for a man who had left her feeling lacking. One of those pathetic losers, he speculated, who covered their own failings by saying 'It's not me, it's you'?

'So it is a non-issue. You're safe. There will be no embarrassing incidents. I won't be pushing any... This is not an issue for me.'

'I am difficult to embarrass.'

'That I can believe,' she said with feeling and a wild little laugh. 'But, seriously, I am not going to misinterpret acting for anything else, if that is concerning you. What goes on behind closed doors can be boring.'

He was gripped by a strong conviction that this woman could never be boring.

'You know, I've had a great idea,' she said, her eyes sparking enthusiasm. She placed her hands on the arms of the chair he was sitting in and leaned forward as she lowered her voice to explain. 'You thought I was pregnant when you saw me. Why don't we let people think...? Not lie,' she added swiftly. 'Just more don't deny it if people assume... It would at least give some sort of reason for you to marry me.'

'You mean people will believe you lured me into your bed when I was drunk and incapable and—' He watched her enthusiastic smile become a horrified frozen grimace.

She registered she was standing too close. She also recognised there was a strange reluctance in her to rectify the situation.

'You're right,' she agreed with a sigh.

'I am?' he said cautiously. The scent coming from her

warm body, or maybe the hair that hung around her face, was distracting…addictive.

'It was a stupid idea. Your family will look at me and know I am not capable of being sexy and seductive.'

'My family…' he began.

'What?' she prompted, struggling to interpret the odd, almost driven expression on his face.

She was too surprised to react when, without warning, he took her face between his hands and, pulling her down towards him, covered her mouth with his cool lips. She gave herself over to the slow sexual seduction and let everything else vanish… For a few blissful moments it was just texture, heartbeat, taste, tactile, sensual and outside her experience.

Lizzie had been kissed, she had actually enjoyed kisses when her brain could detach from what was happening and explain it away, but this was different, very different.

His lips, the way they moved with slow seductive skill across her mouth, the dip of his tongue and the wild need to meet it, the need to explore and taste were new, scary and exciting territory.

Then it was over and after a moment of deep breaths and eye-clashes she straightened up and took a hasty step back.

'Well, that was—' Probably the most erotic experience of her life, which she supposed made her a sad case.

'Nice?'

His smug mockery stung. If he thought she would say he'd rocked her world he was going to be disappointed, even if it was true.

'Passable.' God, he was so up himself and she was so… Well, actually not being too dramatic, she was doomed.

Every detail was indelibly imprinted into her memory. Every tiny detail recorded, the texture and strength of those long fingers framing her face, the addictive lemony spice scent of his soap. Soap—it sounded so prosaic but so wasn't.

She'd thought she had been kissed before but now she knew she hadn't—not really.

And that mind-expanding, physically debilitating kiss, which meant nothing more to him than, well, shutting her up or proving that he was irresistible. Either option was unpalatable and he'd succeeded on both grounds.

She took a second step backwards when he rose to his feet in one supple fluid motion. She told herself for a split second that she was in control and gave up the exercise of denial because she really wasn't.

It was chemical!

It was insane!

As he watched her Adonis was aware of the predatory pulse inside him. It was attuned to every minute shift of expression on her face. He could almost feel the pulse beating under her skin... He could smell her arousal.

It was basic, primal.

It was all so out of his comfort zone, and then some. When was the last time he had struggled to get his libido in check or needed the effort it now cost him?

He wanted to peel away the layers, quite literally, and discover what this woman had that bypassed every logic circle in his brain.

Was this how his parents functioned—all instinct and no brain, no logic...animalistic?

The thought sent a warning kick to his belly. The chilling idea that he had wandered into his parents' world enabled him to shrug it off. A kiss, as they said, was just a kiss, and she did have that mouth.

So he cut himself some slack.

'You really don't have to worry. I know where we stand and I think we can hold hands and I can laugh at your jokes without being overcome by wild animal passion. I agree it is good to think ahead, but…' She took a deep breath. 'I am not one of your—your groupies, so please remember that in the next weeks.'

'So no more kissing.'

'It's a matter of context, I suppose, and I'm fine with that,' she lied glibly. 'Deb was…' She paused. 'I know,' she continued gently. 'Gosh, she was a hard act to follow but one day… Sorry,' she added, knowing she had strayed into areas with massive no-go signs. Obviously he was still in love with Deb. She didn't have to labour the point.

His expression did not suggest that he appreciated her delicate negotiation of a difficult subject at all.

'Will there be a prenup?' she said, immediately feeling foolish for querying the obvious. It was normal for a man like Adonis to protect his interests, and that went double when the marriage in question was less one of convenience, more mutual inconvenience, a few weeks or months out of his life to enable his grandfather to die a happy man.

Whether his grandfather deserved this sacrifice was not the issue for Lizzie. She had been a child and helpless to do anything but, when her mum had been dying, she would have broken every rule in the book to make her mum smile…just for a moment.

She wasn't judging him, but she didn't forget that he was not a child, he was a powerful and ruthless man.

'Well, more a post-nup. You will not lose out financially by this.'

She froze. 'I don't want your money. I earn my own money.'

'I thought you volunteered at these stables?'

His patronising undertone set her teeth on edge. 'Felly Edge. Yes, I did work there when I left school, but now I write.'

'Have you had anything published?'

She nodded, telling herself that boasting was a bad thing, although wafting her last royalty statement under his nose at that moment would have given her a lot of satisfaction.

'It is hard to make a living as a writer.'

'I know.' She gritted her teeth, for the first time understanding a little of her team's frustration as she was forced to bite back the literally amazing number of books her series had sold.

Something about him released the dormant boastful voice in her that wanted to be released, that wanted to scream, *Forget about self-deprecating. I have sold a shedload of books. I have earned the praise, the kudos.*

Even if I still feel a fraud.

'What sort of books?'

'Romance.'

'Ahh…' The way he said it made her teeth ache but that might have been the clenching.

'So you are a romantic?'

'Not at all. If you think I am looking for love you could not be more wrong.'

'So you are not looking for love and marriage.'

'There are lots of kinds of love, but it's not love I have

an issue with, just the blind belief that love will make everything OK.'

Buried memories aside, she knew that her dad had loved her mum, but he hadn't been able to protect her. Marriage was a formula for…well, not happiness anyway.

'Not really relevant, is it, in this instance?'

At the shrill sound of his phone he pulled it out of his pocket and glanced at the screen. 'Excuse me. I need to take this.'

Left alone, Lizzie began to pace the room.

What had she done?

What had she agreed to?

CHAPTER FIVE

'What are you doing?'

Lizzie waited until she had pulled her sweater over her head. 'I'm going home.'

'You can't go back to your cottage. I will arrange for someone to close things up for you and collect your documents. If you are thinking clothes, you will need a new wardrobe anyway so—'

'What is wrong with the clothes I have?'

His eyes moved in a disparaging sweep from her feet to her face. 'Do you really want me to answer that?'

She flushed. 'I won't let you dress me.'

A disturbing smile played across his sensual lips as he studied her. Despite the smile and the mockery in his dark eyes, she sensed a tension about him as he gave his throaty response. 'Husbands are normally more concerned with undressing their wives.' He paused and laughed. 'You blush like a virgin.'

What would he say if she said she was?

She moistened her lips and decided not to find out.

'Do not look at me like that.'

She blinked in bewilderment.

'You are entering into this of your own free will.'

'I know that. Don't flatter yourself that you could force me to do anything.'

'I promise you I have never forced a woman.'

The male arrogance made her laugh. 'No, you just overwhelm them with your wit and charm. Course, you're rich, but I'm sure that has nothing to do with it.'

After a moment's shocked silence he laughed. 'You really don't take prisoners, do you?'

'I didn't mean Deb,' she blurted.

He arched a brow. 'Didn't you?' To her relief he left no gap for her to respond before adding, 'The fact remains you can't go back to your cottage. The press are camped out.'

'How do you know?'

'Why risk it? I think it would be best for you to stay here.'

She laughed. 'That is not happening. I have a cat, which will need feeding when I have organised—'

'You can't stay in your cottage. You will be a target for—'

'I'm not going to stay there. I'll go home. The estate has good security and high walls.'

'So you have a cat, I do not see the relevance. Someone can deal with your cat and have him housed.'

'Mouse is—'

'Mouse? I thought you said you had a cat.'

'I do have a cat. Her name is Mouse. If I'm going to put my life in storage there is no way in the world I am going to allow some stranger to walk into my house and literally pack my life away.'

'Very well, but you will not leave here until it is dark.'

'That's ridiculous!'

'That's the deal and, if it makes you feel any better, I will not be here. Dmitri will see you safely home and then take you to your father's estate.'

'I'll drive myself.'

He clenched his teeth over a robust retort. 'Won't it be awkward for you to see your father just now? What did he say when you said you were coming?' It really didn't seem the best plan to him or, for that matter, any plan at all. He studied her face. 'You didn't tell him you were coming.'

'He won't be there.'

He arched a brow. 'You know this how?'

'I know my father. Look, it's my home but he really won't be there. Dad always vanishes when there is something he doesn't want to think about.'

'Vanishes?'

'Well, not vanish, more removes himself. When Mum died he went on a six-month cruise.'

The expression on Adonis's lean face made Lizzie regret the confidence.

'He took you with him? How old were you?'

'I was twelve and, no, he didn't take me with him. He couldn't cope with me crying. He sent me postcards though.' A smile played across her mobile mouth as she thought of them lined up around her dressing-table mirror.

Adonis had never been much impressed by Deb's uncle on the occasions they had met, but this artless confidence made any ambivalence vanish. What a loser!

'If you have things to do…?' she said pointedly.

'And deprive you of my company?' he taunted. 'Actually, now is as good a time as any to put things in motion.'

She shook her head. 'What things?'

'A marriage doesn't arrange itself.'

'Oh, I suppose not.'

'I'll keep you up-to-date with the arrangements.'

'Don't bother, I don't need to know the details.' It wasn't as if knowing would make any difference. 'Just do it.'

Lizzie's furtive return to her own home under the cover of darkness made her feel like some sort of thief, even if it was one with a key.

'Was it really necessary to go round the block three times?' she asked Dmitri as they drew up, and immediately felt guilty for the sarcasm because she had no doubt that he was following orders. 'Well, you can tell him there were no ninja warriors hiding in the bushes.'

'I think the odd pap is what worries him most.'

'Well, thanks, I can take it from here.'

She let herself in and, walking to the window to close the blinds, she saw the four-wheel drive still sitting outside. No doubt he'd been told how long to wait—maybe all night? She was considering going outside to inform him when the car drew away, making her glad she hadn't made a fool of herself.

Dmitri parked up and took out his phone again, ensuring he wasn't driving before he spoke. 'Hi, boss,' he said, settling back into his seat. 'The place was clear, no sign of any journalists, and she's safe inside. I've parked at the end of the street, got a good view of access.'

'Thanks for this,' Adonis said. 'Let me know what time she starts out.'

'You want me to follow her?'

'No, I'll arrange for someone to wait for her to arrive then we can stand down. The Sinclair place apparently has pretty good security.'

* * *

Six a.m., the text had said, and the rat-a-tat knock at the door came exactly at six.

Lizzie fought against the tempting idea of ignoring the summons, turning the lock and whisking away upstairs. Maybe there was more of her dad in her than she had thought.

Her prediction that he would have absented himself—his usual way of dealing with unpleasantness—had been proved right. After his initial message to say he was playing golf in Portugal there had been radio silence.

Last night had been the first night in her own bed for a week, and maybe the last for a long time. The knowledge made her tummy muscles tighten.

After the second knock Lizzie unclenched her fingers one by one and took a deep breath. She tried out several versions of a cool and collected smile in the mirror and settled on a scowl, which came naturally, as she sidestepped the pile of luggage crammed in the small hallway. It was not the set of designer luggage that had been delivered along with a wardrobe of designer clothes brought by a duo who appeared to have been waiting for her return in a van bearing the name of an expensive department store.

Most of the contents of the glossy bags, wrapped between tissue paper or on hangers, were now in the motley collection of her own mismatched bags and holdalls.

True, it was a pretty feeble sort of rebellion, but it went a small way towards making her feel she was in charge of something and not some puppet. Feeble or not, it seemed a principle worth holding onto, and lessened the gut instinct that told her she was being managed.

Heart thudding, she pulled the door open a lot more

violently than she had intended. She immediately lowered her line of vision a good four inches—the man standing on her doorstep was not six three. The anticlimax was intense.

'Hello, Miss Sinclair.'

'Hello again, Dmitri,' she said, responding to the greeting in an overly bright voice. 'Does my carriage await?' she asked. Her gaze moved beyond him to the massive four-wheel drive with blacked-out windows parked outside her gate just as the passenger door opened and a woman with short bleached hair spiked around her head appeared.

'My wife, Jenna. We're the witnesses.'

'Oh, that's…good. Well. So, no bridegroom?'

'He's meeting us there.'

She didn't bother asking where there was. It seemed a bit late to take any interest in the details at this stage.

As the broad-shouldered figure picked up several of her bags she grabbed a rucksack and slung it over one shoulder.

'I'll take that,' he protested.

Lizzie ignored him and picked up Mouse, who was looking through the screen of her carrier with an expression of fastidious disgust.

'A cat?' He looked nonplussed.

'Yes, this is Mouse. She's a very good traveller,' she explained, deciding to eliminate all the potential objections straight off. 'And she's got a passport and is up to date with all her jabs.' She strode down the path to the car, not waiting for a response.

'Hi, I'm Jenna.' The openly curious woman looked her up and down. Lizzie assumed the brightly coloured kaftan-style maxi she was wearing was not normal office wear, unless Adonis kept a very informal office, which, considering his sharp suits, did not seem likely.

To Lizzie's annoyance she heard herself say, 'I've got shoes in the bag,' when the other woman reached her seen-better-days trainers.

'Good-looking cat. Do you want to sit up front?'

'No, we're fine in the back,' Lizzie said, warming towards the woman who had admired her cat. 'Oh, the key...' she added, glancing at the baggage-laden figure striding down the path. She put Mouse in the back seat and reached into the front pocket of the rucksack. She was afraid that if she went back into the house she might go inside and lock the door to shut out this insanity.

She was on her way to her own wedding!

'You'll need these,' she said, throwing them to Dmitri, who had finished putting the first load of bags in the boot and was going back for more.

He caught them casually one-handed and nodded.

He made short work of the rest of her bags and Lizzie watched him lock her door. The mundane action seemed scarily symbolic.

It was still home, she reminded herself as she accepted the keys and put them in her bag. When this was over she would be able to walk back into her old life, or reclaim a new life where her dad was not in danger of going under.

She couldn't allow herself to regret her choice. Some people could rebuild their lives after everything went pear-shaped—they could come back bigger and stronger. But her dad was not one of that number. The humiliation of bankruptcy was not something her dad would ever recover from.

'All set back there?'

Lizzie nodded, then realised that no one could see her. 'Yes,' she lied.

'Have you ever been to Gibraltar before?'

'Gibraltar?'

Straining in her seat belt, the older woman twisted around the side of her seat to look at Lizzie. 'Honest to God!' she exclaimed indignantly. 'I made up an information pack for you. Didn't he give it to you? Typical!' she brooded waspishly.

'Information pack?' Lizzie echoed, thinking, *Oh, be still my beating heart...how romantic!* 'Aren't we going to a register office on the way to the airport?'

'Airport first then wedding. Adonis has been in Gibraltar setting things up for the past few days. It's less complicated to get married at short notice there as a tourist. Didn't he mention that when he rang?'

'He didn't ring, but then,' she added with a bright smile, 'he didn't need to. We hardly chat for hours every night, and I'm not counting the hours until I hear his voice.'

Lizzie stopped abruptly, discomfort spreading in her chest as she tried to read the expression on the other woman's face.

In her desire to make it crystal clear she was not blinded by his smile or besotted by his sexual charisma, she had gone too far. She had also spoken out on the assumption that this couple knew everything, but was this the case? She fretted, her anxiety communicating itself to the cat, who began to miaow loudly.

Jenna also seemed to pick up on Lizzie's unease. 'Don't worry, we both know what's happening,' she said, sounding sympathetic. 'Well, obviously as much as we need to know.'

Probably they know more than I do…

Lizzie felt a stab of resentment. She might have basically said just do it, but that had been a figure of speech. She hadn't meant she wanted to be left in the dark about basic stuff. Adonis was clearly a man who had no problem taking control without any encouragement, and she had encouraged him.

'Can I call you Lizzie? Or do you prefer Elizabeth?'

'Lizzie.' She forced a smile. The other woman seemed friendly and it wasn't her fault. She was obviously just the messenger.

'Do you want to drop the cat off somewhere?' Adonis's PA asked as she pulled back into the front seat.

'No, she's coming with me.'

'She's got a passport,' Dmitri supplied in a voice devoid of all intonation.

'Is that even a thing?' his wife asked doubtfully.

'Yes, it is.'

Lizzie saw the couple exchange glances and her chin locked in stubborn determination. There was no way she was leaving her cat behind.

This was non-negotiable.

Lizzie had not acquired a cat. The cat, a bedraggled, underweight creature when she had arrived, dragging one injured leg behind her, had chosen Lizzie.

No Mouse and there might never have been any bestselling books. She had modelled her feline heroine on the stray who had worked her way into Lizzie's heart.

It was a short flight and, though her dad did not own his own private jet or a fleet of them like the Aetos family, he hired them. It was his preferred form of travel, and

Lizzie, who had flown in private jets before, was not overawed, and she wasn't a nervous flyer.

Lizzie had worried a little about how Mouse would adapt. The two times she had taken her cat abroad before it had been by car and ferry, and with the help of a mild sedative—luckily she had had some left over from the last trip, but had not so far administered it. To this point the cat had taken it in her stride.

Released from her carrier once they had taken off, much to Jenna's alarm, the feline had actually enjoyed the attention from the crew, who had fussed over her during the short flight.

Lizzie was not a newbie when it came to flying, but she sat with her nose virtually pressed to the window as they came in over the sparkling waters of the bay, the Rock behind them, and landed on the runway.

It was stunning.

'Incredibly short runway,' Dmitri, who was sitting on the opposite side of the plane, supplied.

'Totally incredible,' Lizzie breathed. 'I felt as though we were going to end up in the sea!'

'Shut up, both of you. You are not, either of you, normal. It is horrific,' Jenna had declared, grabbing her husband's hand in a death grip as they hit the tarmac with a jolt that drew a scream from her.

'Jenna is not a good flyer.'

'I hate you,' his wife said firmly. 'Both of you.'

Lizzie, laughing, unfastened her belt and discovered that the cat, who was safely secured back in her carrier for the landing, was asleep.

'So what happens now?' Lizzie asked, thinking, That was the fun bit, now comes the nightmare. *Man up, woman*, she snapped out in her head.

'Jenna usually throws up.'

Lizzie laughed. She might not like her future husband, but the people who worked for him were another matter. Unbuckled, she stood up and smoothed the silk of her short blue skirt while Jenna talked her through the immediate schedule displaying brisk efficiency and no visible signs of nausea.

'Through Customs, shouldn't be an issue. Adonis will be meeting us. Nowhere is far from the airport on the Rock. If you want to freshen up or change, Adonis has been using the owner's suite at—'

'He owns a hotel?'

'He does, several actually—he believes in diversification. But the one here belongs to a friend of his.'

Friend covered a lot of territory. Were they talking friend or was it shorthand for old or maybe even present lover?

She pushed the intrusive thought away. Those were not the sorts of questions that came as part of the territory of temporary fake wife.

'But if you don't need to stop, it's straight to the wedding venue, a celebrant and a private setting, for the ceremony. Then it's back here and you fly direct to Xania. You'll be on the island for dinner.' Seeing the expression on Lizzie's stunned face, she paused, seeming to realise she was delivering a lot of information.

'Are you OK?'

'Finding it a bit hard to process,' Lizzie admitted. 'So we are travelling directly to Greece.'

'It isn't a long flight.'

'Then transfer to the island?'

'We can fly direct. It's a recent addition and more an

airstrip than airport. Previously you did have to land on the mainland and get a helicopter transfer to Xania, which was a nightmare.'

'Have you stayed at the island much?' She had read up on the Aetos family's private island and seen the photos. 'Island paradise' was an overworked term, but in this instance, if the photos told half the truth, the description was deserved.

'A few times. Not at the house. We stay in one of the bungalows.' Jenna flashed her husband a secret smile. 'It's one with all the facilities we need for Robert when he comes. He just loves it there.'

'Robert?'

'Our son, well, my son. He has some complex needs, but he is spending this week in respite care. He loves it at the farm. He goes there several times a year. We are so grateful to Adonis; the breaks help us.' Lizzie watched the other woman's eyes fill with tears before, after a short struggle, she regained her composure. 'Though of course he says he is the beneficiary of us functioning...' She gave a light laugh. 'That's sort of true. He forgets sometimes that not everyone has his energy levels.'

Lizzie digested this information in silence, gripped by unfamiliar and uncomfortable emotions. Whatever else her future husband was, he inexplicably appeared to inspire fierce loyalty from his employees.

Inexplicably, mocked the voice in her head. You mean other than his being sensitive and thoughtful?

Any problem could be worked through if you broke it down into manageable pieces. It was a philosophy that Adonis applied in practical terms every day of his life.

It was the same attitude he had approached his prospective marriage with, and so far everything had gone according to plan. He rejected the voice in his head that suggested this was only because he had avoided Lizzie Rose during the interim.

With her sharp tongue and her wicked sarcasm, not to mention that mouth, she was a disruptive influence to his peace of mind. He had never experienced a person who... He felt her presence like an internal pressure.

Obviously he could negate this, but it seemed reasonable to delay any time-consuming conflict until after the contract was signed.

Pushing the problem ahead does not make it go away, scorned that voice in his head.

The scornful voice was proved correct when he saw her walking towards him.

She hadn't opened her mouth yet and he was chained to the spot by nothing more complicated than lust as he felt a scalding streak of heat slide like a blade through his body and settle in his groin.

He had suspected what his bride had spent a lifetime hiding, but the reality was more in every sense of the word than he had imagined. And all of that more was showcased by the outfit she was wearing, a skirt and cropped jacket ensemble in pale blue.

The skirt that managed to swish and cling to her bottom ended three inches above her knee and showcased really incredible legs, which he instantly decided would be criminal to hide. The jacket was fitted with a tiny peplum that showed off a tiny waist and the feminine flare of her hips. Beneath, the cream corset affair was held together with a row of tiny pearl buttons; it had a square neckline that didn't distort the full curve of her dramatically incredible breasts.

He recognised the moment she identified him—her spine went significantly stiffer and her chin rose before she paused for a moment, putting down a basket she was carrying. She balanced on one leg while she removed a crepe-soled trainer and slid on a slingback spiky heel she had produced magician-like, then the balancing-on-one-foot routine was repeated.

The ground under her feet was even but Lizzie felt as if she were on a tightrope as she walked towards the tall waiting figure. Elegant to the nth degree in his dark formal suit and snowy white shirt, he looked as though he had just stepped out from the pages of a fashion shoot intended to make the gullible male believe if they too used this brand of hair product they would become utterly irresistible, have a beautiful woman in their bed and drive a designer car.

She blamed it on the heels, except of course no glossy fashion shoot had ever projected the sort of earthy sexual aura that Adonis did.

'Hello, nice day for it.' It wasn't but, as the other option had been help or, even worse, wow, Lizzie settled for gentle sarcasm.

He did look wow!

Actually, wow was an understatement. Lean and muscular, his carved features could have graced a statue, but they were real, glowing, alive.

She held herself tense as dark, heavy-lidded eyes that seemed to hold no expression flickered over her.

'You are not wearing the wedding dress.'

'Very observant of you. It's lucky I'm not, really, as I

would have looked every kind of lunatic wafting through the arrivals lounge in white lace and frills.'

'I didn't think of that and there should not have been frills. I specifically mentioned that.'

His ready admission took the wind out of her lofty superior sails. She fell back on attack, it being the best form of defence, she really hoped, against the hormonal overload that was nibbling away at her ability to string words together that made sense. 'Well, neither did I, think, that is, because I didn't know I was about to get on a plane, because you didn't have the courtesy to inform me of your plans.'

'You told me to do what I liked. You were not interested,' he pointed out.

'Well, I didn't mean this...' She faltered, annoyed with him for paraphrasing her own parting shot against her. 'And Jenna went to the trouble of putting together an information pack for me and you didn't even bother to pass it on!'

'Did she?' he said, pretending ignorance. 'It must have slipped my mind.'

He had actually been on the point of pressing the send key on that information pack when he had hesitated, Jenna's comment when he had requested the schedule springing to mind.

'Most brides would prefer flowers.'

There was a balance between formal and flowery, and maybe the timetable was not hitting it, but then flowers would have been overkill too and possibly thrown back in his face. Decision-making was not something that Adonis struggled with, he didn't like the paralysing indecision, and in the end had opted for doing nothing.

He should have known that lack of action would not save him from her sharp tongue.

Lizzie snorted. 'You mean you wanted me to feel even more helpless and out of my depth than I already do!' She immediately regretted the fact she had just admitted a vulnerability to him that she had managed to deny even to herself.

'I don't want you to feel that way.'

'I don't,' she countered.

'You look stunning.'

Her defensive stance melted, as did her insides. Blue eyes met dark and the world seemed to still for the space of several heartbeats, until she brought her lashes down in a protective shield and mumbled, 'You look OK too.'

His brows lifted. 'Thank you, yes, we make a handsome couple, I think,' he concluded, making her think of some sort of preening, self-satisfied jungle cat sheathing his claws before he swiped her verbally with one satiny sharp paw.

'Jenna said there is an option of pausing to redo my lips, but it won't be necessary.'

Her comment brought his eyes to her mouth just as she moistened her lips nervously with the tip of her tongue. The flickering action, unintentionally erotic, sent a surge of reckless lust through his body.

Dmitri repeated his question three times before Adonis, thinking about how she would taste, reacted with a vague, 'Ah yes, fine, you go ahead, we'll follow.'

CHAPTER SIX

As he turned back to Lizzie he focused his attention on the basket at her feet. 'What is that?'

He looked so bemused that the tension that had been building inside her vanished. This was a conversation she didn't mind having because there was only one outcome. The knowledge made her feel in charge.

'My cat.'

His thick dark brows knitted into a pattern of disapproval. 'You have brought a cat to a wedding.'

'Well, I couldn't leave her on the plane.'

She spoke kindly, as though she were addressing someone slightly slow on the uptake.

'Why was she on the plane in the first place?'

'Because we come as a package deal.'

Her tone, in fact her entire body language, suggested she wanted to instigate a fight, just for the hell of it, meek mouse… He felt quite wistful for the time when she was neatly filed under that heading in his head.

'Do you know how absurd you sound?'

'Do you actually think I care about what you think about how I sound or, for that matter, look?' She frowned, not liking the look of comprehension that spread across his face.

'This is about my remark at that awful dinner, isn't it?'

She opened her mouth to deny this and closed it again. 'You were extremely rude, but that came as no surprise.'

'You were wearing a tent-like garment, which for a woman with your shape is—'

'What's wrong with my shape?' she flared.

'Nothing in the world except the fact you try and hide it.'

Her pugnacious stance disintegrated in the space of a single thud of her heart, and her insides melted as she stared at the compelling earthy perfection of his carved patrician features.

'You should not try to hide your femininity. You should celebrate it.'

This advice, coming from a man who had never been seen in public with a woman who didn't have hip bones you could hang a coat hanger on—in fact, she decided viciously, women who were coat hangers—struck her as the ultimate hypocrisy.

'We were talking about my cat, not my body,' she reminded him coldly.

They might not be talking about her body, but he was thinking about it. The thoughts combined with the subtle citrusy scent of her perfume, and the surge of desire and something more complicated that he fought hard against all but consumed him.

'You were talking, correction, you were itching to start a pitched battle. You brought your damned cat. Fine. I have no view on it at all.' His dark eyes flickered to the basket she was brandishing like some bloody weapon. 'How about you and your pet get in the car and let's get married?' snarled the groom.

She fixed him with a killer glare.

'How can I resist such a charming invitation?'

She sat in the air-conditioned luxury barely registering it, or the scenery through the window, but there was only so long a person could sit stiff-backed without being in pain.

'I'm a bit nervous about this. I never thought I'd get married, let alone to someone who…to someone like you,' she said, her eyes trained on her interlaced fingers as her bottled-up feelings burst out. 'I keep telling myself it's not real, but it bothers me so much that I am… It's cheating.'

She leaned back into her seat, her temper burned off, and a sadness remained.

He flicked her a sideways glance, noting the traces of blue shadows under her beautiful eyes, the quiver of the blue-veined pulse in her temple. He redirected his eyes to the road ahead, his brain shifting gear to cope with the surge of protectiveness her vulnerability shook loose in him.

'Who are we hurting, Lizzie Rose?'

She blinked, her eyes swivelling to his achingly perfect profile. 'It's… I…' She paused, struggling to put her complex feelings into words. She couldn't bring herself to say that marriage was a sacred thing because that would have made her sound naive.

'You can walk away at any moment.'

Nostrils flared, she sucked up a quivering breath and pushed out a resentful, 'Yes, I know you're right.'

He laughed. 'That must have hurt.'

'Yes, actually it did, but the last week has been…not easy.'

'Tell me about it.'

Her brow pleated into an uncomprehending frown until understanding dawned and the feeling in his voice made sense.

Just because he was pushing this didn't mean he liked it. How could he? He was facing a fake marriage of inconvenience with Deb's dumpy little cousin while he was still grieving for his lost love. It had to be dredging up all sorts of painful memories of the wedding day he had been robbed of.

'Sorry, it must be hard for you.' Did he feel disloyal to his lost love?

'Sorry?' He slid a mystified glance her way before focusing on the road ahead.

'I know... Well, I don't know.' How could she? She had never been in love. 'Deb was so beautiful, and your wedding would have been... This one isn't real.'

And when it was for real another man would unlock the fiery passion he sensed inside her, a fiery passion that he was sure that her lovers to this point had not tapped into.

Of course, with it came the stubborn streak, the awful dress sense and her misplaced empathy.

'The traffic is though.'

She clamped her lips. 'OK, sorry.'

'You've already said that. Sorry for what, exactly? You feel cheated from the big wedding you have always imagined?'

'God, no!' she came back with a horrified shudder. 'I have never dreamt of a wedding at all, ever, but you...' A frustrated sigh left her lips. His attitude was making it very hard to hang onto her sympathy.

'You had Deb. It must be hard after you planned your perfect wedding. The contrast with—'

'Marriage is a contract.'

'Well, ours is, obviously, and I know it might not seem like it now, but one day you might—you will—meet someone.' And Lizzie for one did not envy the woman he would marry for real, not when competing with a ghost who would never gain a few inches around her waist or have a bad hair day.

'If you want to set me up with another woman while we are married, you might raise a few eyebrows.'

'I'm not trying to set you up. I'm being sympathetic,' she pushed out in an offended rush. 'I won't bother.'

'That news makes me very happy and, for the record, if I want a woman, I have never needed a cheerleader.'

'That is... You are...'

'Being very restrained. You notice I did not say pimp for me. So are you still up for this or shall I just, as they say, call the whole thing off?'

The question hung in the conditioned air between them for a long moment. She hardly trusted her voice as she sent him a poisonous sideways glare. 'No, let's do it.'

Adonis's firm lips turned up at the corners. He had known many women over the years who had been willing to go to any lengths to extract a proposal from him and he was marrying a woman who approached marriage to him with the enthusiasm most people reserved for a root canal or leaping into a lake of freezing water.

'In that case, have a look in the glove box. There's a ring. Put it on.'

'I don't need a ring.'

'It's not about need.'

Lizzie stared at the ring, nestled in red velvet, the sapphire surrounded by twinkling diamonds. A very expensive piece of window dressing, like the wardrobe of clothes.

'People will think I'm a cheapskate if you don't have an engagement ring.'

She flashed him a sideways look and warned, 'It won't fit.'

But it did.

Obviously it didn't, but it felt to Lizzie as though the long corridor went on for ever. The sound of her heels on the marble floor had a dreamlike quality as she fell into step beside Jenna, who looked almost as nervous as Lizzie felt.

Adonis was walking a little ahead, his head tilted as he made conversation with the person who appeared to be the celebrant. In truth, Lizzie had no idea because she had only heard one word in three when the woman had introduced herself above the static buzz that had taken up residence in Lizzie's head along with Adonis's distinctive deep voice and jumbled snatches of conversation.

One rose to the surface above the others.

He'd said she looked stunning.

She purposely dampened the illicit little glow of pleasure that came with the memory, reminding herself that he was not talking about her, he was talking about her clothes. She was still the same person she had been two years ago, he had just admired the fancy wrapping.

Which was of course shallow, but she had to admit that actually the feel of expensive silk and natural fibres against her skin was sensual... Normally, she was a sports bra fan, but the underwired piece of silk she was wearing was pretty and gently supportive.

She was still thinking about underwear and how he'd known her size when the corridor ended, and they reached a large arched metal-banded door.

There were no more thoughts to distract her from

the moment. Her brain had effectively gone into frozen freeze-frame.

The celebrant stood to one side and Lizzie felt everyone's expectant eyes on her. The space next to Adonis was hers for the taking.

How many tall skinny women out there would envy her and feel quite rightly that they would be a better fit for that spot, for the ring on her finger? Her flickering gaze was captured by the ring as she began to tug panicky at it.

'What are you doing?'

'You can use this as a wedding band.'

'I have wedding bands for us both.'

'Oh, right...' It seemed he had thought of everything except the fact that no one would believe that he had picked her out for his bride.

The elephant in the room had never been properly addressed. The argument that should have been front and centre. Nobody was going to believe they were a fit. Everyone would see through the ruse. This would all be a stupid waste of time.

'Do you need a glass of water?'

That was Jenna and then another voice said something about nervous brides.

'I'm fine.' Her voice sounded as though it were coming from a long way away and her feet felt heavy as she finally walked towards him. Her stomach was a mess of butterflies as she kept her gaze low under the mesh of her naturally dark eyelashes.

She fell in beside him, close, but not quite touching as they walked through the arch into a flower-filled paved quadrangle enclosed by richly glowing stone walls, beyond which you got iconic glimpses of the Rock against a cerulean-blue sky, the Rock that dominated Gibraltar, that pretty much was Gibraltar.

Her heels on the stone sounded loud but the water falling from the fountain was louder.

'You've got no flowers,' Jenna suddenly exclaimed, sounding horrified.

As if flowers were the only absence in this wedding, Lizzie thought, turning a bitter laugh into a cough.

'There are plenty of flowers here,' she soothed, amazed that she sounded calm, almost normal. But it was true: a riot of colour spilled out of the raised beds, herbs flourished in the cracks between the stone slabs, filling the air with their aroma as they were crushed underfoot.

'She has a cat.'

Lizzie had hardly forgotten he was there but the sound of his deep voice made her jump.

'Give him to Dmitri.'

For once it didn't sound like an order. If he'd pushed it she would have hung on, but he didn't so she handed Mouse over, telling her to be a good girl.

'It's her, not him.'

'Would your cat like to run around? There is a secure area, the smaller garden, more intimate, some couples prefer that... If you like she could be released there to stretch her little legs. Suitable for animals. A couple last month had their rescue dog deliver the ring.'

'Oh, how lovely! So romantic!' Lizzie exclaimed, enchanted and at the same time depressed because of the contrast to her own wedding, but she still hesitated. 'It's secure? She couldn't escape?'

'Oh, absolutely not. Shall I?'

She nodded her permission to Dmitri, then smiled at the older woman. 'Thank you so much.'

While desperately aware of him at a cellular level, Lizzie didn't look at Adonis through the entire mercifully short ceremony—maybe because she was so aware.

If it hadn't been for the rapid rise and fall of her incredible breasts, he might have thought she had stopped breathing. She radiated stillness as she delivered her responses in a soft, barely audible voice, and not until the final moment did she abandon her still-statue pose and he saw a myriad emotions move across the surface of the vivid little face lifted to him.

She appeared almost to be compensating for his lack of emotional reaction. His teeth ground in frustration. It was almost as if she was trying to guilt-trip him.

To be cast in the role of villain to her victim did not sit well with him. She had not walked into this with her eyes closed, she knew what she was doing, he thought, feeding his anger to drown out the noise from his irrational guilty conscience. Totally irrational!

But she looked so lost.

He pushed the thought away. Just because a woman had big blue eyes and narrow, fragile wrists did not make her weak. He was not attracted by weakness in a woman, and Lizzie Rose was anything but weak. She had tenacity and a temper, which were two of the reasons he liked her.

He liked her.

He buried the acknowledgement that felt like a weakness and told himself that she would be better off moving forward, thinking about the next stage of their plan and the big reveal with his family instead of broadcasting every little thing she was feeling. Everything.

Theos! It appalled him that someone wore their emotions so close to the surface. How did she survive like that, wearing her vulnerabilities like a neon sign, like an open invitation to take advantage?

Like you did?

'You may kiss the bride.'

He angled his head, bending down as his big hands landed on her shoulders, his intention clear.

She didn't panic, a fact she was proud of. Instead she brought her hands palm outwards at chest height and whispered quickly, 'You really don't have to.'

'It's kind of obligatory to kiss the bride,' he retorted drily, smothering a fresh flare of annoyance that he was the one putting the effort in. She had as much invested in this working as he had. 'It's just a kiss. Just close your eyes and pretend I'm the man of your dreams.'

She heard the undercurrent of irritation in his soft-voiced aside and was not fooled by the loving hand that tenderly stroked the loose strands of hair from her face and curled around her cheek. He was right, of course. She was making it a big thing when it really wasn't.

You carry on telling yourself that, Lizzie.

'I think there's standing room only in that particular club and I'm not good with crowds.'

'Ouch!' he huffed under his breath, relieved to see the antagonistic spark in her eyes as he moved in closer, the action effectively capturing her hands between their bodies.

At the first brush of his lips her wide blue eyes closed and she swayed towards him as though responding to some sort of magnetic tug.

The soft brush of his lips over hers could have stopped there had her lips not parted slightly... Did she kiss him back?

It was hard to know who was responsible for the clash of lips, teeth, and tongue in the hot breathless moments before his hands fell from her shoulders.

It was a mistake, obviously. There was no argument. But she tasted like strawberries, and her lush lips were silky and soft. He hadn't been able to resist exploring them...and the moist inner aspects of her mouth. He had wanted to explore every inch. The jolt back to reality was like an ice shower, physically painful.

They simultaneously stepped back. Her knees were shaking, and she looked at the two rings that now lay on her finger.

'I wasn't expecting...' Her glance lifted, her eyes zeroing in on his mouth. 'It's beautiful, the courtyard,' she tacked on, saving herself from further embarrassment.

He virtually had to prise her mouth away.

Her body burned with the shame of it, though actually if it had just been shame that she burned with, ached with, it would have been a lot simpler.

'I wasn't expecting it to be outdoors,' she elaborated. 'So pretty,' she trilled, senselessly.

The next part was a bit of a blur, laughter, the chinking of glasses—at least she retained the residual sense of self-preservation and settled for orange juice.

It was actually a relief to get back in the private jet. Mouse had obviously exhausted herself in her brief moments of freedom, so she curled on Lizzie's lap and went to sleep. Nobody had ever said she was not a survivor.

Lizzie envied her.

For God's sake, Lizzie, less of the drama-queen stuff. It's not like you're flying towards your doom, she told herself sternly as she shifted restlessly in the comfort of her deep leather seat, causing the cat to flex her claws in protest against Lizzie's thigh.

'Sorry,' Lizzie soothed after an ouch as she stroked the soft, silky fur, turning her gaze to the window and the stream of clouds wafting by.

Fatigue held at bay by nerves washed over her in waves, receding and advancing until the long surreal day caught up on her and her eyelids closed.

Adonis walked into the cabin, intending to update Lizzie on what to expect when they landed in Xania, but she was asleep, the darned cat curled up on her knee.

Considering he had decided the cat had been brought along for the ride just to irritate him, he felt rather good he had not risen to the provocation; it opened one eye and regarded him with disdain before closing it again, the purring audible from where he stood.

He studied Lizzie Rose's sleeping face, slightly flushed in repose. The lashes on her wide-set eyes cast a shadow over the smooth curve of her high cheeks. Her relaxed mouth was stretched in a soft half-smile, a few strands of glossy hair lay across her cheek, and the jewel-encrusted slide that had pulled her hair away from her face on one side had slid down to the end of one silky strand.

He could only suppose that his lengthy celibacy was responsible for the ribbons of heat that threaded through his body as he looked at her, thinking of the warmth of her lips.

Initially the celibacy had been a natural reaction to Deb's sudden death and then later, when there was widespread speculation about the woman who would be her replacement and apparently heal his broken heart, he had felt a disinclination to fuel the media and gift publicity to the first woman to make it to his bed.

Or then again, maybe he had been too lazy to make the effort. Sex had become too easy, almost mechanical, boring.

There was nothing lazy about the kick of his libido as his eyes followed the long, graceful curve of her neck where the skin looked smooth as warm silk, and then lower, where one of the tiny pearl buttons had slipped free of the loop of fabric, exposing a modest but fascinating glimpse of her bra and an even more fascinating section of cleavage.

It could not be considered a bad thing to lust after your own wife, but it could, given their unique circumstances, be considered a complication. His fingers flexed as he pushed them into his pockets, the compulsion to touch so strong it was almost overwhelming.

Lizzie Rose's passion was buried beneath prickles and contradictions.

She opened her eyes. He saw the confusion in the deep blue depths and heard her wince as the cat, annoyed at having its sleep disturbed, dug its claws into her thigh.

'Ouch, Mouse...' She pushed her hand through her hair and herself up in her seat.

Adonis caught the jewelled hair clip before it hit the ground and handed it back to her.

'Thank you,' she said as he dropped it into her open palm. 'I must have fallen asleep.' She sat upright from her slumped position, smoothing the cat's fur as she did so, the action making her aware that her skirt had ridden up, showing far too much leg.

Surreptitiously pulling it down, Lizzie angled a small cautious smile up at him, noting that he was no longer wearing a jacket and the tie was gone, leaving a small vee of butterscotch-coloured skin exposed at the base of his throat.

She looked around the cabin and realised they were alone. 'Where are Jenna and Dmitri?'

'They stepped out for a moment. There were only two parachutes, but they said they'd meet us there,' he explained, deadpan.

'Very funny.' She sniffed, arching an interrogative brow.

'They have gone through to the bedroom, to take a Zoom call.'

She wrinkled her nose at the explanation. 'That sounds very high powered.'

'No, personal. Their son, Robert, he needs routine. When he is in residential care, seeing them at the same times every day helps.'

She nodded at the explanation. 'I suppose having a disabled child can put a lot of strain on a marriage,' she mused.

Adonis took a leather seat opposite her as one of the attendants approached with a tray bearing coffee and sandwiches.

'Thought you might be hungry,' he said, before adding, 'I am.'

As the attendant left he leaned back and crossed one ankle over the other, letting his long legs stretch out. Despite his claim to be hungry he seemed in no hurry to address the food.

'Jenna's first marriage broke down because the father couldn't cope. Dmitri loves the kid. He is a great dad.'

Lizzie took a sandwich and waited until she had swallowed a bite before speaking. 'Will your parents be there on the island?' What were they going to make of his unlikely choice of bride?

'My parents? That is extremely unlikely.'

Something in his tone made her ask. 'You don't get on?'

'Get on?' he mused, looking at her over the rim of a coffee cup. 'We get on fine now that I am no longer an inconvenience.'

She shook her head. 'I don't understand.'

'My parents always found that having a child in the picture got in the way of their great epic love story.' He heard himself explain and immediately wondered why he was revealing this private part of his history.

Some of the tension bunched in his shoulders fell away when a logical explanation for his soul-baring almost immediately revealed itself: they were about to play a couple who had just eloped—it made sense that she would know something about his history.

He turned a deaf ear to the annoying voice in his head that inconveniently pointed out that the only thing Deb had known about his parents was that, according to her, they both looked far too young to have a grown-up son.

'Your father resented the attention your mother gave you?' Lizzie tried to keep her disapproval out of her voice. Not easy—the idea of a jealous manchild filled her with angry contempt.

Adonis laughed, and the discordant sound made her nerves jangle.

'If my mother has maternal instincts they are well

hidden. My parents both thought that having a child was the worst thing they ever did, though, I have to hand it to them, they did not allow my existence to ruin their lives,' he explained with a cynical shrug. 'They packed me off to school when I was seven and I spent most holidays on Xania.'

Horrified, Lizzie didn't know how to respond. After a moment she pushed out a troubled, 'Hands-off parenting is a thing, I suppose,' struggling to think of anything non-judgemental to say to even partially excuse his parents. 'But I'm sure they didn't really feel like that.' Even if that were true, it was truly terrible in her eyes that they had made their child think they did, made him feel he was unwanted.

An image of a young Adonis, dark eyes and a mop of jet hair, slid into her head and her anger heated once more.

'I am not reading between the lines. They told me on more than one occasion that they wished I had never been born.'

He watched her eyes fly cartoon wide before narrowing into furious slits. Nostrils flared, she put the rest of her sandwich in her mouth and swallowed without chewing.

'How? Well, they are…?'

'In love,' he drawled with a sardonic grimace of distaste. 'A narcissistic match made in hell. They are totally obsessed with one another to the exclusion of the rest of the world. Their fights are things of legend and their making up—' He caught her horrified expression and clamped his mouth over further unnecessary reveals. 'Don't look so devastated,' he added, thinking there was a big difference in discussing some family details so she could act the role he had brought her here to play and serving up a sob story with a side-order invitation to wander around in his head.

'I actually liked school. It taught me to be independent.'

'I've heard people say that.'

'And you don't believe it.'

She shrugged. 'I hated school,' she revealed abruptly. 'Well, secondary school at least.' Maybe if she had not just lost her mum, her dad hadn't gone on his cruise because looking at her reminded him of his dead wife, and the only female influence in her life hadn't been the well-meaning housekeeper whose ideas of suitable clothes and guidance for a pre-teenage girl had been firmly rooted in the fifties, it might have gone better.

She had not complained to him, but maybe her dad had sensed she was unhappy when he had persuaded Deb's mum to allow Deb to transfer to the same school, reasoning that her presence would help Lizzie. It hadn't worked out that way. Deb had arrived and instantly been the popular girl that everyone wanted to be with. Lizzie hadn't minded her cousin ignoring her. In fact it had been preferable to the occasions when she'd led the bullying.

'Why?'

'The usual,' she said, avoiding his eyes and shrugging. She was already regretting opening up this far.

'You are not a very trusting person, are you, Lizzie Rose?' he observed, studying her with an intensity that made her shift uneasily in her seat.

'I don't have much reason to trust you, do I? I don't really know you!'

The utter absurdity of saying this to the man you had just married struck her forcibly. She paused, biting her full lower lip between her teeth as she gathered her calm around her, pulling it tight like a comfort blanket. Now was not the time for thinking about what she had done. That time had gone. She just had to deal with the reality of the present.

'My mum died just before I started secondary school. I missed her.'

He watched her expression close down and realised the world of hurt behind the composed words.

'That must have been tough.'

Her jaw clenched as she thought, *Do not be nice to me.* Nasty she could take, but nice cut through the protective layers that she had built up over the years.

'I was not...cool. The school didn't have a uniform and, well, my clothes sense then was pretty much the same as it is now. I was a swot, and, well, you get the picture. But you learn coping techniques...' Her voice trailed away as she articulated this for the first time.

'Such as?'

'Never let the bastards see you cry.' She flashed him a defiant look. 'Oh, and, of course, when you're the butt of the joke play dim and laugh with everyone else. It comes in handy even now,' she mused drily.

The wave of protectiveness that rose up in Adonis was shocking in its intensity. 'Bastards,' he murmured. 'Or should that be bitches? Was your school mixed?'

'Mixed, and I went from flat-chested to...not flat-chested overnight.' Avoiding his eyes, she got to her feet and made a show of looking around for the cat. 'Where has she got to?'

On cue, Mouse revealed herself by leaping onto a startled Adonis's knee.

'Theos!'

His bass rumble of alarm made her laugh. He was looking at the cat with the sort of expression normally reserved for an unexploded bomb.

She silently thanked her scene-stealing moggy for affording a distraction.

'Let me take her.' She bent, loose strands of her hair brushing his cheek as she gathered the purring cat up in her arms. 'How long before we land?' she asked, looking around for the cat basket.

'Probably time to put it—' he caught her eye and corrected himself with a half-smile '—her in her basket.'

She nodded.

'You're nervous?'

Lizzie laughed, secured the cat in her basket and turned, staring at the rings on her finger and feeling a contracting wave of fear swell in her chest. 'Of course I'm nervous. People will never believe that—'

'They will,' he contradicted, rising in one fluid motion to his feet. Towering over her, he placed his hands on her shoulders. 'They will believe because they will all want to believe. They will look at you and think you are exactly what I need.'

'What, someone plain and homely? I don't even know who they are other than your grandfather.'

'Homely?' he echoed before he threw back his head and laughed. He was still laughing when his hands dropped from her shoulders and he fell back into his seat in an elegant sprawl, all long legs, coordinated grace and off-the-scale sex appeal.

Lizzie planted her hands on her hips and glared down at him, using her anger to hold back the panic that was tight in the pit of her stomach. 'I'm glad you think this is funny.'

CHAPTER SEVEN

'NOT FUNNY. Tragic if you really believe that.' Adonis had stopped laughing and looked inexplicably annoyed. 'What have the men in your life been doing if you don't know that you are gorgeous?'

'I don't need men to tell me—' Lizzie stopped, colour flooding her face.

Gorgeous?

He made a sweeping motion with his hands, his dark eyes lingering on the sensual curves of her lush body. 'You are sexy, you have tremendous legs that you never allow anyone to see, you envelop your figure in tents and dull colours, but your body issues aside—' He pushed away the subject as though it had been nothing more controversial than the weather forecast.

'Aside from my grandfather, my two aunts will be there and their husbands, or in Elena's case not her husband yet, her divorce has not come through. Elena and Lydia are my father's twin half-sisters, considerably younger than him. They both have daughters, a set of twins apiece, teens.'

Lizzie blinked, taking the details on board. 'So what did they say when you told them we were coming, that we are...' she cleared her throat, finishing on a shrill '...married?'

'Nothing.'

She looked at him blankly.

'I didn't tell them and I hadn't confirmed I would make it for the birthday party.'

'Birthday party?' she said, trying to stay calm.

'My grandfather is eighty today.'

She stared at him, then gave an incredulous bubble of laughter and sank back into her seat.

'So you are just going to walk in and announce…?' She gasped, shaking her head in disbelief. 'You really do like making an entrance, don't you?' Not for one second did she think the timing was accidental. 'For the record, I don't.' But then she reflected, shaking with the strength of her feelings, Adonis was not interested in what she liked, wanted, or needed.

Before he could respond, Jenna and Dmitri reappeared.

Adonis turned his head. 'How was Robert?'

Jenna nodded and smiled. 'He's settled in really well. Right,' she added with a grimace. 'Time to belt up?' She sighed and closed her eyes. 'Wake me when it's over.'

'Adonis.'

He turned back to his bride and found azure-blue eyes fixed unblinkingly on his face. 'Lizzie.'

Her lips tightened. 'Let me get this right—we are going to crash a birthday party and tell your nearest and dearest we are married.'

'That's about right, though first you can get changed. I picked out a couple of possibles and laid them out on the bed.'

'I'm not letting you pick out my clothes!' What her voice lacked in volume, it made up for in outrage.

He responded with a teeth-grating gorgeous smile that made her want to hit him.

'Why would you do this?' she despaired. 'Why land me on them this way? Couldn't you come up with something less...dramatic?'

'You forget that our engagement has already been announced, even if not by us, so it's hardly going to be a drama. There might be some ruffled feathers that we robbed them of a wedding, but eloping has the cachet of being romantic,' he drawled with a lip curl that suggested he did not share this viewpoint. 'The old man had the element of surprise. He'd taken control of the narrative but now it is our turn.'

'Don't include me in this,' she said, leaning forward in her seat to fix him with a killer glare. 'It has nothing to do with me.'

'The ring on your finger says otherwise,' he countered. 'Look, what is the issue? Keeping this a secret rather defeats the object of the exercise.'

'Obviously I didn't want to keep it a secret.'

He arched a sceptical brow. 'So what is the problem?'

'You playing some sort of game with your grandfather, proving you are in charge, watching people dance to your tune. You are as manipulative as he is.'

Her chest heaving as she struggled to contain her feelings, she slid a cautious sideways glance at the other couple in the cabin and was relieved that they seemed oblivious to the war of attrition being waged across the aisle.

'Did it occur to you for one second to imagine how I am going to feel being thrown to the lions this way?' she hissed resentfully. 'A family party!'

'No one is going to eat you. You will be fine,' Adonis said, his infuriating attitude of lazy indifference tipping over into impatience as he advised her to, 'Just relax and fasten your seat belt.'

A glance through the window told her the tarmac was empty apart from another jet with the distinctive gold Aetos logo on its side. It would seem that there would be no massive queues to negotiate and the only officialdom for a man who literally had his name written on everything would involve bowing and scraping, she concluded cynically.

'Aren't you coming with us?' Lizzie asked, hiding her panic under a smile when Dmitri and Jenna made their farewells.

She struggled to hide her escalating dismay when they explained they would be going straight to the bungalow they were staying in for the duration.

'We're officially on holiday now,' Jenna said, adding a comforting, 'You'll be fine.'

Lizzie nodded and made her way to one of the bedrooms—apparently the jet boasted two—where there was a selection of the promised outfits laid out on the bed.

She stripped down to her bra and pants, feeling as creased as the suit she took off and hung on a hanger. After a short internal debate she ignored the shower in the en suite but felt slightly fresher after splashing her face with water and refreshing her make-up.

It didn't take long—a few minutes later she was viewing the results with a critical eye, the fresh gloss of lipstick, a smudge of shadow on her lids and, because she did look desperately pale, a light dust of blusher on the apples of her cheeks. She decided she looked less ghost-like, though the sprinkling of freckles across her nose and cheeks still shone through.

Bending her head forward, she shook out her long hair. The silky and tangled strands almost swept the floor as she bent down and began to brush in long, rhythmic strokes that made her glossy rich hair crackle with static. After one final brush, she straightened up, pushing the mane of hair back from her face with one forearm as she stepped into the bedroom.

The breath left her lungs in a sibilant hiss as Lizzie found herself looking at her new husband, who was in the act of fighting his way into a fresh white shirt. It hung open, revealing the carved musculature of his tanned chest complete with a light sprinkling of body hair and the muscle-ridged corrugation of his flat washboard belly. She licked her lips, unable to stop her eyes following the narrow directional arrow of dark hair that vanished beneath the belt of his dark tailored trousers.

In seconds the creeping heat in the pit of her stomach became a flaming inferno, the tug of her sex between her legs a throbbing ache and inside the silky cups she could feel her nipples shamelessly harden into tingling peaks.

Sensing that his dark hooded eyes had landed on this shameful physical response and painfully aware of the liquid heat in her pelvis—it felt as though she were being attacked on multiple fronts—she lifted her hands in a defensive gesture to cover her breasts, stopping midway when she realised it would make the situation a million times worse by drawing attention to her weakness.

Mortified, confused and angry that it was now of all the times for her libido to come out of hibernation, she drew in a ragged breath and lifted her gaze. Unfortunately the level of her thoughts did not follow.

'Sorry, I... Sorry,' she mumbled, not caring if she sounded stupid, just glad whole words came out.

Adonis didn't hear what she said. His mind was filled with the imagined sound of her gasp as his tongue slid between her lips. The muscles in his brown throat worked visibly as he held her gaze in a blank burning stare while inside his head he was seeing those soft curves plastered up against him. There was a whole series of incrementally more erotic fantasy images being projected by his imagination onto his retina.

He had thought of her as a revelation, but now he knew that barely came close to describing her body. How could any man look at her and not think of sinking into the softness, feeling her warmth close around him?

'I left my shirts in here,' he finally pushed out hoarsely, glancing at the crumpled discarded shirt on the bed then back at Lizzie, immediately seeing her on the bed, her arms outstretched to him.

Adonis could feel his control unravelling faster by the second. He knew he had to remove himself from this situation or... Before he could come up with the or option, there was a tap on the door.

As he pushed it open to reveal one of the male attendants standing there looking apologetic, Lizzie grabbed for her robe and moved out of view.

The conversation was short and inaudible to Lizzie, who had regained a crumb of her composure. When he stepped back inside, she coached the belt on the robe another painful hitch tighter.

'Take your time. No hurry, we are not on the clock.'

'Thanks, yes, of course...'

He vanished and she lowered herself to the floor in a cross-legged posture that spoke a lot for her core strength. Lizzie was not thinking about core strength, she was not thinking at all, she was stunned, shocked and... She had never felt anything approaching that before, not the wanting to touch, to taste... She wanted to surrender not just to the need inside her but to him.

She took a deep breath and told herself to get a grip as, with thoughtless elegance, she rose to her feet and focused on the practical.

She needed to get dressed.

She didn't take her time. She didn't even look at the dresses laid out on the bed. Heart hammering—what the hell had just happened there?—she grabbed the one nearest.

Like you don't know, mocked the voice in her head.

Maybe the colour caught her eye. It was a deep jewelled turquoise blue; the heavy silky fabric skimmed elegantly and didn't cling but managed to show every dip and curve of her body.

Still feeling dazed, she glanced in the mirror and a stranger looked back at her. She would have walked past this Lizzie in the street and not recognised herself, not that walking past yourself was an option unless you had a twin. With a supreme effort she closed down her tangled jumble of thoughts and looked properly. Ignoring the sultry glow in her eyes and the light all-over flush on her skin, she took in the simplicity of the dress that ended with a sensual swish four inches above her knee.

It was a simple tunic in cut but subtly shaped to show her narrow waist, the deep vee on the back showed her shoulder blades, and it was high in the front but still revealed the delicacy of her collarbones. The pleated cap sleeves that floated when she moved provided the drama.

She had never imagined she could look either elegant or sexy, but in this dress she looked both. The spiky heels with the pointy toes and the frivolous bow didn't diminish the effect. She really did have quite decent legs, she decided as she contorted to see her rear view in the mirror.

The effect could have given her confidence, and it did, to a point. It helped with the illusion she was acting a part. The problem was that she hadn't been acting just then. Her stomach flipped, and her body thrummed with the memory and intensity of those moments. She had felt attraction before but not the inexorable tug of animal magnetism, chemistry. Come on, Lizzie, she told herself impatiently. Sex.

She was inexperienced but she was not stupid or blind and he had felt it too, or something. Even as she remembered the feral heat in his eyes, the tension that surrounded him like an aura sent an illicit thrill of fluid heat through her body.

She exited the plane alone, apart from Mouse in her basket. Lizzie held onto her tight, as though she were her only link to reality, to who she really was. Adonis was already in the sleek car waiting for her. Thinking he might be watching made her determined not to trip, so she focused on putting one foot in front of the other.

So long as she thought about feet she would be OK.

'That cat travels well.'

Her eyes flickered to the basket wedged by her feet. 'She is resilient, one of life's survivors. Are there any other cats in the...?' She paused and realised she didn't have a clue where they were headed. The sun was dropping, the sky illuminated by streaks of gold, and every so often she had a glimpse of the sea tinged with gold.

'Villa,' he supplied, aware in the periphery of his vision as she crossed her legs; the silky rustle that went with the action aroused him to a painful degree.

'I really don't know. When you hand him over to the kitchen staff...'

Lizzie embraced her anger with a kind of relief. It was marvellous to be able to think he was shallow and lacking in any sort of empathy, not how gorgeous and incredible he smelled.

'I am not about to hand her over,' she snapped, outraged at the suggestion.

'You do know that you are being ridiculous.' The residual tension from the moments when she had been standing there in her very provocative underwear had lessened but not diminished. It had more coalesced into a tight fist of frustration and resentment in his gut.

Lizzie turned her head, intending to project cold ice queen, but an iceberg could not have cooled the angry frustrated heat inside her. If her eyes had been lasers his perfect profile would be seriously damaged. 'I'm not discussing this.'

'Fine, my suite... The sitting room opens out onto a quadrangle, totally enclosed. Will that suit you and your blasted animal?' he asked in a clipped tone.

Lizzie's lips tightened in response to the sarcasm in his voice. 'Yes.' She stopped. 'Your suite? Where will I be?'

'We are arriving a married couple. Where the hell do you think you will be?'

Her breath coming in shallow laboured puffs, she didn't say a word for a moment. 'I hadn't thought that far ahead.'

'Sometimes it is better not to. Thinking is not all it is hyped up to be. You can't always factor in the...' The fact that he wanted her, so badly that it felt like a weight in his chest. 'Look, we are married. We will be sharing a room. Let's work out the logistics later. It might not be an issue.'

She let the heavy silence lie for a moment. 'What do you mean?'

An exasperated hiss emerged through his clenched teeth. 'You know exactly what I mean. I am attracted to you and you feel the same way. It could make the next few weeks enjoyable or it could make them a lot less comfortable. Frustration makes you quite tetchy.'

'I'm not frustrated!' she exploded. 'I'm confused. Someone like you does not want someone like me.'

'For pity's sake, move on!' he bellowed.

She closed her eyes until he had negotiated a bend at what felt to her like reckless speed.

'I don't know what the guys you have been sleeping with have been doing.' His lips curled in disgust. 'But I promise you they have been doing it wrong if you don't know... *Theos!*' he grated. This woman was driving him to places he had never been before. His brief sideways glance was at the upper end of smoulder. 'How incredibly sexy you are.'

She sat there, the numb shock giving way to a sense of power she had never experienced before, a power that came from knowing that a gorgeous man wanted you.

Well, he had to. She could think of no reason for him to lie.

'And you'd do it right?' she heard herself throw out recklessly.

If the stare he aimed at the road ahead had been directed at her, Lizzie imagined she would have ignited.

'Damned right I would.'

His arrogance should have offended her. It didn't because she believed him with every fibre of her being.

The car jolted, sending up a shower of loose gravel as he brought it to a halt.

At her feet the cat squealed, but Lizzie didn't have time to soothe it. She opened her mouth but the sound was smothered by his lips, lost in the heat. The carnality of the way he claimed her mouth, licked into the moist warmth, flicked, teased and sucked. The sheer undreamt-of dizzying pleasure left her shaking.

Adonis looked into her glazed eyes, gave a fierce nod of satisfaction and restarted the engine.

She had to say something, and he had been upfront about the fact he was some sort of sex god.

'I'm a virgin.'

The car came to another screaming halt, followed by a stream of invective in several languages that you didn't need to be a linguist to translate as not polite.

'You're a…?'

She nodded, deciding she would remember Adonis looking shaken because she doubted it occurred often.

'How is that even possible?'

'It wasn't a criminal offence last time I checked,' she snapped back, not enjoying him acting as if she was a freak, even though there were occasions she felt she might be.

'I refuse to believe you have an issue with sex.'

Well, if she ever had, that ship had quite definitely sailed now, she thought, moistening her tingling lips. 'No, I have an issue with…well, the emotional bit…love… and I wasn't sure that I could have one without the other. I might,' she added, looking at his mouth, 'have been wrong.'

It was true he was the last man in the world she would have fallen in love with, but she could definitely have sex with him so long as she knew he wasn't thinking of Deb. That would for sure be a lust killer.

'Love?' he said as though he needed her to translate.

'I am not brave enough to love someone and then lose them for whatever reason. Why would anyone open themselves to that world of hurt?'

'I don't sleep with virgins. I have never slept with a virgin.'

She lowered her eyes, making a supreme effort to be adult about the rejection. 'A bit like skiing, I suppose. Nursery slopes are a bit boring for people used to going off-piste.'

He vented an incredulous laugh. 'You do know that you say the most… I think an hour in your head would make any man…' His voice trailed off as his mind made the leap from head to bed, razor blades of lust leaving a zigzagging trail of destruction in their wake. 'I think we should have this discussion later.'

When he was not fantasising about back-seat or, for that matter, front-seat sex. What was he, a teenager? A virgin. He had never spent much time thinking about virgins. There was an abundance of women who were not, and the responsibility was something he had always avoided. He had always prided himself on being more evolved than men who got a kick from the idea of being a woman's first lover.

It turned out his smugness had been misplaced. He wasn't so evolved, after all. All it took was the perfect storm, and a particular virgin.

It seemed to Lizzie that there wasn't that much to discuss but she shrugged and made no objection when he restarted the car.

Conversation was sparse on the rest of the journey—actually it was non-existent—but as the Aetos residence came into view Lizzie gasped.

The building, a sprawling white affair, had a low profile. It seemed to be built into the hillside, organically almost a part of it, but designed so that most every window in the place, and there were many, appeared to face the sea.

He had slowed, appearing to appreciate the impact that first glimpse offered.

As they got closer she took in the other details in the fading light: the softly terraced gardens that ran right down to the beach, the paddocks below the escarpment the house was built into with horses galloping, tails up, as they passed. The glimmer of a swimming pool behind a row of sentinel pines against the darkening night sky.

'You spent your childhood here?' She didn't wait for him to respond. 'It really is a paradise.'

As he pulled up onto a gravelled forecourt and walked around the car to open the door for her, Lizzie could hear the sound of music drifting on the soft, salty, pine-tinged breeze.

She stepped out carefully on her heels, murmuring comforting things to Mouse, who was sniffing the air.

Adonis, outlined against the darkening sky, looked

heart-stoppingly gorgeous as he took her elbow in a light supportive grip.

'You OK to do this?'

He watched as the turquoise silk reacted to her deep breath, making the fabric quiver deliciously and causing his libido to strain against the shackles he had imposed. Then the little chin lift that for some crazy reason made things inside him soften as she responded to the challenge with a 'bring it on' smile that didn't reach her eyes, which remained shadowed with trepidation.

Not enjoying his perceptive appraisal, she shrugged her narrow shoulders. 'I'd prefer root-canal work, but, as we're here, let's get it over with.'

Theos, this woman had balls, he decided with reluctant admiration. She was the equal of any adversary he had ever come up against, and she was on his side…for now.

He liked the idea of it staying that way. From somewhere surfaced a feeling he had never experienced before: he wanted her to like him.

Someone appeared before they had reached the massive double oak doors, which swung open.

'The place is wired for sound,' he whispered, still holding her elbow as they stepped forward.

Lizzie had no idea if he was joking or not, but she couldn't have laughed at that moment if her life had depended on it.

'Luisa…' The rest was Greek to Lizzie, quite literally.

After a few moments back and forth Adonis appeared to remember her existence.

'This is my wife, Lizzie Rose. Lizzie, this is Luisa, who has known me since I was…?'

The woman held her hand a little above knee level.

'I was never that small.'

His grin was so natural, so uncomplicated and so warm, it made him seem unfamiliar. Lizzie felt her chest tighten with an unnamed emotion.

'You are welcome. It makes my heart light to see Adonis with you.' She stepped back and pressed a hand to her chest. 'Yes, I can feel your love.'

Emotional tears stood out in her eyes.

Lizzie didn't dare look at Adonis. She hoped he felt as uncomfortable and guilty as she did. It was one thing to trick his grandfather, but not this nice woman. It seemed too unkind.

This was not a good start from her point of view—for starters, she was a terrible liar.

'We are here for the party. Are we too late for the fun?'

Without picking up on the sarcasm Lizzie could hear in his voice, the woman rushed in to cheerily assure him. 'Never, never. I will organise... Oh, this will make your grandfather so happy.'

Well, his grandfather might be a monster, but he obviously had one fan at least. The woman's sincerity was unmistakable.

'How is he today?'

'The pain,' Luisa began with a grimace. 'It makes him short-tempered.'

'Shorthand for he has been giving everyone hell.' Adonis frowned, his voice hardening as he tacked on, 'Does he not have adequate pain relief?'

'That I cannot say, but the doctor has been with him most of the day. He is here tonight as a guest. I do know your grandfather does not take his medication always as he should. He says he needs to stay alert.'

Adonis dragged a frustrated hand through his dark hair and ground out something angry in his native tongue, a look of grim determination spreading across his lean face as he nodded in thoughtful response to this information.

'We will see about that. Oh, Luisa. Lizzie's cat.'

The woman, who Lizzie was assuming held the role of housekeeper, looked at the cat basket that Lizzie had placed on the floor for the duration of the interchange.

'Shall I take him?' she said, moving forward.

'No!' Lizzie said before softening her abrupt response with a smile and adding, 'I prefer to keep her with me.'

Adonis restrained the impatient response on the tip of his tongue. He was learning that Lizzie was not someone who reacted to orders well. 'I think the small sitting room in my suite might suit her until she gets her bearings, and the courtyard. Would you say that is a safe space?'

'Oh, yes, definitely.'

'Fine, then. Our luggage is in the car.'

'That is already being attended to.'

'Actually, Mouse is not an escape artist—she doesn't wander,' Lizzie said in defence of her pet.

'In that case might she not be more comfortable being released while we eat dinner?'

She tipped her head in reluctant acknowledgement that he was probably right. 'All right.'

'Then we will detour on the way to dinner.'

'Shall I tell your grandfather you are here?'

'No, let's not spoil the surprise.'

'This way, Lizzie.'

From the square hallway with its cool marble floors and cedar-panelled high ceiling, Adonis led her through a network of wide corridors, many with windows that revealed glimpses of spotlit gardens and moonlit sky. The floors underfoot were a mosaic of tiles or wood, and art on the walls provided blasts of colour and texture that she could have spent hours perusing. It went by in a blur.

'This is the link corridor to my private apartments,' Adonis explained as they entered what appeared to be a glass-walled box. Beyond her own reflection Lizzie could see the sea, silver in the moonlight apart from a few fingers of red that remained from the sinking sun, which vanished as she watched.

'That was…is beautiful.'

'Yes,' he murmured.

When something in his voice made her lift her head she found he was looking at her, not the silvered sea. His eyes appeared dark shadows, but the fierce tension stamped in the planes of his handsome face sent her stomach into a deep dive.

'Come.'

The spell was broken so thoroughly she thought she had imagined it as she followed him through the glass box. The door on the other side led into what appeared to be a study with book-lined walls, a large table and a big leather chair positioned to face a wall of French doors. He walked through it and into an adjoining room.

'This is the sitting room. I thought it might be appropriate for your cat.'

It would have been appropriate for visiting royalty, Lizzie reflected, looking curiously around the minimally but tastefully furnished generous space. Like the previous room, there were French doors and, beyond them, she could make out a space that made her think of their wedding.

Was it really only hours ago?

Her eyes alighted on the fluffy little cat basket she had packed and Mouse's food and water bowls.

'How did this get here already?' she asked, putting the cat basket down and giving a sigh of relief.

'A heavy comfort blanket,' he mused, watching her.

'She is—' she began and stopped. 'OK, maybe a bit,' she admitted, thinking that she might as well invite him into her head because he had a disturbing habit of appearing there uninvited. 'How did all this get here before us?' she asked, opening the cat door.

'Luisa runs an ultra-efficient ship. She's not coming out.'

'She is essentially lazy and very adaptable. Any place with food and me is home for her.'

'You are her home?'

'Well, you know what I mean.'

He shook his head. He didn't. The idea of a person rather than a place being home was an alien concept to him.

'The bedroom is through there,' he said as he saw her staring curiously at the ajar door. 'Check it out.'

Lizzie didn't immediately react to the invitation.

'I never ravish women before dinner.'

She refused to blush. 'Well, that's so civilised of you. The press tell so many lies about you it's scandalous.'

He grinned, immediately looking impossibly attractive, and waved a hand in gracious invitation.

Struggling to fight off a smile, she accepted the invite, walking past him and into another high-ceilinged, massive room.

While she was determinedly not looking at the huge

four-poster bed that dominated the room, she immediately saw more illustrations of the efficiency Adonis had spoken about.

Through the open doors of the walk-in wardrobes she could see her new clothes hanging, other items neatly stacked on shelves.

'This is the bedroom,' he said, rather unnecessarily.

She didn't turn. The feeling of him so close was making her deeply uneasy.

'There is a dressing room through that way. I do not encourage people to unpack for me.' He opened a door and she saw his luggage on the floor. 'And the bathrooms are off that corridor,' he added, pointing to the right. 'The guest bedroom and bathroom are behind that. I don't need much space.'

Lizzie hid a smile. The scale of the rooms was…well, generous hardly covered the cavernous proportions. What, she wondered, would he consider generous space?

Walking back into the sitting room, she wondered whether he had noticed the discreet litter tray that was an addition to the elegant room, but decided not to mention it. The cat was sitting on the back of a sofa, cleaning herself.

'Be good,' Lizzie said before she pasted on a smile and blew a kiss her way.

CHAPTER EIGHT

LIZZIE REALISED THEY were retracing their steps, then they weren't, and she was hopelessly lost. The place was a beautiful maze. There were few steps, but the floor beneath her feet occasionally sloped.

Adonis could feel the tension coming off her.

'Greeks are friendly people. They love strangers.'

'Pardon my scepticism, but you are the only example I have.'

He conceded the strike with a wry grin. 'We love them so much we have a word for it.'

'A word for what?' They had reached a set of open double doors, and the echo of music she had heard was now a solid sound. Lizzie could see a jazz quartet at the far end responsible for the mellow sounds.

'For our love of strangers. *Filoxenia.*' His eyes brushed her pale face, lingering on the pulse beating at the base of her throat. 'OK?'

As OK, she thought, as she was likely to be. 'He won't believe that we are—'

'What he believes is not relevant, the point is he can't disprove anything, unless we tell him.'

'You must really not like him.'

'I love him. I want him to live his last days and weeks

with the hope that there will be a grandchild and the challenge of disproving it will give him endless pleasure.' A distraction from dying, Adonis thought, his expression sombre.

'That seems perverse,' she observed, shaking her head.

'Possibly,' he conceded with a lazy grin. 'But that is the sort of family we are. Are you ready to do this?'

She nodded, thinking, I hope that room is filled with a lot of *filoxenia*. 'This is what I signed up for.' Obviously she had not been in her right mind.

She was glad of the encouraging hand on the small of her back as she stepped forward. The room was dominated by a long table lit by a row of chandeliers that picked out the silver and crystal, illuminating the edges of petals in the flower arrangements that were starting to wilt.

Lizzie really identified with those petals!

She wanted to shrink into his side, but pride stopped her.

Adonis appeared to have no problem with being the focus of attention. He ignored the various levels of bleats and gasps of surprise as he walked down the table to the head where a thickset man sat. He had a head of dark hair liberally streaked with silver and a face that cynicism had etched deep lines into.

'Happy birthday, Papou.'

'You have brought me a present?'

Lizzie felt the dark eyes move over her in an assessing sweep that made her want to crawl out of her skin.

'I have.' Adonis made a flourishing gesture towards Lizzie, like a magician pulling a rabbit out of a hat. 'My wife. And my thanks for introducing me to her. Lizzie

Rose. Lizzie—' the fingers on the small of her back spread, as did the comforting warmth she needed at that moment '—this is my grandfather, Spyros.'

The silence was total. Even the musicians, awake to the drama of the moment, had stopped playing.

'Happy birthday. I hope you don't mind us gatecrashing?'

The elderly patriarch got to his feet, the hand tight on the arm of his chair the only indication that it was not easy for him. Despite his obvious ill health, he was not a man it was easy to pity.

'Welcome to our family.' He tilted his head towards Lizzie and gave what she supposed was his version of a smile. 'Elizabeth.'

'Lizzie.' He took the correction with a shrug that made her think a little of Adonis. 'I think you might know my father?'

She looked such a picture of innocence as she threw out the challenge that Adonis had to fight back an admiring laugh.

His grandfather didn't miss a beat. 'Indeed, I do. Welcome, Lizzie. Welcome to our home and this family.' He gestured in a grand fashion to the family seated around the table, who obediently echoed him.

'Sit by us, Adonis, sit by us!'

Lizzie was surprised the plea came from the two youngest of the family members. She had never thought that Adonis would bother to make himself popular with youngsters.

His grandfather responded to the children in Greek. His imperative gesture making it obvious that if anyone was going to have Adonis's ear it was him.

The girls, after a quick glance at the woman sitting opposite them, subsided into sulky silence.

'Let me make the introductions. Lizzie, this is my aunt Elena.' He pointed out the tall, elegant woman whose dark hair had a striking silver streak. She nodded, her expression curious but not unfriendly.

'Her girls, Cora and Chloe, and her husband, Nik.'

A balding middle-aged man got to his feet and tipped his head in Lizzie's direction. *'Kalispera.'*

'This is my aunt Lydia.' The other woman had the silver streak but her face was much more rounded. 'And her girls—or should I say young women?'

'Yes, you should.'

'Definitely you should.'

'Hi, Lizzie,' they both said in unison. Then the one who had shaved off the sides of her hair added, 'I love that dress!'

'And this is Iris and Areti.'

'I'm Alex,' the man sitting closest to her said, getting to his feet and extending his hand. 'Better known as Iris and Areti's dad.'

'My soon-to-be ex-husband,' Lydia added as her husband sat down. 'And this is my partner, Adrian.' The handsome young man sitting next to her sent Lizzie a dazzling smile. 'Dr... Baros, is it?'

A tall, thin man wearing spectacles got to his feet and inclined his head politely to Lizzie. *'Yassas.'* He turned to Adonis. 'Congratulations.'

'And that is the lot, except, of course, for Grandfather.'

The music began at the same time as groups of servers began to unobtrusively lay extra places at the table and the rest of the family discovered their voices.

Lizzie exhaled, finding the low buzz of chatter a relief.

Adonis ushered her to one of the new place settings and pulled out the chair for her, bending low to speak encouragingly into her ear. 'All OK?'

The whisper of his warm breath on her skin sent a distracting wave of heat along her nerve endings as his dark eyes held hers for a moment. She was incapable in that moment of doing anything else but nod—she would have nodded to anything he suggested. This piece of self-knowledge she could have done without and did nothing to soothe her jangling nerves.

'When you have finished, Adonis.' His grandfather gave a sharp nod to the place that had been set beside him.

Before Adonis had taken his seat, Spyros pushed out a peremptory question, making no attempt to lower his voice. 'Now tell me, is it true? Are you actually married or is this one of your—?'

'We are married.'

'Oh, when?' one of the older twins asked. 'We could have been bridesmaids.'

'Today.'

The look of astonishment was shared by everyone at the table.

'You got married today? Where? How?' His grandfather continued to look sceptical.

'Gibraltar.' Adonis produced a paper from his pocket that Lizzie hadn't known he was carrying. Clearly he had anticipated some scepticism. 'The official licence will follow in a couple of weeks.'

'You eloped?' Lydia gasped.

'That is so romantic,' one of her daughters inserted, her twin nodding in vigorous agreement.

'Exactly, and Adonis is not one of life's romantics,' her mother responded, looking across the table to her sister for confirmation.

'It's true, he isn't.'

'I am pleased that I have enabled you two to agree on something.'

His aunts glared at him.

'So the engagement announcement was real?'

The doctor scraped his chair on the floor. 'Perhaps I should leave the family—'

'Sit down, man!' his patient instructed. 'If you breathe a word of what is said in this room, I will sue your pants off.'

Flushing, the medic sat down.

'The engagement announcement was true?' Elena said slowly. 'None of us believed it.'

'Neither did we,' Adonis said, sending Lizzie an intimate smile that left her shaking and reflecting on what a loss he was to the acting profession.

'Look, I really don't know why this marriage is anyone's business but our own. When you, Papou, conspired to push Lizzie Rose and I together...'

All eyes went to the figure at the head of the table, who simply shrugged.

'It was both our intentions to tell you to go, very respectfully of course, to hell. However, being thrown together as we were...the unique circumstances. I had never met a woman like Lizzie.' The last observation had the ring of truth because, he realised, it was the truth.

One of the teen twins gave a sigh. Lizzie struggled to

put a name to the pretty face but the names were still interchangeable in her head. 'I think that is so romantic.'

Unlike the teen, Lizzie had heard the deliberate ambiguity in his sentence, but she also heard the caressing lie and, even knowing it was a lie, she felt herself reacting to the fake warmth even though they had no intimate bond and never would be likely to have.

'We are planning on spending the rest of the summer here—'

'I'm not planning on dying yet,' the old man snarled.

'That is good to hear,' Adonis said smoothly, glad to see the spark of defiance while planning to discuss that subject with the doctor, who was looking fixedly at his plate as though wishing himself elsewhere.

Not an encouraging sign.

He had actually been shocked to see the changes wrought by the cruel disease that had had his grandparent in its claws the past few weeks. The clothes that hung on his broad frame, the sallow cheeks and dark shadows under his sunken eyes.

'Papa,' began Lydia.

'Do not "Papa" me, woman. I can't be doing with weaselly words. We all know I am dying.' He rose unsteadily to his feet. 'I will go to bed.'

His daughters both jumped to their feet.

'No, you can walk with me,' he said, waving an imperious finger at Lizzie.

'Papou…' began Adonis, rising to his own feet, his height and physicality highlighting the older man's frailty.

'No, Adonis,' Lizzie said calmly as she pushed her chair back.

'You haven't eaten—'

'I'm really not hungry.'

His eyes held hers, a question and concern in the dark depths. 'Sure?'

She nodded, determined not to let anyone think that she needed protecting, although the fact that this had been his instinct sent a warmth through her.

'My grandson seems mightily protective about you,' the old man commented as he paused to catch his breath after a few yards.

'I think he's worried I'll say the wrong thing... I do that.'

The admission drew a rumble of laughter from the old man's chest, which was followed by a bout of wracking coughs.

Lizzie waited.

'You are not much like your cousin.'

'No, Deb was very beautiful.'

He scanned her face as though searching for something. Lizzie endured the fierce scrutiny in silence.

'So you don't have a lover in the wings?'

Lizzie was more confused than offended. Her brows went up. 'A lover? I don't—'

'I wouldn't want my grandson's heart to be broken.'

Lizzie shook her head. 'I won't break Adonis's heart. I can promise you that,' she said.

'And do you always tell the truth?'

'That depends.'

'So you don't think that honesty is always the best policy?'

'Not if the truth hurts someone and would not achieve anything.'

Though he didn't immediately respond, Lizzie had the feeling she had said the right thing.

'So would you lie to my grandson?'

'Adonis is not an easy man to lie to.'

Her reply brought a quiver of a smile to his lips. 'Neither am I,' he added, banging on the door with his cane, and a woman wearing white scrubs appeared.

'My nurse,' he said, his lip curling at the description. 'Or what passes for a nurse these days.'

'What can I say? There were no oil lamps left,' she said, casting a professional eye over her patient and detecting the signs of strain in his face.

'Have you thought of using a wheelchair?'

Two pairs of eyes swivelled Lizzie's way.

Ah, well, she thought philosophically, she had to say the wrong thing at some point.

'The last person who said that got this cane thrown at them.'

'Wow, I can see where your grandson got his tolerant disposition from.'

The old man fought off a smile. 'At least you have good child-bearing hips!'

It was so outrageous that Lizzie laughed, and before she could denounce this sexist comment he vanished through the doors, leaving the nurse to throw an apologetic look over her shoulder.

Did that go well?

Lizzie wouldn't go that far, but it hadn't gone badly as such, she decided as she began to retrace her steps. She passed musicians carrying their instruments on the way and by the time she reached the dining room it had emptied.

The only person there was Adonis, who was seated at the piano that lived there, his fingers moving quite professionally across the keys. The moment he saw her, his fingers came crashing down on the keys with a discordant clatter.

He rose and walked quickly across to her.

'The party broke up early?'

'It did.'

'Can't say I'm not relieved.'

'So how did it go?'

'You mean did I say the wrong thing?'

'No, I mean how did it go?' He could hardly blame her for doubting his concern was genuine. It came as a shock to him as well.

'It was OK, I think, right up to the moment I suggested a wheelchair.'

Amusement sparked in his dark eyes. 'Did he throw anything at you?'

'No, he just told me I had good child-bearing hips.'

The comment drew his eyes straight to the area in question, where her tight bottom was lovingly outlined beneath the heavy smooth fabric that he had noticed flowed in an arousing way when she moved. Who was he kidding? There didn't need to be flowing involved. She just aroused him, full stop. Maybe it was the fact she made no attempt to seduce that made her inherent sexiness all the more powerful?

He had to admit that powerful barely covered the hunger she had awoken in him. He felt he was hovering on the edge of a loss of self-control continually.

The knowledge she was a virgin should have simply drawn a very clear line in the sand. Instead it was a very faint line that he kept making rational excuses to step over. Without the disturbing, yet also, he had to admit, arousing virgin tag hanging over her he would have skipped tonight altogether and they would have spent it in bed.

'I think that was meant as a compliment.'

'I didn't take it that way.' Despite her claim, she gave a tolerant smile. 'And anyway, it's probably true.' She sighed as her eyes flickered to the piano. 'You play well.'

'No, I play adequately,' he said, a half-smile tugging at his lips. He retrieved the jacket he had slung across the back of a chair and shrugged it on.

'How very self-deprecating of you.' She stopped, shock flickering into her eyes. She was teasing Adonis Aetos. It was strange, she reflected, how quickly their relationship had developed.

'You made an impression tonight.'

'Good, bad, indifferent?'

'The consensus appears to be that I am a lucky man.'

She felt the heat climb to her cheeks.

He studied her face. 'Why do compliments make you so uneasy.'

'They saw the clothes, not me.'

'They saw you, in these clothes, which is quite different,' he retorted, standing aside to let her walk through the door before him. 'Lizzie, I think it's time you let that miserable little girl who was teased by stupid boys and jealous girls go.'

She stared at this cool analysis of her teenage years, opening her mouth and then closing it again.

'Does the therapy come with the rings? Or do I pay extra? I didn't mean in bed or anything,' she said, digging herself deeper into a mire of confusion. 'Obviously not. I wasn't suggesting—'

He looked at her, and the hard expressionless stare sent her stomach into free fall. 'I know you weren't.' If he hadn't known about her inexperience, he would be wondering about it now. 'It's free, no strings.'

She brought her lashes down in a concealing fringe as she fell into step beside him.

'I'd never find my way back on my own.'

'I'll give you the guided tour tomorrow. You'll soon find your way around.'

He turned on a lamp and the room was immediately flooded with soft golden light. Lizzie stood there, nerves jangling. 'Where is that cat?'

'Do you want a drink?'

She shook her head. 'Best not.'

He nodded and moved away, she was not sure where to, but the tension went with him. When he came back a few minutes later, she was standing where he had left her, statue still.

'If you are still looking for the cat, she is asleep on my cashmere sweater.'

'Oh, no!' She gasped with a horror way out of proportion to the situation. 'I will go and get her—'

He caught her arm as she rushed past him, spinning her around to face him.

'Leave it, she's fine where she is.'

For a long moment, neither moved. Tension zigzagged in the air between them.

Her eyes were drawn to the contracting ripple of muscle in his brown throat before he released her arm.

She didn't step away.

She didn't breathe.

'Will you stop looking at me like that?' he ground out.

'Like what?' Her throat felt achy. She could only whisper.

'Like you're seeing us naked in bed.'

'I wasn't, but I am now.' Her own boldness shocked her.

His eyes darkened. Her honesty was a massive aphrodisiac. 'And how does that make you feel?' he asked, his voice low and sinfully seductive as he bent in close enough for her to feel the warmth of his breath on her cheek, close enough to make her head spin.

Could a person forget how to breathe? she wondered as she stood frozen, her heart pounding as he bent his head. There was no barrier as he slid his tongue between her lips before plunging it in deep, the action drawing a keening sound from her throat.

The heat between them was instantaneous.

Lizzie rose on her tiptoes, her hands sliding up his back, feeling ridges of muscle before she raised her arms to link her fingers behind his neck. As she kissed him back, pressing in closer, a wild, inarticulate need pulsed through her body.

As the kiss grew frantic there was nothing in her head but burning need, nothing but his muscles and hot hard body, the male scent of him, the heat of him.

Breathing hard, Adonis broke the kiss and, looking into her glazed blue eyes, placed his hands on her narrow waist. Her half-closed eyes flickered wide when he lifted her off the ground as though she weighed nothing.

Reacting on instincts she hadn't known she possessed, Lizzie automatically wound her legs tight around his waist, the action dragging words of approval from his lips.

They made a staggering progress backwards through

the open door, mouths still sealed as they kissed frantically.

Lizzie was shocked by the primal ferocity of the need that coursed through her, shocked and excited as her heart thudded like a hammer against her breastbone as he laid her down on the bed.

Panting, she stared up at him, the raw power he exuded overwhelming.

'You sure about this?'

She nodded, not trusting her voice.

He knelt beside her and brushed the hair from her face, the tenderness contrasting with the fierce glow in his deep-set eyes. Somehow the fact his hand was shaking made her feel safer, the knowledge that this wasn't just happening to her.

She turned her head and pressed an open-mouthed kiss into his palm.

'I need to hear you say it.'

She reached up and framed his face with her small hands. 'I want this. I want you.'

He lowered his head again, and this time she met the thrust of his tongue.

His chest heaving, he pulled back. 'One taste of you would never be enough.'

Emotion lodged in her throat, and she pushed her reply past the aching occlusion. 'You can have as much of me as you want.'

With a growl he covered her beautiful, sensuous mouth, feeding the flames with every stroke and thrust of his tongue, every greedy nip and clash of teeth.

She gasped and twisted as his hands slid under her

dress, along the soft smooth skin of her thighs. His hands felt cool on her overheated skin.

He suddenly pulled her into a sitting position, one hand on the small of her back.

'You look beautiful in this dress, but I really want to see you without it.'

The idea of being naked in front of the most beautiful man on the planet ought to have set off warning bells in her head, but it didn't.

Dry-throated with anticipation, she lifted her bottom as, holding her eyes, he tugged at the fabric until it bunched around her thighs, then pulled it off in one swipe over her head and, not taking his eyes off her for a second, threw it over his shoulder.

The way he stared at her, the searing heat, made her feel as though he were staring right into the heart of who she was. When he pressed a hand to her chest she fell back bonelessly, her heart thudding as she waited for him.

'You're beautiful,' he rasped, feasting his eyes on the soft pale curves of her body, the full breasts inside the lace covering, the flare of her hips and the lovely line of her slim, shapely legs. Thinking about them wrapped around him while he was inside her raised his internal temperature a few more painful degrees.

Adonis was a man who prided himself on being in control of every aspect of his life, but as he stared down at her so hard his vision blurred he didn't even try to pretend he was in control.

He'd thought he knew sex, loved the uncomplicated simplicity of it, but this was not the sort of sex he was used to.

It was raw. His feelings were raw. It was different and

not just because he was her first—the difference was in him. It was as if her vulnerability connected with something in him that he hadn't known was there. This level of intimacy was beyond anything he knew.

The knowledge made him hesitate but only for a second. The need in him was too strong. His breath escaped in a deep shuddering sigh that lifted his chest and made the sinews in his neck stand out.

She watched as he stood up, pulling at his own clothing, weak with lust as he stripped until he stood there wearing just a pair of boxers.

There was not an ounce of surplus anything. He was all hard, sculpted muscle, lean sinew and strength, the essence of masculinity. Golden and utterly, absolutely perfect. Looking at him made the muscles in her pelvis tighten and her nipples tighten and peak.

She reached up as he came to kneel on the bed beside her, her palms flat on his damp skin, loving the firm texture and fascinated by the iron hardness. Reacting to a primal need, she pulled herself up to taste the salt on his chest, sliding her arms around his back to support herself as she licked lower and felt dizzy with power as a groan was ripped from some place deep in the barrel of his chest.

She was barely aware of him unclipping her bra, not until he began to peel it from her shoulders and her full breasts spilled free. She gave a voluptuous little shudder as he stared, rapt, at the quivering globes of flesh.

'Theos...' he groaned, bending his head to take one pink pouting nipple into his mouth.

The scalding pleasure made her back arch. Her fingers sank into his hair, then he pushed her back onto the tumbled bedclothes, the first skin-to-skin contact as his chest crushed her sensitised breast, his hair-roughened legs pushing into her thighs, was beyond anything she had imagined.

She pushed against him to increase the friction as they kissed, triggering a frantic, feverish battle of clashing tongue and teeth.

As he lifted slightly off her, her protest turned to a low keening cry as he began to slide down her body, leaving an erotic trail of open-mouthed kisses, of clever caresses, until it felt as though every nerve ending in her body were screaming.

When he reached the apex of her legs, the soft curls there, she realised that she was wrong—there were more nerve endings, more of everything.

'You're so hot and ready for me,' he whispered into her ear as he slid a finger deeper into her while continuing to rub the sensitised throbbing nub with his thumb.

Her hand slid down his belly. His skin was damp with sweat. 'I want...' she husked.

'You will, you will. I'll show you everything I like, but now I can't take any more of this,' he rasped, shaking with need. He had never wanted a woman this much in his life before.

As he slid a knee between her legs she opened up for him, tensing slightly as the silky hard tip of his erection nudged her hot, sensitive flesh. But as he whispered things she had never imagined any man saying to her she relaxed, and when he entered her slowly it was a relief and then so much more.

As his big hands cupped her bottom, exerting fierce

control, each stroke sent her deeper into herself, the pleasure like a drug as, snug inside her, he continued to move.

He held on until he felt the first contraction of her body around him and then let go.

He watched her face as her body slowly relaxed, her eyelashes fluttering like butterfly wings against her flushed cheeks. She opened her glowing eyes and looked at him, gave a smile, and he felt himself captured totally by some emotion he had never experienced before.

She lay there panting while he removed the condom she hadn't even been aware of him putting on. When he rolled back to her she snuggled into him, laying her head on his chest.

She felt him stiffen but only for a moment. His arms came around her and she sighed out her pleasure.

'Who needs love,' she said happily, 'when you have sex?'

She had verbalised pretty much his philosophy on life but for some reason he felt a chink of dissatisfaction slide into his afterglow.

CHAPTER NINE

LIZZIE SURFACED FROM a deep sleep and stretched, cat-like, relaxed until the events of the night filtered into her sleep-soaked head. She tensed and slowly opened her eyes, lighting on an empty pillow beside her on the bed.

An overwhelming sense of loneliness swamped her, which was crazy. She'd been waking up alone all her life. Last night had been incredible but she had to keep it in proportion. She couldn't act like a teenager who had discovered sex and felt as though she was brilliant at it.

Which she was.

Reviewing last night, beyond the pleasure and his utter gorgeousness was the total lack of inhibition she had felt. After a lifetime of hating her body she had actually discovered it was possible to like it, love it even, because Adonis gave every indication that he did.

Whatever happened in the future she would always be grateful to Adonis for breaking her free of her self-imposed prison. She pushed the thought away, not keen on thinking too far ahead, determined to enjoy the moment. It would be a much nicer moment if Adonis were here.

As she felt the cold bed beside her, she remembered him saying at some point during the long night that he had arranged to speak to his grandfather's doctor this morning.

She prised herself from the warmth of the bed and walked through to the bathroom where Mouse was lying full-stretch on the heated marble floor, purring.

She smiled. Inside, she was purring too.

She stepped into the shower and stood there for a long while letting the jets of water ease the tightness in muscles that were complaining, muscles she hadn't known she possessed until last night.

She brushed out her wet hair but couldn't work up the enthusiasm to do anything to it, and, after applying some suncream, she glossed her lips and left it at that. Even barefaced, her dark brows framed her face, and the natural dark of her lashes intensified the colour of her eyes.

For the first time in her life she looked in the mirror and felt lucky. Humming softly to herself, she dressed quickly, selecting a pair of linen wide-legged trousers from her new wardrobe and topping them with a square-necked white tee shirt. She shoved her feet into a pair of leather sliders and, calling the cat, walked into the sitting room.

The first thing she noted after she opened door to a generous enclosed green space, where stone benches were set around what appeared to be a herb garden, was a note propped on the table. She bent down to pick it up while the cat wound his way around her legs.

Sorry I had to leave. I fed the cat. See you for breakfast.

There were no kisses attached to the note, just his name written in a bold flourish. The idea of him feeding her cat made her smile. If miracles carried on happening with this sort of regularity, where would they be in a week?

She hoped in bed. She had a lot of years of abstinence to make up for.

'So come on, Mouse, let's go for a walk, sweetheart. See if there are any local felines you need to show who's boss.'

As if she understood every word, the cat fell in by her side, tail high as they walked down the corridor. She found the dining room from the previous night and gave a self-satisfied smile, hoping, as she pushed open the door, this was where she was meant to be.

It was. Several family members from the previous evening were already there.

'Yassas,' she said. It had seemed only polite to learn a couple of Greek words, but she had almost exhausted her vocabulary.

'Yassas,' came the group reply, which seemed a positive response to her effort.

'Coffee is there.' One of the older twin girls pointed to the long low serving table down one wall. There were jugs of juices, platters of breads, bowls piled high with fruit, thick, creamy Greek yogurt and pots of honey, and that was before she had looked under the domed lids of the multitude of serving dishes.

'I can call for fresh tea,' her twin added. 'If you want some and if you need anything fresh cooking, just say.'

'We do self-service on the holidays,' Lydia explained, sounding apologetic. 'Did you sleep well?' she asked as Lizzie picked the lid off a bowl of creamy-looking scrambled egg.

'Mum, of course she didn't sleep.' The teenagers giggled, rolling their eyes at their mother.

To Lizzie's relief, Mouse provided a distraction just by being herself.

'Get down, Mouse,' Lizzie said, pushing the marauding feline off the serving table.

'She has a cat!' exclaimed one of the diminutive twins excitedly. 'Cora, look—a cat!'

'Can we stroke him?'

'Her,' Lizzie said, smiling to see Mouse lapping up the attention plus any stray crumbs that landed on the floor.

'It might not like it, girls,' their mother warned.

'Oh, she'll love it,' Lizzie promised. 'But don't let her persuade you to feed her. She is very greedy.'

'Mouse?' said one of the older twins. 'Like the books?'

'That's cool,' added her twin.

'Did you name her after the real Mouse, the cat in the books?'

'Kind of,' Lizzie said, helping herself to some yogurt and topping it with fruit. She had it halfway to her mouth when Adonis appeared looking every kind of wonderful in faded denim shorts and a tee shirt.

'Adonis, did you know she has a cat?'

'Indeed, I did know,' he said, flashing a warm look towards Lizzie.

'She has the top of her ear missing, like the books.'

Iris and her twin exchanged looks.

'Pink nose, half an ear and the black spot on her back does look like a question mark. She is the Mouse, isn't she?'

'Which would mean,' her twin said, picking up the

story, 'you would be Rose Trelawny?' She gave her head a little shake. 'Not really?'

Lizzie tried to adopt a bewildered expression but she felt the guilty heat climb to her cheeks.

'Have you two read one of Lizzie's books?'

The women in the room turned on him, eyes wide. 'You married Rose Trelawny? This is Mouse the cat?'

'Adonis, is this true?' his aunt Elena demanded.

Adonis looked bewildered. 'She isn't Rose Trelawny.'

'My middle name is Rose and Trelawny was Mum's maiden name. I told you I wrote books.'

'Oh, my God, Adonis!' said Areti. 'She is so way, way out of your league.'

'Will someone tell me what the hell is going on?'

'Rosie's adventures, are they based on real life?'

'Areti!' gasped her mother, who had read the book. Despite her outrage, she could not hide her interest in Lizzie's reply.

'I was just asking, Mum. Did you really have sex in a cupboard, Lizzie, or should we call you Rosie?'

'Lizzie.'

'Sex in a cupboard,' echoed Lydia's youthful lover, who had strolled into the room. 'Wouldn't there be a space issue?'

'Depends how flexible you are...' his lover pointed out.

'Mum, ugh!'

Adonis leaned back and watched as his bride fielded questions about the heroine all present seemed to assume was her alter ego.

Lizzie had had very little contact with fans before, outside online reviews, and she had preserved her anonymity, which made it a lot easier to laugh off the more out-there questions. Being pelted up close and personal was proving difficult.

'No, he was fictional. I've never dated anyone as awful as Damien and he really wasn't that awful.'

'Are you kidding? He was a f—'

'Areti!' warned her mother.

The girl grinned.

Finally she'd had enough.

'Adonis, make it stop!'

Adonis rose to his feet. 'Right, you lot, out. This woman has not finished a meal since she arrived and she gets very cranky when she is hungry. Also, stop feeding that cat!'

'She's hungry!' his little cousins protested.

'No, she is an opportunist. Out!'

'If you're not careful she will put you in her next book,' was Areti's parting shot.

'You were very rude, but thanks.'

'Eat,' he said, taking a seat opposite Lizzie.

'You're not eating.'

'I already have.'

'You had your meeting with the doctor?'

He set his elbows on the table. 'I did.'

'Don't stare like that, it puts me off my breakfast.'

'Not noticeably,' he drawled, the laziness in his voice as he watched her scoop a spoonful of yogurt into her mouth in dramatic contrast to the dark hunger in his eyes.

'So, the doctor?'

'Later.'

She studied his face and noticed the shadow under his eyes, which added to, not detracted from his general gorgeousness. They might not be entirely due to a long athletic sleepless night. She felt a sharp stab of empathy. She had been only a child but she remembered all too well how much her dad had dreaded his meetings with the doctors.

'My mum was ill for a long time. I was young but I know my dad grew to dread the doctor's appointments.'

'It was early onset dementia?'

She nodded. 'Yes… We kind of lost her bit by bit. It was hard as a kid to understand why she did the things she did.'

'I'm sorry,' he said, something twisting hard in his chest when he thought about Lizzie, a little girl, watching her mother vanish and her father so wrapped up in his own grief that she was left to sink or swim.

'Maybe that's why you have such a vivid imagination. You escaped into a fantasy world?'

'I never thought of that, I suppose little bits of yourself do come out in your writing…' she mused. 'Once,' she began, then shook her head. 'There are lots of good memories too.'

'So, my family seem convinced that your stories are based on personal experience. A cupboard,' he said suddenly. 'Really?'

She gave a gurgling laugh and then sobered. 'Once I got locked in a cupboard, so I let my heroine have sex in a cupboard…sort of therapy. It didn't work though. I still hate enclosed spaces.'

'But not sex.'

A slow smile illuminated her face. It faded when she found herself wondering if it was just sex or sex with Adonis.

'No, not sex,' she said quietly. 'So thank you for that, Adonis.'

'No thanks are required, I promise you, *yineka mou*.'

She stared at him, a question in her big blue eyes, a question he didn't want to acknowledge even to himself.

'The famous cat is eating the smoked salmon.'

She leapt to her feet. 'Oh, no…bad girl.' She shooed the cat away from the dish, and Mouse jumped down, retreated to a corner and gave her a dirty look.

'So you are famous?'

She looked uncomfortable and arched a brow. 'I really hope not.'

'Why didn't you tell me?'

'I did,' she protested.

'The lie was in the omission. Why do you downplay your achievements?'

'I don't…' She caught his eye and dragged a hand across her brow before shaking her head, the action causing her high ponytail to flick.

'Your father must be proud of you.'

'He is.' She heard the shrill insincerity in her voice and winced.

'My dad wanted a son. Don't get me wrong, he has always loved me and been a good dad, but I gave up trying to impress him a long time ago. You pick your battles, the ones that matter, the ones you can win.'

'I've not noticed you showing much restraint when it comes to arguing with me.'

'Oh, that's because I know I can always win those arguments. Right being on my side.'

Her pert response drew a throaty laugh from him. 'Is that a fact?'

'It is.'

'So will you put me in a book as one of your long line of loser boyfriends?'

'You're not my boyfriend.' He was her husband. Even after last night that reality felt too surreal to put into words.

'No, I'm not, am I? Perhaps it could be the start of another bestselling series. The husbands my cat warned me about.'

'It is fiction, comedy... Besides, my cat approves of you, and I haven't had a long line of boyfriends, loser or otherwise. It is fiction, you know, made up,' she mocked gently.

'This bestseller list must have made you a rich woman?'

'I don't know—well, obviously I know I've made money. I told you I bought the house. I have an agent and accountant who handle that side of things. I did run the idea past them of helping dad,' she admitted. 'But they said the bulk of my investments can't be touched without six months' notice.'

If she believed them, who was he to disabuse her? If she had known the first thing about finances she might not have spent last night in his bed.

'If you want to talk about whatever it was the doctor said...'

He tipped his head and got up. 'You finished with the food?'

She nodded.

'You said you worked in a stable so presumably you ride?'

'I do.'

'Then how about a horseback tour of the island?'

A smile spread across her face. It made him think of the sun rising.

'I can only see one issue…the cat? Can you bear to be parted from her?' He arched a brow, a smile that made her heart flip hovering across his lips.

'Do not let appearances deceive you. Admittedly she is slightly overweight, but my Mouse is an alpha cat. She will want to establish her supremacy and also find the kitchen, where she will give a very good impression of a starving animal. Mouse is a survivor.'

'So are you.'

She blinked and pushed out an embarrassed, 'I'm fine.' The idea she had painted herself as some sort of victim horrified her.

'I know you are. Go get changed. We are going for a ride. I have a couple of things to sort—shall we say half an hour in the stables? I'll get Georgiou to show you the way.'

She had no idea who Georgiou was, but she nodded her agreement.

CHAPTER TEN

THE BOOTS WERE her own but she was pretty sure that the jodhpurs, which clung in all the right places, had not been there when she left for breakfast. She suspected that one of the twins might have donated them but she decided not to question the appearance in case they had belonged to another personal female guest he had brought to the island.

She didn't want to dwell on the idea, but it was too late. She had left the suite but she had to go back and change, exchanging the borrowed jodhpurs for a pair of jeans. They were less clingy in a sexy way than the discarded jodhpurs but she didn't feel queasy wearing them.

Georgiou turned out to be an enthusiastic young man who was working the holidays before he started university. He was a mine of personal information, and by the time she got to the stables—a quadrangle of purpose-built buildings housing some impressive-looking animals who watched her from their stalls—Lizzie knew all about Georgiou's ambitions in life, and the life story of his sister, who was on a dance scholarship funded by the Aetos family and, according to her fond brother, a future prima ballerina.

The boy saw Adonis a little after Lizzie had spotted the tall, elegant figure who was wearing a white open-necked shirt, his long legs encased in snug-fitting jeans and the boots polished but well-worn.

The boy waved and left as Lizzie walked towards Adonis, who was holding two horses. The taller of the two, a black Arab, was pawing the ground, the smaller, a delicate mare with a blaze, seemed much more placid.

'So you can ride? Not like donkeys-on-a-beach ride?'

'I love donkeys.'

'I thought you might,' he said, silently adding dogs with missing limbs, anything ugly, animals that were blind, and literally anything rejected by anyone else. Lizzie Rose's perception of the world was like learning another language.

It conflicted with any perception he had ever had, and yet at the same time was oddly attractive.

'She is beautiful,' Lizzie exclaimed, softening her voice as she stroked the soft muzzle and murmured approval to the little mare with the blaze. 'Beautiful girl.'

He handed her a hard hat, which she fastened. 'Want a leg-up?'

She nodded and found herself boosted into the saddle.

Beside her she could see Adonis control his horse gently with skill. He was totally in tune with the animal, in harmony rather than control. The two moved as one, and his attitude relaxed as the high-spirited animal caracoled.

Adonis's last remaining concerns faded as he saw her in the saddle. As he looked at her he felt the neat, emotionless boundaries that had always been in place with the women in his life dissolve. His expression sobered as he recognised the danger. The last thing in the world he wanted was a relationship with no boundaries, the sort of relationship that his parents shared.

His horse broke into a canter, and behind him he was aware of Lizzie catching up with him. She flashed him a smile that didn't seem at all dangerous, a smile full of just the joy of the moment and utterly uncomplicated.

After an hour they had covered a lot of ground and a dozen terrains. She remarked on this to Adonis when they paused to stare at a particularly spectacular vista.

'Yes, the island packs a lot into a small area.'

'It's very beautiful. I can see it must have been a marvellous place for a child to grow up.'

He touched the rim of the leather herder's hat he wore, a hat that hid his eyes from her view.

'In those days, a long way away from medical assistance when you break an arm, or a leg, or have a concussion.'

'Sounds like you were reckless.'

'Grandfather's attitude was if it hurts you won't do it again and if you do you get zero sympathy.' Without a word he dismounted.

Lizzie followed suit and stood there, reins in hand.

'The doctor tells me there is a clinical trial. A new drug or combination of them.'

'A cure!' she exclaimed.

'No, not a cure, but for patients at stage four it can mean a significant extension of life.'

'Well, that's good, isn't it?'

'Apparently, the old man doesn't think so. The doctor has asked me to persuade him, but the thing is... Do I have that right? He has been through a lot of treatments and not all pleasant,' he added with a sombre laugh. 'A man should decide his own fate.'

Her heart ached for the moral dilemma that was clear on his face.

He swept the hat off his head and a lock of hair fell in his eyes. 'I shouldn't be asking you this. It's not your problem, except of course it does affect you. If my grandfather lives longer you would stay married to me for longer.'

She flinched as though he had struck her. 'When have I ever given you a reason to think I am that sort of person?'

He turned and tilted her face up to him. 'Never. I know you are not that sort of person, but I am. I am selfish and I have to own that the idea of having you in my bed for longer makes it hard for me to stay objective about this.' He unfastened her helmet and pulled it off. 'It is good, isn't it, the sex?'

She nodded, not understanding why the acknowledgement should make the emotional tears rise up in her throat. Without a word he took the reins from her hand and tethered both horses loosely on a nearby branch. Returning to her, he took her hand and led her to a spot where the moss was deep and springy.

Turning her to face him, he kissed her. She could feel him shaking with the strength of his restrained passion. Together they sank to the ground.

'You must be sore...last night...'

She shook her head and wordlessly took his hand, fitting it to her breast.

It was slow and so tender that she cried when it was over, her head against his heart, hearing the sound of the life force in him and realising she had fallen in love with a man who did great sex but not love. His heart still belonged to Deb. Would it always?

'What's wrong?' he asked, levering himself into a sitting position as she paused in the act of gathering her clothes.

Lizzie froze and turned her head towards him.

When you make love to me...you don't kind of close your eyes and think of Deb, do you?

For one horrific split second she thought she had said the words out loud.

'What's wrong?' he repeated, his frown deepening.

Lizzie shook her head.

'Nothing... I think something stung me,' she prevaricated.

'I didn't hurt you.'

She paused in the act of fastening her bra. 'No, of course not.'

His frown smoothed, relief sliding through him, though he searched her face, horrified at an almost visceral level at the idea of hurting her.

Lizzie was fully dressed by the time Adonis had retrieved his shirt. He continued to watch her as he fastened it.

'You sure you are all right?'

She nodded as she clambered over a large rocky outcrop.

'Be careful,' he called out sharply. 'There's a drop.'

Lizzie had already taken several steps back. 'So I see,' she said as he joined her, his shirt still hanging loose.

'It's beautiful!' she said, staring from a safer distance at the ocean stretched below, blue hitting the blue of the horizon.

The light touch on her shoulder broke her free of her transfixed contemplation of the dazzling seascape.

They retraced their steps and Adonis bent low to sweep up his discarded hat.

'I love horses,' she said, leaning low over her mount's mane to pat her shoulder when they were both back in the saddle. 'Honestly, if you had ever seen how much confidence it can give a kid who feels like an outsider.'

'You?'

'Gosh, no,' she disclaimed immediately. 'The stables I help out at work with children with disabilities. In a wheelchair people look down at them, in the saddle they are equal.'

'You understand people who feel like outsiders?'

She flicked him a look from under her lashes, not liking his perception. 'Should we be getting back?'

'Are you going to tell me what's wrong?' he asked, looking down into her face. 'You were going to say something back there.'

'You never talk about Deb, and I understand it must be hard, but I just wanted to say,' she continued with a small, understanding smile of encouragement, 'that I can listen. I mean, if you wanted to, talking helps sometimes, remembering the good bits.'

He stared down at her, his expression inscrutable. 'I don't want to talk about Deb.'

She immediately felt embarrassed. The sex was so intense it had created an illusion that they were much closer than they were. His closed-off expression was ample proof they were not.

'No, of course not. I'm… Well, I'm here. Thanks.'

CHAPTER ELEVEN

THE TWO TEENAGERS hugged their grandfather before they ran around the table to where Lizzie sat nibbling at a piece of toast. She got to her feet and was swallowed up in a hug.

'I can't believe the summer is over!' Areti, her skin tanned to a deep gold, cried as she pulled Lizzie in for another hug. 'God, school next week!' she moaned. 'I can't bear it.'

Her twin rolled her eyes and took her turn hugging Lizzie. 'Listen to her. She loves it, captain of everything going, whereas I—'

'Are a swotty nerd.'

'Granted,' her twin acknowledged with a grin. 'Our last year. Next year we will be free spirits or more likely terrified of starting uni.'

Lizzie remembered her last term at school. The sixth year had been less traumatic than her early years and by then her main tormentor, Deb, had left. The invitation to a holiday with the cool girls had made her feel her life had changed. Then her bikini top had pinged off. She should have laughed it off, she could see that now. But she hadn't had the twins' confidence so instead she had layered up and never really stopped layering until she had seen herself through Adonis's eyes.

She wanted to say 'don't wish your life away' to the twins, which made her feel very old, but she restrained herself.

'You'll come and wave us off?'

'Of course,' Lizzie promised, retaking her seat.

The room seemed still after the girls' exit. The place was going to seem empty after the summer bustle of activity. Elena had taken Cora and Chloe back at the beginning of the week and all the men had gone back last week.

It was hard to believe that she had been here seven weeks.

Though Adonis had made several trips back to London and to Athens he had spent every night, or what was left of it, in her bed.

He was working from here, establishing his work base in an office away from his private suite.

'Less distractions,' he had said.

They spent a lot of time together swimming and riding, making love. They were idyllic moments she would always treasure. Thinking of them ending was the only cloud on her horizon.

'Are you going to eat that?'

Lizzie, shocked out of her dreamy contemplation of the plate she had piled with scrambled egg, looked up and found Spyros staring at her from his place at the head of the table.

Everyone had been delighted when, without any prompting, he had decided to take part in the treatment trial, which he appeared to be, as the doctor had phrased it, 'tolerating well'. That, along with his new pain regime, had put him in a much more mellow frame of mind—mellow for him anyway—and the fact he had agreed to use a motorised wheelchair meant he was much more mobile.

'I've had enough,' she said lightly, aware that the shrewd eyes fixed on her missed very little.

'You haven't had any.'

She waved her piece of toast and smiled. 'Filled up on toast.'

Spyros grunted. Since he had discovered that Lizzie was, as he put it, an adequate chess player, she saw him most days outside the noisy communal mealtimes and she'd grown very fond of him.

'You want to continue our game later?'

She gave an apologetic smile. 'Maybe not today. I'm feeling slightly off colour,' she admitted, not quite meeting his beady eyes. 'I'll just go and see them off.'

'You do that.'

'Adonis is sorry he couldn't see you off,' Lizzie said, embracing Lydia as the remainder of their luggage was stowed on the jet.

'Don't worry, he said goodbye this morning.' She took Lizzie by the arms. 'We are all so happy he has you. You do know that?'

Lizzie didn't say anything. What could she say that wasn't a lie or, even worse, the truth?

With a sigh she gave a last wave to the faces in the window of the plane and got into the waiting car.

She didn't go up to the house, instead she went to the beach. Over the weeks they had fallen into a daily pattern. Adonis tried to make himself free around this time and they swam in the warm blue water or sometimes just walked and talked.

It would have been easy for anyone watching to think they were a happily married couple for real.

She stripped off her blue cambric sundress, underneath which she wore a blue bikini.

She wandered down to the water's edge, not wading in, just allowing the waves to gently break over her feet. She closed her eyes, allowing the image of Adonis, barechested in a pair of cut-off denims, to form in her head.

It was so vivid that when she opened them she was shocked he wasn't standing there.

Enough of this, she decided, her chin lifting as her expression became resolute. She couldn't keep delaying. She had to know.

Half an hour later she was standing staring at her own pale face in the mirror, the third test strip in her hand. It wasn't really a shock, she'd suspected it for a full week—longer, even. All the signs had been there.

The irony was she had what Deb had wanted: Adonis's wedding ring on her finger and now his baby.

Except she didn't have his heart. That still belonged to Deb. Her face crumpled as a sob gathered in her tight chest. She pressed a hand to her flat belly, realising after weeks of denial that that was what she wanted: his heart.

She loved her husband.

The harsh hybrid sound that emerged from her pale lips was part sob, part laugh.

She loved her husband, and she wanted her mum, but she couldn't have either. She sniffed and pulled her shoulders back. This was her problem and she had to deal with it.

How would Adonis react?

She pushed away the question. She couldn't deal with that now. This was happening to her. She had to sort out her own thoughts before she faced him. She would tell him, obviously, but…but…he'd stay with her because of the baby, she was sure of it, and that wasn't enough.

She pressed a hand to her head, which felt as though it were going to explode. She needed space.

The thought had barely formed when her phone pinged. She saw the name and shook her head, then, her expression thoughtful, she picked it up and read the text.

It was pretty much a repeat of the previous half-dozen she had received from her publisher, detailing the PR tour for her latest book they were trying to sell her on.

'Why are you sitting in the dark?'

Lizzie blinked when one of the bedside lights was switched on.

'What's happened? What's wrong?' His concern growing, Adonis's glance moved from Lizzie's pale face to her clothes. She was fully dressed. 'It's half one. I thought you'd be in bed.'

'Sorry, I lost track of time. I've only just finished packing,' she said brightly.

'Packing?' The dark hooded glance shifted to the bags lying on the floor and the cat sitting in its basket.

She nodded. 'Yes, it's so exciting. They want me to do a PR tour for the new book and I thought, well, I've been here a lot longer than either of us anticipated, which is great, but Spyros is on the new course of treatment and I'll be back before you know it.'

'You'll be back?' he said in a voice wiped clean of any

emotion, and then, in a voice that was no longer empty, instead filled with fury, he continued, 'So how long have you been planning this?'

'Not planning. It just kind of happened.'

'We had a deal.'

'I know,' she said miserably. 'But things have changed.'

'I haven't changed.'

'I know.'

That was the problem: he hadn't changed. He still loved Deb, and Lizzie would always be second best. She really didn't want her baby to have a second-best mum.

'I thought you were happy.'

She said nothing. How could she be happy when she loved a man who didn't love her back?

Her silence fed the outrage, the sense of betrayal building inside him. He had trusted her and she had thrown that trust back in his face.

'Fine! Go. I'll get the jet fuelled up. It is at your disposal. I'll get a driver to take you to the—'

'Everyone is asleep, Adonis.'

'Then they can wake up!'

'I want to say goodbye to your grandfather.'

After a moment of nostril-quivering, jaw-clenching staring he gave a curt nod. 'As you wish.' And he was gone, leaving Lizzie to cry with no one but Mouse to hear her muffled sobs.

Lizzie snatched a few hours of uneasy sleep and woke early to throw up. So far pregnancy did not have a lot to recommend it, she decided as she examined the dark panda shadows circling her puffy eyes.

Had Adonis, true to his word, organised the jet?

She didn't have a clue. She just knew that she really couldn't face him again right now.

She knew if she had told him he'd stay married for the sake of the baby, but she didn't want that. She was not about to settle. She'd had enough of pretending.

'He doesn't love me, Mouse,' she said as she shoved the indignant cat into the travel basket and got a scratch for her troubles. 'Nobody loves me.'

Dashing the self-pitying tears from her face, she gave a loud sniff and went to the only person other than Adonis she knew could get her off the island.

She wasn't very coherent, but Spyros seemed to get the main point, which was she wanted off the island.

'The PR tour is a marvellous opportunity,' she explained brightly, hoping the concealer around her eyes was hiding the worst of the damage caused by her tears.

'Couldn't Adonis organise that for you? Didn't he get back last night?'

'He said he would, he might have, but he might have forgotten, and I don't like to disturb him. He's very busy this morning, what with everything...' she said, her voice starting bright before it trailed away into a whisper.

'The jet will need refuelling.'

'Oh, will that take long?'

'It's a big plane.'

She nodded. 'But when it is ready?'

'It is at your disposal.'

'Fine and I'm sorry that...' Shaking her head, she hugged the old man before she picked up the cat basket and her rucksack.

* * *

When she had gone, Spyros pressed a buzzer that brought assistance running.

'No, I'm not dead,' he snapped. 'Get me my grandson. Tell him I'm dying if you like. I need him here now.'

Five minutes later the door was flung open and a white-faced Adonis rushed in. His eyes widened when he saw his grandfather standing there. 'I was told you were dying.'

'Theos!' Spyros bemoaned. 'These people take everything so literally. Well, we are all dying, some of us sooner than others, but not today.'

'What is wrong?'

'You, if you let that woman run away.'

Adonis's expression froze. 'She has work commitments.'

'You are an idiot, you know that? You can't see what is right under your nose, what everyone else in the house can see.'

'And what is that?'

'The woman is in love with you. If you don't love her back, let her go. She deserves more.'

'Our marriage, as I am sure you have worked out, is an arrangement. Love is not part of the deal.'

The old man folded his arms across his chest and raised a bushy brow. 'If you say so.'

'I do say so,' Adonis shot back, clinging to his restraint in the face of his grandfather's interference.

'Ah, well, you know best,' he said in a tone that implied the exact opposite. 'You told her about Deb dying with her lover, did you?'

'That was not relevant.'

'I can see why you feel a bit of a fool.'

Adonis clamped his jaw.

'She thinks you still love the other one, and, the way I see it, that suits you. It means you don't have to admit to your own feelings because, well, basically, you are—and I hate to say this about my own grandson—a coward.'

His face reflecting the tangled mess of emotions in his head, Adonis sank into a chair. 'She has deserted me.'

The old man smiled. He could hear the lack of conviction in his grandson's voice.

'I'm worried about her flying. She's not been looking too good most mornings for the past couple of weeks.'

Adonis's questioning gaze flew to his grandfather's face. 'Are you saying...?'

'I'm not saying anything. It's not my place.'

Adonis shot to his feet and nodded. 'It's mine, and you are a manipulative old bastard,' he observed, slanting a half-smile at his grandparent.

'Good to know I've still got it. Nurse!' he bellowed. 'I need my meds.'

'You've already had your medication.'

'This boy is upsetting me,' he said, missing plaintive by a country mile as he added, 'Your mess, you fix it, own it, or you are not the man I thought you were. Oh, and the plane will take a long time to refuel today.'

'Excuse me, but I really think your grandfather needs his rest.'

Adonis ignored the woman, tipped his head in respect towards his grandfather, and hit the ground running.

Own it. The words went around in his head on a loop as Adonis made his way to his car.

He had spent the night telling himself that when she was gone he was free and good riddance.

His satisfaction was marred by the mocking voice in his head that said, *Free or maybe just scared.* And that voice was the truth. He could see he was a man who had been too chicken scared to invest in a relationship in his life.

Would she be there when he arrived or would he be too late? The question tormented him as he floored the accelerator.

Lizzie sat with Mouse plaintively meowing as she waited in the warm morning sun beside the runway.

With a hissing sound of exasperation, she pulled off her sun hat and put it on top of the cat carrier. 'All right. I'd ask someone if I could but there isn't anyone here!'

There was.

She hated that her heart swelled at the sight of him.

'What are you doing sitting in thirty-five-degree midday sun? You want to get heatstroke?'

'I'm leaving.'

'How? Sprout wings and fly?'

'The jet is refuelling. Your grandfather said...'

The anger and doubts suddenly fell away as he looked into her eyes, red-rimmed and bloodshot from crying. He wanted to wrap her up and keep her safe. 'My grandfather says whatever suits him but he isn't important right now. I'm an idiot,' he said.

'Yes,' she agreed.

'And I love you. I think I've loved you from the first moment I saw you.' She stared at him, wanting to hear him say it again, not letting herself believe that this was real... She had been in the sun a long time.

'You love Deb. I understand.'

He gave a hard laugh. 'I don't love Deb. I never loved Deb. I was marrying her because I didn't love her and she didn't love me, less a marriage and more a spreadsheet,' he mused, mocking himself. 'But it turned out she wasn't as clinical as it seemed. When the helicopter went down there were not two fatalities, there was a third, her long-term lover, a married man. Spyros buried the story, God knows how.'

'Is that true? Oh, God, why didn't you tell me? Why did you let me feel like second best?' she wailed.

'It was a pride thing. Deb had taken me for a fool, which I have been,' he admitted readily. 'I have never ever been in love with your cousin and you could never be second best to anyone or anything. I knew that, I think I always did, but I've spent my life staying in control. I know now that what I feel for you bears no resemblance to my parents' toxic love. You have no idea how liberating it is to know that I am nothing like them. We are nothing like them!'

'Of course we aren't.'

'Lizzie, I'm trying to tell you I love you and I want to stay married because my life without you in it looks like one dark empty road, smooth, no bumps or twists or turns. Boring. I know I've been an idiot and I hope you can forgive me... And if this PR thing is important to you, your career matters. You should do it.'

'You'd be OK with me being away for six weeks?'

'I will come with you.'

His response made her laugh. 'I forgive you, Adonis, and it's lucky you love me because you're going to be a father.' Holding her breath, she watched the emotions move across his face before settling into an expression that banished any lingering doubts about his reaction. 'Also your feelings are totally reciprocated.'

'You love me?'

'I do.'

He exhaled deeply, his eyes sliding to her flat middle, before repeating, 'You love me?'

She nodded. 'And, yes, I really am pregnant this time,' she teased as she fell into his open arms and felt them close around her.

When the long, deep, draining kiss ended he rested his forehead against hers. 'The old man was right.'

'Spyros?' She gasped, drawing away a little to angle an astonished look up into his face.

Adonis nodded, smoothing his hand around her face and gazing lovingly into her eyes. 'He implied you were pregnant. The old reprobate doesn't miss a thing.'

'I would have told you about the baby. I just needed some space to sort it in my own head first. I would never have kept the baby from you, but I didn't want to stay with you because of the baby.'

'I know that, and I know we will not be like my parents. We will always be there for him or her.'

'It's a deal.'

It seemed appropriate to seal the deal with a kiss, which was interrupted by loud cat cries.

They broke apart, Lizzie laughing at his expression. 'Just accept it. Mouse always has the last word.'

'I know my place in the scheme of things. Perhaps you can train her to carry your ring when we renew our vows here.'

'I think that might be beyond... Renew our vows? Are we going to do that?'

'I think our family deserves to have the wedding we cheated them out of, don't you, *yineka mou*? Besides, I want to show the world how beautiful my bride is.'

She sighed. She felt beautiful. 'I'm so happy I could explode.'

'Kiss me instead.'

'I can work with that!'

EPILOGUE

'Here, you hold Atticus,' she said, passing the swaddled infant with the mop of dark hair to his father. The baby looked at his father with big, interested eyes. 'I just need to, yep, done,' she said as she wiped around Lucas's mouth. He didn't open his eyes.

They were very different, in personality at least. Atticus was louder, demanding attention. Lucas, five minutes older, was more placid, but when he did lose his temper he really did lose it!

Most people could still not tell them apart. Lizzie had always been able to see the subtle little differences, the angle of Lucas's eyes and the deeper dimple in Atticus's right cheek. At six months, they were even more obvious than they had been at birth.

'Have we got time to…?'

'Plenty,' her handsome husband assured her calmly. 'It's not like they can start the christening without us, or the boys at least.' His glance slid down to her shoes, lingering a little on the way on her stupendously excellent legs. 'You going to be OK in those shoes?'

'Fine,' she promised him patiently. She had grown accustomed to his overdeveloped protective instincts during the pregnancy. He was better since the birth but still inclined to see dangers that weren't there lurking around every corner.

They took their time walking up the incline to the place where Spyros had been buried the previous week.

Once he'd known the twins were on the way, he had seemed to gain a new lease of life, and the extra months the treatment had given him had meant that he had lived to see and get to know his great-grandsons.

It had been sad when he had passed away in his sleep but, as he had said when he'd got to hold the babies for the first time, it was all about continuity and, as far as he was concerned, he was holding immortality.

Lizzie handed Lucas to his father as she laid the wildflowers on the grave, which was marked with the simple cross Spyros had requested.

She straightened up and moved in close to Adonis's side, aware of the protective warmth of his presence that made her feel shielded from any harm.

'Thank you, Spyros,' she said quietly.

In response to the unspoken question in her husband's eyes, she said, 'If he hadn't meddled and manipulated we might never have met.' The thought of that filled her with horror.

'Oh, we would have,' Adonis responded with total conviction. 'We were meant to be together. I truly believe that.' He bent his head and brushed her lips with his, then kissed both babies in his arms. 'They look like little angels, but you do realise that as soon as we walk into the church they are going to scream the place down?'

'Oh, I'd say that is a sure thing.' She laid a hand on his arm. 'You are not upset that your parents didn't turn up?'

'Not especially. Actually, not at all. I have everything I need right here.'

* * * * *

PREGNANT, STOLEN, WED

LORRAINE HALL

MILLS & BOON

For all the amazing NICU nurses out there.

PROLOGUE

REBECCA MURPHY HAD never been so happy to see the sights of home, even if the drive to her parents' cottage was a bit bumpy and therefore painful on her poor, shattered hip.

Oh, she'd been through the surgery and recovery so that she could walk and do most things. Certainly go back home.

And the Desmond Estate *was* home. Maybe her family wasn't the wealthy, estate-owning type, sharing it generation to generation, but she understood the history of the land and the horses, and felt she belonged exactly here.

She liked to think, despite her modest upbringing, that was what Patrick Desmond had seen in her. She smiled a little, despite the pain.

Patrick had promised a ring when she returned from Cork, and to announce the engagement to his family. Though Rebecca had been a bit…concerned about how his father would take the news, the Desmonds knew her, knew her family. They'd helped fund her equestrian Olympic bid.

Cut short now.

She ignored the pain in her leg—both physical and emotional. Everything would be fine. She would be Patrick Desmond's wife, and that would take up her time. She would *throw* herself into the role. She would be everything he—and they—wanted.

She instructed the driver to let her off at the main house

rather than her parents' cottage out by the stables. Patrick could drive her out there, and they could share the happy news. Hopefully it would cushion her parents' worry and concern over her recovery *and* the loss of all their dreams.

And maybe more than that... She needed something positive to keep her going. Something to look forward to. If she didn't have that concrete promise from Patrick, returning home with her Olympic dreams shattered into a million tiny pieces might end her.

She knocked on the door and grinned at the woman who answered.

Who shrieked in excitement and threw her arms around Rebecca. "Oh, our little Rebecca. Back home. Just where you belong."

Rebecca desperately wanted to believe that as Maeve's arms held her tight. Yes, she belonged here. On the Desmond Estate. At Patrick's side. Maybe she'd never ride professionally again, maybe it would be years before she could ride at all, but she'd been leading a new, different life.

"Is Patrick here? I'd like to speak with him."

"Oh." Maeve's hug stayed tight for another moment, then she pulled back, looked away. "I take it you haven't been down to see your parents?"

"No, I just wanted to..." Get this crossed off the list, she supposed. Have something happy to bring them.

Before she could really read into Maeve's strange response, Patrick appeared. "Maeve, I thought you were going to..." He trailed off when his dark eyes spotted her. He stopped midstride, there in his nice suit, looking perfect.

And shocked.

"Rebecca."

He didn't smile. He didn't cross to her. He stood there, looking at her like she was a ghost.

Which made Rebecca feel suddenly…in the wrong place. At the very wrong time. Which was ridiculous. "I texted…"

"I didn't…" He shook his head, then looked behind him. "Rebecca, you shouldn't have come here. Not yet. We need to… It's only that…"

"Pat?" It was a woman's voice. One Rebecca didn't recognize.

A vision appeared. A willowy blonde on the highest of heels, dressed in the kind of perfectly tailored and gorgeously pastel sundress that likely cost more than what it cost to feed the horses on the Desmond Estate.

There was a ring on the woman's left ring finger. Bright and sparkly. It seemed to wink at Rebecca as the woman wound her arm around Patrick's. "Who's this?" she asked, smiling brightly with lots of cheer, but there was a suspicion in her eyes all the same.

"Love," Patrick said, patting her hand on his shoulder. His expression was…blank, as he called this woman *love*. Right here. Right in front of her. "This is our horse trainer's daughter, Rebecca."

Horse trainer's daughter.

Rebecca glanced at Maeve, but she had her head down, staring at her shoes. Something was happening, and even though deep down Rebecca knew what it was, she couldn't seem to access the brain cells needed to stop it.

"The almost Olympian?" The woman smiled brightly, and Rebecca felt all the worse because the woman didn't seem to *mean* to be cutting. Perhaps she didn't know how much that *almost* hurt and echoed through her.

She was an *almost*. Now. Forever.

Rebecca couldn't manage any words. She stood absolutely still and mortified, trying to work through what was happening.

Love. Almost.

"I know you've been a dear friend to Patrick, especially after his mother passed. We simply *must* see you at the wedding."

The wedding. She looked from the woman, to Patrick, to the ring on the woman's finger again.

The wedding.

Not *her* wedding.

Their wedding.

"How kind," Rebecca managed to mutter. "I'm sure it'll be lovely. Congratulations."

The woman beamed, then bussed a kiss across Patrick's cheek. "Well, you two catch up. But don't take too long. I need you to play peacemaker between me and my mother once we get to flowers." She sent Rebecca a sunny smile, then sailed back from where she came.

Patrick stood there, and to his credit, Rebecca supposed, he looked miserable.

"I'm sorry. I… My father…" He stood there, looking a little contrite. But only a little. "Bridget is…the right choice."

"Of course she is," Rebecca agreed. Her voice even sounded like she believed it, though her face no doubt betrayed her. So she worked as hard as she possibly could to smile. "You have a nice…life, Patrick." Then she turned and left.

She wanted to run, but she couldn't without hurting her aching hip. So she walked.

And cried the whole way home.

CHAPTER ONE

"You don't have to go."

Rebecca fixed her mother with a calm, pointed look. "Yes, I do." She surveyed herself in the mirror. She had spent more money than she should have on the dress, but she wasn't about to be shown up *and* labeled as the help.

Her family had been invited to the wedding reception as *guests*. As *friends of the family*, even if they were employees. The Desmonds were loyal to the *help*, even if they didn't want their son to marry one.

Rebecca was grateful she didn't have to put on a brave face for the ceremony itself, and determined she would have *fun* at the party. She would not give anyone the satisfaction of thinking she'd miss it because Patrick had crushed what little had been left of her hopes and dreams.

She had her father's pride and her mother's stubbornness. That's what everyone always said.

So she was going. She wouldn't cry. She wouldn't run away. She had to be brave and strong.

Patrick was married. All her dreams were dead, and she'd struggled to find a new one in the months since. Maybe she wasn't there yet, but she was going to get there…somehow.

She waltzed into the elegant, sprawling reception outside on the rolling lawn, the weather perfect, the sun setting like Patrick and Bridget had paid heaven itself.

She kept her head high, knowing that she looked damn good. She smiled. She greeted. She *sipped* the champagne offered on roaming trays.

And she avoided the receiving line like the plague. They would know she was there. She didn't have to pretend to congratulate them. There were a couple of people from the stables here as guests, and she'd hunt down Hank or Sullivan to dance with, just to be seen. Just to prove she was *fine*.

She was doing just that when she found herself face-to-face with the second-to-last person she wanted to have to deal with.

"Mr. Desmond." She tried to make herself smile. She tried to relax her shoulders. She tried not to stare at him, wide-eyed and nearly hysterical. He'd always been kind to her. He'd never made her think he'd disapprove of her with Patrick. Disapprove so much that he'd find Patrick a new bride while she was off getting her hip surgically repaired and going through all the rehab that required.

"Rebecca," he greeted with his usual warm smile. "I hope you're enjoying yourself."

"Of course," she replied, as if by rote. "You put on quite the wedding."

"Oh, that was the bride and her family's doing, of course." He cleared his throat, looking around them. Rebecca looked too, but no one seemed within reaching distance. It was like they were their own awkward island out here.

He didn't excuse himself. Instead, he stepped a little closer, leaned in, making it impossible for Rebecca to escape.

"I know you and Patrick…" He trailed off, gruff and uncomfortable. "It's best this way," he said. Carefully. Like he was letting her down gently, when the past six months had been stab wound after stab wound.

And still she smiled, nodded at him, like she couldn't agree more. "Of course, Mr. Desmond. The absolute best."

She watched as his gaze momentarily fell to her hip. No doubt thinking about all the ways his investment in her hadn't paid off. She should be grateful she still had a job.

"Enjoy yourself, Rebecca." Then he moved away.

She wanted to hyperventilate, but she couldn't. Maeve and her mother were both looking at her with sad, pitying eyes from where they stood next to each other. So she kept her brittle smile in place, carefully moved away from them and searched.

She couldn't escape, not yet, but she could hide. She knew the places to hide, even out here. Out *here* was where she and Patrick had spent most of their time. She hadn't seen it for what that was then. She'd been blinded by love.

But he'd never wanted her inside where her station might leave a stain.

There were trees, hedges, benches that would eventually be in shadow as the sun dipped below the horizon. She just had to find one and get ahold of herself.

Then she'd find some more champagne, and a rich, handsome stranger for a dance partner. God knew the reception was crawling with them. Someone to toss all her cares away on.

She never expected such a man to find *her*. But not half an hour later, tucked away on a little bench under an arbor, just in the falling shadows enough to hide her from anyone looking, a man approached, slid behind the same canopy, then came to a short stop when he saw her sitting there.

He was the opposite of Patrick. Tall and broad. Dark-haired and-eyed. Oh, he had that same *moneyed* look about his clothes, but there was an elegance to this man that Patrick could not have been taught. It was...innate, Rebecca decided.

And she *liked* it.

"I'm afraid you'll have to find another hiding spot," she said to the stranger with a wry smile. "This one is taken."

His gaze moved over her. "You wouldn't consider sharing?" His voice was dark, almost abrasive. Velvet, she would say, textured and not fully soft, but not rough. In an accent she couldn't place. Certainly not from anywhere in the UK. And it had an interesting fissure of heat spreading through her.

God, she wanted some heat. Something to think about besides her poor, battered pride.

"That depends, I suppose." She peered out at the guests milling about beyond the canopy. "What are you hiding from?"

He glanced back out at the grounds dusted in golden hour, perfect and beautiful. Dancing was off to one side, drinks and socializing off to another. "A woman with talons who thinks I'd be *perfect* for her daughter." He sighed. "I am out of practice warding off preying mothers."

Rebecca was really beginning to hate the word *perfect*.

But then his dark gaze returned to hers.

"What about you?" he asked, with enough interest she felt a strange and compelling warmth overtake her.

She didn't want to think about Patrick or his *wife*. She didn't want to think about anything except that exciting and unique pull to a dark, mysterious stranger. She tried out what she hoped might be an enigmatic smile. "I'm not sure I should be trading secrets with strangers in the dark."

His mouth curved, but just on one side, so that her gaze was caught there, which seemed to be the only spot of *soft* on him. A lovely little spark warmed inside her.

He held out his hand between them. "Theo," he offered.

She decided then and there she did not want to be herself tonight. Not the gifted and dedicated athlete who thought of little else. Not the careful and studied woman who thought she'd one day be lady of the manor.

No, she wanted… Something else. Including a different name. "Becca." Different-ish, anyway.

"See there? We are not strangers now." He took her outstretched hand and brought it to his mouth, keeping his eyes on hers.

And she liked *that*. The way his mouth touched her skin, a chaste enough kiss no doubt people of his station exchanged all the time, but his eyes never left hers as his lips barely brushed her knuckles. Excitement shivered through her, all physical reactions born of just that. *Physical.* She had never had that kind of reaction to a man before, and it was like an antidote to all the horrible emotional poison that had been sitting inside her.

She wanted more of it. "Perhaps we could even solve each other's problems," she offered, allowing him to keep her hand in his.

"Oh? And how might we do that?" he returned, clearly interested. "Are you going to share your bench?"

"Maybe," she offered, smiling as she stood. "But first, I think we should dance."

Theodorou Nikolaou had not planned on enjoying himself at the Desmond wedding. He'd only come to appease his father, and perhaps get a break from his father's disturbing *new leaf.*

This kind of event was usually Atlas Nikolaou's purview. The rubbing elbows, the networking, that jolly way his father had about him, easily parting people from their money.

Theo tended to handle the details. His father had fondly called him *katharistís*, because Theo had spent most of his adult life cleaning up after his father's messes.

But the heart attack last month had left Atlas more about *hearth and home* lately. Luckily wife number four—or was it five? It was hard to keep track since his mother was none of the wives—was happy to see to his every need.

Unluckily, Theo was now thrust into the obnoxious spotlight. Atlas wanted to spend time at home. He wanted to "discover himself." Which meant Theo was now the face of Titan Banking, his father's financial conglomerate.

Atlas *liked* being the face of things. He *loved* women being thrown at him, as his four or five wives could attest. Theo preferred to do the choosing rather than fend off the gold-digging horde. He distrusted flattery, interest and pretty packages with little substance. He preferred to be in control rather than in the spotlight.

He had spent most of his adult life avoiding just that and fashioning his life the way he liked, more or less.

It shouldn't have been a surprise that Atlas would find a way to upend it. That the mess he would make would require a rearrangement of Theo's carefully arranged life.

Theo looked down at his dance partner. He supposed he could find a way to make the best of it—he usually did.

Becca did not give the impression she knew who he was. No one *he* knew flagged her down or looked at her with even a flash of recognition. Only a kind of avarice, like an undiscovered jewel being brought out into the light.

He was not *so* unlike his father that he did not enjoy being the one who held out the jewel to shine. As long as it was his hands on her.

"How do you know the happy couple?" he asked. Perhaps

if he could puzzle out how she fit into this tableau, he could determine whether she knew who he was or not.

He was not *famous*, exactly. His father held more of the renown, but because of Atlas's money, his penchant for splashy marriages to famous women and his larger-than-life personality, there *was* interest in his bastard and only heir.

Theo preferred women who did not hold that interest.

His dance partner seemed to consider this question, her gaze darting to where the fair couple stood chatting with someone or another. "Do you think they're happy?" she asked thoughtfully.

To him, the couple looked as though they could be brother and sister, but mostly they looked like any other couple on their wedding day. Smiles and excitement. Was it from *happiness* or just the moment? Theo did not know. Or care.

He shrugged. "They are rich and the center of attention as was likely the intention with an event such as this. Why shouldn't they be happy about it?"

She laughed, the sound low and husky and like a shot of fine Irish whiskey in and of itself. Because she was interesting. Not tall, exactly, but lithe anyway. An athlete's body, he'd characterize it as, though he couldn't quite imagine what sport she'd fit into. Her Irish lilt and coloring was soft and alluring, but didn't speak of the grit and determination required of athleticism.

But there was something underneath all that external soft. A hint of something sharp. In that laugh, in the way she looked around the spectacle, in the way she moved in his arms, sure and certain.

Whereas his father preferred the soft and easy, Theo had always relished the sharp and complicated. A challenge to be met and prove that he was equipped to handle.

She looked up at him, that pretty lush mouth curved into a smile, her eyes dancing with possibilities.

He had not *planned* on a wedding tryst, but he was not one to reject such an interesting prospect. Particularly if she didn't know who he was and wasn't motivated by what kind of funds or fame she might be able to get her hands on.

So he pulled her closer in the dance, their bodies brushing, heat that slow unfurling creature inside his chest, deepening the pink in her cheeks. He slid a hand up from her hip to her back, where her dress was tantalizingly nonexistent.

He skimmed his fingers up her bare spine, then back down again. Smiled, when she leaned closer, teasing, inviting. He splayed his hand there on her bare back and enjoyed the little catch in her breath before she sighed.

They danced through three songs, closer and closer. Teasing, with brushes of bodies, hands, arch looks. Until he was hard and aching and ready for more than *teasing*.

He made sure his lips just barely skimmed her ear as he spoke quietly into it. "I have a rental in town."

She considered this, not meeting his gaze. "Where?"

He told her.

She nodded, her blue eyes finally lifting to meet his. "I'll meet you there."

CHAPTER TWO

IF IT WAS a mistake, Rebecca was determined to enjoy it. And she was gratified that it didn't feel like some kind of misplaced revenge.

No, she was excited. She didn't give much of a passing thought to Patrick once Theo opened the door to his rental house. She thought of the way this man's hands had felt on her bare skin as they danced. The way he smelled of expensive cologne, but something else. An earthiness. A *realness*.

Maybe it was in *reaction* to her life falling apart, but she wasn't doing it *for* that. This was for her.

"Can I offer you a drink?" he asked in that low, rumbly accented voice of his. Very polite.

Rebecca decided she didn't want polite. She didn't want patience or control. She wanted to shed everything she'd held on to—certain it would give her the life she wanted.

She wanted to be bold. Reckless. She wanted to lean into every impulse instead of always fighting them—for better form on a horse, a higher jump, Patrick's ridiculous approval.

"No, thank you," she offered. Pausing in the prettily appointed living room. Wealthy, but cozy. And just a rental, so it didn't really matter, but she liked it. "You didn't wish to stay in one of the hotels? A B&B?"

"I like my privacy," he returned, easily enough, but he

also turned to look at her. And she was done with small talk. She had come here for a reason, and she wanted to have it.

Keeping his gaze, she reached behind her and began to unzip her dress. He did not move, as she shimmied out of it. His eyes flared, as he stood there, looking like some kind of bronze god, angry and vengeful, but she knew it wasn't anger that stamped itself across his austere face.

It was desire. She did not wear a bra, and the underwear left little to the imagination.

Rebecca was no shrinking violet, but she'd never allowed herself to be so bold. Maybe she never would again, but for tonight, it was everything she was. She was determined, and Rebecca determined was always a dangerous thing.

That choice was rewarded when he stepped toward her. He murmured something in a language she didn't recognize. Maybe Spanish, but she didn't think so. And she didn't have the wherewithal to puzzle it out when he crossed the little distance between them and put his hands on her.

Everything in her body seemed to sigh with relief. As if he was the great antidote to all she'd been feeling. As if something *special* existed in sharing her body with a stranger.

And then he kissed her, and it *was* a revelation. Something different from anything she'd ever experienced. There was no hesitation, no carefulness.

He swooped in. He took. He conquered. His mouth was hard, but his lips were soft. He demanded, and she still had enough athlete in her to relish meeting every demand. To push it, every line, every end goal.

And as his mouth found new and inventive ways to send her body into overdrive, his hands did the same. Moving over her, molding over her. So she did the same. Reaching up to unbutton his shirt, push it off his tall, broad shoulders.

A sound escaped from low in her throat. He could have been an athlete himself with how carefully each muscle was honed. He was hard and rangy. A testament to raw, masculine power. She let her hands revel in it, then moved lower, even as his hands cupped her breasts, teased until she was as breathless as if she'd run a mile.

She did not manage to get his pants unfastened and lowered before he whisked her up into his arms and was moving with purposeful strides through the house. He took her into a dark room and laid her out on a soft bed that smelled of laundry soap.

She expected him to join her, quickly and assuredly, rush this along, but he did not. She moved up onto her elbows, somewhat confused, but he switched on a lamp, filling the room with a warm low light.

He stood there at the end of the bed, his gaze raking over her like a touch. When the dark depths met hers, he nodded shortly. "Take the rest off."

He did not phrase it as a question. His tone brooked no argument. A man used to issuing orders and having them obeyed. Rebecca had become accustomed to orders—both at work, and in her former life as an equestrian, but she also gave them. She believed in *partnerships* and equality.

And still, she shimmied out of the lacy underwear so she was completely naked on the bed, waiting for him, and not demanding anything of him at all.

His eyes took her in. "What a gift you are," he murmured, some awe in his tone rather than the hard-edged order from before.

The words landed somewhere in her chest, where they shouldn't. The words of a stranger couldn't—wouldn't—matter. And it was easy to believe that when his body ranged over hers. His hands, his mouth. He seemed content to explore every inch, to drive her desire to a fever pitch until she found herself begging.

Even when he laughed darkly against her neck, the sound reverberating through every point their bodies touched.

Then he finally touched where she needed him to.

"Ah, yes," he murmured. "You like to beg, don't you?" He stroked as he spoke, and she moved against him, desperate. So desperate she wasn't sure she cared what he said. What she did.

Yes. Please. More.

The orgasm ripped through her like falling into a chasm. Endless. Sightless. Just the overwhelming ebb and flow of a pleasure so bright and bold, she wasn't sure she would ever fully catch her breath again.

"Theos mou," he said on a growl. *"Omorfiá mou.* What a treasure I've found here in Ireland."

For a moment, his weight moved off her. She almost reached out for him and begged, but he had opened a drawer and pulled out a condom. In quick movements, he had protected them both and then moved back on top of her. His rough palms spreading her thighs wide, settling himself at her entrance.

For a brief moment, a bit of panic had her thinking *too much*, but then he was deep inside her and it would never be enough. *Never.*

Since her experience was all of *one* man, she knew she didn't have anything to compare it to, but she'd never had any complaints when it came to Patrick. Sex had been good.

Or so she'd thought. Turned out, that had been the virginity talking.

Because *this* wasn't just kind of fun and enjoyable. It wasn't a little sigh of pleasure and one mild crescendo.

This was all-encompassing. *This* was what those books her mother loved to read spoke about.

Fire and wildness and changing the chemistry within. She didn't have to know a thing about this man to enjoy the way he seemed to innately know his way around her body, how to stroke sparks into fire, pleasure into ecstasy.

The way he fit inside her like they'd been made to come together. His hands were rough on her, his gaze fierce and a little wild, but each careful thrust was controlled, purposeful.

And when the climax came, it was like that moment of jumping on a horse, when nothing touched the ground, when she was all but flying. It was like that freedom, that thrilling, addicting excitement of not knowing what might happen in the aftermath.

And not caring. Pleasure pulsed, exploded, engulfed. And his eyes burned into hers, two little center points of perfect freedom.

And then he moved them, in easy, swift moments, so that she was sprawled on top of him. Gazing down at the hard planes of his body, him still seated deep within her. But at a new glorious angle.

She let out a little huff of breath, half pleasure, half amusement, all wonder.

Who was this man? Who was *she*?

His hand moved, gently, over the scars on her hip. There wasn't much pain anymore. Not externally. But the near reverent touch made them pulse with *something*. Not pain. Not pleasure. A strange kind of belonging.

And still he moved her against him. That same inexorable pace. Ruthless, just on the edge of freedom. Of everything they both wanted, but he had control she could not claim to have in the moment. She wanted to race forward, and he would not let her.

She made a sound of frustration, and he *laughed*. "So impatient." He murmured a few more words in his own language, and they sounded exotic and romantic.

And since she was just that, impatient and needy despite all the peaks she'd already climbed and flown across, she sought to find something to break his rhythm. His control.

Her nails bit into his shoulder, and he hissed out a breath, then pushed deeper inside her. So this time she used her teeth. The sound he made was primal and shot an impossible thrill through her.

His hand became a clamp on her hip, his movements wild, glorious, perfect. She cried out, shuddering into oblivion. And then she was under him.

There was no more laughter now. There was a fierceness. There was only the race to his end goal and she relished the frantic pace, the way it whipped her back up and exploded…just in time with him.

He didn't collapse on top of her exactly, but she didn't quite feel real, pressed between the mattress and his hard, gasping body.

After a few moments, he rolled off her, both of them little more than pulsing bodies and struggling lungs.

She could have left then, once her breath was back. Perhaps that was the cosmopolitan thing to do. Slip out of bed, grab her dress and heels, and disappear.

But his arm was around her, and when she made a move to be that sophisticated one-night-stand woman she was pretending to be, his hold tightened. He pushed up on his elbow to look down at her, eyes dark and fierce and *thrilling*.

"No, *omorfiá mou*, I am not done with you quite yet."

And that sounded *perfect*.

***

She was gone in the morning.

Theo had the oddest sensation of not knowing what to do with *that*, when he knew what to do with everything.

Always.

Luckily, he did not need to worry himself over it. He was leaving today. Back to Greece and work and dealing with all that came with his father's *new leaf.*

So it was for the best he didn't have to extricate himself from an uncomfortable morning after. He had no use for pretty Irish sirens beyond his short visit here for the wedding.

Needs met, he would head back to Athens to attend to business and forget all about the charming Irish woman with her wild hair and sad eyes.

Yes, he'd forget all about Becca whatever her last name was.

He was sure of it.

CHAPTER THREE

Four months later

REBECCA DID NOT forget about Theo. She tried, but her recovery still kept her off horses, and Patrick's happy marriage loomed over the estate like a ghost. Bridget *Desmond* was now the head of the house, and she was making *changes*.

Rebecca couldn't quite shake it whether she was dealing with the Desmonds' horses alongside her father or running into a friend in town. Everyone wanted to talk about the sweet, glamorous Bridget.

And that was the worst part. She was sweet and kind and glamorous. She fit in the Desmond House like she'd been born to be its mistress.

It sat in Rebecca like a sickly thing. Sometimes Rebecca was almost certain she'd come down with some kind of virus, then she'd simply feel better for a few days and be certain she was moving on with her life.

Only to wake up back in the sickly pits again for a few days. So she tried to think of Theo, of their remarkable night—because it *had* been remarkable. So much so, though, that it felt like…some fairy tale. A dream that wasn't real.

Everything around her right now was far too real. But if that night had been possible, there was more possible for her out there. She did not have to stay hung up on stuffy Patrick Desmond.

She wished she'd had the presence of mind to hook up with a local. Someone who could continue to take her mind off things. And at least make it appear as though she'd moved on.

But what local could have made her feel what Theo had? That had been...revelatory.

She supposed she could make a casual inquiry into the guest list. Figure out who he was.

And then what? her inner critic demanded. *You'd just ring him?*

He clearly wasn't residing in Ireland.

Miserable, and frustrated with her own misery, Rebecca sat on the floor of the bathroom not sure whether she should attempt to get up or not. The roiling nausea really liked to play its little games with her.

She supposed she was going to have to go to the doctor like her mother had been pushing for. Of course, she half expected to be recommended to a psychiatrist for simply being pathetic and incapable of getting over her heartbreaks.

It didn't *feel* like heartbreak. Not over Patrick, not even over the Olympics. It was more like being stuck. Sunk into a quagmire she couldn't quite claw her way out of. There was sadness, regret, some anger, but mostly she understood life was not fair and she needed to move on.

And she couldn't.

Because she had no goal. No focus. She needed one. She needed—

"Rebecca."

She looked up at her worried mother standing in the doorway but waved her off. "I'm all right, Mam. I must be coming down with the flu or something. I'll go to the doctor, like you asked, but I'm sure it's fine."

Her mother's expression went very grim as she stepped

forward. "I don't think it's a flu, *a stór*." And then her mother did something that felt completely insane in the moment.

Held out a pregnancy test.

"Mr. Nikolaou."

Theo didn't look up from his spreadsheet. His assistant, Dmitra, would hopefully get the hint that now was not the time unless she had something urgent.

She did not get the hint. "Do you recall those…strange messages we've been getting and ignoring?"

Theo stared at his assistant, working through the heaps and heaps of work he'd been attending to. *Strange* was just a way of life as his father attempted to upend everything. Atlas's natural greed and business savvy had turned into a deep and abiding need to be charitable and *good*, like he could buy his way into heaven now that he knew he had a faulty heart.

Theo rubbed his temple. He preferred it when his father had been a careless rogue. Not because he enjoyed his father's recklessness, but because *he* had been in control of Titan. As long as their profits climbed, Atlas left him be to do his work of organizing the company while Atlas played.

Now, his father was dialing into meetings, starting a million fires Theo had to try and put out.

"No, I don't remember any messages," Theo said irritably, because he remembered *everything*. Had to in order to keep up with the promises his father was making that might bankrupt them all if Theo didn't find a way to smooth things over.

"Ah. The personal ones," Dmitra replied, clearly uncomfortable, which was not her usual way.

Theo frowned. He hadn't had time for *personal* in something like four months, and the memory of that was still too deeply stamped on his mind and he did not have time for that.

But now that she mentioned strange messages, he did recall. "Yes. Right." He snorted. "The cryptic need to get in touch. What about it?"

"Apparently she has decided to get in touch...in person."

"She?" The last thing he had time for was some woman wanting to get in touch. The last thing he had time for was—

A woman stepped into his office. A woman with that reddish hair, snapping blue eyes and fair skin. A woman he recognized immediately. So immediately he felt struck dumb for a moment, completely frozen still.

"Becca."

She stood there in his office, the Irish siren he hadn't been able to fully forget. So much so that, even though he'd blamed it on the influx of work, he hadn't been with another woman since.

She moved forward. "You see, when you told me your name was Theo, it did not occur to me that it was short for Theodorou Nikolaou, heir to the Nikolaou fortune."

He wanted to believe that, particularly since she seemed irritated about it, but the usual chill spread through him. "And yet here you are."

"Yes. Indeed. Greece." She laughed, and it sounded strangely bitter. "Who knew *this* would finally get me here?"

Theo did not know what to make of this, of her, of the wild, twisting thing inside him that wanted to reach out and touch, but whatever it was, he did not want to do it in front of his assistant. "Dmitra, I will see to Ms...." It occurred to him then he hadn't a clue what *her* last name was. "I will handle this."

"Of course." Dmitra beat a hasty retreat.

Theo studied the woman he had not quite been able to

forget. That he had drowned himself in work to pretend he had. She was dressed in a kind of oversize sweater that no doubt suited the weather in Ireland more than here in Greece. Her hair was piled up on her head, and he remembered all too well his hands tangled in it.

She had haunted him, he had to admit now with her standing in front of him, with that damnable heat curling through his bloodstream like an expensive liquor. Even knowing this could not bode well for either of them, her sudden appearance all these months later.

The oddly potent pull of a woman he'd spent *one* night with *months* ago frustrated him, so he did what he did best. Focused on the problem at hand and pushed away his own wants, needs or complications. "What is *this*?"

She did the most incomprehensible thing then. She spread her hand over her stomach, cupped the slightly rounded surface that had not been round before. "Do you recall wearing a condom during our night together? After the first time, that is. Because I think there might have been a hiccup somewhere in the middle."

It wasn't embarrassment, exactly, that had him striding forward and closing his office door with a snap. It was how he could remember all too well, every moment, and if he looked back upon it, the *hiccup* she spoke of.

He'd had her, over and over again, and there had been a moment in there when he had not cared about anything except feeling her lose herself around him, and he had forgotten, momentarily…everything.

Which was not acceptable, *obviously*, and added to this unsettled frustration. Why was she *here*? Surely she didn't mean… "I am not certain this is an appropriate setting for… this discussion."

"Maybe I'm just handling it wrong." She pressed a hand to her temple, and she *did* look tired. A little pale.

Beautiful as ever.

But those eyes, direct and potent, met his gaze and said words that took their time to penetrate. "I'm pregnant. The baby is yours, as I haven't been with anyone else. Since I couldn't get a personal phone number for you, or through to you on a professional one, and dropping the news in an email to some faceless corporate name seemed wrong, I came here to tell you."

Everything rattled around in his mind like loose tacks. He tried to shake his head to clear it. "And you just expect me to…believe you?"

Her face got very hard then, but her words were not. "No. I don't expect you to, I suppose. I don't need you to, either."

She made absolutely no sense, on every level.

"You are claiming I am the father of your baby." He didn't allow the words to form a picture, to truly penetrate. Partially because he was completely and utterly upended by her standing here. In his *office*.

She rolled her eyes. "If you want to put it that way, sure. Now you know. And I've done my duty, so…bye."

He moved in front of her out of instinct more than plan, blocking her exit. She could hardly drop this…accusation, then say *bye* as if it did not matter. "This is…madness."

"Madness seems a bit much. A surprise? Unexpected? Yes. But I did not come here to…make claims or have arguments. I thought about not telling you at all. It would have been easier." She lifted a shoulder, as if this was a casual conversation about small, unimportant things. "But… I guess it just didn't seem right you didn't at least *know*, but I don't need help. I don't need…involvement. I won't fight for you to be a part of this. I don't need to."

He tried to make sense of her words, but there was *no* sense. She had come all the way from *Ireland* to tell him he was—allegedly—the father of her unborn baby, and yet she wanted no demands, no involvement, no fight?

No, it was a trick. Somehow. Why else come all this way? She knew he had money. She wanted it. Like all of the women his father fell for, forever throwing money at anyone who smiled at him.

But there was no arguing this woman had done more than *smile* at him, and while it *had* to be a trick, he did not know how to fully settle into that belief.

He took a deep breath, centered himself. "And if I should *like* to be a part of this?" he asked, pleased with how mild and accommodating he sounded.

Since he felt and would enact neither of those things.

"Well." She frowned a little. "I suppose we will have to figure out how that should work. I'm not leaving Ireland." She looked around his office. "Though you probably have the means to make the trip whenever you'd like."

Yes, indeed he did. But that had nothing to do with a child.

A *child*. Potentially…his child. But he couldn't determine how he might feel about that. First, there were particulars that needed to be taken care of, and like everything else in his life, he needed to handle them calmly and stoically until he had *all* the facts.

Then maybe he could deal with *feelings*.

"I am a wealthy man. Even if I chose to believe you by merit of…something, considering I know nothing about you except you are Irish, I will need proof. In order to move forward. In order to…" Clean up this mess.

He had never truly considered being a father. He would have had to consider a marriage first, and while his father certainly made marriage seem easy and *disposable*, Theo did not view it as such. He held too much responsibility to be as free and easy with such things as his father.

He held himself to too high a standard, and any future wife would have had to have met that standard, and he'd certainly never met anyone who came close.

He stared down at the woman who claimed to carry his child. He did not know her at all, so there was no way to determine if she met any standard.

"I understand you might want proof, but I just don't care enough, *Theo*. You can go ahead and not believe me. And I can go back to my life. I did what was right, and I don't need to…" She shook her head, and to her credit, she did not look overwrought. Just tired. But certain. "I won't prove it. I don't need to. I said what I need to say, and now I'll go."

"You came all the way here."

Her smile was small. Sad. "You wouldn't answer my messages. It felt like the only way to move forward. Now it's done. I got a glimpse of Athens. I told you what I needed to tell you. And now I can go home, conscious clear."

"And this baby?"

She put her hand protectively over her stomach, and her eyes went fierce. "Will be mine."

He had the pointless, ridiculous impulse to wonder if his mother had ever stood there, hand over her stomach with him in it, and called him *mine*.

No. It was clear she had not. She had birthed him and washed her hands of him as one might a puppy. Theo supposed he hadn't *been* there, but his mother's silence across the years while she perfected her life as a royal had made it clear.

And he had no business sitting in the past when his present…perhaps his future, stood in front of him. Becca, her hands cradling the child she grew.

A bastard. Abandoned by its parent.

No. The cycle would not repeat.

"We will have the test."

"I told you—"

He stopped her with one quelling glare. "And I am telling you, we will have the test. I will know if this child is mine, and if it is, it will be mine."

"What the hell does that mean?" she demanded, temper fraying the edges of her control.

"It means we are going to have a test." Because every mess had to be cleaned up one step at a time.

This would be the first step.

CHAPTER FOUR

REBECCA REALLY HADN'T known how this would go. She had a million different scenarios and plans that she'd thought through once she'd decided to actually come to Greece. She had even considered that a man such as Theodorou Nikolaou might offer a marriage proposal. Rich people were so touchy about *heirs* and such. She had been prepared for threats, demands of paternity proof and so on.

But she hadn't expected any of it to *matter* or move her any. She'd known she could reject a marriage proposal, no matter how far-fetched such an offer had seemed. She didn't need any tests when she knew the truth. She could raise a baby on her own. She kind of preferred the idea, all in all, rather than deal with some *stranger*.

She would raise her fatherless baby at home. It wasn't a terrible prospect as she'd had a lovely childhood. Her parents would help. She *liked* her life, more or less, and adding a baby to it had given her... Well, it was scary, sure, but she liked the prospect of it. Having something to protect, guide, *love*.

And without a man in the picture, there would be no concern that one day she would arrive home to find him marrying someone else entirely. Her child would need her. She could not afford to be crushed again.

There was the practicality of money, and the hitch this

trip had put in her savings, but she had a steady job, a steady family. They could scrape by.

The idea of Patrick and Bridget passing judgment did give her *some* pause, she couldn't lie to herself about that. She didn't *relish* the idea of financial insecurity, or putting her parents in that position.

Regardless, she would handle this. On her *own*. Even if Theo didn't react as she might want him to.

She was becoming concerned she really didn't know how to handle *him*. And it was very concerning to realize that her body's *reaction* to him was not dulled by time, circumstance or pregnancy.

Still, she didn't want to take any tests, even if she understood why he'd want or even need them. She didn't *want* to. She wanted to go home, duty done. She wanted to pretend there was no father. It was just her and her baby. Safe.

Instead, she found herself being ushered into a car and zipped off to what she assumed would be some kind of doctor's office. No doubt the wealthy had a doctor on hand for just this type of situation. No doubt, this wasn't Theo's first pregnancy scare as it was hers.

She certainly hoped it was his first scare that actually ended in his *child*, though. She should hate to be *one of many*, or have her child be.

"How many paternity tests have you forced upon women in your life, Theo? Or should I call you *Theodorou*?"

She could tell the question irritated him—both questions—by the way his jaw set, then his teeth almost seemed to grind together in frustration, even as his expression remained otherwise blank.

"It seems you will be my first, Becca."

Becca. Becca was someone else. That fairy-tale night

she'd created for herself. But Rebecca had to deal with Becca's consequences. "Rebecca."

"Syngnó mi?"

It was Greek. *He* was Greek. She was somehow here in Athens, a place she'd only dreamed about. A place that seemed as foreign to Ireland as it could be, and yet it was the same, essentially. Buildings. Cars. People. Life.

Of course, their lives looked nothing alike. He was richer than even the Desmonds. Some sort of investment banker billionaire.

And she was… "My name is Rebecca. Rebecca Murphy. I go by Rebecca." She looked at her hands. It didn't matter. It wasn't like *Becca* was all that different, but it felt necessary and important to ground herself in reality right now. Rebecca Aoife Murphy. Former equestrian, current stable girl.

Pregnant with this billionaire Greek's baby.

"You told me Becca," he said like an accusation.

"I did," she agreed, even though that night felt like a lifetime ago. Or maybe a fairy tale she'd dreamed up. "Because I wanted to be someone else that night. But a person doesn't get to just *be* someone else, do they?" She looked up from her hands to him. She wondered if he understood such a sentiment, or if that could only be understood by someone who'd had to struggle for something.

He made a noncommittal noise, staring out the window as the car sped along. His face was sharp, hard, unreadable. It felt…impossible she had allowed herself to spend a night with this *stranger*, and yet…

Even with everything they would now have to wade through, she understood *why*. He was fiercely handsome. Potent. There was something about him in particular that made her feel…bigger than she'd ever been. More alive and vibrant. *Something* woke up when he looked at her, and the only other place she'd ever felt that was on the back of a horse.

She sighed, heavily. "It will not matter what this test says," she ventured to say, to explain. She wouldn't have her life upended by *him*. Her baby? Yes. Him? No.

"I will know if this child is mine," he said darkly, fiercely. In a way she almost admired. Because she felt fiercely protective of the child growing inside her, and maybe it was good he might feel the same.

And she understood, she supposed, where his fierceness came from. Even if she hadn't expected it. Because once she'd figured out who he was by making a few subtle inquiries about the wedding guest list, and realized she knew of his family name even if she didn't know much about *him*, she'd made it her business to find out what she could as she tracked him down.

While his father was a well-known, boisterous and tabloid-friendly investment banker, there was no talk of Theo's mother. The gossip wasn't that she was dead so much as never in the picture. Theo had grown up as his father's protégé, in his father's home with an ever-revolving number of women or off at boarding schools. No mother in sight.

So, it made sense, she supposed, that a child being his might mean something to him. She didn't know what it was like to be abandoned by a parent, how that might affect feelings on the matter.

She wished he'd be more of a careless asshole who wanted nothing to do with the whole endeavor, but if she allowed herself to set her feelings aside and be *practical*, it was hardly a bad thing that a billionaire would want to be involved in his child's life. It would offer the baby a life without financial burden, and wouldn't that be something?

The car rolled to a stop, but not anywhere she'd expected.

It wasn't a medical office. It was a modern-looking house, all sharp lines and bright white, tucked away in trees and bushes to give the illusion of some privacy amid the city around them.

Rebecca didn't like the way nerves settled in her chest. A terrible foreboding like nothing would be the same after she stepped out of this car.

But everything had already been upended. Everything had already changed. So she let Theo open the door for her and help her out of the car.

For a moment, they both stood there, her hand in his, the warm Greek air surrounding them like a bubble. They regarded each other, and Rebecca could admit she was surprised by the potent arc of their own heat that seemed to pass between them.

Like that night hadn't been a one-off born of her disappointment in Patrick and her hip. Like it had been something…more. Something as big as it had felt at the time.

Theo dropped her hand, and she was glad for it. So glad, she followed him inside without lodging a complaint or concern. Anything to leave that feeling behind.

"The medical team will be here shortly to administer the test," he said, leading her into the sleek, impersonal house. "I will show you to a room. You may make yourself comfortable. Once the test is done, we will await the results."

"I suppose you can pay for that kind of quick turnaround."

"Indeed," he agreed.

The bedroom was nice. Still very white and impersonal, but the bed looked soft and she wouldn't mind a nap. Her gaze went from it to him, and thoughts went from a nap to memories of *that night*.

In the immediate months that had followed, she hadn't minded the memory. She'd kind of enjoyed going back over it, knowing what she could be without Patrick. Without all the plans she'd made for herself. She'd looked at it as a kind of celebration of independence.

Then she'd taken that test her mother had handed her, and she hadn't allowed herself to think back to the night. She'd focused on the reality of the *present*.

But back in his orbit, she could too easily recall the way his hands and mouth had felt on her, the reactions he had brought out in her body. It throbbed in her now, and she might have been embarrassed, but she saw a flare in his eyes that was *also* recognizable.

Until he blinked, and it all chilled away. "The doctor will be in shortly." And with that, he turned on a heel and left her there.

Rebecca sank onto the bed and wondered what the hell she'd gotten herself into.

Theo waited with what he considered impressive calm. In his mind, this could go either way. He would not be shocked if this *Rebecca* was a liar. He had always been too careful to allow such machinations to be lodged against *him*, but he had watched his father. There had been paternity tests, lies, schemes. His father had fallen for some, swiftly cut others off at the pass.

His father *lived* for the drama of it all. Theo did not, and *would* not.

If she had figured out who he was and figured one night owed her a certain monetary compensation, he would not allow himself to be surprised, taken off guard and dragged into a drama.

She hadn't *asked* for that, and her calm resignation as the doctor had entered the room didn't mesh with that possibility, but Theo could not yet rule it out.

But he would also not be surprised if she were as she seemed. That he was indeed the father of the baby, if there was a baby. They *had* shared a night together, and if he looked back on it, perhaps he had gotten...careless.

The one thing he had spent his adult life avoiding. The one thing that terrified him. He would not be his father. He would not consider every possible outcome.

So, that's what he did. Rather than beat himself up for a...misstep, he used the waiting time as an opportunity to learn about his Becca.

Rebecca Murphy, he found, sitting at the desk in the office of his Athens house. He didn't spend much time here. He preferred his island estate about two hours away. Private. Isolated. His and his alone, but sometimes work required he stay here.

If it turned out she was telling the truth, they wouldn't stay here. They would need more privacy, more...distance, in order to figure out a way forward.

And he would figure out a way forward. First, he needed to know her.

The first surprise was that she was an employee at the Desmond Estate, not a true wedding guest. The second was that she had been an equestrian. Had won all sorts of championships in Ireland and then other places in Europe. It seemed there'd been some kind of Olympic bid, before she'd had a terrible fall with her horse.

There wasn't much on what had happened after, but there were murmurs of a long medical recovery. It explained the scar he'd seen on her hip that night, an unfortunate memory. Because it brought to mind other moments.

The way she'd smelled of spring rains and something earthy that he'd never been able to identify since. Something unique to her, or maybe Ireland.

The way her pale skin had felt under his palms, the way that scar along her hip and leg had added an interesting point of imperfection amid the otherwise perfect.

He scowled at his thoughts. No one was perfect, himself included, more was the pity. The night had no doubt taken up residence in his head like an apparition because it had been…out of character. Because she had not been a carefully vetted romantic partner.

She had been a moment of weakness, and while he'd been fine with that in the moment, he had not expected it to have consequences.

As if on cue, a knock sounded on the doorframe and Theo looked up to find the doctor there. The man had spent most of his career in his father's employ, and Theo didn't love the fact he'd had cause to use the man, but he knew he could trust him. There would be no whiff of Becca or his child until he was ready.

"Paternity is positive, Mr. Nikolaou. The baby is healthy, measuring at about nineteen weeks. The mother is healthy as well and has been receiving good care and taking care of herself."

Paternity is positive.

Even though Theo had been half expecting that outcome, it did something to him. Something unwieldy. But he pushed it down, offered the doctor his thanks, showed him out of the house.

Then took a few moments standing in the entry to decide how to move forward. While breathing through the tendrils of *something* that tried to wind around his lungs.

No, there would be no *thinking*. No *feeling*. Action was needed. He strode through the house to the room he'd left Becca—*Rebecca* in. Things needed to be decided.

Things needed to change. He could hardly allow her to go back to Ireland. She carried his child.

His child.

The reality of that was too complicated to parse, so he had to focus on the practicalities. She would need to stay in Greece. His child would be born here, where his money and influence would matter and give the child the best of everything.

He wasn't *so* arrogant he thought Rebecca would agree to this quickly and easily, but surely she would see with little argument that it only made sense.

He opened the door of the room. It didn't even occur to him to knock.

Rebecca had been lying on the bed, but now pushed herself up into a sitting position, regarding him with cool blue eyes. "So, congratulations. You're a father." There was no feeling to how she delivered those words, and still they landed like little, painful blows.

A father. There was a child. *His* child. And it brought to mind all the ways his own father had failed him. All the ways his mother had abandoned him.

All the ways he would not fail or abandon his child. He refused.

"But you don't need to be one, Theo," Becca continued, something like entreaty in her tone now. "I can go back to Ireland, to my life, and you don't need to concern yourself with this."

She was serious, and she was offering him the easy way out. It was insulting, for many reasons, but he did not allow himself to sound affronted or angry. His voice was calm and firm and brooked no argument.

"You are not going home, Becca."

She blinked, then frowned, pushing to her feet. "Yes, I

am. I will do what I want, and I will be returning to Ireland. *Tonight.* If there's something you'd like to discuss, we can arrange a…a…meeting. Later."

"I am afraid that cannot be arranged. Instead, you will stay." But it had to be more than that. It had to be everything. If he was to have a child, his child would have *everything*. "And we shall marry."

The noise she made was some mixture of a gasp and a shriek. "No we *shall* not. What the hell is wrong with you?"

He shrugged. "I do not think much, frankly. This cannot function with you in Ireland and me here. I have a job here. Responsibilities here. So we will stay here."

"I have a job."

"Come, Rebecca, at best mucking stables is a hobby. You live with your parents. I run a billion-dollar company, and every estate I own is mine and mine alone."

"Well, *la-dee-da*."

For a moment he was so surprised by her dripping disdain, he found himself at a loss for words.

But he found them, as he always did. "You will stay. We will marry. It's the only way forward."

She shook her head, not just bristling but fuming now. "You're delusional." She tried to push past him, but he would not be pushed. He looked down at her.

"No. But I am powerful."

"What, you're just going to keep me here against my will?" she demanded, her hands fisting on her hips as she glared up at him. "Marry me against my will?"

She was getting a bit hysterical, so he remained calm. He lifted a shoulder, held her wild gaze as he continued to bodily block her exit. "If your will is wrong, then I will have to."

CHAPTER FIVE

Rebecca knew how to fight. She considered her angles now, as rage and frustration and something softer she did not want to identify wound through her.

She could land a punch, but the reach up would make it difficult to put any heft behind. She could get a sharp elbow to the chest, but she knew from firsthand experience the kind of muscle his perfectly tailored suit covered.

A knee lifted to the groin was the only option, but it would require getting closer. She considered, looked up at him.

For the first time since her arrival, his mouth curved upward, ever so slightly. "You could *try*," he said silkily, clearly seeing through her.

"You cannot hold me against my will. That is kidnapping."

"Óchi," he returned, shaking his head. "I have not taken you anywhere against your will. You seem a bit hysterical. No doubt the travel and the stress of a test. We must think of the baby. You must be hungry."

"No, Theo, I am *panicking* because a man I barely know is holding me hostage."

"Hostage?" He laughed. "Do not be so dramatic, *omorfiá mu*. We are simply in a stalemate until we make decisions together."

"You sound like a psychopath trying to reason out your horrible actions."

This accusation *also* did not seem to faze him. He kept talking in that damnable *reasonable* tone.

"If I do, that only means you sound like a hysterical overwrought woman, and I do not think you are that. So let us take a breath. You must be exhausted and starving. I will have the kitchen fix you a plate."

She was *all* those things and felt a bit like crying, too. But she could not simply…give in to him. She had to maintain some control. Some autonomy. As exhausting and painful as that seemed. "Theo, I am going home."

"Becca. You are not." He said it in the same implacable tone. "We have many things to discuss. To work out. You cannot come all this way and think you will simply waltz back to Ireland without having to deal with the fallout."

Oh, how she was so very tired of dealing with fallout. Of having everyone else make decisions that *she* had to come to terms with. Whether it be the universe, a horse and her doctor, or Patrick and the perfect *Bridget*. Nothing ever got to be her own choice, did it?

She closed her eyes against the wave of powerlessness and exhaustion. Tried to squeeze the tears back with it.

"Over the next few days, we will work out an arrangement," he said. Firmly. With complete assurance. Like he knew just what to do. Like *he* would deal with the fallout, and everything would be fine.

Dangerous ground, Rebecca.

But it felt…reassuring in some way. That he'd have answers. That he would have a plan. Her parents just kept asking her what *she* wanted to do. They supported her, but they expected her to have answers she just didn't have.

So far her plan had been, weather everything. And tell him. Love her baby. The end.

But he...had answers, or so it seemed.

"A plan we both agree with," he continued. "But it must be done in person. I think you owe me this."

That pricked at her temper. "*Owe* you? I didn't get pregnant alone."

"No, indeed. So you shouldn't be making the decisions alone. It appears you have chosen to have this child, so if there is to be a child, I have a say. This is not unreasonable."

No, it wasn't. Which didn't seem fair. But... He seemed to know what to do.

As if sensing her softening, he moved for her. "You will rest. I will have dinner made and then you will eat. Then we will sit down and begin the discussions." He put his hand on her elbow, as if to usher her back to the bed.

His hand on her arm was a shock. Because it was like being swept up into carnal memory. She wore long sleeves, and still she knew what his palm would feel like on her arm. Smoothing over her breasts. His fingers inside her.

She tried to breathe normally, tried to hide her reaction to him, to his memory. She thought she might have succeeded...until he turned her to face him.

When their eyes met, held, she knew he saw the same things she did. Even felt them. His grip on her arm tightened, his eyes flared with all that glorious, dangerous promise.

She couldn't want this again. She didn't even *know* him. One night at a wedding to exorcise some heartbroken demon was one thing, but it was completely another now when he was making demands and orders and...

The father of your child.

But all those feelings, reactions, whirling thoughts kept

attacking her and she couldn't center herself enough to find a word, a denial.

If he kissed her, she would kiss him back. If he touched her, she would beg for more. She didn't have to like it to know it was true. There was something about this man that undid her foundations.

She gently pulled her arm away from his grasp, settled her hand over her stomach as she'd grown accustomed to doing. Because this baby had given her a strength, or a reason to rediscover her strength. That didn't allow her to give into him, no matter how hard her body pulsed or ached.

"Very well," she said, trying to sound firm, though she didn't think she succeeded. "I will rest. I will eat. We will discuss. But I am going back to Ireland once we've come to an agreement. I am not staying here. I am not *marrying* you."

He made a noncommittal kind of noise she wasn't foolish enough to take as agreement, but when he reached out for her elbow again, she climbed into the bed rather than be touched by him again.

Of course it was soft and comfortable, and her body practically sighed into it. Her eyes were already drooping, so she didn't have to fight to keep from looking at him. She just let her eyes close.

She was asleep before he'd even left the room.

Theo stiffly went to the kitchens, requested an early dinner and a tray to be put together for his visitor. He would deliver it himself.

No matter how the thought of them together in that room now felt like the threat of a dangerous storm.

He had not meant the touch to be anything more than a guiding gesture. Hand on elbow, move her over to the bed, ease her into it. She needed rest and he'd just been trying to push her in that direction.

Then her eyes had met his, and he had *seen* all the heat there. Reflecting in her blue eyes seemed to be images and memories of their night together.

The soft velvet of her skin, the floral perfume he'd found in her hair, in the crook of her neck. The taste of her like an addicting liquor, and much too easily, he could remember exactly the noises she'd made as she'd lost herself around him.

It was an affront to find himself tense and hard. He never allowed his wants, his passions to rule him. He had taught himself to be the antithesis, and maybe savior of his father. He had learned to push himself physically, emotionally, to always know his control center point.

He had taught himself from a young age to do everything with purpose, with calm, with control.

He could delve into the psychology of that some other time.

Right now, he had to focus on that control. On the ability to push all memories, all *desire* away.

But it was so visceral, this reaction to her, regardless of her dress or the circumstances. He understood lust—he'd once been a teenage boy eager to discover the pleasures to be found in a woman's body—but it had never had some kind of *choke hold* on him like this.

He wanted her. Now. To strip her of her drab, baggy clothes. To taste, to touch, to watch her blue eyes darken with need. To hear her *beg*.

And to feel the growth of his child inside her. To trace the new curves with his hands. He did not understand the response, a kind of primitive, biological *satisfaction* that *he* had been the one to make her with child.

Child. She was carrying his child. They would need to marry. Plan a life together. *Sex* was a distraction. Not off the table, but he could not let it be his motivation, his goal. His *goal* had to be making her into the wife he needed.

Perhaps she would meet his stringent standards, though he doubted it, but standards could be taught and met. She'd been an athlete herself. A woman who knew how to set a goal and reach it.

Almost, anyway.

He needed someone who could attend events with him. Converse with the wealthy all over the world. Be sophisticated, controlled. She was a beauty, so there was no issue there, but the wardrobe would need improvement. He did not know how she interacted with people other than him. No doubt she would need to be taught.

Thinking of the practicalities helped ease some of the heat raging inside him, so he continued thinking as he waited for the kitchen staff to put together a tray.

And as he stood there, he acknowledged even as he made mental plans for all of these things, the most important goal she would need to meet would be that of mother. He liked what he saw already. A protectiveness. A sense of fairness in telling him.

His child would have a good mother, no matter what. He did not know what it looked like, but he knew that absence and abandonment was *not* it. And he, too, would have to learn how to be a good father.

Atlas was not…the worst. There was *some* affection there. Some…passing down of things. But mostly it had been a careless, *friendly* sort of relationship. His father had always worried more about the ever-revolving door of women than what Theo wanted or needed.

Theo would do more for his son.

He pulled out his phone, began to do some light research on the finest parenting instruction and was frustrated when there was nothing *definitive* to be found. He ordered a slew of books for the time being. There was time to learn.

And learn he would.

Learn *they* would.

Whether she wanted to or not.

CHAPTER SIX

REBECCA WOKE UP DISORIENTED, except for the nausea. She was very used to that by now. Her doctor had assured her it was normal and would lessen as time went on. She'd taken him at his word.

He had been *wrong*. Hunger and the need to vomit were a constant war all morning long, then just like a switch, afternoon would be fine. Mostly. She got the occasional evening attack if she didn't eat.

Eat. Though her stomach rejected the idea, she realized she had not eaten since…the plane.

The plane. Greece. Theo. She closed her eyes again, just for a minute. Just to give herself the chance for regret.

If her mother hadn't harped on her doing the *right thing*, she'd still be home in Ireland. And maybe mucking the stalls had been an exercise in torture with the morning sickness, the exhaustion, but she hadn't been willing to admit that to her father or the Desmonds. Maybe growing a *child* in her childhood bedroom wasn't exactly a satisfying *adult* endeavor or left her much room to feel like a *mother*, but… It was what it was, like so many other things in her life.

Except now she was here, dealing with the father of her baby, in this pretty if bland room, on an amazingly soft bed, and though nausea rattled at her, she'd definitely slept hard and maybe long. Plus, there weren't any unpleasant smells to make that worse, except…

She pushed into a sitting position. Then gave a little sniff. It smelled a bit like…food. She looked around. There on the pretty little desk—no doubt some extravagant antique—was a giant silver tray full to the brim of food.

Pastries, fruits, cereals. A pitcher of water that had the last vestiges of some ice floating at the top as though it had been sitting there for a while.

A far cry from the oatmeal and herbal tea her mother liked to shove at her in the mornings. Neither of which Rebecca had been able to stomach.

Rebecca didn't know how to conceptualize this whole strange twist on her life, so she had to focus on facts. That was clearly a breakfast tray that had been there for a while. So what time was it?

She couldn't remember where she'd put any of her things, but rolling over a little told her that her phone was in her pocket. She pulled it out, but the screen was blank.

Dead. She would need to charge it, which meant finding a charger. She would need to find out what time it was, and let her parents know that she…

She would stay in Greece for a few days. With some sleep under her belt, she didn't really see any way around that. Maybe talking this out with Theo sounded a bit like torture—especially if she kept having annoying and unrelenting physical reactions to him—but it was the reasonable, responsible, *adult* thing to do. For the *baby*.

Besides, the bed was nice. The food might be nice. And she *had* come all this way. Ireland and home could wait for some answers, some decisions.

Carefully so as not to upset her stomach any further, she pushed out of the bed and moved over to the tray. She made herself a plate of a few of the blander items, poured herself a glass of water. No doubt it wouldn't stay down, but that didn't seem to matter. Most mornings were the same. Eat breakfast. Toss breakfast right back up, and then settle. But not eating meant feeling worse all day.

Then, because she was alone, and because she was pregnant and deserved a little pampering, she crawled back into the bed and settled in to eat. She was halfway through some sort of flaky pastry filled with a delicious cream when the door creaked open.

It was Theo's head that popped in. He regarded her, then pushed the door the rest of the way open and strode in. Without any sort of invitation offered.

She had a feeling he was not a man who often waited for an *invitation*. Particularly in his own home.

"You are awake," he said by way of greeting.

Since it was a rather silly greeting, she raised an eyebrow at him. "Yes."

"And eating."

She waved the pastry. "It appears so."

His expression was unreadable, but she *thought* she saw a flicker of annoyance. She couldn't tell if it was at her existence, or at his own self. "Eating is good. How are you feeling?"

She wasn't sure what to do with the question. It seemed genuine enough, so she answered without being too graphic. "A bit off this morning, but some food should help it."

"Morning sickness, then?"

The fact he knew the term for it was interesting. "You're well-versed in pregnancy symptoms?"

He stood there, tall and broad, and not *stiff* exactly, but unmoving, his hands clasped behind his back. And yet she had the impression of *strength*, that in the blink of an eye he could move and handle whatever he wanted to handle.

"I did some research," he said, then moved over to the tray, surveyed what was left. "All challenges must be met with knowledge. The best way to educate myself was to read, and since you've done nothing but sleep, I had plenty of time to do such." He studied her for a moment, then turned back to the tray. "The sleep was good for you."

She didn't know why those simple words settled over her like a compliment. She knew what she'd looked like when she'd arrived. Tired. Haggard, probably. Though sleep might have done her some good, she couldn't imagine she looked *good* right now. She brought a hand up to her hair. It was half in and out of the band. She no doubt looked a fright.

But he'd said the sleep *was* good for her, not anything about her actually *looking* good.

She didn't need him to. Obviously. But the idea of him sitting around last night reading about *pregnancy* was hard to reckon with. This impressive, austere man. She had not really seen him interact with anyone but her, though. Maybe there was a warmth somewhere he was hiding. Maybe he would be…a good father.

She knew it would be wrong to take that opportunity away from him, and that was why she was *here*. Still… It was a lot to reconcile when he was a stranger she had a ridiculous physical reaction to.

"You may take the morning to acclimate yourself, but this afternoon we will take a drive and sit down with my lawyers and decide how to move forward."

Rebecca set the half-eaten pastry aside, took a sip of the water. The idea of a drive roiled around in her stomach just as moving forward with *lawyers* did. "I will not sit in a room with *your* lawyers, while I have none of my own."

"You may call one."

She snorted. "Don't be ridiculous, Theo. I realize you have money and that makes things complicated, or whatever you privileged lot convince yourselves of. That's fine. But first, we must make decisions as *people*. No lawyers."

She realized with some trepidation how out of her depths she now was. Maybe she understood the rich having worked for the Desmonds, and had a relationship with Patrick, but she did not have access to things like *lawyers*.

How would her family absorb such a cost? No, she had to try to appeal to Theo's humanity and focus on this between the two of them.

She looked at him standing there, his expression hard and determined, like he'd already written out the entirety of the rest of their lives. Like he'd somehow make certain she never left Greece, never had her own life again.

And that should terrify her, but it sounded kind of nice—someone else taking care of everything for a bit. Which was the problem. Maybe she wouldn't mind a little swooping in *now*, but she wouldn't want it always.

She certainly wouldn't want lawyers swooping in, no doubt to make sure Theo got all he wanted and she got nothing. But first, everyone had to decide what they wanted.

Her thoughts took a quick, drastic turn to the state of her stomach. She pushed out of the bed. Barely got the words "excuse me" out of her mouth before she walked into the bathroom, carefully closed the door, then indeed threw up the entire contents of her breakfast.

Theo stood in the guest bedroom with the completely foreign feeling of not knowing what to do.

She was…retching. He'd read this was fairly common, though usually not a symptom that stuck around into the nineteenth week—if the doctor's measurements had been correct. Should he be concerned?

He did not for the life of him know how to react to this. When Theo had been a boy, he had sometimes nursed his father after a dastardly hangover, but usually there was a woman around to do that kind of thing, and Theo had long since grown past the age and urge to do so.

These days, Theo was used to taking care of problems and *things*, not…people.

He could not think of the last time he'd had an upset stomach, but he tried to cast back to childhood. There'd been a few bouts of the stomach flu over the years. What had his nanny done? Soup? Some lemon mint water? A cool washcloth to put over his head?

He sent a text off to the head of his kitchens to bring an assortment of remedies down to Rebecca's room.

She emerged seconds later. She looked…shaky. Not at all like the vibrant woman at the wedding, or even the one who'd walked into his office looking tired but determined.

A foreign sensation spun in his chest. A need to act, in ways he didn't fully understand. But action was good. Better than feeling. He strode into the bathroom, grabbed one of the folded washcloths in the vanity, ran some cool water over it.

She had crawled back into bed when he returned, and he walked over and handed her the cloth. When she frowned at it, as if she did not know what it was for, he scowled and moved forward to place it across her forehead.

She blinked once, then looked over at him. There was *something* in her blue eyes. A kind of wondering, but then something he did not care for at all.

A little indulgent smile. "I do not have a fever," she said gently.

"Nevertheless," he said, hating that she'd made him feel foolish.

She reached up, moved the cloth from her forehead to around her neck. Then she sighed, closing her eyes. "Thank you."

That odd spooling in his chest warmed, settled. The problem was solved, but what had caused it? He looked at the tray of food. "Is the food not to your liking?"

"The food is fine. I just can't keep anything down in the mornings. But if I don't put *something* in my stomach first thing, I'm a wreck for the whole day. So it's just a whole vicious cycle."

He had read about morning sickness, but this seemed… ridiculous. "Surely there is something to be done."

"My doctor back home said if I do not gain more weight by my next appointment, the next step will be an anti-nausea medication."

"Your new doctor will get you some immediately."

She shook her head. "No. No, I don't want to take anything."

"That is foolishness."

Her eyes snapped open. Frustration clear in them, but that did nothing to lessen their impact. Her impact. Nothing did.

"It is *my* choice."

He did not know how to argue with that, though he wanted to. So he changed tactics. "You will need to have your medical records sent to your doctor here."

Her expression stayed sharp and frustrated. His blood swam in response.

"It is not *my* doctor. I am not staying forever, Theo."

He wanted to immediately argue, but he was not the head of his father's company because he did not know how to maneuver people. "Perhaps not, but you are here now. Wherever you are, the doctor should have the necessary information."

He could tell that she had a harder time finding an argument against that. "I suppose I could call their offices and see what needs to be done. But not right now." She closed her eyes, made a face that indicated pain.

"What is it?"

She shook her head. "I'm just so sick of throwing up. So sick of feeling…not myself. Run-down. And so on."

"You are growing an entire human being."

Her hand rested against her stomach, and she sighed. "I know." Her mouth curved ever so slightly, eyes still closed. "Isn't that the strangest thing? People have been doing it since the dawn of time, and yet, it feels like this impossible, improbable undertaking."

Those words made everything different somehow. He had been conceptualizing the child as…a *child*. An entity. And what that entity meant to his life, his future, his choices, but he had not thought of it in terms of…an actual infant. Growing inside her. Being born from her.

He had read about these symptoms, about complications, but he had not…allowed them to penetrate. She was talking about needing medication, to gain weight. She was retching in his bathroom.

Everything suddenly felt so…precarious.

They could not stay here, amid the bustle and demands of Athens. No, she needed rest and privacy and the best he had to offer. She was right, no lawyers. He didn't need logistics, yet.

He needed to win her over, and to do so, they would need to be alone. Truly alone. Away from all the reaches of the outside world, except the team of doctors he would employ.

"Rest. This afternoon, I will take you somewhere private—no lawyers, just us—to discuss how we will handle this. Together."

She let out a long sigh, relief softening her features. She yawned. "I need to contact my parents. My phone is dead and I…"

"You rest, *omorfiá mou*. I will handle everything."

And he would.

CHAPTER SEVEN

WHEN REBECCA WOKE up this time, she felt much better. Sturdier and hungry without the nausea settling at the bottom of the hunger. She could admit to herself now, in the aftermath, that in the days leading up to coming to Greece, she had been too stressed to take care of herself and baby properly.

It had caught up with her. One more good night's sleep tonight, and she'd no doubt feel more like herself. And food. She definitely needed food. She didn't think she'd slept *that* long, but there were no trays waiting for her now, which was a shame.

She once again reached for her phone to find out what time it was but couldn't find it at all now. Not in her pocket, not twisted up in the covers.

She pushed out of bed, found no sign of any of her things, then figured she'd have to hunt down Theo. She left the room, not sure she remembered which way they'd entered, but she could wander. If Theo had a problem with that, he should have left her some instructions or her damn phone.

The entire house was like the room. No doubt incredibly expensive but all a bland kind of white with no personality. There didn't seem to be *any* personal touches here— photographs, collections. If she didn't know it was Theo's, she might think it some rental property. It was nothing like the Desmond Estate—full of history and luxury and ancient personality. Certainly nothing like the tiny home she'd grown up full to the brim with knickknacks, family heirlooms, ribbons and awards from both her and her father's equestrian pursuits.

Before she could determine what that said about Theo, if anything, she was met with a slight man dressed all in black, blocking her forward progress deeper into the house.

"Ms. Murphy. Mr. Nikolaou is waiting for you just outside." He gestured behind her toward a hallway that she thought led out to the front. "Follow me," he said. Firmly.

But Rebecca didn't move. She looked down at her feet, covered in nothing but fuzzy socks that had been better suited to the Ireland weather. "I don't even have shoes on."

"It is of no matter. The things you came with are with Mr. Nikolaou." He moved briskly past her, and she felt no choice but to follow. Theo had all of her things? Where? Had he decided she was too much trouble and he was sending her home?

She wanted that to be relief winding through her. She could go home and handle this on her own, without having to make compromises or worry about an enigmatic *stranger* who claimed he wanted to marry her. She should be thinking: *hallelujah!*

But Rebecca had a bad feeling the sensation coursing through her was a lot closer to regret for not trying harder to find some sort of middle ground with him. For their *baby*.

"Does he have my phone?" she asked, scurrying after the man.

"Likely." He led her outside, to where a large vehicle sat in the drive, Theo standing outside it. When he saw her, he opened the backseat door and gestured her inside.

"I imagine you are starving. Come. We have an assortment of sandwiches for you to choose from," he offered by way of greeting.

"Theo. Where are we going? Where are my things? I need my phone."

He gestured inside the opened door. "Everything you need is inside."

She couldn't say she trusted him, but she wanted her things. So she moved forward, peered into the back seat. There was a basket full of food, the bag she'd brought with her on the airplane. And her phone peeked out of the outside pocket.

Before she could decide exactly what to do, Theo slid into the driver's seat. Which had Rebecca blinking. "You're driving?"

"Indeed. Relax. Eat. The drive will take some time. But I think you'll enjoy the scenery. Let me know if you're feeling unwell and we'll stop and pull over."

"Theo, you can't put off this discussion. Or the fact I have to go back to Ireland. After a few days," she amended, because she could give him a *few* days to really have a conversation about their future.

But that was it.

He made an agreeable sort of noise, though she didn't actually take it for agreement. But her stomach and wanting her phone and to contact her parents got the better of her. She slid into the back seat, the man who'd lead her out of here closing the door behind her before she had a chance to do it herself.

Rebecca grabbed her phone—fully charged now—and noted that her morning nap hadn't been more than thirty minutes, and still Theo had put all this together. Well, no doubt he had a team of people who had.

She texted her parents that she had decided to stay a few days while Theo began to drive.

With her parents contacted, she looked at the basket of food. There was an assortment of sandwiches, and she appreciated there were a few offerings that were fairly bland.

Some more containers held fruits—some apricots, some peaches, already cut up. Some sort of watermelon salad that was completely and utterly refreshing.

Rebecca ate her fill, enjoying the fizzy ginger drink, ice cold. The rich did have a way with food.

She knew she should be concerned about where they were going, especially as she watched Athens pass by outside her window, as they took a road that wound along the coast of glittering blue water.

But it was too beautiful, too relaxing. This area of Greece was as green and blue as Ireland, but the hues were different. Ireland was lush, a deep kind of vibrancy. Greece had the sun to brighten everything and make it sparkle like a jewel.

It nearly made her wish she had some kind of artistic talent so she could find a way to recreate the differences.

The food settling nicely in her stomach for once, the lull of the quiet and the drive, had her dozing off once again. She wouldn't have called herself tired, but it seemed like if she sat still for any period of time in a moving vehicle she just couldn't stay awake.

When she woke, she had no idea how much later it was. Frustration that she'd dozed at all quickly turned to concern as she recognized the strangest sensation. The car wasn't moving, or at least it wasn't *driving*. The engine was clearly off, but everything seemed to sway.

She pushed up from her slouched position and looked out the window. Nothing but bright blue water and the sun most definitely lower in the horizon. She jerked her head to look in the front, but no one was there.

Heart slamming against her breastbone, she flung the door open, and there he was. At the bow of some kind of… boat. A ferryboat. The car was parked on a kind of plank part of the boat, and Theo captained this vessel easily as the wind ruffled his dark hair, and the sun shined down on him like a spotlight on a perfectly bronze statue.

Even having no idea what the hell was going on, his beauty took her breath away. Which was not *fair*.

"What is going on?" she demanded.

He looked back at her, unperturbed. "We are nearly there."

"We are nearly *where*?"

He pointed ahead, and she saw a shore coming up. There were some buildings on a little...island amid all the blinding blue.

"This is my island," he announced, like that was a normal thing to have ownership over. "We will stay here to work out an arrangement. You will like it."

"It's...an island. *Your* island."

"That is what I said."

"I didn't agree to come to some...remote island owned only by you!" Panic and something else thudded inside her. She didn't *like* panic, but it sounded a lot more sane than *excited*. She had never even *dreamed* of being on a private island before.

But it was wrong. He hadn't asked. He hadn't even *told*. He'd tricked her.

"I didn't ask you to agree," Theo said easily, in that way that had her wondering if she'd suffered some kind of head injury and was now living in an alternate reality.

Or he was.

"Turn this boat around. Take me back. I... I... This *is* kidnapping this time, Theo."

"If you wish to consider it such, I suppose you can, though it does nothing to serve our purposes. We will come to an agreement, Becca." His expression was hard now. Fierce. "And neither of us will leave until we do."

* * *

Theo took care of landing the ferry on the shore. Two of his men who lived and worked on the island were waiting, and helped take care of the practicalities of his and Rebecca's things and handling the boat.

Or they would, if Rebecca would *get off*. But she stubbornly refused to get in the car, or even leave the boat. He told her she was being childish. She didn't seem to care.

"At some point, you will need to eat, sleep," he pointed out to her, standing with his driver's side door open.

She stood in the far corner of the ferry, leaning against the rail, her arms crossed over her chest—she still had no shoes on, only socks. The sun glinted against her hair, shooting off little strands of fire amid the rich browns. Her chin tilted higher, like some diminutive goddess warrior. "I refuse."

"Your hunger strike will only punish you. Eventually, you will throw up again, and then you will require *something*. Unless you plan on standing on the boat in your own filth."

Her hands fisted on her hips. "You're being unreasonable."

"*I* plan on driving off this ferry and to my home, if you'd care to be *reasonable* and join me. You could also put on some shoes, *agapi tós*."

Her expression remained stubborn, but he noted a weakening.

So, he pressed. "It is a beautiful estate. Peaceful. Calming. You will have the run of the entire house. You can request whatever meals you like. You will be taken care of, waited on hand and foot. What more could you possibly want?"

"Personal autonomy?"

"Come. You are exaggerating. I haven't locked you up." Perhaps if situations were reversed, he would be furiously raving, but he didn't want to think about putting himself in her shoes. He wanted to think about ensuring he got what he wanted.

Needed.

Access to his child. A marriage that provided all the stability he'd certainly never had. She needed some...convincing, and Theo thought there was no better place than here.

And that was that.

"You've made it impossible for me to leave," Rebecca said, though no hysterics tinged her tone.

"I have made it so we both are together with no distractions until we have decided how to best proceed, for ourselves and our child. This is not the atrocity you are trying to make it out to be."

"You *could* have said, *Rebecca, I have this lovely private island I'd like to take you to so we may discuss our future without distraction*. Instead, you tricked me."

He didn't care for this conversation at all. "Show me the trick. I don't recall lying, tricking. I simply said we'd take a drive so I could show you something. *You* did not ask any questions. *You* got in the car."

He could tell that she did not have any quick-witted response for this fact. And since this was the first time since they'd docked that she seemed to show a weakening, he moved from the car toward her.

"Come, Rebecca." He stood in front of her, reached out and gently wrapped his hands around her upper arms and gave her a little tug. "Let us move forward."

Her scent wound around him. An odd mix of floral and mint, tinged with the surrounding sea. Her blue eyes were wary but looked bluer out here amid the water and sky. He thought of the first time he'd seen her back in Ireland. The light had been in shadows, but still that blue had penetrated.

Hit its mark. He could not fathom *why*. What made this

upended reaction whirl around inside him when she was near. She was just a beautiful woman. There were so very many of those.

And yet none had ever had the effect on him she did. Which was concerning, but at least he could see she felt the same. The wariness had not gone out of her eyes, but something else had entered her expression.

Longing.

"You have two days," she announced loftily. "I will stay for *two* days. Then I am going back to Ireland."

He didn't verbally agree. Saw no point in lying to her. She would not go *anywhere* until he was satisfied. But he gave a slight little nod if only to get her to move toward the car. When she did, he tucked her into the front seat this time, and then *finally*, only a little behind his preferred schedule, drove off the ferry, onto the island and toward *home*.

He'd had major renovations done to the stone buildings on the island when he'd first purchased it in his early twenties. He'd wanted a place to escape his father, escape the *world*. Somewhere quiet and just his—no pretense, no…*drama*.

But he'd modernized much of what had been old. He'd kept the historical charm as best he could. As suited him. The buildings, including his sprawling house, were still made of whitewashed stone and glistened prettily in the sun. The shutters were painted dark, Greek blue every year.

He felt himself settle as he drove up the winding drive. Yes, this was the best place to make decisions that would change the course of his entire life. There would be no demands here. Just him and Rebecca.

He tried to ignore the twirl of carnal want that tried to take hold of him. Privacy did not mean they would give in to the chemistry between them.

What would be the harm?

A dangerous line of thought. But he was a man who sometimes walked the line of danger, as long as he always had one finger in control. He'd lost that one finger back in Ireland for a night, but he could not afford to lose it again.

Except, she's already pregnant.

Frustrated with himself, worried these were the kinds of thoughts that prompted his father to act without thinking, Theo came to a stop in front of the house. He handed off his keys to the staff member waiting, murmured instructions of what to do with their things in Greek, and then opened the passenger door for Rebecca.

She'd found her shoes in her bag and put them on her feet. She clutched the sad little duffel to her chest. Theo tried to take it, but she held firm.

He wanted to argue with her, or jerk it out of her grasp, but he had more control than that. He put his hand on her back to guide her, but the little intake of breath held more punch than he'd like it to. Just touching her brought images of their night together to his mind, in blaring color and sound.

He let a slow breath out as he led her inside. The tile was colorful and unique. He'd taken some of the decoration upon himself. Antiques that appealed to him. Art that interested him. Color schemes he liked. Furniture that was comfortable, window views that were enjoyable—not just impressive. Plus, there was the potted garden outside he liked to tend while he was here.

He had never brought anyone here and wondered what they might think of it. It was him, and he was confident in himself and what he liked, what he wanted. But he found himself turning to look at Rebecca, to see her reaction.

"It's so different from your other place. So...interesting." Her mouth curved, ever so slightly, her finger reaching out to run along the frame of a painting of his home—before he'd modernized it. "*This* is a home," she said, with something that sounded like awe in her voice.

He found himself struggling to find words, both because of the heavy band around his lungs, but also because... He did not know what to say. It was a home. *His* home. He'd chosen much of the decorating himself—where his properties in Athens and London and New York were meant for business, for holding the reins of his father's ever-splintering attention, and reflected that with a kind of austere simplicity.

Even his library was different here, focused on what he *enjoyed* reading over what he felt it necessary to read to be a good businessman.

It was a strange thing for her to recognize it so easily and for that recognition to...mean something.

They were strangers. Strangers with an electric physical connection. That was all.

Well, that and a baby.

"Follow me," he said abruptly, because the things rattling around inside him were foreign and strange and he did not know what to do with them except push them—and her—away, until he could have some quiet to sort it out.

He led her up the stairs and through the hall to one of the guest rooms he'd had his staff prepare. He opened the door, gestured her inside. "This will be your room. Should you want to change anything, add anything, you need only ask me or my staff."

She hesitated a moment but ended up moving inside the room without voicing whatever concern she had. She still clutched the bag to her, but—as he'd hoped—she immediately relaxed and moved for the wall-to-wall window, the curtains opened so the entire view of the beach below spread out.

She let out an awed breath. "My God," she murmured.

The sun was setting now, a pretty, demure slash of pastels in pink, lavender and orange. Still the sea glittered a beautiful blue against the white beach.

"I take it you approve of the room."

She made a sound, almost like an awed laugh. "I suppose." She moved to drape her bag across the cozy chair in the corner, her eyes never leaving the sunset outside her windows. "That doesn't mean you shouldn't have asked."

"Noted."

She managed to tear her gaze away from the window to him, her mouth curved in a smile of that same awe in her voice and a kind of amusement. Now she was backlit by the painting of a scene behind her, and it caught around his lungs, a barbed wire lasso.

Painful, too searing to take a breath. The amusement, the awe in her expression changed. Faded, then sharpened.

She felt this, too. This insatiable thing that he didn't have the words for. Perhaps if she didn't, he'd have the tools to fight it. He moved closer when he shouldn't. She didn't back away when she should.

Fight it. "You've had much travel." His voice sounded and felt like gravel. "I will have someone draw you a bath."

They were so close, a kiss so...*possible*. He knew she was angry at him. Frustrated at herself for finally giving in and agreeing to come inside.

But he also knew she felt *this*. This wild, untamed thing he hadn't figured out how to control.

Control, control, control.

"That would be fine," she said, her voice rough, her eyes wide and on his, even as her breath came in soft little pants.

The moment wound through him as erotic as any strip tease. Just standing here *staring* at each other, a shade too close. Knowing that she no doubt had the same memories running through her mind.

She would taste as fresh and vibrant as an Irish meadow. She would feel as soft as silk under his hands.

He could think of nothing else to do except lower his mouth to hers. He drew out the moment, wondering if sense would reign for either of them.

It didn't. Her mouth met his, a soft, sensual brush. But that softness lasted all of a second before they were grabbing each other, hurtling the kiss into that heat they both knew existed when their bodies came together.

It was the antithesis to the sunset behind her. That was gentle. This was rough. A band snapped. The lashing pain of holding back this whole damn day. She was heat and wonder and the kiss a million chances to find bliss.

He tangled his hands in her hair, angled her head back to deepen the kiss, to have her just the way he'd been wanting to. Not just since she arrived, but since she'd slipped away that early morning.

She'd left some kind of hook in him. Engaging in this behavior hardly ripped it out, but by God he would have what he wanted before he caused himself that kind of pain.

Her, her, her. He wanted *her*.

When he came up for some kind of air, she made a sad little attempt to push him back before her hands fisted in his shirt, keeping him right there.

"We can do this, Theo." She panted it, her eyes meeting his, wide and blue, pupils big. "It changes nothing." She said this firmly, even through her gasping breaths.

She was right, of course.

So why not have what they wanted first? It changed absolutely nothing, risked absolutely nothing, so it was not a loss of control. It was simply getting what he wanted.

And he *wanted*. A clawing need he was having trouble thinking around, through. So he crashed his mouth to hers again, took and took and took. Her body pressed to his. The taste of her invading him once again. He'd never forgotten it. Might never.

He led her to the large bed that dominated the center of the room without ever taking his mouth from hers. His hands streaked under her shirt and he pulled it off her, using the momentary break in the kiss to note how every moment from before broke free from the little box he'd try to put it in.

Her skin felt the same. Her sighs in his ear, the same pounding, unsettling need for something. More than release. More than *usual*. She was just…more.

He laid her out on the bed, a conquering hero over his prize. And she was a prize. So beautiful. So perfect. He peeled off the soft pants she wore, bared her beautiful body to him. All creamy perfection. In his home.

For a moment, he realized *this* was what he'd really brought here for. Not to minimize distractions, but because he wanted to see her in the fading island light in the only place that had ever felt like *his*.

His hands moved down over her breasts, fuller than they had been, beautiful and mesmerizing. Over her ribcage, and the slight rise of her stomach. There was a difference there, a roundness, but not yet like there would be. Eventually she would be ripe with his child.

And she would be *his*.

He gripped her hips and entered her on that thought, felt her shatter around him with just that. On a cry, that beautiful sound that had haunted him through months. The light playing around them a golden haze, making her seem otherworldly.

A ghost. A goddess. A curse. A promise.

CHAPTER EIGHT

REBECCA KNEW THIS was wrong. This kind of pleasure had to be the kind of sin her parents had always warned her about. It made her forget everything. All the ways she should protect herself, her baby, her future.

Everything except him. Everything except *more*.

How many times could he drive her to this peak? This cliff? How many times would he fling her off, always demanding more, more, more.

It should have been a warning. She should have heeded it as one.

Instead she dived. Again and again into him. Into this.

He held her hips in an iron grip, moved into her with a precision, a ferocity that didn't seem fair. Until his perfect, careful pace began to fracture. Until he got that wild look in his eye.

She did not understand it, but there was something inherently gratifying in watching him lose himself. She did not know him, and yet she *knew* that was not a common occurrence for him.

He roared out his release, and the vibration of sound had her spinning into her own final one. A breathless, sensory overload that she knew eventually she would regret. She'd have to.

But she couldn't work up to it just yet.

They lay next to each other on the bed, haphazard and winded. She felt alive. A sparkling, energetic flame of *life*.

Which reminded her why she was even here. The life they'd created and she was growing. She closed her eyes, trying to hold on to a flicker of regret rather than self-satisfied smugness over pleasure.

"We can't keep doing this." That was clear. It was…distracting, and if they *kept* doing it, it was going to complicate things that she could not allow to be complicated.

"I cannot see why not. The damage has been done." He glanced over at her, and his hands reached out, traced the curve of her breast so that her nipple pebbled and sensation that couldn't possibly still stir within her did just that. Especially when his mouth curved into the sharp blade of a smile "And you like it."

So much. Too much. But… "*You* like it," she replied, almost managing to sound lofty instead of *stirred*.

"I would venture to say we *both* more than like what we are able to bring out in each other." He propped himself up on his elbow, looked down at her his gaze dark and intense. His body… *God*, his body was unfair.

"What do you do?" she demanded, gesturing at the hard wall of muscle in front of her. "Lift weights all night?"

"I prefer to strength-train in the morning, actually."

Strength training. She shook her head. It was so clear this man was a stranger. How did she keep allowing herself to be naked with him?

"Listen," she began, hoping for sense even though they were both still naked on *top* of all the bedding. She stared at the ceiling so she wouldn't be distracted by his body or his eyes. "Yes, we both enjoy this. But people enjoy drugs, too. Doesn't make them *good* for you. We are going to be parents." She met his gaze now with a quiet determination, she hoped. "We have to start being responsible."

His eyebrows puzzled together. "I have never been anything but responsible, *omorfiá mou*."

She placed her hands over her stomach, where she needed to remind herself their *child* grew. And that child had to be the most important thing. For both of them. "A surprise pregnancy says otherwise, Theo."

He grunted, some irritation working its way into his gaze. He looked away from her, up to the ceiling now. He crossed his arms behind his head, making no move to leave.

"Perhaps," he finally agreed. "But I have suggested the responsible move forward. Marriage. I do not see the problem." His gaze landed on her again, like a lightning strike. "There is certainly some compatibility here."

"Sexual compatibility. People don't just get married because of *sexual compatibility*."

"I'm sure some have, just as some have gotten married over the presence of a child. In that case, we have two items in our favor."

She shook her head, wondering if there were words that would get through to him or if he was just so…pigheaded, he would keep saying the same things over and over. "We are *strangers*."

"So you keep saying. How about this? We stop being strangers, then."

"Oh, and how do you suppose we do that?"

"You stay. For more than two days. We get to know one another. Discuss what we'd like our child's future to look like. Et cetera. Et cetera."

Rebecca found it frustrating this was not an…unreasonable request. Perhaps he'd gone about it *unreasonably*, and perhaps that would be something she would get to know him and understand.

Or she wouldn't. But she couldn't *know* unless she gave him time. Unless she gave him the opportunity. And maybe...

She'd always dreamed of marrying a man she loved. Her parents loved each other, and though she'd wanted more than a little cottage on someone else's land, she'd wanted that *love* more.

She'd loved Patrick. She'd been able to picture their life together. And look how that had turned out. He'd chosen duty over love and seemed to be happier for it.

Should she do the same? Think of her child over herself? Stay here and... Well, it would be no hardship to stay here. She might miss her parents and her horses, but this was beautiful. Peaceful. She could picture a child here.

Or maybe you're letting great sex make you insane, Rebecca, she told herself sternly.

Because there was a major hurdle here.

She didn't know anything about Theodorou Nikolaou beyond what an internet search had told her and what he could do to her body when they were naked. There was a *lot* of important information in between those two things.

But only time and at least *some* proximity would get her that, this was true. Whether she wanted to admit it or not. Two days was not enough time to get to know someone.

She could give him a week. Maybe two. And then reassess. It would take longer than that, but in a week she should be able to have *some* sense of him.

"I may agree to...get to know you. To stay for more than two days," she said slowly, carefully. But she needed to make it clear that wouldn't end in some kind of shotgun wedding. "But I'm not going to agree to marry you."

He made one of those noises she was supposed to take as agreement and didn't.

"And," she added loftily, not sure why she was trying to make herself out to be a liar, "we shouldn't sleep together again."

His smile was feral in the darkening light. No noncommittal noise this time. "We shall see."

He had the bath drawn for her, and though he was tempted to stay and draw it himself, some things had to be seen to. He had settled everything at the office so that he could take a small leave of absence, but he still needed to address this with his father.

Atlas would be all for Theo taking a vacation, but Theo needed to find a way to impress upon his father he was not to try and make major financial decisions without him.

Theo had nothing against his father's impulses, but they needed to be more than *impulse*. They needed to be vetted, for starters. At least two of the "companies" his father had wanted to ship off money to had turned out to be fake charities. Scams, essentially.

Theo did not understand a man who'd once been a titan of industry falling for such ridiculous schemes, but he could only lay the blame on his father's one weakness: women. In particular, right now, the one he was married to.

Theo hadn't even bothered to learn her name. She was a nonentity to him. And if she wanted to suck Atlas dry, Theo figured that was their business.

But it would *not* be allowed to affect Titan Banking. Not under his watch.

So, he went into his office. Here at home, it was decorated for comfort. He didn't *work* here, per se, but he put out fires when need be.

He sat in the soft overstuffed armchair and dialed his father's private line, already bracing himself for the Atlas hurricane.

"So he *does* know his father is still alive and kicking," Atlas answered in his booming voice, laughter along the censure. Theo often wondered if his father's easy laugh and jovial nature tended to smooth over the carelessness that was at the fiber of his being and made it impossible to *hate* him.

"Hello, Father. How are you feeling?"

"Every day is a gift and a chance for redemption."

Theo grimaced. His father's redemption was as messy and careless as all he'd done to need it. "And your rehabilitation?"

"My nurses have no complaints."

"I'm sure they're very pretty."

Atlas laughter boomed into the phone. "I am a married man, boy. But yes, very pretty. Wouldn't have it any other way."

Theo considered that his requirement of small talk for the day. "I wanted to let you know that I'm at the island. I will likely be staying a few weeks. I've left Christopher in charge, for the most part, but if you need anything, you may call me, of course."

"Is everything all right? It isn't like you to take an impromptu trip to the island."

"It's a…small vacation, is all. You needn't worry. All my best men are handling the day-to-day, and any major problems will be brought to me."

"I am not worried about Titan. I am concerned about my son behaving out of character."

"*I* am worried about Titan," Theo said by way of a sidestep. "I need you to promise me you will not try to bully everyone into one of your…endeavors while I am gone. If you have any ideas, you email them over to me first."

"You shouldn't work on your vacation."

"And you shouldn't work during your recovery. So how about we both agree to keep our hands out of it?"

Atlas let out a huff of breath Theo chose to hope was acceptance. "I heard a rumor," Atlas said slyly after a moment. "A woman. An Irish woman. In your office. With important news. I don't suppose that could have any bearing on the sudden vacation?"

Theo found himself utterly speechless. How had that gotten back to his father? His assistant was always the *most* discreet. His staff at home had no ties to his father. Who would have given him this information?

"The Irish part I found very interesting. Especially when I remembered you'd gone to that wedding. In Ireland. In my stead. Three or four months ago, wasn't it?"

Theo remained quiet. Did his father *know*? Surely not. He'd never paid much attention to what was going on beyond his own nose, unless…

"Dr. Gataki contacted you." *That* was the weak link. He'd used one of his father's contacts, and now Atlas *knew*. Not a tragedy, just…annoying that he could not share the information with his father on his timeline, in a way that would not require…*this*.

Atlas made a humming noise. "Dr. Gataki had some concerns."

The doctor's concern would soon be that Theo would not be consulting him again. Theo would find a new doctor for Rebecca. One who would stay on the island for the duration of her pregnancy. Perhaps longer. One who would *never* gossip with his father.

"Do *you* have concerns, Father?" Theo asked smoothly.

"I, too, was once surprised with the happy news I'd be a father in the offices of Titan Banking."

Theo winced. How he detested the idea that he'd repeated history. Except he hadn't. Maybe there were unfortunate similarities, but Rebecca was still *here*. And she would stay here. She would not be allowed to run off scot-free like his mother had been.

"Congratulations, Theodorou. Being a father is a great joy. Perhaps it will lighten you up some. And I shall look forward to meeting the Irish woman who swept my dour son off his feet." Atlas laughed heartily. "Perhaps Ariana and I will come out to the island and meet—"

"No." Theo bit it off before he thought better of it and came up with a more diplomatic response. "While I appreciate the idea, now is not the time. Rebecca is still dealing with the physical aspects of the pregnancy. No doubt I will invite you and…" What had her name been? "Alicia to the wedding."

"Ah, so there is to be a wedding? I'm sure *Ariana* would be keen to help plan."

"That won't be necessary." Again, too curt. Too clipped. He needed to get himself together. "I will let you know once Rebecca is feeling up to visitors and we will…work something out. But in the time being, I need you to focus on your rehabilitation, on your lovely wife, and leave Titan Banking *alone*. And keep my happy news to yourselves."

"Hmm." It wasn't denial, but a thinking noise that set Theo's teeth on edge. "And you. You'd like me to leave *you* alone."

Theo pinched the bridge of his nose. His father had never once cared what Theo thought or wanted. Not before the heart attack. It never would have occurred to him to consider what *Theo* would like.

He'd lamented it as a young man. Now that he had his father's sudden interest, he lamented that much more. It was easier when he could move through his life as he pleased without dealing with his father trying to…be a better man.

"I have been through what you're going through," Atlas said when Theo offered nothing.

"No, you had a child dumped on you. Rebecca will be a mother to our child. This is not the same."

Atlas made a noise, far too close to the noise Theo made when decidedly not agreeing with Rebecca but not wanting to say so.

But it was *not* the same. They would be married. They would be stable. *They* would put their child first. There would be no upheaval. There would be stability and structure.

Rebecca herself had clearly grown up with it, so she should understand. But maybe she simply took it for granted.

He would explain it to her. She would understand. And once she thought of him as less of a stranger, she would agree to the wedding. She would agree to everything.

"Good night, Father, I will be in touch."

"Good night, Theo. And relax. Enjoy this time. Once the baby comes, everything changes."

But it wouldn't. Not for him. His entire life had been responsibility. Building foundations his father could not be bothered to build. This was just an extension of that.

In a few weeks, at most, Rebecca would agree to marry him. In the meantime, they would enjoy each other physically. Why not? They would be stable. They would be good parents. They would do all this as he saw fit.

Theo would accept nothing less.

CHAPTER NINE

REBECCA DID NOT wake up to any trays of food, which was a shame. The room was still dark, she realized. She reached out for her phone on the nightstand.

Four thirty in the morning.

She supposed it made sense she'd be up early. Despite all the upheaval yesterday, she had spent a considerable time *sleeping*. The bath last night had relaxed her right into sleep fairly early, all in all.

The bath and the orgasms preceding it, you mean.

She shoved that thought away. She needed to focus less on her body and its reactions and more on her *brain*. On Theo's brain. They needed to get to know one another.

She did not believe that meant falling in love and marriage would follow, but she liked to think if they could understand each other, they could build a solid, co-parenting partnership.

Difficult across countries, but the man was a *billionaire*. He could work it out. And maybe this heavy-handed way of just *whisking her off* to places was unacceptable, but there was the strangest lack of *meanness* to it. He was stubborn and hardheaded, but she got the impression he was those things because he didn't realize he *shouldn't be*.

Like a willful horse, he would need to be taught a thing

or two about cooperation. That's how she'd start approaching him. As a difficult mount.

She couldn't think about *mounting*, though. Not right now. Not when she had to focus. Better to imagine him as a horse. The silly image brought a smile to her face.

She dressed in her last clean outfit she'd packed. She'd need to do some laundry before the day was out. She was going to need…more of a plan. But first she needed something to drink. She'd love more of that cool ginger drink she'd had in the car yesterday. Maybe some bland toast.

Her stomach wasn't quite as riotous this morning, but she knew better than to think that meant anything. If she could sneak around and find the kitchens, she could get the normal processes started before Theo even woke up.

The halls were dimly lit, and she roamed, enjoying the solitude to study her surroundings. Like she'd said last night, *this* was a home. So far it still missed the personal touches like photographs of actual people, but there were colors here. Vibrant and muted depending on what part of the house she was in. All sorts of windows, in all shapes and sizes, each one with a view of the sea. Alcoves were dotted with potted plants and pretty bowls, vases and the like—all of which looked old *and* interesting. Paintings on the white walls were often huge, gorgeous landscapes.

If he had chosen the art himself, he was drawn to the *vast*. Seascapes and wide-open spaces. Skies that seemed to never end. There was a sense of freedom in every piece.

Interesting for a man who was outwardly so controlled.
Except in bed.
Honestly, she despaired of herself and her reaction to him.
She heard the faint sound of movement eventually. And the smells of something baking. She moved toward it.

Through a large, sprawling dining room and into a brightly lit and spacious kitchen.

One woman bustled around inside of it, moving from oven to refrigerator to counter in graceful movements. She upended a bowl on the counter, and a fat roll of dough fell onto it with a plop.

Everything smelled divine, and Rebecca's stomach did only a little questionable turn as she stepped fully into the room.

The woman looked up, startled a little bit, but recovered quickly. "*Kaliméra*, Ms. Murphy. You are up early. Breakfast will be ready shortly. Can I get you something to drink? Perhaps you'd like to sit in the dining room and get off your feet? Mr. Nikolaou will join you shortly."

"He's awake?"

"Oh, yes. Mr. Nikolaou is quite the early bird. Always down in his gym before we even get started here. Breakfast is always at five sharp." The woman looked up from where she worked. "For *him*. You are welcome to set your own schedule, of course." The woman's gaze dropped to Rebecca's baby bump for just a moment before she looked back down at the dough she was kneading.

"I don't suppose you'd have something along the lines of ginger ale?"

The woman gave a little nod. "Carbonation feels good when things are upset, doesn't it? And you'll need something to go along with it. Just to settle it all." She tossed her dough into a bowl, draped a cloth over it, then hummed to herself as she bustled around the kitchen. "Go on into the dining room. I'll bring you everything you need."

"May I just sit here?"

The woman hesitated again, but her smile didn't dim. "If that's what you wish."

Rebecca settled herself on a stool at the counter and the woman settled the food and drink in front of her. "Here you are, Ms. Murphy."

"Please, call me Rebecca. And what should I call you?"

"I am Acacia. I handle the kitchens for the most part. Elias is my assistant." She nodded toward the window. Outside, Rebecca could see a young man on the patio drinking coffee and looking out at the sea. "And my son." She rolled her eyes. "Between the two of us, whatever you need by way of food or drink, we will get for you. Right now the schedule is breakfast in the dining room at five. Lunch is at eleven on the terrace. I put together some kind of snack plate around three, then we serve dinner at seven. But, you may request different times for your own meals, whatever snacks you wish."

"Eating with Theo will be fine."

"You let me know if you change your mind. Growing life is a serious and wonderful endeavor."

Growing life.

Rebecca rested a hand on her stomach without fully thinking the gesture through. Sometimes it was so easy to get caught up in pregnancy, in *Theo*, she forgot that on the other side of all this was...*life*. And she had to find a way to ensure her child's life was a good one.

She drank the ginger soda. A little different from the one yesterday. Sweeter, as though it had been mixed with honey. It soothed and settled enough she felt up to eating the delicious-smelling roll of some kind Acacia had put in front of her.

Acacia, for her part, went about her work in the kitchens, making Rebecca feel a pang of homesickness. She should call her parents instead of just text, but she still didn't have any clearer answers for them.

So, she needed to find some.

"Can you tell me where this gym is?" Rebecca asked.

There was a slight hesitation in the woman, but eventually she looked up with that same pleasant smile. Then she let out a sharp whistle that had Rebecca startling.

After only a moment, the young man appeared in the doorway and stepped in from outside. He set his cup down on the counter and looked at his mother.

"Elias, show Ms. Murphy downstairs to the gym," the cook ordered.

"But—"

Whatever his objection, he swallowed it down at the cook's sharp look. "*Naí*, of course. Follow me, ma'am."

Rebecca slid off the stool, thanked Acacia for the breakfast and the company. She thought *maybe* she'd be able to keep it down this morning as she followed Elias through winding hallways and down a dim staircase into a cool basement-type area.

Elias stopped at a door, looked back at Rebecca. "He doesn't usually like to be bothered when he is doing his morning routine. Fair warning."

Rebecca smiled at the young man. "Another reason to bother him, then."

She watched Elias fight with a smile, but he gave a nod and then hurried off. No doubt so as not to be caught in the crossfire.

Not that there would need to be crossfire. Regardless of Theo's *schedule*, they needed to talk, to plan. She couldn't just sit around all day enjoying the pretty scenery. She had things to accomplish, and a whole life to get back to once she did.

She gave the door a perfunctory knock before going ahead and pushing it open. She was met with the sound of pounding music. Not blaring, just a heavy, thudding beat. She immediately recognized the room as a kind of home gym. She'd never liked working out all that much, but strength had been required of her when she'd ridden, so she had some familiarity with some of the machines.

Theo was not at a machine. He was lying on a bench, pushing a bar practically bending with weight up. Sweat dripped from his temples. His T-shirt was darkened in a ring around his neck. The muscles in his arms strained against the heavy weight he pushed up. Then back down. Then up again.

Rebecca watched, dumbfounded. She had understood in some way that the way he looked, the sheer *strength* of him, had to come from somewhere, but she hadn't imagined… this. Or that it would stir things in her.

Then again, what about this man didn't *stir* things in her?

He deposited the bar on some rack above him with a loud metal *clank* that had her jumping, her already overbeating heart thudding against her chest. She must have made another noise as well because he sat up and looked directly at her.

The potency of his dark gaze, the way that connection arrowed through her as viscerally as if he was touching her, deep inside, made absolutely no earthly sense to Rebecca, but there it was. And she was all but panting.

Slowly, Theo got to his feet. He did not cross to her, but he reached behind himself and pulled off the T-shirt he wore, exposing the hard ridges of his abdomen and chest. The hair that dotted both. The sheer perfection of him, as impressive as any statue.

He rubbed the shirt over his face, his hair, wiping away excess sweat, she supposed.

All she could think was he couldn't be real, except he

was. She'd been intimately acquainted with his body multiple times now.

She knew she should stop staring at his chest, at his arms. She needed to make eye contact. She needed to get *ahold* of herself.

"Rebecca."

Just the way he rumbled her name was like a lit match. But she was determined to blow it out. Determined not to jump him every time she wanted to.

"I didn't mean to interrupt," she managed to rasp out, hoping he would stay across the room so she could keep herself from falling at his feet. "I was told you were awake."

"Yes. I have a schedule I like to keep. You are free to join me, of course." He gestured at some of the equipment. "Light weights are safe in pregnancy, I have read."

Rebecca looked around at the intimidating room of equipment, tried not to think of this incredibly strong, incredibly sweaty, incredibly *hot* man reading a book about pregnancy. It was doing too much frying of her senses. "I was thinking of something more like going for a walk. That is what I do at home, but I do not have a beach at home."

He started moving. Toward her. She backed away a little. Not out of any fear of *him*, but fear of her own pitiful lack of control.

"You should come with me," she said on a squeak, hoping it would halt his forward movement. "And we will start to get to know one another." Because that was the point. Make them something different from strangers who couldn't seem to resist each other.

He eyed her, and still approached. She thought there was some suspicion in his gaze, but she couldn't understand why. *He* had been the one to say they should stop being strangers as if it was easy as that.

He came to a stop right in front of her. His eyes were intense, his face and chest covered in sweat. But his eyes pinned her, held her gaze there. It did nothing to stop the frantic rattling of her heart.

Or worse, the insistent pulse deep within her, demanding release.

"Very well. You must eat first."

She licked her lips, trying to wet her dry throat. "I…did. I can't promise it will stay down, but I did eat."

He nodded in approval. "Good." He looked her up and down, and some very stupid part of her wished she'd thought to put an effort into her appearance. "How did you sleep?"

"Oh, very well."

"Dreamless?"

She blinked, not sure what he was getting at. "Yes."

He reached out, traced a finger down a strand of escaped hair. His gaze was dark. And wicked. "Would you like to know what I dreamed of, Rebecca?" he asked in a low, husky voice.

The curve of his mouth was a sensual promise, tales of the dream were, as well.

Yes, she wanted to say. *Tell me. Show me.*

But damn it, she had to have some self-control. Some self-respect. She took a step away from him, swallowed down the hard ball of everything that lodged in her throat.

"N-no. I will…meet you on the beach." And then she turned and hurtled herself away, aching for something she needed to resist.

He met Rebecca outside. She stood on the patio, looking down at the beach below. The wind whipped through her hair and played with the loose fabric of her clothes. The blue of the sky and sea framed her, set her apart, seemed to create a spotlight in which she was the most stunning thing he'd ever seen.

The cold shower had done nothing to cool his bloodstream. He had seen her interest, her desire, her *wants* clearly expressed in those crystal blue eyes. The reality of her, in his space, the same wants and needs careening through her, was a thorn he had not considered.

And he *had* been plagued by dreams of her. Naked and his.

He had sought to exorcise the demon of her through a hard workout. It worked with almost every other problem in his life.

Not her.

He had been forced to use his shower wisely, and held no compunction about picturing her mouth taking him deep as he had dealt with the problem.

But just the sight of her now had him stirring again, like some uncontrolled teen.

Like your father.

At least that idea had him finding some semblance of control within himself. He came to stand next to her. She glanced up at him, a soft smile on her face.

"I still think you should have *asked* me to come here, but it *is* beautiful," she said. "And wonderfully warm."

He grunted in response, then with some reluctance, took her arm. "The sand will make it harder to walk. You should be careful."

She hooked her arm with his but kept a space between them. Like strangers on a first date might act.

This also irritated him, enough so that the pretty morning seemed more affront than solace.

They hit sand and she paused to take her shoes off. She sighed happily and then they began to walk again.

"Tell me about yourself, Theo."

Like this was some kind of job interview. Frustrated with his own raging desires, and the way she suddenly seemed so unaffected by her own, he was curt in his response. "You do realize I know all I need to about you."

"Is that so?" she returned with haughty indifference.

"You are Rebecca Murphy. Born and raised in Ireland on the Desmond Estate. Your parents both work in the equestrian arm of said estate. You showed an aptitude for riding from a young age, and the Desmonds encouraged your parents to allow you to compete. They helped fund your competition schedule. You would have gone to the Olympics, but an unfortunate injury and subsequent surgeries made it impossible. Hence the scars on your hip."

Her mouth had dropped open. "You…did an internet search on me." He didn't know why she was surprised. She'd done the same. Did she think he would not find out a few facts about the *mother of his child*?

"You are not much of a mystery, Rebecca Murphy. And that is only the surface. I could know more if I hired someone to go in depth. All but the scars on your hip were easy enough to discover on my own."

"I hardly made it difficult on you to discover the scars on my hip," she muttered, a mix of amusement and self-deprecation.

He laughed, the sound and the feeling a strange foreign lightness he wasn't used to. Even when she churned him into unrecognizable knots, there was something amusing about her. She had a self-awareness she did not try to hide, try to sophisticate away. He was not sure he knew someone with a sense of self that did not come from money and power.

"You're not the only one who can do an internet search,

you know." She fisted her hands on her hips and glared up at him.

He didn't relish the idea of her finding things out about him that the press reported, particularly in his youth, but she'd already done it, so he waved her to speak.

"No one knows who your mother is. Your father, Atlas Nikolaou, presented you as a baby as his own and there was never any whiff of where you came from, though there are many rumors and stories. None could be proven enough to take hold. Throughout your childhood, your father was married a handful of times and you were alternatively sent off to boarding school or kept home depending on the wife."

He stiffened, couldn't seem to stop himself. He knew his father's many marriages were very public, easy to find out about, but he hadn't expected her to draw conclusions about his on-again, off-again boarding school experience to be tied to which wife was lady of the manor at the time.

"You showed an aptitude in school for many things, but business has always been where you've shined," she continued. "Quickly becoming your father's heir apparent. And it seems very few people can attribute that to the fact you're his only child, because you're just that good at your job."

"Naturally."

Her mouth curved at that, amusement in her eyes. But she didn't stop there.

"Since you were more responsible and dedicated than your father—according to reports—you quickly took on more responsibility as he acted more a figurehead. That is, until his heart attack a few months ago, when you also took on the role as figurehead and Atlas stepped back to focus on his health and family."

Theo's gut churned. It made no sense. These were all things everyone knew about him. Easily found on the internet as she said, and yet the way she recited facts about him, reduced him to a little paragraph, it grated.

She grated.

He began to walk again, not wanting to meet her gaze. "See, a simple internet search and we already know each other. We could be married by the end of the day, and all will be settled."

"We don't *know* each other. We know a list of facts *about* each other. Certainly not enough to form some kind of legally binding union."

"The scars on your hip are not a list of facts."

"You know nothing about the injury. The surgery. The recovery. What it felt like. The surgery is a *fact*. The scars are a reality you couldn't possibly understand without understanding *me*."

He heard the heartbreak in her words and felt twin emotions. He wanted to know all those things. Wanted the find the source of her hurt and fix it.

The other half of him wanted nothing to do with something so complex, so unfixable. Because he could not cure her physical ailments. He could not turn back time and change things so she was able to compete at the Olympics.

So he found himself uncharacteristically speechless. Thankfully, she did not give him much time to live in this discomfort.

"Tell me something no one knows." She demanded this, as if he should jump to whatever she said, and it would not start a disastrous precedent.

"You first," he retorted.

She didn't look angry. Instead, her expression went thoughtful. "I suppose a few people know this, but you don't." Her eyes met his, a kind of challenge. "I was engaged, in a way, to Patrick Desmond."

Theo stood stock-still. He could picture Patrick Desmond, the groom at that wedding that had started all this. The only descriptor Theo could think of for Patrick was *bland*. Soft maybe. There had been nothing interesting about the couple at all.

But he could remember now, Rebecca watching them. Asking him if he thought they were happy.

He looked down at her. With her wild hair and sharp eyes and the light dust of freckles down the bridge of her nose. The idea of her with *Patrick Desmond*, the idea of that man's hands on her, his *ring*, enraged him for reasons he could not and would not parse.

"What does *in a way* mean?"

She sighed, looked out at the water as they walked. "We were meant to be engaged when I came back from the Olympics. He'd said we would be."

Theo watched her face for every little emotion. He saw anger. Frustration. Maybe some wistful sadness. He did not see heartbreak or abject misery there, but he thought back to the wedding. Her easy acquiescence to his invitation. Did it stem from both those things?

Did it matter? Of course not.

"Instead, I was hurt. Patrick was very… Well, he was not attentive after my injury. I didn't read into that. I should have. But I was in a hospital hours away and he was at home. Still, in all that time, he never said anything about *not* getting married anymore. Then when I was able to come home, I went to see him and…"

Theo did not want this story, and yet he stood there memorizing all her features as emotions chased across them. Eyebrows drawing together, the slow downturn in her mouth. Again, anger over any kind of bereft loss.

Or was that a strange kind of wishful thinking?

"Bridget was there. The woman he married. A ring on her finger, draped all over him. And I realized I had been very, very stupid. A fool, really. He was always going to follow his father's decree. I just thought…"

"That because the family had been kind, funded your Olympic bid, and because this *weasel* had told you that you would be married, you would indeed be married."

She blinked once, then looked up at him with a startled kind of expression. "I should have—"

"It seems to me the *should-haves* fall on the Desmonds. This Patrick was a coward. People change their minds, *omorfiá mou*. People cave to pressure. But they should be stalwart enough to admit this to the people who are affected."

Rebecca seemed to mull this over as they walked over sand again. He thought that would be the end of it, but then she spoke. Quiet and unlike herself. A kind of demure searching.

"But shouldn't I have seen the coward in him?" Her voice was little more than a whisper.

She asked this as a real question, and it hung there, as if he was forced to answer it when he was already eager to leave this conversation and his part in it behind. And yet, he found words easily enough. "Perhaps. Perhaps you were blinded by love." He tasted his own bitterness at the word.

"I guess," she agreed, which caused a little pain in between his ribs. Then she shrugged. "For whatever kind of excuse that is. I don't know why love should *blind*. It isn't as if I didn't know he had flaws. I simply loved him in *spite* of them."

Silence between them fell again. The idea of her loving a weak-willed fool who then went on to marry a suitable bride almost immediately settled in him in sharp edges and strange weights. He wanted nothing to do with it, so he introduced a topic that would no doubt change the entire conversation *and* be something that she did not know about him.

"*I* know who my mother is."

Now she stopped walking, watched him in complete surprise. "You do? She's…alive?"

"Alive and well." He thought he had come to accept this long ago. That his bitterness had eased, but the existence of his own child had stoked the flames of bitterness once more.

"Who is she?" Rebecca asked gently.

"It is of no matter," he replied, and meant it with fervency. She would *never* matter. "We have never had contact. We never will. But it isn't as if *no one* knows her identity. I do. She does. My father does." His father had never lied. Never tried to hide the truth. He'd always been quite clear.

His mother did not want them. She wanted her crown and her family. She had deigned to birth him, and that was all it would ever be.

And Theo supposed that was why he never could bring himself to hate his father. At least his father had wanted him. Kept him. It wasn't the best of feelings, but it was better than abandonment.

Which was why he would never abandon his child. He would never allow Rebecca to, either. *His* child would be given everything he had not. *His* child would never doubt his place.

"I have to believe that we are the only ones who know or it would have come out at some point," Theo continued.

"Come…out." Rebecca looked at him, as if she studied him long enough she would see the answer stamped across his face. "But for it to *come out*, it has to matter who she is. So she's famous in some way?"

Had he taken a misstep? Given away a detail he shouldn't

have? He was so taken aback by the idea he'd made a tactical error that he could not find words for long ticking moments. Standing on a beach, staring at this beautiful woman who'd upended his entire life.

You are Theodorou Nikolaou. You will not be upended.

"I think we have walked far enough," he said, knowing the clipped tone would only increase her curiosity. Knowing he should have kept his mouth shut instead of trying to distract her from her own misery.

Knowing, if he did not get ahold of himself, he would make more mistakes yet.

Unacceptable.

CHAPTER TEN

REBECCA WAS MOSTLY satisfied with their conversation on the beach. Maybe he hadn't been particularly forthcoming about his mother, but it was no doubt a sore subject. Besides, he hadn't avoided it entirely, *and* he'd told her something she didn't know about him. That no one, except him and his father, knew.

Perhaps that shouldn't mean so much to her, but it required some level of trust, didn't it? She mulled that over as she went about the rest of her day.

After the walk, he'd excused himself, citing business he needed to take care of. He would see her again at dinner. He gave her carte blanch to explore both the house and the island as a whole.

Not that she *needed* his permission, she'd told herself. If he was going to be high-handed and plant her places she hadn't agreed to go, she was hardly going to wait around for his permission to poke around.

So, that's just what she did. She went through every inch of the house—except his bedroom, because it was locked. And his office, because he was in it.

In one lavish room that she might have considered a living room or sitting room or whatever rich people called the excess of rooms they had, she found a large curio cabinet filled with what she could only call artifacts. It brought to mind a museum. But not in a stuffy way. The antiques were arranged like art—little bowls and silverware, small machines she didn't have a clue as to what they did. In the same room, there was a bookcase full of books about history and architecture—most with a local bent to Greece or this area of it.

She found another room—a complete library—full of more books. They covered a wide variety of topics and had a large fiction section, as well. In here the walls were dominated by beautiful paintings of what she recognized as depictions of Greek gods and goddesses.

She wouldn't say every room had a *theme*, but every room above the basement level was filled with art, books or antiques. It was the complete antithesis to his place in Athens, and she could only draw the conclusion that this place was *personal* to him. The place in the city was not.

She couldn't fathom *why*, though. Theo did not strike her as a man worried about what anyone else thought of him. What he liked or what he did. So why hide away his true self on this completely private island?

There were keys to knowing this man all over, but she still had to find the hidden doors to unlock for any of it to fully come together and make sense. For her to truly be able to move forward thinking about any kind of partnership. Parenting or otherwise.

After she was satisfied with her perusal on the upstairs and main floor, she returned to the basement. There'd been more than just his home gym down there.

Or so she'd thought. Downstairs, she found a second gym in the other room—which seemed overkill to her—but this one held an array of pads, mats and bags she recognized as used for boxing.

For a moment, before she got ahold of herself, she weaved quite the fantasy about Theo boxing.

Then she remembered what she was doing. Figuring the man out. She had facts, and she had *him*. The way he spoke and acted and reacted to things. No, she wasn't about to say they knew each other well enough to decide how to move forward, but she was getting a picture of the man. And more time would continue to fill that in.

How much time did she give it, though? Especially when he thought *marriage* was still on the table. Especially when the baby would be born in a few months. That still felt light-years away, but it would come eventually. And she could hardly just be...living on a private island. No job. No control.

But the island *was* beautiful. After Acacia made her a delicious and filling lunch, Rebecca took another walk along the beach. She loved the way the air felt here, warm and soft. The sound of the waves everywhere she walked. The screech of a bird. The impossible blue, blue, blue of *everything*.

It settled in her, warm and happy. It was just a vacation. She reminded herself of this time and time again. A vacation with a purpose. She certainly couldn't get *used* to it. Soon enough she'd be back in Ireland.

And she *loved* Ireland. The horses. Her parents. She did. She just...couldn't seem to get her life there to look the way she wanted. Not with the ghost of Patrick and Bridget hanging over her. Not in her childhood bedroom. Not in a job that only served to remind her everything she'd worked for was gone in one bad snap of luck.

But that was reality, and this was just...a blip. While they dealt with the very real prospect of bringing a child into this world. And she had to remember that all her choices had to reflect not just what she wanted and cared about, but what would be best for her—*their*—child.

She took a little nap after her walk, a bath. When she went to get dressed for dinner, she opened her closet to find an array of clothes. Not her own. She'd only brought a handful of pieces.

She hesitated. They were for her, but where had they come from? Were they new? Or did he keep an array of women's clothes in his home to provide for whatever woman he kind of kidnapped to stay out here?

She scowled at herself. It hardly mattered. They weren't and had never been in a relationship, so whatever women he'd concerned himself with, or would, was none of her business.

Even if she did foolish things like let him touch her. They were *not* in a relationship.

She settled her hand over her stomach. Well, she supposed they had to develop a kind of relationship. And it wasn't like she could ask him to steer clear of all women, especially since she didn't want to marry him, but wasn't it fair to ask him to abstain until they decided how to co-parent? Wasn't it perfectly reasonable to suggest he stay away from anyone else while she was here?

No, it isn't, and you know it isn't.

That practical, no-nonsense voice in her head sounded an awful lot like her mother. Who was pretty much always right. No matter how little Rebecca liked it.

Frustrated with herself, she found the softest and most casual pair of cotton pants, and the loosest T-shirt to go along with it. She didn't bother with shoes, just pulled on her own fuzzy socks that had been laundered at some point.

Then she went to the dining room, her stomach already growling. After her afternoon, she was pretty confident she'd learned where everything in the house was, so it was easy enough to walk down to the dining room, but when she entered through the archway, she came to a sudden stop.

For a moment, she stood frozen in place. The long, elegant table was piled with trays and bowls of food. There were two place settings—on opposite sides of the table. Candles flickered invitingly, and the smells were absolutely heavenly.

But it reminded her of dinners the Desmonds had served. She'd only ever been invited to one—on the eve of her trip to the Olympic qualifiers. She and her parents had dressed up and eaten in the Desmond home like guests, instead of employees.

And Patrick had smiled at her across the table, happy and proud, and she'd felt like she belonged.

But she hadn't. "Should I have worn a ball gown?" she asked Theo, trying to forget about all that had come before.

He eyed her, but she couldn't tell what he thought of her casual outfit. "You may wear whatever you please. I am in the habit of having a nice dinner when I am here on the island."

"By yourself?"

His smile was slow, and it drew a liquid pull of *want* from the pit of her stomach throughout her whole body.

"That depends," he replied.

She didn't scowl, though she wanted to. But jealousy was a stupid emotion, as stupid as wanting to jump him every time he smiled.

Even if the thought of him having another woman here, touching another woman the way he touched her, felt sharp and ugly. It didn't *matter*, because they weren't in a relationship.

"Are you going to sit and eat?" he asked, and there was

some amusement to his expression, like he could read her thoughts.

Which had a little wriggle of embarrassment creeping through her and into her cheeks. So she lifted her chin, hoping to affect a haughty kind of disdain for him and his suggestions even as she moved forward and took a seat across the table from him.

The very long table.

She looked at the food, down the length of the table to him. He was far away and remote and this was just...

"This is ridiculous," she said out loud, pushing back into a standing position. He did what he pleased so why shouldn't she? "I'm not shouting down a table over piles of food," she muttered. She grabbed her plate, her glass and walked down the length of the table. She settled them both in the place next to him, then sat. "*This* is how normal people eat together."

He looked at her like she was an alien. "Perhaps I don't want to hear the sounds of you *chewing, omorfiá mou*."

She rolled her eyes. "I suppose I was raised in a barn, after a fashion, but I do have *some* table manners, no matter how rustic."

The corner of his mouth curved ever so slightly. And there was something about that, about *amusing* him, genuinely in this way, rather than in any sort of sexual way, that had her chest warming.

Which made her half wish she'd stayed down at the end of the table. Because the sexual pull was there, under everything, always, and she was determined to resist it.

At least until they came to some decisions. Together.

You should be resisting it always, Rebecca.

Should? Yes. Would? Well, that remained to be seen. She'd try anyway.

"Perhaps I am the problem, then," he said, lifting his glass to his lips. She noted like her, his glass was filled with ice water—not wine or something alcoholic. "*Normal* was not in my upbringing."

It was the perfect opening. "And what was your upbringing like?"

He paused for a moment. She had no doubt a refusal was on his tongue, but he thought better of it. He understood this was what she needed, and he was going to try to give it to her. She smiled in spite of herself. Maybe he was highhanded, but he was trying.

"To be quite honest, you summed it up quite simply at the beach. There's not much more to it."

Of course there was, but she wondered if he even understood what she was talking about. Not just the facts, but what his childhood felt like. What it meant to him. So perhaps she had to go first to show him.

"My parents had quite a bit of fertility problems. They never spoke of it, but as I got older I began to realize they'd tried to have other children, but couldn't. So I was their sole focus. In many ways, I was lucky. They are warm and steadfast and supportive. I suppose they spoiled me, as best they could. I don't think they were ever keen on the Desmonds funding my training, but they knew I loved it. They wanted me to have what I loved."

She watched his face as she spoke. There was some discomfort there. She half expected him to fidget. But instead, he began to fill his plate. Carefully. Methodically.

So, she kept talking. About growing up in the stables. About her love of horses. When he handed her the plate he had filled, then took the one in front of her, she didn't object. Though she would have preferred to choose her own foods and portions, she wanted to draw him out more.

She got him to laugh at a story about when she'd been eight, sneaking out in the middle of the night to ride the horses, only to find herself narrowly missing a face-first fall into a pile of manure.

"It is your turn."

"I have no such tales of...*manure*."

She rolled her eyes. "Not manure specifically, Theo. A funny anecdote from your childhood that demonstrates what you were passionate about and willing to break the rules for. I loved those horses and the idea of riding them at night more than I valued not getting in trouble. Those things, even as a child, are a...measure of your personality. Of who you are."

"I did not break the rules."

"Never? You *never* broke the rules? Not even just out of spite or anger?"

"The boarding schools were very strict."

"What about when you lived with your father?"

"I don't suppose there were any rules to break." He lifted a shoulder negligently. "I was far more likely to be the one setting them than breaking them."

She couldn't think of a thing to say to that. It struck her as impossibly sad. Her parents had always been *so* responsible, she'd wished they'd lighten up. But to have no responsibility at all, particularly to a child, well, that was a travesty.

"My father was irresponsible," Theo continued, when she said nothing. "The parade of women... Well, they were not the kind who had any interest in being a stepmother, and I did not want one anyway. When I was home, I sought to find order. Our child will have order."

Order. A stern word, but she thought what he really meant was *safety*. People to depend on. And since she'd always had that, she too wanted to ensure their child did. But there was more to childhood than order. There was warmth and fun and learning from your mistakes.

He must have read the sympathy she felt for him, because his expression hardened. But his words were straightforward enough. "I will expect rules for *our* child."

"Yes. Rules are important. But we should agree on them upfront. And they'll have to change as the child gets older."

They both lapsed into a silence. For her it was because she was thinking now not just about a *child*, a *baby*, but the years and years she would be connected to this man by a child. Not just even for those first eighteen years.

Forever.

It was amazing how new implications for her future could continue to hit her out of the blue. But she realized she'd been thinking of this as a problem to *solve*. *Forever*, though, meant there was no solution. He was the father of her child, and he wanted to be involved, which meant for the rest of her life she would have to deal with him. Somehow try to compromise with him so they both agreed on the best course of action.

For their child.

"I have hired a doctor who will come live on the island for the duration of your stay," Theo announced out of nowhere and with no preamble. "She will arrive tomorrow."

Rebecca stared at him, the forkful of food caught there halfway to her mouth. "I beg your pardon?"

"The doctor we used initially will not work. Too many ties to my father. Dr. Doukas comes highly recommended, her education impeccable."

"I'm sure that's all true, but there is no need for you to hire a doctor for only a few days."

He did not say anything right away. She could all but see him weighing the words he would use.

While something like panic began to beat in her chest.

This was what it would be like forever. Him making decrees. Him taking her places she hadn't agreed to be. *Him* calling all the shots.

Still, despite how her breath struggled to come in and out easily, she spoke carefully. She would be reasonable. She would put her foot down. "I have an appointment in less than two weeks with *my* doctor. They are going to do an ultrasound, and I—*we*—can find out if we're having a boy or girl. You are welcome to come. To *that* appointment. In *Ireland*. With *my* doctor."

"That is no longer the case."

The words got stuck in Rebecca's throat, a lump of rage too hot and hard to speak past.

"I took the liberty of canceling this appointment for you. There is no point to you going back to Ireland. The child must have two parents in his life, and we cannot do that flitting back and forth across a continent. You will come to this conclusion eventually."

Because he spoke of the *child*, she did not let her full temper loose. He was wrong. Everything he was doing was *wrong*, but it wasn't selfishly. Or not fully selfishly—he hadn't offered to move to Ireland, had he?—but this was what he thought was best for the baby.

She just somehow had to get through that thick, self-absorbed billionaire skull and make him realize *she* had feelings and needs and rights, too.

"You are supposed to consult the people you're deciding things for," she managed through gritted teeth. "You do not just get to *choose* for me because *you* think it's best."

"But this is the right course of action."

"It doesn't matter if it's right or wrong. *I* have a say. How would you feel if someone swooped in and told you what was going to be done? Changed your appointments?"

"It depends," he replied evenly. "Are they the correct things to be done?"

It was like talking to a brick wall. She wanted to scream at him. Hurl the entire contents of this table. And then *run*. Back to Ireland. *Her* doctor. *Her* plans. *Her* life.

But this would not solve anything. No doubt he would follow her, stop her. No matter how hard or fast she ran. No matter how *over-the-top ridiculous* she found him, he was still the father of her child.

So, he had to *understand*, and she didn't have the words to get through to him.

But that gave her an idea.

So she stopped arguing.

And began plotting instead.

CHAPTER ELEVEN

Sleep was not an easy thing for Theo these days. He was not used to these struggles *here* on his island, in his sanctuary. He didn't let worry touch him *here*.

Though he supposed it wasn't worry that kept him awake. Nothing as simple as that. It wasn't even that when he *did* find sleep, he often had dreams of Rebecca that had him waking hard and panting.

It was the dreams that did *not* end in desire thwarted that bothered him, stuck with him, made sleep more appalling than lying here staring at the ceiling. It was dreams of her holding a child that haunted him. Their child. With dark hair and blue eyes. And even that, he thought he could have withstood. It was their future, more or less. One he'd accepted.

It was the dreams where they both disappeared—in varying impossible ways, like a puff of smoke, over a cliff, into the sea—that made sleep feel less and less safe.

He could delve into the psychology behind these dreams if he wanted to. He did not want to.

So he lay in bed, trying not to think about dreams. Or that confounded discussion over dinner.

He had seen pity, clear as day, on her face. *Pity.* As if he was something to be pitied when he'd handled everything life had thrown at him. He would not call his childhood a *happy* one, but it was hardly traumatic. So he hadn't had a mother involved? This was true for many people. So his father had been careless? He hadn't been *cruel*. Yes, stability had eluded Theo, and that had been challenging at times, but it had built him into a man who had accomplished everything he set out to do.

He had reached all his professional dreams. *He* had everything a man could desire. And *he* would give his child the things he had not had, tying up a loose end with finality.

Theo should pity *her*, but he knew that wasn't what he'd felt when she'd talked of her childhood in glowing, happy terms. The way she'd spoken about her parents with *love*.

It settled in him like claws trying to rip their way out, because it added something else to his long list of requirements for the future, for his role as a father.

In the years to come, he wanted his child to sit at someone's table and speak of him *and* Rebecca with that same sweet reverence. *That* was the measure of good parenting, and he would be a good parent. His child would have the best.

He was *terrified* that this was the kind of thing he wanted that no matter how he tried, worked, demanded, he might not be able to ensure it happened by sheer force of will.

Except by keeping her here. Except by marrying her. Perhaps he could not replicate what Rebecca's parents had given her, but he could try. And these were imperative steps to that trying.

Because he was a man who set goals. Who met them, no matter the challenges stacked against him.

That was a settling-enough thought that he finally drifted off, into a hazy dream that made little sense. He kept chasing after Rebecca. Around the island. Athens. The Desmond Estate in Ireland. She'd be within reach. Then disappear.

And with each disappearance, the desolation and desperation inside his chest grew.

And even that was better than the end. Where he finally reached her. And she collapsed in a pale heap. Eyes open and lifeless.

He woke with a heaving start, pushing up on his mattress, struggling to breathe. He nearly yelped at the figure at the end of his bed but managed to bite it back in time.

"Good morning," Rebecca sang cheerfully.

It had to be a dream. Just another part of the series of horrible dreams. But he sat in the middle of his bed, his breath heaving in and out, as she stood there, a bright smile on her face looking just fine. *Just fine.*

"What is the meaning of this?" he growled. Because he might have welcomed an unannounced appearance if she'd been wearing something that suggested that she was going to crawl into bed with him. Anything that might allow him to believe she would come exorcise the memory of that dream out of him.

But she was wearing some kind of running clothes, down to the tennis shoes on her feet. Her hair was pulled back in a bouncy tail, and she had a pair of headphones hooked around her neck.

"I have decided that the best thing for both of us is an early morning run every morning," she announced. "You should drink water when you wake up, not coffee. For your health." She moved forward and he realized she had a water bottle in her hand. She slapped it down on his nightstand with a loud *bang*.

He looked at the bottle. Then her. Perhaps his mind was still half-asleep, but he could not fathom what she was talking about. "What are you doing?"

"It's just what I've decided, Theo, and since it is the right thing to do, you should get up and get dressed for running." She smiled at him, but the sunny cheer was an act. There was something icy sharp in her eyes.

And he wasn't a dullard, even if his brain hadn't kicked into full gear yet. On a heavy sigh, he leaned back against the headboard. "I see what you are doing."

"Do you?"

"It is not appreciated."

"But these are all *the right* things." She said this with wide eyes and a kind of wonder to her voice. Excellent acting, all in all. "Parents need to be healthy and take care of themselves. No doubt a habit we need to solidify before the newborn stage wreaks havoc with our schedules."

"Your point has been made, Rebecca." Though irritation was the predominant feeling, there was the flutter of something underneath. Something he really didn't want to label as *amusement*, but his lips twitched, wanting to curve upward all the same.

It was quite inspired, really. A little farce to make her point. It impressed him, he could admit, but it didn't change his mind.

He didn't need her to *like* his proclamations. He didn't need her to see his way of thinking. He knew he was right. And whether she liked it, or he did, what needed to be done would be done.

It would cost him nothing to play along right now. To go on the run. Pretend to be cowed by her point. But it would also cost him nothing to distract her from her little bit of theater. And might in fact be quite enjoyable.

"In fact, you are quite right," he offered, trying to match her sunny tone.

She eyed him suspiciously, as she should. "I know."

He tossed his sheets aside. "Let's go."

"A-absolutely." But she didn't move. She stood there, staring at him as he stood. Completely naked. Her tongue darted out, pressed to the corner of her mouth, but her eyes were glued to where he was growing hard and ready, just for her. "Y-you will need to get dressed," she said, her voice a kind of squeak at the end.

He took his time glancing down at his own naked body. Then he looked back up at her, noting her eyes had taken the same tour. "Will I?"

She sucked in a breath, and he watched as she mustered enough control to bring her gaze up to his. She opened her mouth, but said nothing, as though she'd forgotten whatever it was she'd meant to say.

He nearly grinned, but he tried to keep his expression fairly serious. Even as he took a step toward her. "Exercise is important, of course. Even in your condition, I've read that it's important to move every day. But I think there is a better way to exercise one's cardiovascular system aside from running."

Her eyes were wide and so blue, even in the dim light of this ridiculously early morning. Her cheeks had turned the prettiest shade of pink and her chest rose and fell with quickening breath. She swallowed. Then cleared her throat.

She came up with no words. No grand proclamations or arguments. She wanted him. As much, as obsessively and ridiculously as he wanted her.

He leaned close, his mouth at her ear enjoying the sharp intake of her breath and the way she didn't back away, didn't try to find her voice or deny what sparked between them. He spoke low, right there. "And I have come to an interesting conclusion."

She blinked, confused. "Huh?"

"I think, perhaps you came in here not because you

wanted to prove some rather weak point, but because…" He trailed off, leaning closer. So she could feel his breath. So he could hear hers struggle. So warmth encased them both. "I think you haven't quite come to grips with one very clear conclusion. Maybe you like being told what to do, Rebecca."

The noise she made was like an erotic punch. A kind of sigh mixed with a gasp, all delicious sexual want.

She didn't move away. She stood there, swaying ever so slightly toward him. And still she tried to deny that which was clearly true. "No, I…"

"Yes, I think you do." He lifted his hand, trailed a finger down the elegant curve of her neck with a feather-light touch. "You like me telling you what I want." He let his finger trace down over her shoulder, across her breast where her nipple had already pebbled. "What I demand."

She made a squeaking kind of groan then. "Yes," he murmured, continuing the path of his finger down, across the firm swell of stomach, to the apex of her thighs, where he rubbed lightly. "You want to be told what to do, don't you? Sweet Becca, you love it."

She made needy noises in the back of her throat that nearly sent him over a wild edge. "You want this. You want me. Here. Now."

"I…"

She did. She damn well did. And the edge of need cut through him with such force, he wanted it to cut deeper, to cleave them both in two. So he gave more orders. "Get on your knees."

He felt her shudder. Yes, the order thrilled her, but he still wasn't sure she'd take it. Until slowly, so damn slowly, she began to kneel. She balanced her palms on his thighs as she reached her knees, and then she looked up at him as she reached out with one hand and took him in a fist.

He watched her, trying to hold firm against the battering ram of need and her. She breathed, the hot air against him like a torment. He curled his hand in her hair and urged her forward. She didn't resist. She didn't hesitate. She took him into her mouth in one perfect slow slide.

Her mouth was a new heaven, especially when she looked up at him, took him deep. Everything else ceased to exist except the velvet friction of her tongue, and the roiling need that coiled inside his muscles.

He considered letting this be all. A show of full control. But he wanted more than that. Wanted her writhing and begging. He wanted to feel the impossible, perfect fit of her beneath him.

He drew her head back, smiled when she made a noise of distress. "Get on the bed."

She blinked once, but she otherwise didn't hesitate to follow the order. She got on his bed, and he set himself to unwrapping her from the unnecessary exercise clothes. Once he had her naked, he took a moment just to look at her sprawled out on his dark sheets. A pale perfect goddess.

Her breath rushed in and out. "Aren't you going to *do* something?" she demanded, wriggling there on the bed. Needy and wanton. Every lurid dream brought to life.

He intended to enjoy it.

"Be quiet and lay still, *omorfiá mou*." He trailed his palm down the center of her chest, the mound of her stomach. He spread her legs apart, bared her to him, all while being quiet and still.

The thrill of her acquiescence warred through him. The scent of her arousal beat through him. So he settled himself between her legs and feasted on her with his mouth, his tongue, his teeth, spurred on by the way she writhed against him, the whimpers and moans. When she came apart, she sobbed out his name.

Satisfaction roared through him. Want so sharp it had turned to pain throbbed in his muscles. But he pulled away from her, surveyed her. The auburn hair had fallen out of its band and now looked like a sex-tousled halo around her face. Her skin was flushed all over.

She tried to reach out for him, but he held himself just out of her reach. Something dark and dangerous had wound around him. Some piece of his control when it came to her had snapped completely.

When she'd gotten to her knees and taken his orders. He wanted more of that. He wanted all of her give.

So he looked down at her, spread out on his bed, still so clearly wanting more. Wanting all.

"Beg me."

The words hit the center of her like a lightning strike. Ground zero. She was half-afraid he'd sent her over the edge with that simple order alone.

He'd talked about begging their first night, but that had been before. When it had been a temporary dance with fun and pleasure. Not *now* when responsibility existed right there snuggled into her body.

"Theo." She wanted to refuse. Needed to. But her mind was having trouble holding on to that thought as her body pulsed with too many needs to handle.

"Beg," he repeated, his voice hard and unrelenting.

And she wanted to. She really did. She didn't know what it said about her, didn't have the brain power to determine any *whys*. Didn't have any brainpower to remind herself she had come in here to prove a point, and he'd turned it around on her instead.

And in the moment, she didn't care. Not at all. The only thing she cared about was finding the delicious thrill of Theo inside her.

"Please. Please, Theo."

"Please what?"

"I… I…" She didn't have the words for what she was begging for. *Him. Pleasure. Release. Him. Him. Him.* "Please. I want you inside me."

"Hmm." He still stared at her, his dark gaze a sharp, fierce thing. Still he didn't touch her, didn't move over her. But he kept looking. "And what do I want?" he asked.

But it was a demand, in its way. And she knew the answer to this question. "This. Me." Because this wasn't one-sided. Maybe she wished she had more control, more restraint, but they were in this together. She fixed him with the fiercest stare she could muster. "You want me. So take me."

"That sounds more order than begging, Becca."

Becca. Yes, she wanted to be that woman again. Carefree and in tune with a body that could find immeasurable pleasure. So she set about begging in earnest, until his hands were on her, until he'd arranged her on top of him, and slid home in an easy moment that felt like *finally*.

Impossibly big. Impossibly demanding. Every stretch felt like a tug on wires inside her she had never known were there before she'd met him. A higher and higher climb to something disastrous, and yet…a pleasure so big and bright in the moment she could not care about the consequences.

She shuddered around him. The crescendo of pleasure a deafening, bone-melting high.

He didn't stop. He drove her higher. Her flung her off countless cliffs until she was simply a mass of shuddering, boneless limbs. Only then did his grip tighten, his pace quicken into desperation. Only then did he growl his release deep into her.

She collapsed on top of him, both of them winded and indeed having gotten a *cardiovascular* workout. She didn't know how long she lay there, happily sated on top of him. His hand on her back like some kind of sign of possession.

It should have bothered her. It didn't. Had she ever been possessed? Had she ever felt this wild, irrational power? And still, she hadn't come to his room first thing to do *this*.

"This solved nothing," she muttered against his chest.

"That is wholly untrue. I feel quite *solved*."

She sighed irritably, but it wasn't only irritation. She just couldn't help feeling some amusement, particularly when he sounded so smug and relaxed. When she could still hear his heart hammering against his chest.

And then she felt something else, lying here on top of him, his arms around her. Something warm. Something soft.

Something that felt...dangerous.

She moved off him, trying to catch the breath she'd lost in a different way than physical exertion. For a moment, she lay next to him, staring at the ceiling, trying to understand the unsteady beating of her heart.

Trying to understand how she'd burst in here certain she'd prove her point and had ended up naked and unsure of her point.

Rebecca could admit she was pouting. It was frustrating and lowering to admit that he had the upper hand. That he could turn around her *perfectly reasonable* attempts to get him to see his high-handed ways weren't going to fly.

Maybe you like being told what to do.

She blew out a breath. So she liked being bossed around in a *sexual* way. That didn't mean he had a right to cancel *her* appointments and make new ones. It didn't mean he had a right to demand she stay here if she didn't want to.

Her body throbbed in pleasant, drugging after-shocks as if to argue. Especially considering she didn't want to drag on the tight exercise gear she'd had on. She wanted to exist in robes and never leave her bed now.

But it wasn't *her* bed, it was his.

"I will call to have breakfast brought up, if you're thinking you can stomach it."

She should go pack her damn bags. He was a weakness. What he brought out in her was a weakness. But in the moment, soft and warm and sated, she wanted to delve into a weakness.

For once, just *once*, she didn't want to have to work so hard. So… What did it matter? She'd always had to work hard, be strong and keep a stiff upper lip. And what had it gotten her? Not much.

Why not be waited on? Why not enjoy amazing sex? Why not let someone else make some of the decisions? Why not stay and see if there was some way…some way to make this easier. Not just *on* her, but for their child, too.

So, she held his gaze. And if that made her weak, so damn be it. "Yes, I'd like that."

CHAPTER TWELVE

Theo kept her in his bedroom. Had all her things moved in. They didn't discuss it. He was done discussing. He'd proved his point.

His way was best, and she would follow it and all would be well.

She didn't mention Ireland again. Or leaving. She didn't try to go back to the guest bedroom or argue with him. Theo saw that night as a turning point to getting her to understand that moving forward, they would follow his will.

He took her lack of argument as agreement. What else would it be?

And since he did, he allowed her rather invasive questions about his childhood, his business, his *likes and dislikes*. He told stories about boarding school, or his early business exploits.

He did not delve into his father's many marriages no matter how she poked or prodded. He did not discuss his relationships or lack thereof with the women his father had brought into their home. And he did not discuss his mother's identity.

But he listened to all her stories. About her childhood, her parents, training for the Olympics. He filed away every detail, for the most part, but anytime she brought up her injury, he found himself withdrawing. He could not countenance her *pain*, her *loss*. It churned something within him he did not want to feel. So he never allowed her to get past the initial moment when she'd realized the horse would not make the jump.

If she found this irritating, she did not mention it. In fact, she rarely mentioned any irritations. This also left him on a strange kind of…edge. Always a little unsure if he'd done something wrong.

But she came to his bed every night. She kept meals with him, conversed. Nothing *was* wrong, so he did not understand why it felt like he was walking on eggshells.

When the doctor came for the appointment, complete with scanning equipment that would allow them to determine gender, they had a pleasant appointment. The doctor genial and efficient, answering all of their questions.

Once she had Rebecca settled into a bed, a little wand settled over her ever-growing belly, the doctor made humming sounds as a black static appeared on a monitor she'd brought in. Theo stood next to his bed, watching the monitor with his breath caught in his throat.

What would he see? What would the doctor find? How did one handle this kind of unknown, uncontrollable question mark of a future?

"Well, you are very clearly having a boy." The doctor smiled at both of them. "From what I can see, everything is measuring as it should. Our due date is right on target."

He felt something grip his hand. Rebecca. She'd reached out, curled her fingers around his. Her gaze was on the screen, but she'd reached out to him.

He barely felt the pressure of her squeezing his hand. He had not really thought in…realities. He'd been so focused on the practicalities. On how to set up his child's life how he wanted, how would be *best*, he had not considered…

A boy. He was to be the father of a boy.

Whatever eggshells or edges he'd been walking along now felt like a razor-sharp cliff.

"I'll have the images emailed to you," the doctor was saying as she began to pack up the equipment. "I'll want to see you again in a month, Rebecca. But should any questions or concerns arise, don't hesitate to contact me." She turned to Theo. "Mr. Nikolaou. Congratulations. I can see myself out if you two would like to have some time alone to digest." Her smile was kind.

Her words felt like they were spoken in a foreign language. And then she was gone. So he was left with Rebecca and a looming sense of...doom.

"Now we can consider names."

"Names." He felt as if the entire world around him was echoing information he couldn't possibly process.

"I already have a middle name picked out," she said, as if this new information changed nothing for her. She had adjusted her shirt back into place and was sliding out of bed as easy as you please. "James. After my father. That's a non-negotiable for me, but we can decide on a first name we both agree on." She turned and aimed a smile at him.

A name. For a boy. *His* boy.

"Had you thought of any?" she asked, still so casual and easy as you please.

"Any?" His voice felt like sharp knives against his throat.

"Names, Theo. Perhaps you'd like a *junior* situation." She turned to study herself in the mirror, fixed her hair. "Or just Theodorou James. It sounds kind of nice. We could call him TJ."

"No." His voice was little more than a rasp. His heartbeat was echoing too loudly in his ears, and he wasn't sure the breath he took actually brought in any oxygen. He did not understand what was happening to his body. He only knew that… Everything was wrong.

Him. A boy. A baby boy. His baby boy. Their baby boy.

Rebecca crossed to him, concern in those blue eyes of hers. Maybe he was drowning in that ocean reflected there. Maybe this was all her fault. Whatever was happening to him.

"Theo. Are you all right?"

"Of course," he rasped.

"You seem…panicked."

The word got through to him if nothing else did. He straightened, cleared his throat, and demanded his breathing to even as he took a decided step away from the hand she'd put over his arm. "I'm not *panicked*."

"It's okay, you know. I feel panicked out of nowhere about it all the time." She lifted a hand casually. "Being parents is a pretty major undertaking. I think it's okay to feel overwhelmed by everything we don't know."

"I am not panicked. I am not overwhelmed. We have the books to tell us what to do. We know everything we need to know, or we will."

She cocked her head to one side, studying him. "It's okay *not* to know things. It's, in fact, impossible to know everything. You know, when I was talking to my mom last night and she was telling me how that worry about doing right by your child never goes away. I was actually kind of comforted by that, because if she—"

"We will know what is right for our child, and we will do it. Always." This was the very bare minimum of what he demanded of himself. Of her. For her to suggest otherwise was…appalling.

She kept studying him, but she did not argue with him any further. No doubt she understood that he was right. That they would be better than *worry*. Than not being sure.

Certainty got a person through everything. Determining what was right and making it happen was the only way to survive.

"If you're...struggling with everything, Theo, I can always go back to Ireland and give you some space for a while."

It snapped something within him. Oh, there was no panic now. Only a fury he would need to pound away downstairs with his boxing equipment. "You are not going back to Ireland. Ever."

Her expression shuttered. Cooled. "Theo. I have compromised more than I am comfortable thinking about. I have given you everything you demanded. Everything."

"Because it is right."

"No, because... Well, for a lot of reasons. But I will go back to Ireland. For visits. If I decide I'd like to move back. I am willing to give you, this—*us* time. I have come around to be willing to see how this goes, but I am not willing to go along thinking that you can always just...announce things and they will be so. I will go to Ireland if I damn well please."

It was her burst of temper that had him fully realizing just how much he'd lost control of the moment. Of himself.

He had leaned into compromise. He had gotten her to stay, but he had not pushed for marriage. He had been so happy with one tiny victory, he had forgotten about the whole damn war. He had not insisted on what was necessary. On the certainty and legalities of joining their lives and creating the foundation for their child.

What a mistake.

But before he could lash out, a knock sounded at the door. He stormed over to it, growled on opening.

His butler stood there, looking less placid than usual. "I beg your pardon, Mr. Nikolaou. And I am very sorry."

"For what?" Theo demanded.

"Your father... He is here."

"Here?"

"Apparently they are staying for the weekend."

Theo's expression darkened. His temper chewed at the leash he was barely keeping tethered. *"They."*

"Yes. Mr. and Mrs. Nikolaou are here to visit for the weekend. I tried to tactfully explain to them this was not something we had planned for, but..."

Yes, Theo knew what the *but* would be. His father's inability to recognize when he wasn't welcome. Inability or refusal to.

But it gave Theo something else to think about other than names, and the idea of Rebecca going back to Ireland. The wedding he had not insisted upon that would now need to be expedited.

So, he wasn't sure if it was the best possible time or the worst for his father's appearance. But it didn't matter, because it was reality. And Theo was damn well going to deal with it.

Rebecca had an interesting view of Theo's profile from where she stood in the room. She watched as a million emotions crashed over his usually unreadable face.

He *had* been panicked, whether he was willing to admit it or not. And his response to panic was to double down on control. She'd seen this play out over the past few weeks. She liked to think that the whole time had been a learning experience. The whole point of staying, of acquiescing, was to *understand*.

Every time she thought she was coming close to fully

understanding him, predicting his reactions and moods, something new came along. Because while she'd seen him lean on control like a crutch, she hadn't seen him do...*this*, though. Growl at the staff. Have fury, frustration and *hurt* chase through his dark eyes before acceptance settled there.

Yes, she had no doubt his father had done a number on him, and she wondered if that was what had caused his reaction with the doctor. Had he suddenly been faced with the idea of his own relationship with his father and worried?

She didn't know. He would no doubt avoid the question if she asked. But she knew one thing for certain.

He didn't want his father here.

"Prepare drinks," Theo ordered the butler in clipped tones. "God knows we'll all need them. Bump dinner up to five. Perhaps I can get him out of here before nightfall." He paused for a brief moment. "Stay here," he said before striding out the door.

It took her a full minute to realize that last order had been for *her*. And perhaps she'd shamefully taken her fair share of orders these past few weeks, but she was hardly going to lie down and accept *this* one.

She marched right after him. Down the hall, the staircase and toward the grand entrance of the house.

Two people stood there. Atlas Nikolaou—whom she had seen in pictures and would have recognized easily anywhere. The pictures did not quite do him justice. He wasn't quite as tall as Theo, and he was thicker around the middle, but his shoulders were just as broad, his jet-black hair swept back in a dramatic style, his smile wide and very, very white. There was a dazzling quality in his dark eyes. Like an older Theo with a sheen of sparkle.

The woman next to Atlas was tall and slender. Her dark blond hair was slicked back into a bun that managed to look stylish over severe. Gold winked at her ears, all over her fingers that clutched a bag tightly and her wrists. She was dressed in an effortlessly chic way that had Rebecca feeling slightly foolish for being in sweats.

Theo must not have realized she was behind him, because he went right up to greet the pair without a backward look at her.

Rebecca watched the exchange with a grim kind of fascination. Atlas greeted his son with exuberance and love, but it was not met with such. No, if anything Theo looked a bit shell-shocked. Even as he murmured a greeting to his father and the woman behind him.

"I don't recall inviting you, Father." This wasn't said in the cutting tone Rebecca expected. No, there was a tired resignation to this sentence.

Atlas let out a big booming laugh. "Of course you didn't. You never do." He brushed past Theo and immediately set his gaze on her. "And this must be our Irish lass." He laughed, as if he'd made a grand joke. Theo's head whipped back to glare at her.

But Atlas was moving and talking over any reaction Theo might have had.

"And my grandchild." He moved forward, reaching out. Rebecca was half-afraid this man she'd never met was about to grab her belly, but he dropped his outstretched arms as he approached.

He took her hand instead, pumped it exuberantly. Even gave a little bow. "Atlas Nikolaou, a pleasure to meet the woman carrying my grandchild." He squeezed her hand, leaned close and lowered his voice. "And the woman who has kept my son wholly and utterly occupied." Then he let out that booming laugh again. It seemed to echo through the house, rattle the chandeliers.

She could see how in certain situations it might be entertaining, but it felt loud and out of place in this one. And still, she found herself smiling in spite of herself. He was loud and a little forceful, but it was in such a jovial way there seemed nothing to do but get swept away in his charm.

"Uh...well." Rebecca didn't know what to say. So she only managed, as if by rote, "It's nice to meet you, as well."

He dropped her arm, turned back to Theo and the woman, who stood next to each other, both frowning at Atlas.

"Introductions, my boy. You know better," Atlas ordered.

Theo was so still she wasn't sure he breathed. "It seems you are doing a well enough job. Rebecca, my father, and this is..." He trailed off, looked at the woman next to him.

She stepped toward Rebecca, held out her hand. She was tall, sophistication dripping off her. Rebecca didn't think she looked a day over twenty-five.

"Ariana," the woman supplied. "So good to meet you." The words held no warmth, only a polite kind of ice.

Perhaps because Theo hadn't even known her name. Rebecca looked from Theo—blank and icy, to Atlas—smiling and warm, back to Ariana—polite if a little icy herself. It was the strangest moment she could remember finding herself in.

"We'll only stay for the weekend," Atlas said, sighing dramatically and giving Rebecca a look as if they were somehow co-conspirators for the weekend. "But you must give us *some* time to get to know one another. It's not as if you are busy with work, and you won't let me be."

"Very well," Theo said. "Let us retire to the patio. Rebecca, I know you said you were tired." Theo looked at her pointedly. "Why don't you go rest?"

Maybe she should. She didn't need to get involved in his family drama. But she remembered how he'd snapped out she'd *never* go to Ireland again, which made her feel like rebelling for once.

She also remembered the tired, curt way he refused to go deeper into his childhood in regard to his stepmothers or his own mother. She remembered the detached, almost *tired* way he discussed Atlas as a father to a young man.

He did not know it or want it, but no doubt Theo needed an ally.

So instead, she smiled brightly at him. "I'm feeling much refreshed. Besides, how could I miss *finally* getting to meet your family?"

Because she might want to be his ally, but she also kind of wanted to get under his controlling skin.

CHAPTER THIRTEEN

THEO WOULD FIND a way to punish Rebecca. This was his only thought as he watched Atlas and Rebecca put their heads together and make each other laugh on the patio of his personal, private home.

Atlas's was the loud booming laugh Theo remembered from his youth. Sometimes, back then, it had made Theo laugh and smile in return. But sometime around the first time he'd been sent away to boarding school, thanks to Wife Number Two, Theo had come to see beyond the charm, the laugh, the amusement.

Atlas could entertain a crowd. He was enjoyable to be around, as long as there was enjoyment to be had. He could make you think he cared *deeply* about you and your happiness.

But he refused to deal in any other emotions. So it did not matter if you were sad, upset, hurt, furious. *He* was going to find it funny. He was going to put a positive spin on it, and if you insisted on wanting to discuss and see a serious matter through, he was going to withdraw.

Theo knew this was why the wives never lasted. Though Ariana had been around for some time now. Four years? Five? She remained, despite the past months of upheaval following Atlas's brush with death.

Theo glanced at her, sitting quietly and involving herself in the conversation not at all. She had taken maybe two sips from her glass, and now sat back and kept her gaze firmly on the ocean beyond them. Her hand draped over her stomach in a gesture that irked though he could not put a finger on why.

He supposed he would have to remember her name now. She was in his home. She had been introduced to Rebecca. While Atlas liked to drop by on occasion, sent by whatever whims ruled him, he had never toted along one of his women before. Married or no.

But Theo could see in her eyes, in the faint frown around the edges of her polite smile, she was finding her time with Atlas a lot less entertaining than she had once.

It would all crash and burn again, and who would pick up the pieces? Theo. It was always him. He would have to keep Atlas away from the business *and* his own vices. He would have to hire someone to watch after him to ensure he was following the doctor's orders.

They ate dinner. Theo didn't say more than five words. Neither did Ariana. Atlas dominated the conversation, per usual, though he pulled Rebecca into it because she was new. A shiny thing to pander to.

Rebecca smiled and laughed and puffed up Atlas's considerable ego, which left Theo feeling more and more tense. His staff brought dessert out to the terrace and Theo suffered through the continuing Atlas Nikolaou show—something he hadn't had to do since before his father's heart attack.

Luckily, he had a reason to insist upon an early night. Rebecca was growing a child and needed her sleep. He had the staff show Atlas and Ariana to their room, and hoped he could find a way to send them on their way tomorrow.

Early.

While he marched through the house to their room, Rebecca walked next to him. As they took the stairs, she even linked her arms with his, kind of leaned into him in an intimate gesture he did not know what to do with. It wasn't born of anything that might happen in the bedroom tonight. It was a kind of casual friendliness that made no earthly sense to him.

Nor the warmth that spread through him, the desire to wind his own arm around her, and hold her close just so she was there.

"I have a better understanding of you now," Rebecca said as they walked, and she didn't sound *appalled*, so he supposed he would count that as a good thing. He had to. Tonight had proved to him that he had been...weak. He had let the weeks pass without pressing and insisting on what needed to be done.

He'd allowed himself to consider her staying a win, and it wasn't. It was a tiny step toward what must be done. Forward movement was essential. Locking down the foundation for his child, his *son*, absolutely necessary.

There could be no more pretending.

"Well, that is good," Theo said, frustrated his voice sounded tight and tense instead of simply *sure*. "Because I fear we cannot wait much longer to be married. There will be many legal logistics to work through on that front before the baby is born. The kind of thing that will take the few months we have left."

Rebecca sighed and looked at him with a *sadness* in her eyes he didn't understand. She stopped his forward progress in front of their—*his*—bedroom door. "What will marrying me solve for you, Theo?" she asked. Seriously. Curiously. Not an accusation, an actual question.

But she missed the point.

"It is not about *me*, Rebecca. It is about the child. Marriage—two parents—offers stability. You of all people should know it. You benefited from it."

"I benefited from two parents who loved each other and me." She said this very softly. Carefully. Like a verbal tiptoe.

But the word *love* felt a bit like a stab through the ribs. "Love doesn't matter, Rebecca."

"Theo…" She sighed again, moved into the room. So he followed her as she seemed to struggle to explain something.

She didn't have words, so he gave her his. "I have watched my father fall in and out of love his entire adult life." He unbuttoned the top few buttons of his shirt as they seemed to choke him suddenly. "It didn't keep my mother in place, or any of his wives. Did you watch Ariel?"

Rebecca perched herself on the edge of the bed, watched his movements around the room. He felt like a lion in a zoo. Powerful. King of his domain. Caged and watched.

"Ariana, you mean?" Rebecca asked lightly.

"Whatever. It does not matter, because it was clear she was on her last legs."

"How do you mean?"

"I've been through this routine before. Withdrawn. Uninterested. They start the relationship fawning all over him, laughing at all his jokes." He decided to do away with the whole shirt. Maybe it wasn't late, but he was tired and Rebecca needed her rest. "They're dazzled by him but dazzle doesn't last forever. Eventually the theater of Atlas Nikolaou gets old, and they leave. Have I mentioned that?" he asked, only half paying attention to her because the room was unbearably warm. He strode over to check the vents to ensure they were working. "It's always them that leave. Never him trading them in for a younger model like the press likes to claim. No. They leave first."

Rebecca was unfathomably quiet. He felt the undeniable urge to fill the silence, even when he knew he should sink into it instead. "I know the signs. She's going to leave."

"I think you misunderstood her quiet."

Theo stopped moving, realizing he'd been pacing and he needed to *stop*. He stared at Rebecca. "What is there to misunderstand?"

Rebecca seemed to consider her words carefully as she watched him with shrewd eyes. "I think she's pregnant and miserable."

For a moment, Theo could not find his voice. He could not fully grasp her words. Clearly she was wrong. Confused. Swayed by her own pregnancy. "You... My father is nearly fifty-five years old."

"But Ariana is not," Rebecca replied, a kind of gentleness to her tone that seemed to sweep out the foundation of all his denials.

Pregnant. His father had not impregnated any of his wives. He had not doubled down on *that* mistake. And now...

She was wrong. She had to be wrong. "You're wrong." Even as that picture of Ariana sitting on the patio, pale and tight-mouthed, her hand draped over her stomach in a gesture he realized irked because it was one Rebecca often made.

Rebecca shrugged. "Maybe I am," she agreed. But it was *patronizing*.

It bothered him that she wouldn't even argue. Because it left space for him to look back at the evening. The fact Atlas had brought her here. He hadn't paid her any attention when he'd been in full entertainer mode, but there'd been a physical carefulness with her.

No. *No*.

"I'll even say, I hope you're right," Rebecca continued. She got to her feet, crossed to him and rubbed a hand over his shoulder as if to comfort him. "Your father is very charming, but he is very…self-absorbed. There's not a meanness to it, but it's shallow. I can't imagine he was a very good father to you as you were growing, any more than he was a very good husband to the array of women he married."

"He did not abandon me." Theo moved away from her hand. "There is that."

"Do you think that means you owe him? Because I'm pretty sure raising his own son was the very least he could do. And he only did it when it suited. Sometimes he sent you off to boarding school."

"Boarding school is not a punishment. Many people of my station go to boarding school. It's an important experience."

She made a sound that wasn't agreement. He scowled at her. "You wouldn't understand. You did not grow up with money. With a business legacy to uphold."

"No, but I grew up adjacent to it. Patrick didn't go away to boarding school."

"Patrick Desmond is a fool and a nobody," Theo spat. An emotion he refused to accept was jealousy roiling through him. "The Nikolaou empire spans the globe, Rebecca."

Again she made that *agreeable* noise, her dark blue eyes watching him as if she absorbed everything, even the things he didn't say out loud. Even the things she shouldn't see. "You don't like your father. Why do you defend him?"

"I am not defending him. I am laying out the facts. Was he a poor father? Yes. A poor husband? I can only assume. So what?"

"It affected you."

"No, *omorfiá mou*." Nothing *affected* him. He used the building blocks he'd been given to shape himself into everything he was. "I used it to make me into who I am."

Rebecca watched Theo roam the room. He pretended to be doing things. Dressing for bed. Charging his phone. But she *felt* a kind of anxious frustration pounding off him.

She understood parts of it. There was something about Atlas that had left even *her* feeling on edge. There was a demand inherent in his good nature. Like you had to go along with it or you might be punished in some way.

It was interesting, because Theo was far more severe, far less genial, and yet he never made her feel as though she could make a wrong step. They could have a disagreement. She could get mad at him. And they would...*deal*. Not retreat. Not...punish.

And this contrast had left her feeling protective of Theo. She wanted to bundle him up and tell him everything would be okay—not that he'd ever allow it, not that he could admit to himself that things *weren't* okay, but the need to soothe was there.

How did you soothe someone who refused to admit they were upset?

"We will have the wedding here," Theo announced out of nowhere, as if she'd agreed. "A small affair. You may invite your parents, of course."

She wasn't even surprised by his sudden return to insistence on marriage. She realized now he saw it as some kind of...insurance for their child. He didn't view marriage as a partnership. He didn't believe in love. He thought some legally binding contract would create a foundation for their child that he'd never had.

And because she now understood that, she didn't feel

angry by his insistence or heavy-handedness. She only felt sorry for him.

She wasn't going to marry him out of *pity*, but arguing with him over it would get them nowhere right now. Maybe she should just go along until she found the right time to…

What? Change his unchangeable mind?

She would simply get swept into marrying him just as she'd been swept into staying here. And her anger, fear, reticence over that kept…leaking away.

Maybe it was crazy. Maybe she was falling for him, and it was just like Patrick all over again. Put a rich man in front of her who showed her even a drop of interest and she weaved foolish poor stable girl fantasies.

But she had settled into a life here and she *liked* it. She could picture a bassinet in the corner of her and Theo's room. Walking with the baby strapped to her along the beach. Hand in hand with Theo.

It was a ridiculously romantic fantasy that she knew couldn't possibly come true. Theo's determination that he was always right would ruin it. This wasn't *love*. Maybe she was getting to know him. Maybe she liked him and spending time with him quite a bit. The sexual chemistry certainly hadn't dulled, but clearly she was the same fool she'd been when Patrick had begun to show interest in her.

And even if she somehow convinced herself this was different—though it wasn't—Theo didn't believe in love. He thought it as fickle as his father.

He wasn't proposing a loving marriage anyway. He was essentially proposing a business merger—the business being their child. And Rebecca knew that he was in for a rude awakening when the child was born—when their *son* was born. Rebecca may not have ever *had* a child, but she understood children had their own personalities. The boy wouldn't be something they could control with the right environment, with the right legal partnerships in place.

Theo would never accept this. No matter how hard she had tried to get through to him about attempting to impose his will on her, it had gotten her nowhere. Trying to show him he was wrong hadn't done a thing but land them in bed. She ended up doing what he wanted, always.

If it was *just* her, maybe she would have—pathetically—gone along with it. But she had a son to consider. To love. To protect.

So she needed a new tactic. She needed to learn a damn lesson. Which is when it finally occurred to her.

She couldn't do this alone. She had hoarded her relationship with Patrick. Though her parents had been aware, they hadn't been involved. Even Mr. Desmond had been *aware*, but he'd kept his distance and then thrown a new bride in front of Patrick the second Rebecca was out of the picture.

This time around, she needed help.

"Before I could possibly marry you, I would need my parents' support. Which means, you'll need to come to Ireland and meet my parents. Get to know them and vice versa."

She expected excuses. She expected him to balk. But he turned to her, gave a sharp agreeing nod. "Consider it done."

CHAPTER FOURTEEN

THEY LANDED IN Ireland a week later. Theo had seen his father off, been relieved when there'd been no pregnancy announcements from Atlas and washed his thoughts of his father away.

He had a woman to marry. Which would mean charming her parents. Earning their support. He had no doubts this could be done in the course of twenty-four hours. Forty-eight if they were the stubborn sort like their daughter.

The Desmond Estate was exactly as he remembered it as the driver entered the gates. A lush kind of wealth settled deep into the fertile Irish ground, dotted by stately trees and ancient buildings.

But instead of heading up the main drive toward all that, the car took a left and drove out along the edges of a fence, for ages, until an array of agricultural buildings came into view. They drove up to and then around them. Behind the pastures and stables and occasional horse next to a fence, settled back into a copse of trees, was a small house. It was made of brick, certainly showed its age, and yet it had clearly been meticulously kept for decades if not longer.

As they approached, the pretty green door opened and out stepped a woman. She had black hair streaked with a steely gray. In just about every other way, aside from a few lines around the eyes, her face looked almost exactly like Rebecca's.

A taller man with a slight stature came out next. He had a cap pulled low on his head, but he moved to stand next to the woman.

For a moment, Theo could only stare at them as though they were some fairyland creatures brought to life. But they were just two people. Standing in front of their home.

Nothing to feel strangely about. Certainly nothing intimidating.

The car had only just barely rolled to a stop when Rebecca flung her door open and all but leaped out. She jogged across the pretty yard as Theo stiffly exited the vehicle.

In no time at all, Rebecca had reached them and threw her arms around her mother. Her mother hugged her back tight. They swayed together, both talking over one another, and then laughing happily about it. Rebecca's mother put her hands on Rebecca's rounding stomach and beamed.

James Murphy, a name Theo only knew since Rebecca had informed him their son's middle name would be James, crossed to Theo, hand outstretched.

"Mr. Nikolaou," he greeted, in his thick Irish brogue. "Welcome to our home."

"Please call me Theo, Mr. Murphy," Theo said, fixing a smile on his face and offering a businessman's shake. Because all in all, that's all this was. A little bit of business. Win over the parents. Move forward with the wedding. Solidify his son's future.

How hard could it be?

"Oh, sure, sure. And you'll call me James." He squeezed Theo's hand once before dropping it. Then he gestured toward his wife. "This is Sharon."

"So good to finally meet you," she said. Her accent was softer, her expression cooler. The *finally* was pointed. But her smile was present so no one might have picked up on any minor hostilities if they weren't looking. "You'll both come in for some tea."

It was not a request.

Mother and daughter linked arms, moving inside the house already chattering, and father followed. Theo knew he should, as well. He'd been invited in for tea. He had some charming to do.

But for a moment he couldn't get his muscles to move. He watched the family disappear inside as a unit, and he knew he did not belong. He would never belong in such a scene.

But this mission was not about belonging. It was about ensuring what must be done. He could worry about creating that kind of familial warmth for his son once Rebecca married him.

Everything required one step at a time.

So he ducked in through the door, was met by warmth and charm and a coziness. These were not things he had a lot of experience with. It felt a bit like stepping into the beginning of a gauntlet. Except he had no idea what kind of beatings to expect.

Every room was small. He felt like an oversize ogre. And still he was struck by how…*something* it all was. He didn't have the words for this. In many ways, it was not all that different from his own home—the walls and surfaces were decorated with antiques and items that clearly reflected the interest of the owners. Horses, mainly.

But there was a difference, because no doubt the violin hanging from a hook on the wall was not some collector's item hunted down at auction, but a family heirloom. The needlepoint hanging in the dining room no doubt done by one of Rebecca's relatives.

At his home, his things were not his. Not family heirlooms. Not items with stories that were his own. They were all collections. Things he was interested in, enjoyed, admired certainly. He supposed that was some element of *personal*.

But it didn't feel like this. Perhaps a reflection of what he liked, but not a reflection of who he was.

He tried to shake that thought away, even as his gaze got caught up on a row of framed pictures hanging along the wall in a line. Rebecca through the years—from a drooling baby to a school-age child with that same rich auburn hair, braided to hang at either shoulder, bright smile missing two teeth. To a poised young woman, holding a ribbon and standing in equestrian dress in front of a horse.

He found himself unable to take his gaze off the tableau of Rebeccas, until Mrs. Murphy said his name and pointed him to a seat at a sturdy dining room table where everyone else had already arranged themselves.

Stiffly, feeling a bit like this was all an odd dream, Theo lowered himself into the seat next to Rebecca. She was looking at him, and he expressly did not meet her gaze. Until he had full control of these odd sensations rolling around inside him, he was not about to look at her and allow her to see it.

"We're so pleased you've come for a visit. We've missed having our Becky about," James said. He had a cheerful demeanor that should remind Theo of his own father, but it didn't.

Because the humor wasn't to bring attention to James. It was…something else entirely. Just…warmth.

Mrs. Murphy poured the tea into fussy cups—no doubt "the good china," brought out for guests.

"You've been getting some sun," she said to her daughter.

"Oh, yes. Theo and I take walks on the beach just about every day. It's so pretty. Relaxing."

"Relaxing is good," James offered.

"Pregnancy is such an important time," Sharon agreed. "You must make certain she's taking care of herself, Theo. Our Rebecca has always liked to push the envelope."

Theo had to clear his throat to find his voice. "I do try."

Sharon nodded firmly in approval. "It's the best any of us can do."

They had a nice conversation over tea, though everything seemed to bring Rebecca and her father back to the topic of horses. Theo knew *some* about the animals, but clearly not enough to follow the conversation.

And even once they were done with tea, it seemed horses dominated everything. Rebecca grabbed him by the arm.

"I'm going to show Theo the horses," she announced to her parents. "We'll be back in a bit."

She led him outside. "I thought the point of this visit was to get your parents' approval on our marriage. Not…cavort with animals."

She led him across the grassy yard. She tilted her head slightly, surveying him. "Are you afraid of horses, Theo?"

"Don't be ridiculous."

"Some people are, you know."

"Good for them. I am not afraid of much, *omorfiá mou*."

She laughed, the sound rich and bright in the afternoon sun. He found himself mesmerized by how the red hints of fire teased out of her hair in the light. The way she walked with a lightness in her step. The excitement in her eyes as she dragged him into the stables and began to go down every stall and introduce him to each horse like they were people.

Throughout the day, and into the next, Theo came to a startling realization.

Rebecca was different here. With her parents. In her home. With her horses in the stables. Something in her…

bloomed. She chattered. She smiled more. She laughed, a deep, husky one that matched her father's.

He found himself existing in silences he never had before. Simply watching her, absorbing her.

Did she belong here?

It didn't matter.

He had to see his plan through. Because his child would have both parents. They would be married.

And they would give their son everything.

Regardless of where anyone *belonged*.

It was so good to be home. Rebecca was surprised at how happy it made her. How fun it was to drag Theo around and show him all the different parts of her childhood.

Even so, with all the enjoyment and joy over being home, seeing her parents and so on, Rebecca wasn't thinking about staying. About raising her son here.

She, in fact, couldn't imagine it now, which shocked her. She could picture life with Theo and baby at the island in Greece, though, which made this visit feel like…a memory. Nostalgic, enjoyable, lovely even. Something she'd want her son to *see*, but not live.

She didn't want to live in her room at the end of the hall. She didn't want to wake up every morning and make breakfast in the cramped kitchen with her father grumbling over one of his puzzles while drinking his coffee before heading out to the horses.

She didn't even want to find a place in town. As much as she'd love her parents closer, she didn't want to call this place home anymore. It had become a place to visit, and that was strangely painful, even as it was freeing.

She tiptoed down the stairs first thing the second morning to potentially get started early on breakfast. She paused at the door to the room that her mother had put Theo in. Unmarried guests certainly couldn't share a bed under the Murphy roof, even if one of them was pregnant with the other one's baby.

She could go in there now. See what he looked like sleeping on an old mattress, surrounded by her mother's craft supplies and her father's horse magazines and books.

She knew he'd wanted to stay in town, but her parents would have been offended, and while this was all a bit of a farce—she didn't *need* her parents' approval to marry Theo, or not, for that matter—that didn't mean she wanted Theo to make a *bad* impression.

He hadn't complained. He'd been…subdued, she decided. But she didn't know what to make of that, so she continued downstairs. Disappointed if not surprised to see her mother had already beaten her there.

Sharon gave her a sharp look. "You should be getting more rest."

This was another reason she was grateful for her time in Greece. Her mother's worrying had been thousands of miles away. Rebecca understood it—Mom had suffered many pregnancy losses, and she couldn't fault her mother for it, but she preferred not having to prove she was fine.

She walked over to Mam, reached out and grabbed her hands. She settled her mother's hands over her belly. "I can feel him fluttering now and again. Not strong enough to feel from the outside, but he's having a little blast in there."

Mom's smile curved. "You look healthy, I'll give you that. And you'll eat a good breakfast. Both of you."

Both of you.

They hadn't really had much time alone. Theo was usually about, so Rebecca couldn't quite read what her parents felt about Theo. It was strange to realize she was a little nervous about it.

Because, of course, it didn't matter. If she *did* marry him, which was a big *if*, it was only because… Well, she *did* want her child to have a solid foundation. She didn't want to have to worry about two households and custody agreements.

But she worried that made her selfish.

"He is very polite," Mom offered. She gave the porridge a stir, then began cracking eggs.

"Mam. That's the blandest nice thing you could have possible said," Rebecca replied, smiling. She moved to help with breakfast, taking a loaf of bread and beginning to slice it for toast.

"Well, he *is*," Sharon insisted. "He has a kindness to him, but it's hidden deep down, under a very fine layer of manners."

Kindness.

Rebecca had to admit she was relieved her mother saw it. Theo had been polite. He'd even had glimmers of being charming. But he was very quiet. He stayed back. She often felt him just…*watching*. A bit like a visitor at a zoo.

Intrigued, but not part of it. Faintly puzzled, but not enough to find out *why*.

"He is kind. I don't think he'd ever describe himself as such. He fancies himself more big bad alpha boss who *always* does the correct thing, in the correct moment, to create the correct outcome."

Mam chuckled. "Well, in that case, I can see why you are well suited."

Well suited.

She hadn't expected her mother to say that. "You can?"

"I realize losing your chance at the Olympics had you lose your grip on the reins a bit, dear, and this baby as well, but you are not so unlike what you just described. Determined to do what you think is right. To create an outcome that you want. You have always had intense focus and goals you refused to fail at reaching, no matter the fear you might have had in getting there. It's what made you so good at your jumping events."

Rebecca realized her mother said all that in a past tense, and it hadn't even caused a sharp, blinding pain like it might have a month or two ago.

She wouldn't have been able to do her events pregnant anyway, so perhaps that's what softened the blow. But Rebecca wasn't sure. She thought maybe… Maybe she was learning to let that go, because her life had taken an interesting turn that she could not wish away.

No matter how frustrating Theo could be.

"Well, I suppose it doesn't really matter about suiting. He wants to get married for the baby's sake. For *foundations and stability*. I can't disagree with him that it would allow for both, but I still don't know if it's the right thing to do. Is it a stable foundation without love?"

Mom stopped what she was doing, stared at Rebecca for a good full minute.

"What?" Rebecca demanded.

"Rebecca, you are clearly in love with him," Mam said, as if exasperated with her.

She wanted to argue with her mother, but she didn't. Because sometimes she wondered if that's exactly what she was. But…

"It just seems so convenient. To fall in love with him. To jump from loving Patrick to loving him in a blink." She pulled a package of sausage from the refrigerator, the age-old dance of making breakfast together.

But she did not meet her mother's gaze.

"Oh, *a stór*, you didn't love Patrick."

Mam said this as though it was some obvious, *true* fact.

"Of course I did. I was… Mam, I was going to *marry* him."

"You were dazzled by Patrick, by how different he was than your life. And he was intrigued by you. But you both… I watched you both grow up, Rebecca. If his mother had not died when she had, if you had not been kind to him when everyone else around him had been drowning in grief, that boy would have never looked at you twice. And you would have realized it was nothing more than a dazzle. A crush. Patrick was an easy dream—Patrick the package, not Patrick the man." She sighed. "I mean no disrespect, but Patrick Desmond is a spineless lump of hash. He was never any match for you, darling. You liked the idea of the life he offered, not *him*."

It hurt, and she didn't think it would hurt if it wasn't true. Patrick was a bit spineless. Not in a mean-spirited way. He just sort of…went along with what he was told to do. Rebecca had always kind of liked that. She had been in charge.

Until his father had swept in and determined whom he would marry. No doubt Patrick hadn't even put up a fight. Maybe the thought shouldn't depress her since her mother was not *wrong*. Marrying Patrick wouldn't have given her what she wanted. But…

"Theo is rich. Maybe I'm dazzled by that package, too. An easy dream that we'll have this boy and live happily ever after."

Then her mother laughed. Just *laughed*. "I realize I do not know him as well as you do, but nothing about your Theo strikes me as *easy*. Certainly not spineless. Perhaps you are dazzled by his wealth, but that isn't what I meant about Patrick. I meant… You liked the idea of running things here."

Mom gestured as if to encompass the Desmond Estate. "You liked the picture of what your future might look like more than you liked the man himself. For who he was."

Rebecca couldn't find the words to disagree with that, but she just wasn't convinced that wasn't what she was doing with Theo. After all, she'd known him for a short time. And yes, she understood his childhood scars, wanted to help him find a way to heal them. She enjoyed his dry humor and *everything* about the way they were together physically.

But did she know him? Could she live with a man so determined to do things only his own way? Could she love a man who didn't believe in loving her back?

The answers were more complicated than yes or no and Rebecca hated that. The stairs creaked and the sound of Da and Theo's voice wafted through the house. They both came into view, deep in conversation.

"The man has sorrow in his eyes," Mom said quietly, leaning forward so only Rebecca would hear it. "Old sorrow. But it softens when he looks at you."

Rebecca snorted. "Trust me, Theo does not love me. Likes me? Sure. Maybe. I guess. But he doesn't believe in love."

"Love doesn't need to be believed in to exist."

Rebecca looked back at the living room. Theo was listening along and nodding to whatever her father was speaking animatedly about—horses no doubt, but his gaze moved, met hers as her mother spoke.

"Sometimes, Rebecca, when someone has not been loved, they think it cannot exist. Not for them. But they're always wrong," Mam said, still quiet. "Many years ago, your father told me that."

Rebecca's gaze jerked to her mother. Mam did not often talk about her childhood. Rebecca only knew what she did—that her grandfather had used his fists on his wife and children, that her grandmother had stayed because the alternative was abject poverty—from having overheard bits and pieces of conversations over the years when an aunt or uncle came to visit.

But Sharon Murphy did not discuss such hardships. Certainly not with her daughter. She never complained. She just didn't bring it up.

So it was startling she would do so now.

"And he has proven it to me every day since," Mam continued. "I had always hoped you would meet someone who would prove it to you, as well as I hope we have, but perhaps because we did, you can be the person to prove it to someone else."

Mam reached out, brushed a hand over Rebecca's hair, a rare expression of physical affection, though Rebecca had never once doubted her mother's love and devotion to her. She knew she was her parents' pride and joy.

She didn't think she knew how to be so…strong. So determined. Yes, she'd once applied those things to her goals, but that had been…just her. It hadn't rested on anyone else but her.

Still, she could hardly argue with her mother's uncharacteristically vulnerable words. "Maybe," she murmured, leaning into her mother for a moment.

She looked at Theo.

Maybe…

CHAPTER FIFTEEN

ON THE FOURTH DAY, Theo decided it would be the last. He had dutifully slept in an uncomfortable bed in a tiny office room stuffed to the gills with piles of crafts and books. He had eaten every meal at the Murphy table. He had taken the daily walks to the stables. Hell, he knew some of the horses by name now.

It was enough. It had to be enough.

Sharon mothered him. She tutted when he didn't eat enough, when it looked like he hadn't slept well. She asked about his business, but more than that she asked about his *life*—and it was this that he tried to avoid like the plague.

He had work. Now, he had a child on the way and the mother to marry. There was no *life* outside that.

And he'd never realized it before.

Theo had to go back to his real life. Where *he* was in charge, at no one's mercy and in the beam of no one's... It wasn't *care*. It simply felt like it. The Murphys had a...cozy, warm way about them. Theo was simply unfamiliar with it.

But it didn't matter. He'd done what he set out to do. He would secure James's official blessing today and return to Greece by nightfall.

In the morning, when he asked for a moment of James's time in private, James had surveyed him with a surprisingly shrewd look, then nodded.

James hadn't wanted to talk inside but had led him out of the house and over to the stables instead. Inside the smells of horse and hay, Theo was led to a little room at the end of the long row of stalls. Apparently this was James's office.

It was a tiny closet of a room. A desk was jammed into one corner, a chair with a split down the back pushed under it. While the horses had the best of everything, it seemed James took the scraps. James walked over, pulled the chair out and settled himself on it.

There was nowhere for Theo to sit, so he had to stand in front of the man. He was shocked to realize this was very much on purpose. He wouldn't have expected this kind of gamesmanship from James at all.

James crossed his arms over his chest. He did not smile jovially. He did not crack any jokes or try to ease the tension in the room. He said nothing at all as he regarded Theo with Rebecca's cool blue eyes.

Theo felt unaccountably…uncomfortable. But he shoved that away and focused on what needed to be done. What would be done.

"I would like your blessing to marry your daughter." He smiled charmingly, secure in his belief the blessing would come with joy and approval. The Murphys clearly liked him and—

"I note you are not asking my permission." James's voice was uncharacteristically tough. There was no smile on his face, no mischievous twinkle in his eyes. He was dead serious.

Theo felt himself shift. Horrified, he realized he'd wanted to *fidget*. This man who talked of horses like they were gods on the earth, who worshipped his wife and daughter and did whatever they said, now had the look of a shrewd, ruthless businessman.

"My son will have both parents, married and in his life, a stable, certain foundation. So no, it is not permission I ask for. These things *will* be done. But your daughter wishes for your blessing, and I am more than willing to request it."

James nodded thoughtfully, his sharp gaze never leaving Theo's face. His arms never uncrossing. After long moments of silence—something there hadn't been much of on this visit to the Murphys—he finally spoke.

"Rebecca is the most precious thing in the world to her mother and me. She will be a good mother, because she had one of the best. Tell me, Theo, will you be a good father?"

The question filled him with an icy kind of dread. But of course he would be a good father. That was the entire *point* of this. Marriage. Foundations. Security. A father gave their children these things—James had given his own daughter this and should understand.

Theo clasped his hands behind his back, because he was not about to stand here and not know what to do with them.

"I do not have any good examples. But I like to think that in it of itself is an example. My father was not cruel, but he was careless. I will not be careless. My son will have everything—not in a monetary, spoiled way, but in the way of a good, stable life. I will ensure he has everything he needs, everything that is right for his proper development."

James' expression changed, but Theo could not read it. Nor did he know what to label the strange, elevated beating of his heart or the odd heat that seemed to center itself on the back of his neck.

"And will you be a good husband to my daughter?" James asked after another long beat of silence.

Husband. Such a strange word. He had not thought the role had any weight. He had only seen men treat such a title with careless indifference or outright hostility. Until he'd come to Ireland and watched James Murphy with his wife.

There was a tenderness there. A joy. Even when they were bickering about something or another. They had built a house in love and everything they did seemed to reflect it.

Husband. He had never considered how he would be as a husband because whatever it was would be better than the examples he'd seen.

Until this week.

Theo found himself having to clear his throat to speak. "Rebecca will have everything she needs to be a good mother. We will give our son all that we can, together. I… want my son to speak of us as your daughter speaks of you and your wife." The words came out raspy, and Theo could not fathom why he'd said them.

He felt like a babe himself. Immobile and helpless. It was the first time he could remember feeling such a way since he'd been a young boy, not at all certain why the new woman in the house looked down at him with such distaste.

The potency of that awful memory, this current moment, left him utterly stuck in place when the only thing his brain wanted him to do was *run*.

"A blessing is a serious thing, Theo," James said, and his voice was softer now. There was a gentleness to it. "But Rebecca can make her own choices. We will always support her in them. It is hard to watch your child make the wrong ones, but sometimes you have to let them. Sometimes, they have to learn by failure. She always has our blessing to make whatever choices she wishes."

It *sounded* like an accusation, and yet James did not deliver it as one. He said it with a warmth Theo could not fully grasp or understand.

"There will be no wrong decisions, Mr. Murphy," he said,

but not with his usual certainty. Not with the force of his will behind it. He couldn't seem to manage to be *himself*.

He blamed Ireland. Tea and horses and the pictures of Rebecca as a child that would haunt him forever.

Her father smiled, an edge of sadness, an edge of wisdom Theo felt uncomfortable with. "Life is full of wrong decisions, Theo. That's why people love. To soften the blow of those wrong decisions."

Theo knew better than try to explain that *love* had nothing to do with this. That *love* was flighty and thoughtless and more selfish than selfless. This was the only kind of love he knew.

Except, that wasn't true anymore. For the past few days, he'd watched a love that he did not recognize. It was warm, and full of *care*. It was…stable.

Perhaps it was something born of years. Years of making the right choices. Yes, that must be it.

Because James Murphy was wrong—had to be—wrong decisions weren't inevitable. They were to be avoided at all costs.

And so he would marry Rebecca, with her parents' odd blessing.

Rebecca cried when she said goodbye to her parents. She blamed hormones. She'd had a wonderful time, but she was also ready to go. And yet saying goodbye felt bittersweet. She wanted space and freedom again. She didn't want to leave them.

She tried to get ahold of herself on the drive over to the airport. She could feel Theo's gaze on her.

"There will be more visits," he said eventually, as if trying to comfort her.

She sniffled, amused by his efforts, because clearly he

was uncomfortable with her tears. "Yes, I know. I'm not sad to be going back to Greece. I'm kind of relieved, actually. My mother's anxiety weighs on me after a while. But I'll still miss them both."

"And Ireland?"

She looked out the car window. "Some days, I suppose I will. But I missed Greece while we were here."

"You did?"

He sounded genuinely surprised, and she supposed she had been surprised, as well. But she didn't know how to explain why, or what it meant to her. So she kept it simple. "I like your island, Theo."

He blinked once, that rare show of being taken aback, but it was quickly gone and he was leading her from car to plane. In no time at all, they were in the air. Headed back to Greece. Much of Rebecca's sadness had faded, moving into excitement to be back…

She sighed heavily. The island felt like *home*, Theo felt like *home*, and she knew that they had a lot of work to do to make that actually be an acceptable feeling.

Worse, she wasn't sure he'd ever fully acknowledge her feelings. Or his own—whatever they were. She was still wading through how she felt about what her mother had said in the kitchen that morning along with her own insecurities that she was more than just attracted to him because he had money and was the father of her child.

She napped on the plane, woke hungry and disoriented to Theo's dark gaze on her. She managed a sleepy smile. "Are we home?" she asked.

He did not reply right away. His eyebrows drew together, as if she'd asked something terrible. But before she was fully awake, his expression smoothed out. "We have landed. We must move to the ferry now."

She yawned and stretched and opened her mouth to say she was hungry, but he held something out to her.

"You should eat."

It was a little bag of mixed nuts. He also had a little bottle of the ginger drink she enjoyed so much. He missed little, thought of everything. And if it was just little things like *this* maybe she could convince herself her love was misplaced. He cared only about the baby.

But he'd spent *four days* in her parents' home. He hadn't voiced one complaint. She said she needed her parents' approval. He'd earned it.

He didn't have to do that if all he cared about was the baby. Just like he wouldn't be concerned by her tears earlier, if he did not care.

She wondered if he'd ever cared about anyone after his parents, or if he'd cut himself off even then. A young boy, abandoned by his mother, none of his emotional needs met by his father or any subsequent stepmother.

No, she didn't think he'd ever put himself out there after that. Which meant she had years and layers of protection to fight her way through. A daunting task. But she ate the nuts, drank her soda and let him usher her to the ferry.

She would fight for him. For the little boy, and the man he'd become. So that *their* little boy could have everything. Not just the stability Theo thought marriage would magically bring, but the *real* point of having married parents.

Two people in a partnership to lead a child through the first eighteen years of life in the presence of love, compromise, compassion and joy.

They didn't talk as they took the ferry over to the island, the drive up the house. Rebecca was still trying to determine *how* she got through to the old broken heart inside the hard-shelled man when they walked into the house.

She stopped abruptly as she felt a strange *pang* inside. Not a pain. Movement, she realized. Harder movement than she was used to. She reached out to grip Theo. Not because she needed balance, but because she needed to hold on to something.

She could have sworn she felt a hard jab, right there against the inside of her stomach.

"What is it?" Theo demanded, worry in his expression.

"Oh, the baby kicked. But… I think you might be able to…" She trailed off, reached for his hand and pressed it firmly against her ever-expanding middle. "Did you feel that?" she asked, as their son rolled about in her stomach.

Theo frowned darkly. "No."

"Hold on. Be patient." So they stood, her hand pressing his into the side of her stomach where she thought he might actually be able to feel it from the outside.

Minutes passed and she was about to give up when she felt a light little jab and Theo's hand jerked, then pressed back to her stomach. "I… I felt it," he rasped.

She watched his face. The awe in it. That slight flicker of trepidation she felt anytime the whole *baby* thing felt overwhelming.

But it didn't right now. It felt like they were in this together. It felt like… She knew he would be a good father. Oh, he would make mistakes, and he would struggle with that. He did not have her own father's easygoing demeanor, that was for sure.

But he wanted, so badly, for their child to have the good he did not have. It made her heart swell, her eyes fill. How much he wanted to give his child. And her, whether he wanted to admit that to himself or not.

Maybe she was delusional. Maybe his care extended to her *because* she carried his son, but she didn't think so. From the first moment they'd spoken, something had sparked between them. Souls…recognizing each other.

Her mother, the most practical woman she'd ever known, believed in things like that. Why shouldn't she?

She loved Theo. It swept through her in every quiet moment, in the four days he'd spent with her parents, in their passionate evenings and calm, cozy dinners.

Loving him had nothing to do with Patrick or money or even this baby. The baby had just allowed her to see beneath that heavy armor Theo carried over himself, forever trying to shape the world around him into something that wouldn't hurt those old, vulnerable wounds.

She wanted to soothe them, love them, find ways to heal them as they raised their son together. She wanted…him, a life with him. That stability he was militant about giving their child, but with the safety net of all this *love* she had underneath it.

As if he could read her thoughts and they made him uneasy, he stepped back, let his hand fall. "Movement is good, I have read."

"Yes. I can feel a lot more than you can feel from the outside, but the books all say it gets stronger. You'll be able to feel all sorts of kicks—feet, knees, elbows."

He said nothing for a while, then turned. "We should get you off your feet." He moved to her again, took her arm by the elbow, like she needed to be guided carefully up the stairs.

She decided to let him. Figured it settled him to feel in control. He took her up to the bedroom, then nudged her into a sitting position on the edge of the bed.

For a quiet moment, they only regarded each other. Then he stepped back. Away. He pulled his phone out of his pocket.

"Did your parents let you know they gave their blessing?" he asked. His gaze was on his phone, no doubt checking business emails and the like, but she got the sense he was holding himself very still as if guarding for an attack.

"They did."

He lifted his dark, haunted gaze. "Then we shall be married. Soon."

He said this like a challenge.

"Are you sure that's what you want, Theo? Because you will be well and truly stuck with me then."

"I have no intention of changing my mind. This is the right course of action."

She looked up at him and then she knew what must be done. She couldn't be afraid. She couldn't wade through a million what-ifs or insecurities. She had to be bold. She had to make sure her wants and needs existed in this space, too.

She wasn't *going along* this time. She wasn't fighting him, either. She was just going to stand her ground, in her own space, and not let him control *everything*. Certainly not her feelings.

"The right course of action," she repeated carefully, as if mulling it over. "Maybe it is. But there's one very important fact you don't know that you should before you start making any plans."

"Nothing will change my mind, Rebecca."

"All right, try this. I'm in love with you."

CHAPTER SIXTEEN

THEO DID NOT grasp the words. For full-on minutes it felt as though she'd spoken to him in a foreign language.

It was her chin up, that *challenging* glint to her eye that finally shook him out of the shock of this all.

He'd felt his child move under his hands.

Rebecca loved him.

The ground he was so sure of, the foundation he'd built himself up on, seemed to tilt dangerously, reminding him too much of being a small boy, never sure of what his foundations were.

She only *thought* she loved him. Because, of course, that was ridiculous. Sexual chemistry could not be confused with love. Love made things perilous. Decidedly *unstable*.

"You are mistaken."

For a moment, she reacted not at all. Then she threw her head back and laughed. And laughed. She wiped at her eyes. But she was not crying in anything but amusement.

What the very hell?

"Theo. Honestly." She chuckled again. "Why would I be *mistaken* about how I feel?"

"You are simply confusing good sex—"

"I'm not some teenage innocent virgin," she said, cutting him off, all humor gone. "I'm a grown woman. With at least one heartbreak under my belt. I know what love feels like, because I once thought I was in love and wasn't."

Theo wanted to *sneer* at the idea of this Patrick. Whether she'd loved him or not, the very idea of her being with someone else…

It didn't matter. She was simply mistaken, and she needed it pointed out to her. "What is it you think you love about me, Rebecca?"

She moved to him, and he hated the sympathy in her blue eyes. He wanted to move away from her, but he wouldn't let her win whatever manipulation this was.

That's all it could be. All he'd ever known it to be. Love was used to get what a person wanted. Every wife his father had ever had had used the love he'd felt for her to get what she wanted—bigger homes, brighter jewels, Theo shipped off and away.

Rebecca simply wanted some kind of power over him, and she thought this would do it. This would give her some upper hand.

He refused.

"Is it that you think no one could love you?" she asked, with such gentleness it took the meaning a moment to hit like the stabbing pain it was.

He wanted to throw back his head and laugh as she had done. He was sure that's what he would do, but he found his head would not move, a laugh would not emerge.

Instead, he struggled to breathe around a searing pain lodged between his ribs.

She put her palms to his chest as though she could see the injury and knew her touch would soothe it away, but there was nothing soothing in her words.

"I'll admit, you need improvement," she said, her eyes serious, her mouth curved into a soft smile. "You're far too bossy and the obsession with the *right thing* gets old. Especially when you've suffered enough blows to know it doesn't matter how many *right things* you do, mistakes still happen."

Theo remembered, far too uncomfortably, what now felt like a dire warning from her father.

Life is full of wrong decisions.

But this was inaccurate. Because he had been making the right ones from the moment he'd had full control of his life. Maybe he had not *meant* to spend a night with a beautiful Irish woman at some ridiculous wedding, and he'd certainly always *meant* to use protection, but the subsequent pregnancy and Rebecca in his life was not a *wrong decision*.

The *wrong decision* would have been ignoring her. Turning his back on her. Or worse, allowing her this idea they could have separate lives their child was shuttled back and forth between. Those were the wrong choices.

Theo had made the right ones.

That was all that mattered. Not shortcomings or thinking she was in love with him or whatever *this* was.

Not that he needed to argue with her. What did it matter if she fancied herself in love with him? She would not have that kind of power over him. He wouldn't allow it.

They always leave, Theo. It's never enough.

The old memory of his father crying into his bottle of whatever had been his drink of choice at the time, the first night Theo had been back from the first boarding school, was something he hadn't considered in years. He would have said he'd locked those kinds of ugly memories away.

The way everything had changed every time a new woman had come into the house. Every time his father fancied himself in *love*. With Theo never holding enough of that love to make anything matter.

Still, memories were just that. Old things that had happened. Lessons, if you were smart enough. Theo knew as well as anyone that his father's *enough* was never more than exactly what he wanted. So whatever he'd blubbered about had been about his own shortcomings. Not the women he'd chosen.

Theo was not like Atlas. He made choices not about what he *wanted*, but what was correct.

So Rebecca's *love* was neither here nor there. Certainly something not to worry over if she *could*. It was irrelevant.

He would tell her that. Once he found his voice. Once she stopped *touching* him like he was something precious to her.

"But there is an innate kindness underneath all of that control," she said, fitting her palm to his cheek. "There is a desire to comfort and care for. There is a *desire* to make things better for others than they were for you. I happen to think that's very admirable. You will be an excellent father. Not perfect, but good. No one's perfect. No one's right all the time. That's what love is for."

Her father had said that. What dream world did the Murphys live in? Not in a real one. Not in a substantial one. They could hide in their cottage and with their horses and pretend the world wasn't hard. People weren't cruel. That love mattered.

But they were *wrong*.

Rebecca had loved her horses, her training, and where had it gotten her? Nowhere.

Love was irrelevant. Pointless. Useless.

"Will you still marry me?" she asked him, still with that gentleness that was some foreign entity to him. He did not recall anyone treating him like this. He did not like it or want it. He was certain he didn't.

"Knowing how I feel?" she continued. "That every day will be me trying to get you to admit that you love me, too."

His chest felt tight. His palms hot. She made no sense and neither did this, so the only answer was to focus on the simplest fact he knew.

They would be married. It was the right choice for their child. Beginning and end of story.

"You may love me or not, Rebecca," he said, wondering if that was really his voice that sounded so thready. "It really doesn't matter. Love isn't the point. Of anything."

"If love is so pointless, Theo, why does it terrify you?"

"Terrify?" he scoffed, taking a step back so her hand fell off his chest, off his face.

He was not *scared*. He had stepped away from her because…because… Because she was trying to push something, and he wouldn't be pushed.

"We will be married, Rebecca. As soon as the arrangements are made. I care not one bit how you think you feel, or what you think you'll try to get out of me. Our feelings are not important. Everything we do will be for our child."

"Because heaven forbid we try to make something work out for ourselves," she said quietly, all accusation and yet not scathing or mean in delivery. All that damn gentleness. "Heaven forbid we think the right choice is our own happiness. But you'd have to believe you could find it. You'd have to believe you deserve it." She sighed, her dark blue gaze never leaving his. "It's all right, Theo. I'll show you."

"I have work," he muttered, retreating. Not because he was wrong, or she was right. Not because he was *terrified*. But because this was *pointless*.

And she wouldn't show him a damn thing.

He planned the wedding quickly, as if her declaration of love—something Rebecca repeated every night before they went to bed—was a wildfire coming for him and the only way to outrun it was to say *I do*.

Rebecca supposed that's why she allowed him to make the decisions. Until he admitted he loved her, this wedding was not real. Yes, she would go to the altar in a white dress and say *I do* in front of both their parents. And yes, she was mostly doing that because she loved him and thought...he had to love her, too. In some way.

But the wedding wasn't *about* love. Not yet. First she had to find a way to get through to him.

It was proving to be a little harder than she'd anticipated, which she could admit was her own fault. She'd thought love would win the day, but she hadn't counted on all the past traumas she'd have to fight through to get him to even admit love existed.

She didn't really have a clue where to start, so she just showed up every day. Every night. And every day, her stomach got a little bigger. Their son's kicks grew stronger. Sometimes she grabbed Theo's hand, placed it against her stomach and watched his expression. Soften and marvel, for a brief moment or two before he came back to himself and drew his hand away.

He loved. Oh, he would label it something else. Duty probably. But he loved. He was capable. It was in him. She just had to find a way for him to acknowledge that those things that chased across his face—for their child, for her— were love.

And love was not pointless. Or something to fear. Because he was edgy, grumpier than he'd been before, short with almost everyone around them.

Rebecca knew all that frustration was just fear he couldn't admit to himself.

The only topics Theo would discuss were the wedding,

plans for their son and deliciously dirty things in bed together, because neither could stop the physical attraction that raged between them—even when she said she loved him, even when he refused to say it back.

If she tried to discuss anything else, even something as inane as the weather, he changed the subject.

Weeks went by like this and she let it. She didn't know what else to do but give it time. She supposed she could leave him, but that felt counterproductive. He'd already been left—by his own mother, by any of the women that had come into his father's life, and in a way, Atlas had left him, too. To fend for himself as a young boy.

Leaving would not prove her point, but as the wedding approached, she was no closer to determining what would.

Her parents arrived. Atlas and Ariana arrived. The four could not have been more different, and yet they got on well. Rebecca watched it with some amusement. Theo did nothing but scowl.

Then, she woke up alone on her wedding day. She had not gone to bed that way. But there was no time to dwell on it. People swept in to begin getting her ready for the afternoon wedding.

Once her hair was done, her makeup applied, the dress pulled on, Rebecca surveyed herself in the full-length mirror while her mother sat off to the side watching her.

Rebecca smoothed her hands over the pretty dress and the ever-widening baby bump. She knew she looked pretty, and yet she didn't feel excited. She wanted to. Wanted to enjoy today. Wanted to believe that she could find a way to reach Theo, and that agreeing to marry him was a necessary part of that.

Still, she wasn't nervous. More resigned. Determined maybe.

Mom came to stand behind her, brushed lint that wasn't there off the pretty silken flutter sleeve.

"Are you sure?" Sharon asked.

She met her mother's gaze in the mirror, lifted her chin. Because maybe she wasn't excited or nervous or even happy, but she *was* sure. Maybe she'd taken a page out of Theo's book. This was what was right, so she'd see it through. "Yes. He needs this. I won't be able to get through to him until all his plans are in place."

"And once they are?"

"He'll have to deal with love."

Mam's other hand came up to her other shoulder. She gave Rebecca a gentle squeeze. "And if he doesn't?"

"I don't give up, Mam."

Not until bones get crushed, anyway.

But she didn't want her mother worrying about how she might get crushed.

One thing Rebecca had learned that she did not think her parents understood—at least when extended to *her*—was that losing her Olympic dreams had taught her something.

You could be crushed and keep going. You could be crushed and find something new and wonderful in the rubble. She couldn't see a way forward that wasn't *trying* to make this work. She didn't want to be at odds with him, constantly trying to run away from his focused machinations to make everything right.

At least here, in the circle of his plans, she was with him. She had some chance to get through to him.

She placed a hand to the side of her stomach, where a twinge of pain accompanied a kick. She decided to take it as approval from baby. Why not?

They married in an old chapel that had been abandoned since before Theo had bought the island, but he'd had it meticulously renovated and brought back to life. He had determined they would be married here, their child would be christened here, and Rebecca had loved the idea that he would create a sacred place, a place of good things and memory, just for their family.

Because that's what they were and would be, once he accepted love.

And he would.

She walked the aisle on her father's arm. She could tell from her parents' quiet that they weren't quite *approving*. It was how they'd been when she spoke of marrying Peter. Never quite *approving*.

But they supported her. And even if it all went terribly wrong, they would be there to support her with no recriminations.

It wouldn't go wrong. She wouldn't let it.

She met Theo at the end of the aisle, beamed at him. His expression was guarded. Maybe there was even a little tension around his mouth. But he took her arm as they turned to face the officiant.

The man spoke of love and duty. Marriage as sacred. He had them exchange rings, light a candle, and then blessed them both for a happy future. When he committed them as husband and wife, extended the invitation to *kiss* the bride, Rebecca turned to Theo.

He was so handsome, even stern and detached. But that was a sign in and of itself. He was holding *something* back.

Still, he lowered his head to dutifully kiss his wife.

"I love you," she murmured, before pressing her mouth to his. Because when he looked back on today, he would not get to pretend she was here for any other reason but love.

They proceeded to a nice dinner out on the terrace with her parents and his father and Ariana. Atlas and James were jovial, Ariana and Sharon a little more reserved. Rebecca was even more convinced that Ariana was pregnant considering the very loose dress she'd chosen, but she didn't think today was the time to bring it up to Theo.

There was a stillness to him. An alarming finality to the way he moved and spoke. After everyone had retired for the evening, the fathers a little heavy in the drink, Rebecca turned her attention to their wedding night.

When they entered their bedroom—because it had been *theirs* for almost two months now—she expected him to cross to her. Kiss her. Take the dress off her and take her to bed. She didn't think her expectations could be that far off. Obviously she wasn't expecting declarations of love or an invitation to have a conversation. That would come later.

But he didn't even look at her.

Instead, he crossed to the closet and rolled a suitcase out.

Confused, Rebecca frowned at it and him. "I didn't think we were taking a honeymoon."

"We are not. Now that we are married, I will return to Athens."

She didn't really want to go to Athens, but... He'd said *I*. "Wh…? Wait. What?"

"I will attend my business there until the child is born. You may stay here. You may stay at my estate outside of the city. If you wish to go to Ireland, I'll have to insist you take Dr. Doukas with you and return before travel is risky. My child will be born here."

She couldn't find her words, not for full, quiet minutes as he gathered his things. Gathered his things to *leave*. Leave her. Right after their wedding. It made absolutely no sense, and maybe that's why she said something she would have been better off keeping to herself if she wanted to keep her pride.

"And if I want to stay with you?"

"That is not possible."

"Why not?"

He moved for the door. "I have created the environment I want for our child. It does not require us to be together before he arrives, and I have much work to catch up on."

Hurt twined inside her, making it hard to breathe. But she had to see through her own surprise and pain and see this for what it was, even when her eyes filled with tears.

He was *running*.

"It doesn't change anything," she told him, desperately trying to keep the tears at bay. "I'll still love you. It'll still be there when you come back to be a father. You can run away from it for this little time between now and then, but it changes nothing."

He didn't even look at her. "Believe in love if you wish. Love me if you must. But these things are irrelevant to me. They are irrelevant to the choices we must make for our child. Someone will contact me once you go into labor."

One tear slipped over. She couldn't stop it. He sounded so cold. So sure. Maybe she…had misread everything. Maybe she didn't understand him at all.

"I won't…live like this." She could hear the panic and desperation in her own voice, but this wasn't… This wasn't the plan. This wasn't what she'd expected. She needed time. Time *with* him to change his mind, to open him up. So she lashed out with the only weapon she had. "I won't stay married to you like this."

He didn't even look back as he strode out the door. "Yes, you will."

CHAPTER SEVENTEEN

THEO WAS MISERABLE. It frustrated him beyond belief he could not deny this simple fact. He had been back in Athens for nearly a month. He did not trust himself to work on anything important, so he simply trudged about the offices, a grumpy, demanding ogre.

And no amount of *knowing or understanding* what he was doing could get him to stop. Because the only solve was to go back to the island, to face Rebecca, to hear her say *I love you* every damn day and he didn't know how to weather it.

She had looked like an angel in white in the chapel. For a blinding moment, he thought he'd finally been saved.

Then he'd remembered. There was no saving. There was only the right choice. The introduction of love to their union, even if it was only her own delusion, made everything precarious when he wanted everything solid and stable.

For the sake of his child's future, he could not be around her until he got himself under control. Love had been the destabilizing force of his entire life. He would not allow her to love him, to ruin everything.

He would not allow himself to love her, to jeopardize the stability and safety of his child.

Because that was all love ever did. He was certain of it, had lived it. Everything had centered on whom his father had loved and lost. *Love* made everything quicksand—for him, for his child. He *knew* that.

But now he had the specter of the Murphys and their cozy, *loving* life haunting him, poking at all his certainty and life experience.

Could he make *love* less of a threat? With Rebecca... Could it be *good*?

He missed her, with an ache that was bone-deep. He woke reaching for her, even though she'd never spent a night in his bed in Athens. More than once he had lifted his phone to his ear, dialed his assistant to demand the plane and ferry be readied, only to hang up in the nick of time.

He was considering his phone right now. He could go there. He could demand she stop telling him she loved him, since she most assuredly did not. He could demand it. Ensure it. He could...

His office door opened, no knock, which meant the only person brave enough to be the one striding through the entrance was his father.

"Father," he greeted, surprised by his father's appearance here after so many months away. Surprised he did not feel relieved this unexpected appearance had kept him from making a mistake.

Atlas walked straight to a chair, settled himself in it and fixed Theo with a stern look Theo didn't recognize.

"There have been complaints, son."

Theo winced. At the sentence. At being called *son*. At his father being the one to bring him *complaints*.

"Shouldn't you be home resting?" he asked his father rather than acknowledge the comment.

"The doctors gave me the all-clear to return to work full-time if I so chose. And I think Ariana would like me to find something else to worry about for at least part of the day."

"Worry about?"

"We didn't want to say anything that might bring attention to us rather than your wedding, your baby."

The way Atlas said *your* baby made it clear. Rebecca had been right. Ariana was pregnant.

Dear God.

"We'll come back to that," Atlas said, sounding firm and in control, which was odd. There were no jokes. None of his usual joviality. None of even his pre-heart-attack business focus.

He just seemed serious. "I know you find my change of heart little more than a nuisance."

"Perhaps because it has been." An honesty he wouldn't normally have bothered verbalizing, but he was losing his grip on everything.

He and his father would have a child the same age. Who wouldn't be a little rattled by that?

"Perhaps it has for you. I apologize. Genuinely, Theo. I have strived to fix my mistakes after the attack, but you are the mistake I could not figure how to handle. I could easily, or at least to me, ease my conscious about greed. But it was the people I had wronged that felt…impossible to rectify."

"You hardly wronged me, Father. No need to be dramatic about it."

"I don't think you understand me, Theo. You think my change of heart was temporary. Based in fear, and I suppose in a way it was. But it was more than that. It's not temporary. I lay there, before Ariana found me and called the ambulance, thinking I would die, knowing that no one would care. Ariana was getting ready to leave me, I could feel it. You… You might have felt a pang or two, but I knew we did not have a relationship that would allow you true grief. It felt terrifying, to die knowing no one would care. And none of that fear, that terror, came from *business*. It came from the way I'd been with the people in my life."

Theo felt…uncomfortable. He didn't want to hear this. Explanations or heart-to-hearts or whatever nonsense. It didn't…matter. He didn't want to mine the complexities of what he felt about it. None of that was…clear-cut. A right way forward. It was just messy and…pointless.

Yes, pointless. Irrelevant. Like love.

"When they told me I would survive, with change in diet and exercise and what have you, I told Ariana I knew she was going to leave, and she should." Atlas inhaled, looking as vulnerable as Theo had ever seen him.

He wanted to run. Only pride kept him rooted to the spot.

"She told me I should stop trying so hard to stop the hurt before it landed." Atlas looked up at Theo.

The eye contact with the words was like a spear to his chest. A terrible understanding. As though every step he took, every decision he made for the *rightness* of it all, was little more than this:

Trying to stop the hurt before it landed.

Theo tried to shove this thought, this feeling, this terrible reckoning away, but Atlas kept speaking.

"I look back at how careless I was. At the wall I kept between us. I didn't realize it then. I think it's something you can only see in hindsight when you're finally forced to consider your mortality. But if I look back at it, if I analyze it, I realize that I knew someday, whatever I offered would not be enough. Just like with your mother. I knew someday you would become old enough to blame her for leaving, because I blamed myself for not being what she needed. I realize now, older and wiser, that was her choice. Her title over love. It had very little to do with *me*."

Theo had never believed his mother held any special place

in his father's heart. He had gone on to marry so many times since. *Love* so many times since. What could she have mattered to him?

But maybe older and wiser and actually giving it some thought, he could see it for what it was. Running away from a hurt.

"Her decision to leave us changed me. Not for the better, and that's not her fault…something I am learning with help. I'm in therapy, you know."

Theo didn't know what to do with any of those words.

"And we're exploring the ways I have made it harder on the people around me, on anyone who might love or depend on me, on purpose. Namely you."

Theo couldn't meet his father's gaze. The idea of Atlas discussing *him* with some therapist left him feeling…itchy and vulnerable.

"Therapy was Ariana's idea, naturally," Atlas continued. "But I didn't accept it until Ariana told me she was pregnant. I… I can't stomach the idea I will make the same mistakes all over again. Especially as old as I am now. I won't have what feels like a lifetime to try to make it up to this one."

"There is nothing to…make up to me. We are fine."

"Fine." Atlas laughed, but it was not his booming laugh. It was almost sad. "We are that, Theo. But I would like to be more than fine. I am proud of what you are. In spite of me. In spite of your mother and some of the…less kind women I married along the way. It is clear how much you love Rebecca, and that will go a long way in making you a much better father than I was on the first go-round."

Atlas stood, skirted the desk behind which Theo stood. Breaking the barricade Theo held himself behind. Even as Theo held up a hand as if to ward off an attack, Atlas wrapped his strong arms around Theo.

"Stop punishing those around you. Go back to the island. Go back to her. Don't be like me, Theo. Don't waste years being afraid, pushing real love away and grasping after fleeting feelings that are safer because they end." He squeezed hard. Stepped back. "We'll talk more when you get back."

But Theo wasn't going. He wasn't. He *wasn't*.

Oh, whom was he kidding?

Rebecca's parents had gone back to Ireland after the wedding, but that had only lasted two weeks before Mam had returned—insisting on coming and staying when she'd found out that Rebecca was having some false labor contractions.

It had been nice. To have her mother here for the past two weeks. To be fussed over. To talk about baby things. They picked out a room for the nursery, started ordering things and decorating.

If she'd been left to her own devices, she might not have. She might have thought she should wait for Theo. She might have wallowed, like she had the first two weeks. But she wouldn't wallow in front of her mother, and that made it easy to move on to the next part of her…grief, she supposed.

Determined. Focused.

She could not control Theo. She could not make him feel the way she wanted. And this was familiar. She had not been able to magically heal her hip, make it do what she wanted it to do on the back of a horse after her injury. She'd had to accept her own limitations.

So, she would accept his. And she could accept it without hardening her heart to him, because she would focus on pregnancy, on preparing for the baby, and once they were a family…maybe.

Maybe.

So she did not discuss Theo with her mother, and Sharon never brought him up. They happily planned for the future with a baby and *only* a baby.

Until her thirty-two-week appointment. Rebecca didn't tell her mother she'd been having pain all morning, because she figured she could discuss it with the doctor and not worry her mother, but the minute she told the doctor, everything…changed.

The doctor took vitals she'd never taken before. She seemed serious over cheerful. Even though Rebecca had said she didn't want her mother in the room, the doctor insisted.

"You're pale," her mother said quietly while the doctor consulted something on her laptop.

"Mam."

"I know you're talking care of yourself, darling, but that does not ensure everything will go well. You need someone here who cares *about* you, not just for you."

"I have a doctor."

"You need love."

They couldn't discuss *that*, because the doctor said her name. In a very serious manner that had Rebecca's heart sinking.

The doctor's face was calm, but she didn't flash her usual reassuring smile. "Rebecca. Between the contractions, the blood pressure, the swelling, I think it best if we go to the mainland."

The words didn't make sense. "What?"

"This isn't false labor, it's real. And I don't think I can stop it. You need a hospital. And more importantly, your baby will. Better to go now, while it's not an emergency, than wait until it might be."

Rebecca's hand shook, but her mother took it, squeezed. "Then that's what we'll do," she said to both Rebecca and the doctor. Firmly. Determined. "I'll go talk to the staff and make arrangements."

The doctor nodded. "I'll call the hospital so there's a room ready for us." She stepped out of the room first.

Mam squeezed her hand again and then released it, heading for the door to make those arrangements.

But Rebecca knew she'd also contact Theo and… She didn't want that. She didn't want him there until she knew for sure she was in labor, and they couldn't stop it. She didn't want him…hovering about before the baby was born. "Mam. Don't call Theo."

Sharon's face got pinched with disapproval. "Rebecca."

She shook her head. Determined. "I don't want any pity visits. If the baby comes, we'll contact him. Otherwise, he can wait."

Sharon sighed. "Very well."

CHAPTER EIGHTEEN

THEO SAT WITH his father's words. His father's *apology*. He could not fight it off. And worse, the thing that had once haunted his father, as his death flashed before his eyes.

If he died, would anyone care?

Rebecca would.

Or would the month away have cured her of her love for him? Had he ruined it? Had he used his father's own methods and stopped the potential for hurt and ruined *everything*?

No. No, he did not give up. He did not. He *would* not. If he had ruined things, he would fix them. He always fixed them. Right steps, and she...

God, Rebecca was right. Everything about her. Everything she said. She was the rightest thing he'd ever known, and to keep his distance from that wasn't just wrong... It had been cowardly.

He would not be a coward for his son. For Rebecca. And maybe even...for himself. The boy who had learned to be careful in the shadow of his father's carelessness.

Theo lifted his phone from his desk, but before he could dial the number to order his plane to be readied, the phone trilled, actually startling him.

But not as much as the caller. It was Rebecca's name. He answered, words tumbling about in his head, so many things to tell her, but he could only manage her name.

"Theo, this is Sharon."

Sharon. Calling from Rebecca's phone. His heart sank like a heavy stone. "What's happened?"

There was a pause. "Rebecca has gone into early labor. We are at the hospital now. Your son is in the NICU, but he is doing well."

Your son. NICU. He'd read about the NICU. Something about premature babies and… "He's…here. Now?"

"Yes. If you come to the hospital, you may see him."

"What about Rebecca?"

"What about her?"

"What caused this? Is she all right? I want to see her. Never mind. I will see her." He tossed the phone aside, half out of his mind with terror. He yelled for his assistant. When she asked what hospital, he realized he hadn't asked for details.

But his assistant must have recognized his panic, because she took care of everything. Got him into a car with a driver who seemed to know where he was going. He was dropped off in front of a hospital and heard nothing, saw nothing, thought of nothing, except finding her.

He went to the first desk he saw. "You will tell me where Rebecca Murphy is."

The nurse raised an eyebrow at him. "I beg your pardon."

"Rebecca Murphy. Where is she? What room? Do not make me tear this hospital apart of find her."

The nurse sighed, almost bored. She moved to a computer, typed a few things. Then shook her head. "We don't have a Rebecca Murphy. Are you certain—"

Even though he wasn't certain at all, he needed her to be here. Needed it. "Yes, you do. Do not lie to me. I—"

"Theo."

He whirled toward the Irish accent, half believing it

would be Rebecca. But it was Sharon who stood there. He crossed to her in two long strides.

"Where is she?" he demanded.

Mrs. Murphy lifted her chin, so much like her daughter his knees almost gave out.

"She will see you, but you must be calm or I will not take you to her."

"I am calm."

"Son, you aren't even breathing."

It was the *son*. The accent. Rebecca so near and so far from him. His son. His *son*. Everything crashing together at once. How did he hold it all?

"Inhale," Sharon said gently, placing her hand on his shoulder. "Then exhale."

He followed instructions because he didn't know what else to do. Everything whirled inside him. He was going to lose it all. Everything. Because who was he to have it all?

"Both are well," Sharon said in her calm way. She began to lead him down a hall. "The babe will have to stay in the hospital for a bit, but the prognosis is good."

Prognosis. A prognosis meant there was a *problem* to be solved.

Sharon stopped at a door. "She has been through a lot today. You will be calm, or I will drag you out myself."

"Yes, ma'am," he rasped, feeling like a child again. She opened the door and Theo stepped in.

Rebecca sat in the hospital bed. She looked pale. Her eyes red-rimmed as though she'd been crying. Exhausted, clearly. But she sat there and met his gaze, chin raised.

"The baby is in the NICU," she said, reciting facts. "You will have to have a chat with the nurse before you can see him."

Him. Baby. Son. Her. Her. *Her.*

"Rebecca." He crossed to her bed. He had no words. He had nothing. She had done this without him.

And he'd deserved that.

"Rebecca," he said again. "I… You should have called."

"No, Theo. You should have been there."

Yes. He should have been. He never should have left her. But how could he face it? All this love? All this need? Everything she brought out in him was something he had learned not to trust.

Except he trusted her. "Rebecca, please…"

She shook her head, cutting him off, which was good since he didn't know what he'd been about to say.

"I don't need your change of heart. You don't love me, Theo. You're just scared of losing me and the perfect image of family you think will protect you from hurt. It won't."

It mirrored, in many ways, what his father had said. Would he be receptive if his father hadn't been in his office this morning?

Or should he take this as a sign? A sign that it was time to do some of the healing and growth his father was trying to find?

Because, of course, he loved her. It terrified him how much. How easy it was to lose. How fickle everyone was. How love had upended his life more than it had ever stabilized it.

Except when it came to her. She had swept into his life and upended it, but that had made it *better*. He was miserable without her. He wanted her.

He *loved* her, and she didn't think he did or could. So he would have to find words. Somehow. He let panic and fear and the last month of misery drive him.

"I love the way you look in the morning, before you open your eyes. I love the way you take my hand, place it against your stomach and watch me. Your love of horses, and the courage it took to build a new life for yourself after your dreams were unfairly taken away from you, simply from an accident."

She had stilled, her eyes going wide. But he couldn't stop the torrent of words.

"The courage it took to go to that stupid wedding when you felt your heart was broken. Your pride. But it isn't like mine. It doesn't…isolate you. It gets you through the hard things."

"No, Theo, love has gotten me through the hard things. All pride did was…" She shook her head. Her face was clouded with pain, and it was lowering to realize there was nothing he could do to fix that. "I guess it kept me putting one foot in front of the other sometimes."

"I love that about you, too. I have been miserable. Loving you and not wanting to."

Her face hardened.

"I need you, Rebecca. Not for a perfect life, a stable, right life for our child, but for me. I have taught myself not to need. It feels terrible to need. But I love you. I need you. Please, Rebecca. Don't walk away from me. I do not know how to love. I do not know how to be anything other than what is *right*, which seems less than you and our son deserve."

"It is, Theo." She touched him, finally. Just her fingertips to his cheek. But it was enough. "So why not try to be what we deserve?"

The NICU was a startling reminder in just how lucky she was. *They* were. Theo James needed very little intervention. A little machine to make it easier to breathe, and a tube for vitamins and food until he gained a few more pounds.

There were many little bundles here connected to machines, tinier than even TJ, as they walked toward his corner of the NICU. They came to a stop on either side of his little crib. Inside, their tiny baby slept.

"He is too small," Theo said roughly.

"He will grow." Rebecca said it as much for herself as for him.

Then she watched as his gaze snagged on the nameplate above the baby's head on the outside of the crib. He frowned. "Rebecca."

It read *Theodorou James Nikolaou*.

She shrugged. "It is what is right. You can't get mad at me deciding when it is right."

For a few silent moments, he just stared at her. So many emotions warring there in his gaze. "How do you know it is right?"

Her mouth curved ever so slightly. "Look at him, Theo. His little patch of dark hair. Even though his eyes are kind of blue like all babies are when they're born, they're a very deep blue. I think it will turn brown. He is yours."

"He is ours."

"Yes. Ours. And he shares his name with two very good men. Come. Sit. You can hold him. I've had the honors already."

She got him settled in the chair. Since she was still shaky from labor, and connected to an IV, the nurse came over and lifted TJ out of his bassinette and handed him over to Theo. TJ was just shy of four pounds, the tiniest bundle she'd ever seen before the NICU, but he looked even tinier lying on Theo's broad chest.

Theo closed his eyes. The strain of it all sat on his face, but she watched as he just sat there and absorbed the steady rise and fall of their son's breathing against his own. As his big hands spanned almost the entire baby with a gentleness that spoke of deep, abiding love.

The kind she understood because of TJ. The kind that allowed her to forgive. Because this… This was the future they could have. Parents. Love. Family.

A tear slid down her cheek. She would have this moment forever. This memory. Father and son. These two men she loved so much.

When Theo opened his eyes, they were dark, shiny almost. His voice was rough. "I do not know how *to* love, but I do know that is what this is inside of me. This overwhelming loss of control, and the warmth and joy that fills in that empty space. It is terrifying and wonderful, and I love you both. I will always, *always* love you both."

She swallowed, more tears following as she crossed to him, bent down to press a kiss to his cheek. "We will all always love each other."

EPILOGUE

Theo had kept TJ's first birthday present a secret from even Rebecca, as it doubled as a present for her, as well.

Theo sent James a text that they were ready for the unveiling as he surveyed the little beach party. TJ and his uncle, Atlas Juno, otherwise known as AJ, crawling about on the big blanket, while Rebecca and Ariana watched them. Atlas and Sharon stood off to the side, discussing something or another.

Perhaps in a strange twist of fate and timing, Theo and Atlas were learning how to be good fathers side by side, and in doing so, repairing some of what remained broken between them.

Theo chose to believe in that hope, day after day. Especially when Ariana had asked if they, too, could move to the island. Ensuring that TJ always had his uncle as playmate, and that family permeated everything they did.

The Murphys visited often, and Theo and Rebecca had taken TJ to Ireland just last month. They would travel there more frequently once he was older, Theo was sure.

James was the one who'd picked out the horse for him and been in charge of transporting the beast to the island and keeping him occupied this morning until it was time for the party.

He appeared now, so Theo knelt next to Rebecca and

picked TJ up and settled him so he could see the horse coming. "Here is your present coming for you."

Rebecca frowned a little, turned her head, then her expression went fully slack. Before tears filled her eyes and she looked at him. "Theo…"

"It is a present for you both, I think. Come, take our son for a ride."

She brushed away tears and let him help her to her feet with his free hand. As a family, they walked over to the horse.

James helped with a knee so Rebecca could get on the horse, then Theo handed TJ up to her, and she settled him between her legs. TJ squealed in delight, even louder as Rebecca urged the pony into a trot.

After a little jaunt up and down the beach, she switched TJ for AJ and gave him a ride, as well. It was easy to see both boys had fallen in love, and Rebecca was exactly where she belonged.

Atlas boomed out a laugh with James, while Ariana and Sharon sat in the sand with TJ. Rebecca beamed on the back of a horse, with her baby brother-in-law in her lap.

Because they were a family. Not perfect. Not *right*.

And somehow exactly perfect. Exactly right.

Because if there was love, everything was perfectly right.

* * * * *

MILLS & BOON®

Coming next month

THE HEIR AFFAIR
Heidi Rice

'Poppy,' he shouted.

The girl's head whipped around, responding to her name. Joy exploded in Xander's chest, as the need shocked him. Those eyes, that face. It was her. But as she turned toward him, depositing the tray back on the bar with a clash of glasses, his greedy gaze swept down her figure.

His steps faltered. And he blinked, exhilaration turning to shock, then confusion, then another blast of hunger. A compact bulge distended her apron where he had once been able to span her flat, narrow waist with a single hand.

He reached her at last, but it felt as if he were walking through waist-high water now as he tried to make sense of all the warring reactions going off inside his head.

But then his gaze snagged on her belly again—and the only question that mattered broke from his dry lips.

'Is it mine?' he demanded.

Flags of color slashed across her cheeks, but all he heard in her tone was the sting of regret when she whispered, 'Yes.'

Continue reading

THE HEIR AFFAIR
Heidi Rice

Available next month
millsandboon.co.uk

Copyright ©2025 Heidi Rice

COMING SOON!

We really hope you enjoyed reading this book. If you're looking for more romance be sure to head to the shops when new books are available on

Thursday 28th August

To see which titles are coming soon, please visit
millsandboon.co.uk/nextmonth

MILLS & BOON

FOUR BRAND NEW BOOKS FROM
MILLS & BOON MODERN

The same great stories you love, a stylish new look!

WED IN A HURRY
KIM LAWRENCE — LORRAINE HALL

Bound & Crowned
LOUISE FULLER — CLARE CONNELLY

Love to HATE HIM
JULIA JAMES — MILLIE ADAMS

RECLAIM ME
CATHY WILLIAMS — DANI COLLINS

OUT NOW

Eight Modern stories published every month, find them all at:

millsandboon.co.uk

afterglow BOOKS

Afterglow Books is a trend-led, trope-filled list of books with diverse, authentic and relatable characters, a wide array of voices and representations, plus real world trials and tribulations. Featuring all the tropes you could possibly want (think small-town settings, fake relationships, grumpy vs sunshine, enemies to lovers) and all with a generous dose of spice in every story.

@millsandboonuk
@millsandboonuk
afterglowbooks.co.uk

#AfterglowBooks

For all the latest book news, exclusive content and giveaways scan the QR code below to sign up to the Afterglow newsletter:

SCAN ME

afterglow BOOKS

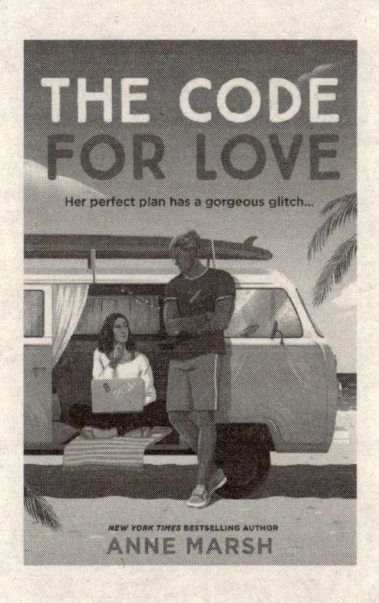

THE CODE FOR LOVE

Her perfect plan has a gorgeous glitch...

NEW YORK TIMES BESTSELLING AUTHOR
ANNE MARSH

✈ International

⛅ Grumpy/sunshine

🏃 Fake dating

OUT NOW

To discover more visit:
Afterglowbooks.co.uk

LET'S TALK
Romance

For exclusive extracts, competitions and special offers, find us online:

- MillsandBoon
- @MillsandBoon
- @MillsandBoonUK
- @MillsandBoonUK

Get in touch on 01413 063 232

For all the latest titles coming soon, visit
millsandboon.co.uk/nextmonth

OUT NOW!

TEMPTED BY DESIRE

THE TYCOON'S AFFAIR COLLECTION

USA TODAY BESTSELLING AUTHOR
ABBY GREEN

Available at
millsandboon.co.uk

MILLS & BOON

OUT NOW!

A DARK ROMANCE SERIES

Thorns of Revenge

TARYN LEIGH TAYLOR · ABBY GREEN · JACKIE ASHENDEN

Available at
millsandboon.co.uk

MILLS & BOON